Rodney Savage was the last member of his family to serve in India – the fourteenth and final generation of Savages. The first of his ancestors to reach India had stepped ashore in 1628. From then on the Savages were bound to the continent by a tie which grew stronger down the years . . . Rodney Savage had known India as a soldier, a hard drinker, a womaniser, an adventurer – India was his life. Now all his efforts were concentrated on coming to terms with the new India, proud and prickly in her independence. Danger, hardship and poverty meant little to Savage – as long as he could stay in the country he loved . . .

Also by John Masters

COROMANDEL
BHOWANI JUNCTION
THE LOTUS AND THE WIND
THE RAVI LANCERS
PILGRIM SON
BUGLES AND A TIGER
THE VENUS OF KONPARA

and published by Corgi Books

John Masters

To The Coral Strand

CORGI BOOKS
A DIVISION OF TRANSWORLD PUBLISHERS LTD

TO THE CORAL STRAND

A CORGI BOOK 0 552 10078 1

Originally published in Great Britain by
Michael Joseph Ltd.

PRINTING HISTORY
Michael Joseph edition published 1962
Corgi edition published 1976

Copyright © 1962 by Bengal-Rockland Inc.

This low-priced Corgi Book has been completely reset in a
type face designed for easy reading, and was printed from
new plates. It contains the complete text of the
original hard-cover edition.

Conditions of sale
1: This book is sold subject to the condition that it
shall not, by way of trade *or otherwise*, be lent, re-sold,
hired out or otherwise *circulated* without the publisher's
prior consent in any form of binding or cover other than
that in which it is published *and without a similar
condition including this condition being imposed on
the subsequent purchaser.*
2: This book is sold subject to the Standard Conditions
of Sale of Net Books and may not be re-sold in the U.K.
below the net price fixed by the publishers for the book.

This book is set in 10pt Baskerville (Intertype)

Corgi Books are published by Transworld Publishers Ltd.,
Century House, 61–63 Uxbridge Road,
Ealing, London, W.5.
Made and printed in Great Britain by
Hunt Barnard Printing Ltd., Aylesbury, Bucks.

For Alan and Nancy

This book is wholly a work of fiction
and no reference is intended in it to
any person living or dead, except
that a few public figures are
mentioned. Geographically, a few of
the places mentioned are, of course,
real – for example, Delhi and Bombay;
the great majority are imaginary.

J. M.

Chapter 1

Margaret Wood walked slowly down the centre of the path, between the deep ruts of cart wheels. The sun streamed through the trees on her left hand, but the earth seemed dark.

Was it evening, then? She passed her hand in front of her eyes, and for a time afterwards could see nothing. She began to fall, and grasped a tree for support. Later, light returned, and she limped forward. Her shoes were red, and the red mud stained her bare legs.

The jungle fell back on the right and tall shapes began to glow among the trees. The sun spread an aura of orange light over the twisted façades and towers of four temples. All four stood on a stone platform raised a few feet above the level of the earth. The summits of the towers rose a little above the tops of the tallest trees. She leaned dizzily against the stone platform.

Was it evening, then? Twenty-four hours since he had died. Ten since the red earth rattled down on his coffin. Nine since she started walking.

The part of the platform where she rested, near the track, was almost undamaged. The nearest temple stood there, too, seemingly complete. Behind, tree roots and bushes grew through cracks in the stone. One of the other temples was little more than a ruin, another leaned crazily against the bole of a peepul tree which had grown up from the earth below. The light shone, under a flat lintel, into the interior of the temple which leaned against the peepul tree. It illumined a stone pillar, polished and glowing, the side facing her carved with the curved lines that turned it from a pillar to a phallus. The other three towers repeated the shape. Every tower rose by soaring steps, and every step was composed of a torrent of human beings in stone, but alive. Every human being coupled sexually with another, or others. Close to her head, where she had laid it on the stone, a girl bent over, her long hair sweeping her bangled ankles, and a

7

man powerful in his desire held her hips from behind. The stone girl smiled straight at the living woman.

Margaret closed her eyes and wept soundlessly. God had taken Henry from her and she was alone. Why? Where was His infinite mercy? Alone against this overpowering, thrusting animalism, which Henry had so despised . . . and feared. Alone, by herself, without his simple goodness, that had been able to shame her out of all passion.

She straightened her knees, and began to walk again.

'Been having a look at the local pornographic exhibition?' The man's voice was a little high-pitched, pleasant, slightly nasal. She jerked her head up and the words snapped out before she had time to think. 'Yes . . . No, of course not.'

The man stood in the road five feet from her, a walking-stick in his hand and his head bare. Through the blur of her recent tears his face sprang into violent focus, evenly lighted, grey against the orange glow among the trees. She stepped back a pace, and another, raising her arms. 'Keep away,' she gasped. 'Don't touch me!'

A shadow of astonishment crossed the man's blue eyes, then his expression altered. 'You're ill. You're out on your feet.' He took a pace towards her.

She backed away. The trees swayed and the earth heaved. 'Don't . . . ' she began, and stopped. She stared more closely at him, one arm still raised. Was it possible that she had been mistaken? He stood there for inspection, his thin lips parted and his forehead wrinkled in an anxious frown. He was quite tall, clean shaven, his hair thick and dark, his eyes pale cold blue. His face was long and narrow, tapering to a strong pointed chin, his mouth wide. His khaki shirt flapped outside khaki drill trousers, and his desert boots were covered with the same red mud that covered her shoes. He held the walking-stick in his left hand, and his rolled sleeves showed thin muscular arms thickly covered with black hair, a silver wrist-watch strap round his left wrist.

She had not been mistaken. This was the man.

'Now, please,' he said. 'Let me help you before you fall down.' He smiled. 'I assure you I never assault women unless, in one way or another, they invite me to. You must be Mrs Wood.'

'My husband,' she began, and stopped. The red earth

glowed at her feet, and the sky was turning red. 'My husband . . . is dead.'

She saw him stepping quickly forward, his arm outstretched, and then the red light filled her eyes.

She was lying on her back, water on her face and in her eyes and hair. She sat up, feeling an arm supporting her, and looked dimly around. It was almost dark. A stream purled and splashed past her feet and she saw a dim white shape to the right. 'That's the old Forest Rest House,' she muttered, 'and this is the stream, the Shakkar.'

'Yes,' he said. 'I carried you here. You weigh quite a lot.'

'I'm not fat,' she said indignantly, sitting up straight..

'That's better. No, you're not fat, but you're not a sylph . . . Can you walk now, if you lean on me? If not, I'll get my car. I could be back in half an hour.'

'I can walk,' she said. He helped her up. Her knees trembled so that she almost fell. 'I think so. I've been walking a long time.'

He said, 'I apologise for my flippancy. I just parked my car in Lapri and walked straight past your mission. No one told me.'

She began walking, his stick in her hand. He walked at her side, comfortably matching his pace to hers; and as he walked, he talked – He was with McFadden Pulley, had been for a year. It's good, interesting work, he said, and worthwhile. He had never realised how much pioneering the British business firms did, and with no help from Government. At the moment, indeed, it was worse than that – there were prospects of active hostility from the socialistic-minded Congress. But McFadden Pulley would show them! At this very moment M.P. were on the track of new ore sources which, properly exploited, would create a whole new industry for India.

'What ores?' she asked involuntarily.

'Mainly manganese,' he said. 'Do you know anything about metals?'

She did not answer. His manifest enthusiasm had momentarily aroused her from her lethargy. But Henry was dead, and how could she care what *this* man did or thought? Anyway, he was only talking to keep her awake.

He rambled on. He was staying at his firm's Sabora quarries, just down the main road. She had visited them, of

9

course? 'No . . . I mean, yes, once.' He loved this central Indian countryside. He had been in these parts before. How long had she been in India?

'I landed in Bombay on August 15, 1947,' she said, and turned her head to stare at him, trying to see his face. There was no reaction.

'Independence Day,' he said. 'You've been here a year, then. I've been here seventeen years. There's a legend that a remote ancestor came here first in 1620, or thereabouts. Quite a long time.'

He turned to other subjects – the trees, the flowers, the wild animals. He asked her how much Hindustani she had learned and cross-examined her with Hindustani words and phrases.

Two miles, she thought. Two miles down the gently winding road, empty as a churchyard at this hour of the evening. Last time she met this man he'd been a lieutenant colonel in worn jungle-green uniform, with two rows of medal ribbons, and he'd been drunk. It was in Bombay, not far from Sir Andrew Graham's flat – Sir Andrew was the managing director of McFadden Pulley. Perhaps he'd just come away from the flat, too, or was on his way there to be interviewed for a job in civilian life. He'd obviously got the job – but surely not *that* day, in that state?

Her thoughts blurred and wandered. She wished she could lie down and sleep.

'Shall I carry you?' he asked. 'I could, you know. You're not really a bit heavy.'

'No,' she snapped.

His supporting arm pushed and joggled her, and she stumbled on. She didn't even know his name. He knew hers, because someone at the Sabora quarries must have mentioned the missionary couple buried in the jungles up the road, just over the border in Chambal State. Mentioned it, but not bothered to mention that Henry was dead. Perhaps they didn't know. Or care. Quiet, shy, Henry had never been anyone's hero. And now he'd gone, silently, with no one but herself as mourner.

A yellow light shone ahead, and the man said, 'Nearly there.' He raised his voice and called, *'Koi hai? Iddar ao, jaldi.'*

10

'There's no one,' she mumbled. 'No servants. We are missionaries.'

'But there is someone,' he said.

She recognised one of the nurses, a convert, walking towards them, lamp upheld. She heard the man's rapid talk as the two of them helped her up the steps. Now he had lifted her, and was carrying her to the bedroom. Last night she had knelt all night in the chapel, praying over Henry's body ... and before that she'd lain alone here while he crept towards death in the front room, where he had insisted they put him. Now she was really alone. She wanted to cry out, Don't leave me. The nurse was a dirty, unwilling girl, her face sulky even in this extremity. Margaret had learned enough Hindustani to understand that the man was saying, 'She's just tired. Stay with her. Give her something to drink, warm milk or tea, if she wakes up.'

She opened her eyes with a last effort. 'Thank you. What's your name?'

'Rodney Savage.'

When she awoke it was full morning and she was alone. She got up, and only then felt the blisters on her feet. She raised them and looked incuriously at the water-filled lumps spreading across the balls of her feet and between and under every toe. She prepared breakfast, ate hungrily and drank deeply, and went into the glare of the sun.

Her aching feet led her slowly down the dishevelled drive, a few yards along the road, and then left, towards the tiny chapel. Beside the chapel stood seven crosses. Six, the graves of men and women who had died in the mission hospital, were marked with simple stone crosses. Henry's had a wooden cross. Later, she must go to Sabora and ask the masons at the McFadden Pulley quarry to make her a tall, beautiful one for him. No, not bigger, just the same as the others: he would have wanted that.

She stood for a moment at the cross, looking down. What am I to do now? Go over to the ward and see the patients, as though nothing had happened? Write letters to the Society in England, asking for instructions? Begin packing my clothes?

Henry gave her no answer, on his grave the red earth lay silent, a little darker than the rest, but drying, fast sliding back into the breast of India.

11

She turned to the chapel. Its door hung open on a broken hinge and she slipped in. It seemed very dark inside, but hot. There were two benches on one side, two on the other, at the end a bare teak table, and on the table a wooden cross. The floor was of beaten earth and the whole room was twelve feet square. She sat on one of the benches, staring at the cross, then slipped to her knees.

'Jesus Christ, our Lord,' she began, aloud, and stopped.

Her whisper hung in the enclosed darkness. A bat circled the room, brushing the silence with noiseless wings, and settled with a creeping sound back on its perch.

Henry was dead. His work, his life had been this mission. He had carried it forward through a thousand trials, a thousand disappointments. Now the work was hers. She clasped her hands together so tightly that the nails bit into the palms. She was so tired. Already they had written to her from England, accepting that she must close the mission when Henry's slow, inevitable march to death reached its end. It would be easy to give up, and leave this burning, desolate land to its heathenism, to the pagan sexuality, which could live even in dead stone and seemed to wink and laugh everywhere, just under the decorous surface of life.

'Give me strength to stay. I will not go,' she prayed. The mission, her husband's lifework, must live on in her, where he himself would live, inviolate.

She sat back on the bench, feeling the sweat run down between her thighs and under her breasts.

As clearly as though he were speaking to her now she heard the man's voice, Rodney Savage's voice: 'You've chosen a fine time to arrive, haven't you? Can't you read the traffic signs? One-way only, for us. That way.' And the vivid image of the man saying them, one upflung arm pointing out to sea, face grinning sardonically under the street lamp.

Now it was dawn that morning a year ago, August 15, 1947, India's Independence Day. She stood on the deck and watched the grey hot light spread under the monsoon clouds, and watched the approaching city grow out of the water. Henry lay in his bunk, weak and in pain with the first intimations of his illness. She remembered thinking, guiltily, as the Gateway of India slid past, that it was a strange moment to be arriving, bearing the dour messages of

12

Lancashire nonconformist Christianity, in a country joy-fully celebrating its reunion with its Hindu past. Henry had been here before, of course, many years. Henry felt nothing, no premonition, no despair. But Henry had faith.

By the evening of that day Henry felt a little better, but not well enough to go and see Sir Andrew. She quieted his fears on her account, left him in the cheap hotel, and went herself. McFadden Pulley's cement works at Sabora were close to the Lapri Mission and the firm had always been generous in its help.

It had drizzled slightly on her way, but when she came out after seeing Sir Andrew the rain had stopped. The streets were in pandemonium. Rockets fizzed across the sky, thunder flashes exploded everywhere, and bonfires flared in the road-ways. Without warning a surging crowd, yelling and singing at the tops of their voices, had surrounded her, and she had felt a momentary panic. She found herself pressed against a lamp-post, close to a tall British officer. He was wearing a peaked military cap of pale khaki felt with a black cloth patch behind the big silver badge. The light shining directly on his shoulders showed his rank badges, the black crown and star of a lieutenant-colonel of a Rifle regiment – she had learned all that during the war. A heavy lanyard of twisted black and dark-green cord looped round his neck under the lapels of his tunic, and then divided at the top shirt button, one strand disappearing into each breast pocket. He wore two rows of medal ribbons, starting with the O.B.E. and then the Military Cross with two silver rosettes. Three M.C.s, she remembered thinking – he was a hero. Rodney Savage.

He noticed her, examined her, and after a while said, 'Frightened?'

'A little,' she said, smiling because her panic had gone. 'They seem so . . . wild.'

'Just off the boat?'

She nodded. 'This morning, very early. My husband is a medical missionary. He's been out before, but this is my first time.' She had to shout to make herself heard above the din. 'Have you been here long?'

That was when he said it, 'Can't you read the traffic signals? One-way only, for us. That way,' and the arm pointing seaward. That was also when she realised he was

13

drunk. Nearly paralytic, her long nurse's training added. She found herself examining him with clinical interest. The lamp-post was supporting him, but his eyes were out of focus and his voice slow, the words kept separate by hard effort, each word slightly blurred.

She became frightened again, for her question seemed to galvanise him into action. He took a step forward and stood, swaying slightly in the middle of the crowd. He raised his hand, and bellowed in a tremendous voice, 'Indians! Listen to me.' The people nearest to him turned in astonishment. The noise took a while to die down, but soon he stood in the centre of a dense circle of excited, dark faces.

'Indians,' he repeated, 'you are now independent . . . ' The faces broke into smiles, and a dozen voices rose in eager shouts in a language she could not understand. A tall thin man in a dhoti shouted in English, 'And about time, too, don't you agree?'

The drunken colonel bawled, 'You are taking over this country as a gift from me . . . ' He turned to the man in the dhoti and added, 'It is *not* about time, my friend, because you will make an unholy mess of it.'

She tried to move behind the lamp-post and out of sight. If he annoyed them, they would both be torn in pieces. These people were out of control.

The dhoti wearer translated for the crowd, who murmured loudly. The dhoti wearer said, 'But it is our country! You would not be denying that?'

'Certainly, I do! It is not your country. It is mine. I made it, from a hundred countries, I and my great-great-grandfather, and my great-grandfather, and so on. But don't forget my father, my father, whom you murdered yesterday because he loved you.' He raised his voice still more. 'I am sorry I do not speak Gujrati, but my friend here will translate for you . . . You are ignorant, superstitious, lazy buggers. You don't believe in India, because you're too, too small to understand India. Only understand your own dungheap . . . ' She looked over her shoulder for a way of escape, but there was none. She was hemmed in. The colonel went on, 'Whassa name that little man, no clothes, spectacles, spinning wheel?'

'The Mahatma!' the English-speaker gasped. 'Oh, do not dare . . . '

'He understood,' the colonel shouted, 'so you shot him.

14

Like my father . . . Well, aren't you going to kill me, too?'

The English-speaker hung his head as he mumbled a translation. The crowd fell silent. Margaret watched in numb astonishment.

The colonel threw his arms wide and began to talk in a language she did not then understand, but now knew was Hindi. Simultaneously he embraced the English-speaker and shouted, 'It'll be all right!' In a moment he almost vanished under the yelling, weeping, laughing crowd. She saw him shaking hands, hugging everyone close to him, and kissing women on the cheek.

Slowly the crowd moved on down the street, singing louder than ever. Colonel Savage stood in the middle of the road, alone among trodden garlands and wilting flowers, the smoke of a bonfire drifting past. He raised both arms, palms extended and fingers spread wide and began to chant at the deep, light-flecked clouds over the city: 'Let us now praise famous men and our fathers that begat us. Let us call down God's blessing upon Robert Clive, First and Last Baron Clive of Plassey and of the County of something or other. And Warren Hastings, impeached by the mighty British nation for preserving their profits, extending their dominions, and loving India. And Stringer Lawrence and Eyre Coote, those much-underestimated soldiers. And Nicholson, Lawrence, Lawrence, Lawrence, Hodson, and Edwardes, the Old Firm, the muscular Christian moving men. And Mountstuart Elphinstone, Gent. and innumerable people called Battye and Coldstream, who usually died, without public comment, in places called Rumblebellypore or Rotimakkanganj. And William Hickey, and Mr Justice Elijah Impey, and the great Elihu Yale, sometime chief despot of Madras. And Bobs Bahadur too let us not forget him, O Lord, in spite of his well-known weakness in matters of administration.'

He stopped suddenly and staggered towards her. 'You were frightened,' he said accusingly. 'You'll never make a memsahib. You will be terribly polite, and afraid, and, and – hating them. I . . . I'm rude, and I'm not afraid, and . . . I love them. But it's time to go. That's the whole sad sad story. Time to go. *But I'm not going.* Never. See?'

He stood and examined her thoroughly. 'You're a good-looking woman, wonderful body. Would you care to take

15

your clothes off? Take 'em off, and we'll make love in the street, here. Only proper thing to do, today.'

He put out his hand. She gathered her stunned wits and began to run. After a few seconds, realising no one was following, she looked over her shoulder. The colonel lay alone on his face at the edge of the road, under the street lamp. For a time she hesitated, watching and waiting, then she turned again and hurried to the hotel . . .

It was stifling in the chapel now. She got up slowly, and found her knees stiff. She walked out into the leaden glare of day. Time to go – but, like him, she would not go. She crossed the road and entered the low hut that was the mission hospital's only ward.

Chapter 2

Major-General Ran Singh Dadhwal, known throughout the Indian Army as 'Max', spread his big hands on the table and looked up. '*Achcha,* so what do you propose to do now, Ranjit?'

The man opposite him, across the table, Mr Ranjit Singh, Indian Civil Service, was the Deputy Commissioner of the district. He was about thirty-six years of age, and wore a smart suntan suit with a white shirt and British cricket club tie – the Free Foresters, the general noted. The Deputy Commissioner was a Sikh, and today his long hair was bound up in a puggaree of dazzling pink. A polished steel bangle showed on his right wrist under the sleeve of his coat.

'I think we will have to be quite firm,' Ranjit Singh said. 'If we don't nip it in the bud now we will have worse trouble later.'

The general nodded. That's what he had expected to hear. Sikhs usually liked to be tough on everyone's foibles except their own. Also, there was the I.C.S. tradition. Eight hundred Englishmen hadn't ruled four hundred million Indians by forming committees. They'd gone out and done something, in person, at once. All Indians joining the I.C.S. had learned the lesson.

The general said, 'I can send a battalion down to man-oeuvre in the area while you go in and haul out the ring-leaders . . . but I presume you'll speak to the Governor before that. I mean, about what action is to be taken if they won't come. I don't want my chaps to drift into a battle. I want to know what the policy is before we go in. Otherwise, you'll have to do it with the police alone.'

The light changed and the two Indians glanced up. An Englishman stood in the open double doors, smiling. The general leaped to his feet. 'Rodney! What are you doing here?' He pumped the newcomer's arm. 'My God, it's funny seeing you in mufti again. Just like before the war! Have you made your lakh yet, or is it a crore by now?'

The Englishman grinned and slapped the general's back. 'I am in this area because McFadden Pulley have sent me to study their cement operations. I'm in this dak bungalow because there was gossip that the Courageous General Sahib and the August Collector Sahib – they still use the old titles here, don't they? – were meeting to discuss yesterday's incident at Bhilghat.' He turned to the Sikh. 'You're the D.C.? I'm Rodney Savage.'

'Ranjit Singh,' the D.C. said, smiling.

'How's the policeman who . . . ?'

'Died this morning, in Bhowani hospital,' the D.C. said.

'Poor bastards,' Rodney said. 'They must be desperate.'

The general smiled at the remark. Rodney's instinctive reaction was for the Gonds, who had committed the outrage, rather than for the forces of law and order. Yet he had enforced the law often enough, as ruthlessly as he had fought the Japanese.

Rodney turned to him. 'I'm interrupting a conference – and that's what I meant to do. Look – if there isn't anything secret or high policy about this, can I help? I know Bhilghat pretty well. I was there before the war, and again once or twice in '46. And I've got a sort of family connection with the Gonds there. You don't *have* to listen to me . . . any more . . . ' he grinned, 'but it's just possible that I might say something helpful.'

The general looked at the D.C. This was a civilian party, so far, and he'd have to abide by Ranjit Singh's decision. The I.C.S. didn't take kindly to advice from soldiers at the best of times, and now, with independence so recent, and Rodney an Englishman . . .

To his surprise the D.C. said, after only a small hesitation, 'Please do. Why don't you sit down?'

They all sat. Rodney said, 'In case it leaks out to your superiors that I was at this conference, I was just expressing McFadden Pulley's anxiety over the possible effects on our quarrying operations.'

'The story's simple enough,' D.C. said. 'About a month ago the provincial government, in accordance with the policy of the Government of India, abolished the post of special assistant commissioner for Bhilghat.'

'The best young man's job in the I.C.S.,' Rodney murmured.

'Yes, but against national policy,' the D.C. said, smiling a little thinly. 'The Gonds have always been treated as a separate people, as savages. Their isolation from the rest of India, and other Indians, has been preserved and even reinforced. We cannot accept that. All Indians are – Indians. Bhilgat lies geographically in my district, Bijoli, and it has now been included in it. The Special Assistant Commissioner, who used to be responsible to the Governor direct, is now merely my own assistant. They gave me a new man . . . '

The general glanced at Rodney, expecting a groan or a sign of dismay; those were his own reactions at the time when the decision had been made. But Rodney showed nothing. The D.C. must also have expected disapproval, for he added quickly, 'We had to. The man there, though he was an Indian, had identified himself too closely with the Gonds . . . Yesterday the new man went down to discuss the building and staffing of a school for the Gonds. They opened fire on him, wounded him – he's still in hospital – and one of his police escort, the man who died.'

Rodney said, 'And you're planning to go back with more police, or some of Max's men in the background?'

'I am going to get hold of the headman and the elders, and I'm going to discuss schools,' the D.C. said. 'I don't propose to make much fuss about the affair yesterday, if they co-operate now. If they don't – then . . . ' He shrugged.

Max watched his friend drumming his fingers on the table. He hoped he would come out with some idea that would save the Gonds from further trouble. They were a race of aborigines, living widely scattered over these Vindhya hills of Central India and completely out of touch with the modern world. They were not a relic of medieval times, nor yet of India's Golden Age, but of pre-history. They were pathetic and yet likeable. He wished that their individualism could somehow be preserved . . . but the new policy was right. A new India, a single India, conscious of its oneness, had to be created somehow, and fast.

Rodney said, 'Will you let me go down there alone to talk to the headman?' The D.C. started to speak but Rodney raised his hand. 'Not as an official emissary. Suppose I had heard nothing of yesterday's affair and just happened to be driving down that way. I don't think I'll be in any danger. I wouldn't go if I thought that. My hero days are over.' He smiled again, the wide grin that looked out of place under the cold blue eyes. That grin had always made Max smile, too, and he smiled now.

The D.C. said gently, 'I appreciate your offer, Savage – but I'm afraid I can't permit that. After all, I'm trying to make the Gonds realise that there's a new government of India – and that they're a part of it.'

Rodney said, 'Then why don't you and Max come with me?'

'We will increase the danger of a clash,' Max said.

The D.C. grimaced. 'We will, damn it, though it's an annoying thing to have to admit. And if they shoot me or the general, I'm afraid they will be in real trouble. I had thought of going down alone, of course, and decided it was not fair to them. After all, if they are willing to shoot at Parsad, how much more at me?'

'And to bore holes in a Thrice-Born of the I.C.S. is a heinous crime, indeed,' Rodney said with a straight face. The D.C. looked at him suspiciously, and then laughed.

Rodney said, 'Look, I have no position. But I do know these people. I think I can guarantee there won't be any trouble. If we fail, we'll fail without bloodshed. I believe it's worth trying.'

The D.C. made up his mind quickly. 'All right. When can you start?'

'Quarter of an hour,' Rodney said. 'I suggest we go in my company's jeep – we three, and Ratanbir. He's my orderly – I mean my chauffeur. Lately Havildar Ratanbir Burathoki, I.D.S.M., of the 1/13th Gurkha Rifles.'

The general sat up. 'Ratanbir? Is that the fellow who killed two Japanese officers with his *kukri* the night we – ?'

The D.C. interrupted, smiling, 'We had better get ready...'

'Sorry,' the general said, 'Rodney and I haven't met for a long time. We'll have a good *gup* when we come back, eh? You must come and stay with us in Bhowani. Well, we can discuss that on the trip. Oh, and Janaki's coming out...'

But Rodney had gone, with a wave of the hand, and the D.C. was on his feet. 'An old army friend of yours? He's the man who got K. P. Roy, isn't he?'

The general said, 'Yes. He's more than a friend. He saved my career once.'

20

'Yours?' the D.C. said incredulously. 'I've never heard that you were the sort of chap to get into trouble.'

The general hesitated: but it was important to let the D.C. know what sort of man Rodney Savage was. He said, 'It was in Peshawar, not long after he'd joined – I had seven or eight years' service by then. We were an Indianised battalian, of course, and the fellow next junior to me got into moneylender trouble. He asked me to lend him two thousand chips out of the Treasure Chest or there'd be a stink, a court-martial . . . The stink would have been about a dishonest Indian. I felt it my duty to our reputation – there weren't so many of us in the service then – to help him. He put the lot on the horses, lost it, and disappeared. Then it was me who was in danger of a court-martial, and cashiering . . . one Indian instead of another. I told Janaki. She must have told Rodney, though I specially ordered her not to say anything – I had to face the music myself. Next day he came to the bungalow and gave me two thousand rupees.'

'Did he say where he got it?'

'No . . . I've always believed he stole it, but he never said a word, or I couldn't have taken it. It was bad enough anyway – but thinking of Janaki, what would happen to us, made me desperate.'

'A good friend, but a pretty ruthless character,' the D.C. murmured.

The general said, 'Yes, I suppose you'd have to say that . . . We kept on running into each other after that, on the Frontier. Then we commanded battalions in the same brigade in Burma. He was a hell of a good soldier.'

'Old India family?'

The general nodded. 'Yes. Very old.'

The D.C. said, 'Poor devils. They can't let go, even if they want to. Still, they had a long innings, and a good one, from their point of view . . . I'll be ready in a minute.'

The general picked up his red-banded hat and put it carefully on his head. He must tell his orderly and driver they were to stay here. Janaki was due later this afternoon to see how her Sabora Cottage Industry Co-operative was coming along. And, my God, he'd nearly forgotten – Sumitra was coming too. Not to look at Cottage Industries – out of boredom, more likely, and to preach birth control to giggling, nervous village women. Have to tell the *chowkidar* to get her room ready . . . Funny, Rodney turning up out of the blue. You couldn't agree with Rodney all the time about India. No Indian could. But you knew he loved India. You could fight happily with him. He sighed and went to his room to fill his tobacco pouch.

He and the D.C. were waiting on the veranda when a jeep drove up fast from the direction of the little town down the road. Rodney sat in the front seat beside a short Gurkha wearing khaki trousers, a white shirt, and a small round black cap. As the jeep stopped, Rodney swung easily into the back seat. 'Will you sit in front, Ranjit? Then they'll hit you first. Max and I will cower in the back. Thirty-two miles to Bhilghat – about an hour and a half on this road.'

They drove off. Max found his feet awkwardly placed on top of a large sack, that clinked as the jeep bounced along the rutted, muddy road, little more than a cart track. He cocked his head inquisitively, and the D.C. turned round in his seat.

Rodney Savage said, 'Rum. It helps.'

The jeep bumped on, often in four-wheeled drive and low gear in the deep reddish mud. The general fumbled for his pipe and began to fill it with his favourite mixture, a Benson and Hedges Special, which he ordered direct from London. Won't be getting this much longer, he thought, after the Prime Minister's warning that India must cut down imports.

The road wound up a low rise in short, steep zigzags, the outer edge marked by mud-splashed white stones. Momentarily from the top a long view spread out to the south, the foreground and middle distance all green under the jungle, the background dim blue, the whole filmed with a thin haze that reduced all dimensions to one, like a coat of paint on the surface. For a second the land seemed almost featureless, but, quickly, as the jeep's nose dipped down the far slope, he saw scattered cliffs, which marked the edge of gorges, and lines of rock on far escarpments, and the flash of water in a lake. Heavy white cloud formations sailing over from the southwest covered half the sky. Then they were grinding down in low gear, and he was looking under the ranked trees, where the wet leaves lay thick on the short grass, and there was a flock of goats and a young girl standing guard over them in the shade of a sal tree.

Something about his companion's attitude attracted his

22

attention and he turned his head. Rodney Savage sat hunched forward, staring past Ratanbir's head at the landscape – no, not at it, but through and beyond it. His lips were slightly open and his whole being seemed to be projected forward – out of the bumping vehicle into the patterned sunlight and shadow of the jungle. He began to speak. 'Remember the mahua berries in July?' Max opened his mouth, then closed it. His friend was not speaking to him, nor to any of them.

'. . . They lie sticky and white under the trees everywhere in the jungle. The rain seems to fall directly through the trees then, because the monsoon has made the leaves heavy with all the water they can bear. The raindrops glisten on the berries. If you're near a village you see men and women and children gathering them, like ants . . . bent down, the baskets beside them, gathering up the berries and dropping them into the baskets. And someone has always started to boil them in the village, so if you're coming upwind you can smell the sweet, fermenting smell from two miles away . . .'

He stopped, and when he spoke again it was in a different voice: 'What did that missionary in Lapri die of, Ranjit?'

'Dr Wood? Cancer. Did you know him?'

'No. I'd heard of them, of course. They are on M.P.'s books as worthy objects of our charity – and to leaven our profits with a little godliness.'

'It looks good on the balance sheets,' the D.C. said dryly. 'And, of course, the Raj had to stick together.'

Rodney laughed. 'What was he like – Wood?'

'A good man,' the D.C. said slowly. 'He'd been in India a long time but somehow never came to terms with it. He always looked a little surprised and horrified – at the heat, the dirt, the things his patients and the villagers did or didn't do. He was alone there for years, and then near the end of the war he went back to England and married the most competent nurse in the hospital where he'd been trained himself, years before. She's a good deal younger than he is – was. Northern Irish. Her name was Donoghue. A good-looking woman – good figure, auburn hair, and one of those skins that go with it, creamy and almost transparent but healthy.'

'I know,' Rodney said. 'I met her yesterday by accident.

23

She'd been wandering round the jungles all day, in a daze. It must have been a blow.'

The D.C. said, 'I suppose she loved him. She certainly acted like it, and there must have been *something*, to bring her out here. But, you know, it wasn't what I'd call love. Perhaps it was religious fervour, or faith, or – '

'I met her once,' Max interposed. 'She's like an Indian woman, that's all. She married this man, and accepted him and his life and tried to make it her all. How well she succeeded' – he shrugged – 'no one can know. Perhaps she needed more time, and now he's gone.'

'The poor devil was ill the whole time since he came back last year,' the D.C. said.

'She must be absolutely lost,' Max said. 'And, hey, Rodney, that reminds me – congratulations on your engagement. When's the wedding?'

'October, in Delhi . . . We're getting near, Collector. *Asti janu, choro.* I think I'll stand up, if you don't mind.' The jeep slowed and Max thought, he's as sharp as ever. Calling Ranjit 'Collector' suddenly, like that, established the official relationships, and made an acknowledgement that the Sikh was in charge.

It would be easier if Rodney and the D.C. changed places, so that Rodney could hold on to the windshield, Max thought. But that would put the two Indians in the back seat. 'Here, hang on to my shoulder,' he said. He settled his red cap more firmly on his head, grasped his pipe between his teeth, and began to search the side of the road. They'd just passed milestone 28. If the Gonds meant business . . . The jeep swept round a sharp bend and lurched to a halt, throwing the passengers forward.

A sharp clattering sound from the hood made Max look up, and he saw an arrow turning in the air, to land beyond in the mud. Several large boughs blocked the road.

'No farther,' a voice called from the jungle in accented Hindi. 'Go back, or we will shoot, with guns.'

'Sit still, everyone,' the D.C. said sharply.

Rodney turned his face towards the jungle, from where the invisible voice had called. He spoke conversationally, in Hindi. 'Ohé, brother! Is Badal the *shikari* still alive?'

After a long pause the voice answered grudgingly, 'No, he is dead. Now, go back, or we will shoot.'

'Gulu, then? His younger brother.'

'Gulu's the chief now,' the D.C. muttered.

Rodney said, 'Tell Gulu, the chief, that Savage Sahib is here and wishes to talk to him about hunting. Savage Sahib, great-great-grandson of the Deliverer.'

There was a long pause, and then the voice said, 'I recognise you, sahib. Wait.'

Rodney sat down and said, 'We'll have a long wait. Gulu will be in the village.'

'Who was the Deliverer?' the D.C. asked curiously.

'William Savage.'

'The man who destroyed Thuggee?'

Rodney nodded. 'He spent a lot of time with the Gonds after that. It was nothing to do with the Thugs, as far as I can make out, that they call him the Deliverer. It was the British Government he saved them from, who were going to do something dreadful to them.'

'Build a school, perhaps,' the D.C. said dryly.

They all laughed, and then settled down to wait. Max examined the jungle curiously. There were probably half a dozen small dark men in there, with bows and arrows and a couple of ancient muskets trained on them from no more than fifteen feet – and he could see nothing. At least one man, probably two, had just run off through the heavy undergrowth towards the village – and he had heard nothing. He sighed and began relighting his pipe. If he could train his sepoys to move like that . . .

Heavier clouds piled up in the sky, and he felt hungry. Why had no one remembered to bring food? Probably because Rodney intended to ask the Gonds for it, to establish that they were guests. Who was it who'd written, 'If you want to make a friend, allow him to do you a favour'? Now Rodney would have to eat fried rat and raw ants. Thank God he himself was a Hindu and could properly refuse.

A man stood suddenly in the road five feet from the jeep's hood. He wore a loincloth, and nothing else, and carried a small long-handled axe in his hand. He was short, square, and very black, with short grizzled hair over a wide, angular, wrinkled face.

Rodney stood up. 'Gulu – greetings!' He stepped down from the jeep and walked forward. The two embraced formally, first clasping each other round the shoulders and then standing back and bowing, palms joined.

'May your belly always be full, sahib. You look well.'

They exchanged polite small talk for a few minutes. Then the old Gond said, 'Come to the village, and we will eat and drink. The mahua arrack from this year is good, though fiery, and I have a little left, a barrel, from last year.'

'Thank you,' Rodney said. 'I am with these friends – Ranjit Singh-sahib, Deputy Commissioner . . .'

Gulu the chief folded his thin, strong arms across his chest. 'I do not know him. He may not pass.'

The D.C., his face set, began to climb out of the jeep. Rodney said in a low voice, 'Very easy, Collector!' He turned back to the Gond. 'I think you do know him, Uncle. Whether or no – he is my friend and so is the other, the General-sahib, Dadhwal. And the driver, Havildar Ratanbir, a Gurkha. Him you know, he came with me before, when we were in the army.'

'Him I know,' the chief said. He went forward and embraced the Gurkha.

Rodney said, 'We are unarmed, all of us.'

The old Gond had returned to the middle of the road, arms folded, the axe blade over his right shoulder, his head high, silent, unsmiling.

Rodney said slowly, 'Was it not said, once, that the Deliverer and his seed, from then to the end of time, were Gonds? Free to eat and drink and hunt in all Gond lands? To demand the life of any Gond man, with or without reason? Put their own life into any Gond woman not already pregnant? Were these words only the promise of a Hindu *banniah*, to be forgotten when there is no profit to be made from them?'

God, the general thought, he's being hard on them. The promise must already have lasted a century and a quarter; and the deed Rodney was now helping the D.C. to accomplish would mean the end of the promise and the end of the kind of society that could give and keep it.

The old chief stood a minute longer, then bowed his head. 'It was said. I am sorry. They may come, as your friends. For no other reason.'

'We come as the representatives of the Government of India,' the D.C. said stiffly.

The old chief bowed ironically, and Max thought, we do

not, we come under the protection of an Englishman, in our own country. Well, that's the way it was. Next year, the year after, it would be different. There was nothing to be done about it now, except be patient and understanding.

'Get in the jeep, Gulu,' Rodney said. The old man threw a few words over his shoulder into the silent jungle and climbed in. Two men appeared and dragged away the tree boughs. Ratanbir drove slowly on, Gulu now perched on the back seat between Max and Rodney.

It's all over, Max thought, all over bar the shouting. The Gonds were not fools and the only real problem was to reach them without creating another bloody incident.

As he had predicted, the tension relaxed all day, slowly but steadily. An hour after reaching the compact village – all the huts were very small, and two or three families lived in caves – they ate, and not mice or worms but a fine fish, with curried vegetables and chapatties. Outside the hut a short, heavy rain fell, darkening earth and sky. Inside, they sat on beaten earth and were served in silence by Gulu's grand-daughters. Gulu had vanished and did not reappear until mid-afternoon. By then the rain had stopped, the hot sun had dried the grass, and the appearance of able-bodied men in considerable numbers proved that the pickets and scouts had been recalled.

Then Gulu came, and Rodney talked with him for a long time outside, while he himself and Ranjit pretended to sleep in the hut. It would be undignified for the D.C. to hang around, aimless, while the Englishman talked, and this was a good way out. Rodney and Gulu were not far off, and Max, listening to their voices, caught enough to know that Rodney was not discussing the school, nor yesterday's attack on the Assistant Commissioner's party, but *shikar*. There were a good many tigers over to the west, across the border in Chambal State, the old Gond said. A man who went out from here, or from Lapri, could have good shooting. There was good fishing also – he named four kinds of fish. Then they reminisced about Rodney's last visit, and two or three times Gulu cackled with laughter. Max heard the clink of bottles, and later the gurgle of liquid. He hoped Rodney knew what he was doing. The ice had to be broken, but if the Gonds were still in a state of fear and inner tension they might get fighting drunk. Rodney would be all right, but he

27

and Ranjit could easily finish up with poisoned arrows in their guts.

'Now try the arrack, sahib,' he heard the chief say distinctly. 'That is this year's.' There was a faint female giggle. The grand-daughters were pretty girls, for Gonds, and young; they must be great-grand-daughters. The Gonds often consummated marriage at twelve or younger.

The sounds of talk and laughter increased outside and the D.C. sat up. 'About time we joined the party, I think,' he said. They brushed off their clothes and walked out. Twenty villagers were gathered by then, all men except for the two girls crouched in the background. A momentary silence greeted them, broken by Rodney calling, 'Sit down, Collector. I happen to have brought a little rum with me. Gulu has been telling me about the *shikar* . . . '

Then they all talked about *shikar*, which to these people meant food and life; and from there to the state of the few crops the Gonds grew, a little millet on the cleared hillside, a little rice in the bottoms. The D.C. never mentioned the object of his visit and Max thought, he's good, he has the I.C.S. stamp of confidence and firmness, plus an Indian's sense of community, of not being a stranger, however marvellous. As the dusk fell the girls brought little scraps of toasted, curried meat. Max ate without inquiring what they were. They would not be beef anyway, because the Gonds owned not cattle, only a few goats. Two young men lit a bonfire and at the edge of the circle women began to appear, squatting on their hunkers, loinclothed like the men, bare breasted, the younger ones with at least one baby, sometimes two, at breast, and another in the lap.

The murmuring increased, more food came, more people came. Full darkness crept up from the reed-rimmed shore of the lake. Arrack passed round, in bamboo mugs, teak bowls, and earthenware jars. An hour after dark a young man shuffled out in front of the fire and began to dance. Others joined him. Singing began, guttural and almost tuneless melodies that wandered about near the bottom of the scale. Small drums began to rattle and throb. On Max's right, Gulu squatted between Rodney and the D.C.

The two wide-mouthed girls crouched close behind Rodney. Max felt sure, from their protective, intimate attitude that Rodney had slept with them when he was last here. He wondered whether he would do so again tonight. Perhaps he would have to, to avoid upsetting the Gonds, if they had been offered to him as a special gift or because of his relationship with the Deliverer. Himself, he'd rather not. Gond women were really not attractive, and although Janaki would understand if he had to – he just didn't want to. He'd hardly ever wanted another woman than her. To be honest, hardly any other woman had ever wanted him – unlike Rodney. It must be a problem at times, that animal vitality which could at any moment make any woman, even the most respectable, suddenly think of bed. Ah, well, it wasn't likely to be a problem of his. He puffed contentedly at his pipe, noting that about two more rums would be enough for him.

The D.C. was saying, 'No – he died this morning. It was in his fate.' He spoke equably, as though the murder of a policeman on duty was a mere accident, which might have happened to anyone. Good, Max thought; really, it was an accident. A sudden outburst like that, from the Gonds, was an act of nature. There would be many more such, among many Indian tribes and peoples, before they could all be treated as rational human beings, answerable to a court of law for every action. And now the subject had been broached, and the old Gond was relaxed and full of rum and arrack.

The D.C. began to tell Gulu about the school he himself had been to, as a little boy in a Punjab village. Rodney got up, caught the two girls by the wrists and dragged them out, giggling and shrieking, into the centre of the circle by the fire. 'Now I shall dance,' he cried.

He began to gyrate and twist, his feet shuffling time with the beat of the nearest drum – there were a dozen different beats, half a dozen groups of dancers. Holding the girls tight, he danced with ludicrously suggestive movements, and most of the audience collapsed on to the grass, laughing with painful gasps. The girls dragged free and rushed into the shadow of a hut, where they hid their faces behind their hands and watched, cackling with laughter as loud as anyone.

After five minutes Rodney beckoned, and Ratanbir the Gurkha stepped out into the firelight. Rodney seized a drum from a man collapsed with laughter and began to beat a subtle complex rhythm. Ratanbir, his face downcast and earnest, began to dance. Rodney sang, a haunting repetitive melody.

Max poured himself another rum. The D.C. and the chief, their heads close together, were talking about schoolteachers. Where could they find a teacher who understood the Gond language? How could the village pay for such people? The Gurkha danced in slow grace, his powerful squat body bending and turning as sinuously as a girl's. The audience was silent, except for the murmurs of Gulu and the D.C. The fire crackled and hissed as a few drops of rain fell. The underside of the trees reflected a diffuse yellowish light down on the thatched roofs of the huts, the dark heads, the babies sleeping in their mothers' arms.

Gulu the chief rose suddenly to his feet and clapped his hands with a short explosive sound. Ratanbir stopped dancing. Rodney let the rhythm of his drum die down in two more phrases, soft and softer. Gulu spoke a few short sentences in his own language, which Max could not understand. The D.C. leaned over to him and whispered, 'He's agreed. We won't build the school. We'll give them some money, and they'll build it themselves. We're getting a Gond-speaking teacher up from Jubbulpore. He never gave us a chance to tell him that before.'

The old man flung his arms wide in a motion that said, without the need for words, let joy be unconfined. The drums struck up, the singing redoubled, dancers gyrated wildly on the grass.

Rodney approached and Max got up, his hand out. 'Congratulations, Rodney.'

His friend looked tired now and his smile was a little grim. 'Thanks . . . I don't like it, you know.'

'What, education for the Gonds?'

Rodney looked back at the fire and the dancing figures. 'I don't know. Perhaps not even that. Certainly not bringing out these people's basic warmth and then – stabbing them in the back. Next time you come here it won't be like this. There'll be a political rally instead. Guest speaker – Mr Purshottamdass Tirthankardass, M.L.A.' He went abruptly over to the headman and said, 'Uncle, I am tired. With your permission, I shall go to sleep.'

'Thus early?' the old man said in surprise. 'You did not

sleep at all last time you came to Bhilghat.' The D.C. was looking up at Rodney, his expression compassionate. Rodney said, 'The Collector Sahib wishes to sit up all night, though. All Sikhs are mighty drinkers of rum, and the Collector Sahib is a champion among Sikhs.'

'That's a dirty trick,' the D.C. said in English. 'Well, I suppose even the worst hangover in history would be worth it.'

Gulu said, 'Very well, sahib.' He gestured with his chin. 'Your women are there.'

'Not tonight, Uncle. I could not do justice to them.'

He strode away towards the hut appointed for them. Max made his own apologies and followed. It was dark inside and there was no bed, only three flattened piles of dry grass. As Max entered he heard the rustling of grass and muttered, 'Which one are you taking, Rodney?'

'This one, in the corner.' A match flared and then the glow of a cigarette end. Now also the light from the fire outside, slipping in through a hundred tiny cracks in the walls, enabled Max to see. Rodney was sitting cross-legged in the middle of his pile of grass, the cigarette hanging from his lower lip and his face twisted up in the smoke. He bent forward to untie his shoe laces. Max sat down and followed suit.

Rodney loosened his belt and said, 'That's it. Not a very complicated toilette.' He sat there, just as he had in the jeep, staring towards the open doorway and the shadowed jungle, lit by the fire from the other side. He began to speak. 'Poor girls . . . *She* smelled very different, and she was beautiful where these are ugly – to my eyes – but there was something of the same in her. A different relationship with a man. She was as passionate as these half-savage girls are, and they are like rutting animals, and like them, she'd never found that there was a war between men and women. There was none of the hostility you sometimes feel with our women. The moon was in the same phase as it is tonight, and it shone on her hair, her hair flowing like a dark river so that all I could see was hair and all I could feel was flesh, and all I could smell was . . . India.'

'Who was it?' Max asked gently. 'I don't mean her name, but . . .'

'My first Indian woman,' Rodney said. 'I wonder whether

31

I've had my last. I'm engaged, remember? That's why I didn't go to the girls. Frances wouldn't understand. You know her?'

'No. She's John Clayton's sister, isn't she – the fellow who was your M.T.O. in Burma?'

'Yes. He was in McFadden Pulley's before he volunteered. He got me my job with them when I chucked the Service. His wife went home to put the kids in school, so Frances came out to housekeep for him, early in '47 . . . Almost one year of total chastity for R. Savage. You ought to win some bets on that.' He laughed aloud, the strange mood vanished. 'Good night.'

The grass rustled and Max lay back, pillowed his head on his arms, and soon fell asleep.

Shortly before noon the next day the jeep ground over the brow of the last hill on the return journey, and Max saw the quarries and the pall of reddish dust that marked Sabora in the valley below. Now Rodney was driving, and Max sitting beside him. Rodney turned his head and said, '*Eh, atharsi!* Collector Sahib *lai utha.*'

Max watched, smiling, as the Gurkha gently moved his shoulder. The D.C. sat up, yawning and rubbing his blood-shot eyes. He looked very pale and dishevelled. As he adjusted the pink puggaree more firmly on his head, he muttered. 'God, I feel awful.'

'And two beautiful ladies to greet you when we arrive,' Rodney said cheerfully.

'Oh, no!' the D.C. cried. 'Who?'

'My wife and the Rani of Kishanpur – Sumitra,' Max said.

'Sumitra?' the D.C. said. 'I'd better hurry back to Bijoli, full speed. My wife will give me hell if she hears I've been meeting *her* in deserted dak bungalows at the back of beyond.'

'You must stay for a drink and lunch,' Max said; and then Rodney stopped the jeep in front of the dak bungalow. Max's orderly ran out, followed a moment later by two women. Max walked up the steps. 'Hullo, darling. The excitement's over.' He caught her hand momentarily and as he did so he noticed that she was staring over his shoulder, her body tense. 'Rodney,' she said, 'Rodney Savage!'

Rodney came up then, a half-smile on his face. 'In person.' He held out his hand. 'How are you, Janaki?'

She dropped her eyes. 'This is the Rani of Kishanpur. Colonel Rodney Savage.'

The Rani said, 'Rodney – the famous Rodney.'

Rodney stood and stared at her, the half-smile still on his face. 'Sumitra.'

Max watched, fascinated, as they stood there, looking, gauging, Janaki between them. Sumitra had the classical rounded Indian beauty, wheat-gold skin, her black hair piled in a loose Western wave on top of her head. She wore a pale-blue sari, and high-heeled sandals. Janaki was much smaller, her figure in the patterned red sari seeming almost childlike beside the Rani's full-bosomed curves. Her cheekbones were higher and the eyes wider set in the small heart-shaped face; and she was darker than the other, and her heavy head of hair was swept down from a straight centre parting.

The Rani broke the silence. 'I have known about you for twelve years – since I married Dip. And now we meet.'

'I can say the same,' Rodney said.

Then the D.C. came up, and the men excused themselves and went to a spare bathroom to wash off the mud and dirt of the road and the Gond village.

'I didn't know you knew Kishanpur,' Max said, slapping cold water over his face.

Rodney said, 'That goes back a long time, too – to my great-grandfather. He and the Kishanpurs fought in the Mutiny together . . . on opposite sides. Remember Sumitra Rawan, the Rani of Kishanpur?'

'My God!' Max said softly. 'That one. You really are mixed up with India, aren't you?'

The woman on the veranda was also a Rani of Kishanpur, and she was also called Sumitra; but when you mentioned those names, without qualification, it was taken for granted that you meant the famous heroine of 1857. She had led cavalry charges against the British in the Great Mutiny of that year, and had finally vanished, no one knew where or how. Some said it was to refuge in Nepal or Tibet; some said, into a Hindu *ashram*; some said, to lie unknown among the dead of the last great battle of the Mutiny.

Rodney said, 'She and my great-grandfather tried to kill each other – and fell in love. Things like that used to happen.

3   33

They still do . . . The two families have had a sort of foster-brother relationship ever since. They sent Dip Rao, the present Rajah, to stay with us in England for a time when he was a kid – he and I shared a nanny. The same with our parents and grandparents. But I have not met Sumitra, for reasons doubtless well known to you.'

The D.C. came in, curling his beard with his fingers. 'Well known to the entire population of India, I'm afraid. She's intelligent and, somehow, not selfish, though. And she's not a nymphomaniac. Whatever it is, it's not that . . . though I don't doubt she's – er, interested – and interesting.'

Max dried his hands, shaking his head. It was a sad business. Dip Rai Rawan, the Rajah of Kishanpur, was about Rodney's age – thirty-five or thirty-six. He'd married this girl from an old Mahratta family a good many years ago, about '36 – and hardly seen her since.

The French Riviera knew the beautiful Rani of Kishanpur. Kitzbühel and La Baule and Monte Carlo knew her; Claridge's and the Meurice and the Waldorf knew her – but, only very seldom, and for short visits, the ancient State of Kishanpur. Her love affairs, faithfully reported in shiny socialite papers and by word of mouth, were famous throughout the last years before the war, and during the war – which she had seemed to have spent shuttling between the Bahamas, New York, and Chile. It wasn't the affairs themselves that caused the furore so much as the bizarre objects of them: a Russian count who was certainly an impostor; a middle-aged American con man who'd later gone to jail; a Cuban painter who had almost, but not quite, become famous; a young Croat revolutionary who later suffocated himself in an asylum, using his own shirt . . . The list was long, and full of violent lights. Yet you couldn't help liking her when you met her; and though the big, dark eyes settled speculatively on all men, they had never seemed to Max to be predatory, still less, calculating. Rather they were inquiring, and direct – who are you, what are you, what makes you go? She was at home now, with Dip. He saw a good deal of them, for Kishanpur was only forty-seven miles east of his own headquarters in Bhowani.

'Shall we join the ladies?' he said formally.

'You're going to be my guests,' the D.C. said, 'though I think I shall be sick if I even smell alcohol. I've got a couple of bottles of Black Label. My bearer should have put them out already.'

The three men walked together down the central passage and out on to the veranda. Rodney said, 'I'll be with you in a minute,' and went on down the steps to his jeep, parked in the shade of a tree across the drive. Max turning aside to join the women at the small table set up with drinks, saw his friend lean in over the jeep side and put his hand on his chauffeur's shoulder. Ratanbir smiled ruefully and patted his own head. So even he, a Gurkha, had a hangover. It must have been a long night.

The Rani's husky, very French-sounding voice broke in on Max's thoughts: 'The colonel knows how to handle the natives, I see.'

Max answered shortly, 'When he has to, Rodney can handle anyone – one way or another.'

'So Dip tells me,' she said. 'Except, perhaps, himself.'

The jeep drove away and Rodney joined them. The D.C. rose to his feet, a glass of lemonade in his hand. 'Ladies and gentlemen – as Indians I ask you to join me in a toast to an Englishman, who yesterday saved our government a great deal of embarrassment, and also probably saved a score of lives – Rodney Savage.'

Max quickly poured himself a lemonade and raised his glass. 'You were bloody marvellous, Rodney.'

The women murmured politely and sipped their fruit juice. Max began to relate the whole story, from the beginning. Every now and then Rodney threw in derisive comments and humorous pastiches of things seen, and soon they were all laughing. Max noticed the Rani's steady, weighing look fixed on Rodney. Janaki also was watching him, less obviously, and also seemed to be weighing, and judging, as though she had never met him before – although actually she knew him well. They had met soon after his marriage, when Rodney had first joined the 13th Gurkhas in Peshawar as a very young second lieutenant and he himself was a senior lieutenant of the Dogra Regiment – fifteen years ago, good heavens.

When he finished his tale, Rodney said, 'Taken by itself, without meaning, it was a good time – that trip to Bhilghat . . . That's what people like me love about India. To us that *is* India. We haven't had much contact with people like you, for reasons you know as well as I do – our political dominance, our destruction of your class, your sulking in your tents. But we knew the poor, the peasants, those who live in the woods and the mountains . . . in the past, if you like.'

'Kept there, sometimes,' the D.C. interposed softly, brushing up his moustache.

'Yes . . . but damn it, Ranjit, the Gonds *are* different, so are the Bhils, and the Nagas, and the Mishmis, and . . .'

'And the Lahoulis?' the D.C. asked, naming a hill people who lived on the high northern border, touching Tibet. Those Rodney had named were more decidedly 'tribal,' mostly animist in religion and Stone Age in culture.

'The Lahoulis are a borderline case,' Rodney said. His face was eager and alive, his eyes sparkling.

The D.C. said, 'I'm afraid there can't be borderline cases now. There can't even be enclaves of quaint old customs, needing special handling till Doomsday. We haven't got the time. In England you couldn't accept the idea that the people of Lancashire were a special tribe which had to be specially handled, their speech preserved, schools kept away from them so that they'd always remain isolated. At least you never have. Nor can we accept the idea of "reservations", like the Americans.'

'Suppose they don't *want* to go to school?' Rodney said. 'Suppose they don't *want* to join the modern world?'

'They have no choice,' the D.C. said. 'History is marching in a certain direction, and they are going with it – whether they go willingly or get trampled on.'

Max sipped his lemonade and thought sadly, the D.C. was quite right; the Prime Minister was quite right; nevertheless, it was a pity. How many generations, how many short years, would pass before such a way of life as they had entered last night would vanish forever from the jungles, along with the handmade pottery, the wood crafted by their own hands, the weapons shaped by love and ancient skill? In all that village there probably were not ten rupees' worth of articles that had not been wholly made there.

'Go willingly or get trampled on,' Rodney repeated slowly. He stared into his orange juice. 'You'll have plenty doing both . . . and sometimes the people concerned won't even know which they want to do, or are doing. For God's sake, though, Ranjit, go as slowly as you can, as carefully as you can. A tribal, patriarchal society may be a pain in the neck to you and Nehru, but it means a lot to the people who live inside it. It's all that holds them together – and not only the group, but the man himself, inside himself.'

He finished his juice quickly and poured out a whisky and soda. Sumitra of Kishanpur said, 'You seem to have found a solution without going or getting trampled on.'

Rodney nodded, 'I travel all over India. I have responsibility. In a way, I'm getting many of the advantages of the Raj without the disadvantages – all India to roam in . . . reasonable independence . . . general control from the Viceroy – I beg his pardon, I mean the Managing Director . . . policy from a board room in London. It doesn't seem very different, sometimes. And yet – it's strange, being an outsider. Just watching India, instead of being a part of it. On that basis I can't get trampled on. But sometimes I can hardly bear it. I was not born to be a bystander, not in India. I'd rather have the involvement, like last night – and the trampling.'

The D.C. said slowly, 'I'm afraid that's what it would be.'

The jeep drove up from the direction of the town. Ratanbir came to the veranda steps, saluted, and handed Rodney two letters.

'*Aru chhaina?*'

'*Teti ho, hujoor.*'

Rodney said, 'Excuse me,' and opened one of his letters. Max turned to his wife with small talk, and Sumitra to the Deputy Commissioner. It took Rodney a long time to read the letters, and before he had finished them the D.C. told his servant to serve lunch.

Rodney stood up, folding the letters carefully and putting them in his pocket. 'I'll have to be off now,' he said, smiling. 'Thank you so much for the drinks. And thank you, Collector, for allowing me to come with you yesterday.'

Max rose. 'But, Rodney, aren't you staying for lunch? I thought . . .'

'I'm afraid I'll have to go. Business before pleasure, you know, Mc Fadden Pulley need me.'

'But surely . . .'

He felt a sharp pain in his foot and grimaced involuntarily. Looking down he saw that Sumitra, Rani of Kishanpur, had jabbed her stiletto heel into his instep. 'See you later, then,' she was saying, smiling sweetly, 'I'm going back tomorrow, but Max and Janaki will be here for a week, and you know you have a standing invitation to Kishanpur.'

'Thanks. Yes. Good-bye.' The Englishman ran quickly down the steps and jumped into the jeep. Ratanbir engaged gear and the little vehicle drove away.

Max said, 'I'm sure he said he'd have lunch here.'

Janaki said, 'Darling, you are very dense sometimes.'

'I was never supposed to be very bright,' Max said. 'What's the matter?'

'Couldn't you see? The letters.'

Chapter 3

After dinner General Dadhwal, dressed now in light-weight trousers of black cotton and a long, high-buttoning jodhpur coat of white silk, left the dak bungalow and walked slowly towards the town. Janaki told him he must go and see Rodney; he himself wasn't sure. Janaki said Rodney had had to make a tremendous effort to hide his shock while reading the letters. Janaki said she'd never seen a man hit by a bullet in a vital part of his body, but that's what it made her think of, watching Rodney from the corner of her eye. 'He didn't gasp or wince. I don't think a muscle of his face moved. He turned pale, then fought to get the colour back. His hands began to clench and he fought to make them relax. You must go . . . ' All this in the darkened bedroom after lunch, while he prepared to take a nap.

But what right does a man have to intrude on another man, Max thought unhappily? Women don't understand. They can't hide their misery from another woman, so they don't try to. Every woman is part of the club. Womanhood. Someone's husband runs away, she likes her friends to come and comfort her. We don't. We're all as lonely as the single stag under the shade by the stream.

. . . After ten o'clock, and a hint of the first fresh breeze of the cold weather to come; not here yet, for it was only September, but promising to come, in the clear atmosphere and the fading rains . . .

The quarries, still ablaze with lights, were at the near end of the town, and McFadden Pulley's guest house nearer still, only a quarter of a mile from the dak bungalow. Light poured out from a front window, and there was a huge black car-shape silhouetted in front of it. He came close and saw that it was an old Bentley tourer. He shook his head and whistled in admiration. Those things went about six miles to the gallon. Rodney must be doing very well for himself. He squared his shoulders and walked up on to the veranda, and in through the double doors. A door on the left stood ajar and light streamed out over the coir matting on the hall floor. He knocked and called quietly, 'Rodney? It's Max.'

'Max? There's a man who's always welcome. Come on in.'

Rodney was sprawled in one of the long cane chairs that were the feature of every dak bungalow, club, and guest house in India, its arms extended into leg rests, his long legs raised on to them. Two bottles of whisky stood on the table beside him, one of them three-quarters empty. There were two zinc buckets on the floor, filled with ice and bottles of soda water. Half a dozen empty soda bottles stood in a military rank against the wall.

'Sit down. Pour yourself a drink.' His eyes were bloodshot and his voice a little slurred. 'I don't want to get drunk to forget,' Rodney said ' – only to remember. And perhaps to shake up the machinery inside my head. The old equipment doesn't seem to be able to deal with things quite as efficiently as it used to.'

Max poured a drink and sat down. 'What's happened? If I can . . . Well, damn it, I'm here.'

'Because Janaki sent you, I'll bet. You can hide nothing from a good woman. You can hide anything from a good man – the better, the easier, if you follow me. And you are very very good, Max . . . What shall I do? Rather, what *will* I do? Not what *should* I do. Certainly not! What *will* I do? Me, the ruthless chap looking after poor me. What will Me do? Wait till next week's thrilling instalment . . . Will Me go willingly or will Me be trampled on? Will Me find a new way to Happiness? . . . It was like having a lover, a married woman. You got her by force perhaps in the beginning – not rape-force, just power, and you didn't have to use it. Women like power because they need it. Yet they dislike you for having it, and dislike themselves for liking it . . . So part of her always hated you for that, and another part was flattered. You were strong and the husband wasn't. Then in time you fell in love, and there were enough times of physical ecstasy, power and sensuality fused, so that she fell in love too, a little. You thought it would go on for ever. But it wouldn't, and her husband claimed her, softly, inevitably. You hadn't noticed it, but *the tide was going out.* She floated out and away. She had to. High and dry now, your power's gone, the sheer hypnotic power of the erect and rampant

40

stallion gone . . . You know the feeling, when a woman says sadly, "You'd better go now?" No, perhaps you don't, Max . . .'

'What's happened?' Max asked again, speaking very gently. Rodney was talking about the mysterious woman again, and yet Max was sure it wasn't really a woman. At least, not any one woman. He wondered suddenly whether his friend had become impotent. One of the letters might be from his doctor confirming that there was no cure.

Rodney put his hand in his pocket and brought out the two letters. Max did not think, from the clean folds, that he had looked at them since the first time at the dak bungalow. It was a rare man who could do that. 'This one is from McFadden Pulley. From Sir Andrew Graham, in person. He deeply regrets not having been able to tell us before, but the negotiations were of such delicacy that, etcetera, etcetera. In other words, the other chaps insisted on secrecy . . . McFadden Pulley, private sterling company, is being sold to a public company, Indian owned. The people who are floating the new company have declared as policy that all non-Indian executives will be replaced within five years, three quarters of them within one year. With generous compensation, of course – subject to Indian income tax of, say, 97 per cent.'

He drank unhurriedly, almost lovingly, from his tall glass.

Max said, 'But you've done well, Rodney. They may keep you for the five years.'

'I am the most recently acquired non-Indian, bar two youngsters in Bombay. Anyway, it's only a question of time . . . and I'm damned well not going to go on, business-as-usual, knowing that these chaps are playing Russian roulette with my head. No, I'd have to get out sooner or later, and it will be sooner – because of my addiction to duty. The new owners are a canny bunch. They're giving a nice directorship to an important Congressman. Guess who. L. P. Roy.'

'Oh, my God,' Max breathed. Rodney Savage was one of the few army officers whose name was known to political India. Two years earlier he had hunted down and shot the Communist firebrand K. P. Roy, while the latter was causing riots and sabotage in Bhowani. The fact that K. P. Roy had also attempted to assassinate Mahatma Gandhi, and had

41

caused the deaths of many innocent Indians, had been played down in Nationalist circles; Roy was anti-British, and that was enough. This man L. P. Roy, now to be a director of McFadden Pulley, had made an attempt to have Rodney court-martialled shortly after the incident. He was K.P.'s younger brother.

'A more dangerous character than K.P.,' Rodney said cheerfully. 'I rather liked K.P. He was a Communist, but he had a sense of humour. I haven't met L.P., but of course I've heard and read a good deal about him. His brother was a tiger – this one's a man, a twisted, tortured fanatic. As a matter of fact, it wasn't I who actually shot K.P. Another chap did . . . But it doesn't matter. I'm afraid, Max, it wouldn't matter if they promised to keep me on for thirty years. I've seen Indian businesses at work. This is where I discover I'm English. This is the parting of the ways.'

'You'd have stayed on in the army if they'd let you, wouldn't you?' Max said.

Rodney looked up, grinning with the slightly wolfish grin that Max remembered best about him; it had been most common when he was under strain, in battle. 'The Indian Army,' he said, 'is not an Indian business – yet. It rests exactly in the mode and tradition *we* made it. It will remain that way just as long as people like you are in charge. You don't think or act like an Indian, even though you do put on protective camouflage sometimes, like that jodhpur coat . . . That will change. Your political bosses don't like it now and they'll force the change. In a few years they'll find chaps who think their way, not yours, and they'll push them to the top. The pressure will come from inside, from underneath, too. Remember Iqbal?'

'Commanding the 9/21st Punjabis?'

'Yes. Just after the war nearly all his officers were Indian. His adjutant borrowed a battalion truck for non-military purposes – took his wife and kids to the flicks in it – not five hours after signing a strict order of Iqbal's against such practices. Iqbal sacked him. Well, the adjutant's wife was a friend of Iqbal's wife. Know what happened? Iqbal's wife refused to sleep with him unless he reinstated the chap as adjutant . . . Things like that will happen. There's an *Indian* way of dealing with them, I'm sure, and that's how they will be dealt with. But there's no British way of dealing with them. Iqbal was helpless. Know what he did? Applied for more British junior officers. Of course, there weren't any to be had . . . No, the bell has sounded. I realise now that I've been waiting for it, listening for it, ever since Independence. I got absolutely soused *that* night . . . Perhaps that's what made yesterday, with the Gonds, so particularly wonderful. The roulette game's ended, the revolver's gone off, and I'm dead. *But I won't lie down.* I'm not going to go quietly. I'm going to fight, Max.'

Max poured himself another drink. He felt much more unhappy than Rodney seemed to. 'There must be lots of good jobs for you,' he said. 'You have so many friends here . . . '

Rodney went on as though he had not spoken: 'I'm not going to go quietly, and I'm not going to stay quietly. Not like Great-aunt Mary . . . great-aunt by marriage. She's still here. Running a hill station hotel on the road to Lansdowne. Her friends used to go up and down in tongas and ekkas, and break journey there overnight. She made a good living, and the place was always full of handsome, sunburned sahibs and pretty ladies and rosy children. Then they built a motor road, and the traffic went by without stopping, though most of her friends would at least have a cup of tea. Then her generation got old, or retired, or were killed. Then no one came, except a few Indians, who were terribly polite to her. For ten years no one at all. She's still there, nearly ninety, enormous wooden building, no servants but a crazy cook about the same age, with the same ideas and the same dreams, though he's a U.P. Muslim. She dresses every night for dinner in the gown she wore at Curzon's Viceregal Ball in '04, and eats a can of bully beef once a week, and the dust lies like a dense silent carpet over everything, and all the glass broken, and langurs swinging from the pines behind the house into the upstairs rooms. Is that what you'd like me to do?'

Max made a helpless gesture with his hands.

'What about smuggling? That's more like it, for me. What about armed dacoity? It's all here still, under the surface, the India my great-grandfather lived with, and the ones before him . . . It wouldn't be hard to re-create the Pindaris, motorised. With a little bit of skill and luck a thousand properly led men could take over a province, or a district at least – all in the most proper manner, votes and all . . . and I'd be in the background, just like the old days.'

'You can't turn the clock back, Rodney,' Max said.

'Who says?'

'No one can. Besides, you'd have to go back too far. For the past century and a half you've been building things up here, not tearing them down. You've done the work pretty well, too. *We* might tear ourselves apart – but you couldn't. Anyway, you're joking . . .'

'Believe me, I'm not.'

'Rodney, be patient. Just wait a bit. Remember your friends. India badly needs people like you, and there are enough of us, and we're strong enough not to have to take dictation from anyone, not even Nehru. If you want to stay, we'll find something good, and worthy of you.'

Rodney was looking at him, and seemed to be weighing his words. At last he said, 'Tomorrow I shall probably agree with you. I shall probably do just what you recommend. At this moment I want to fight. I know you've had the feeling. Twice in your life, eh? Once, when that fellow yelled at you to stop playing bloody Wog music in the mess.'

Max nodded. Rodney was referring to the incident which had given him his nickname, and made him popular with the inscrutable English. When he joined his Dogra battalion in 1927 the senior subaltern was a man who disliked educated Indians, though he loved the sepoys well enough. Max, the new second lieutenant, liked to play Indian music on the mess phonograph. The senior subaltern ordered him not to, in the language quoted by Rodney. Max respectfully refused to obey. The feud went on for three years until, in 1930, the senior subaltern seized his pile of records and smashed them on the stone floor. Max knocked him out. Hence the name 'Max', for 'Max Schmeling'; and hence one year's loss of leave privileges. A well-deserved punishment, Max thought. Right or wrong, the fellow was his senior officer, and there were other, proper channels of complaint.

Rodney continued: 'The second time was just after Independence, when Nehru and the boys wanted to promote some of the I.N.A. fellows, and you and Des and N. P. Satish and Chandra went and said that if they were made heroes, after what they'd done to Indian prisoners in Singapore, you were going out.'

Max nodded again. The Japanese had formed the Indian National Army from Indian soldiers who fell prisoner into their hands in Malaya and Singapore. Himself, he had never felt strongly for or against the I.N.A., as an institution. There were many ways of being an Indian patriot in those days before Independence. But he and other Indian regulars could not forgive the I.N.A.'s treatment of such men as Hari Badhwar and Dhargalkar, who had refused to join it. Them the I.N.A. had hung up by the thumbs, tortured, starved for months in solitary confinement. When the Congress leaders wanted to idolise the I.N.A. Max knew again – he had to fight.

Rodney said, 'Well . . . I feel now that I have to fight. And even though tomorrow I may decide not to, the need to fight will be very close under the surafce, just suppressed. Remember that, Max, remember.'

Max said, 'What about the other letter?'

'Ah, that. You ought to read that. It would make you cry. Cry for the gulf between people who are supposed to know each other pretty well. But I won't give it to you, because it is a caddish thing to do, to reveal the soul of a lady . . . This is from Frances Clayton, my ex-fiancée.'

'Ex!'

'It was written before the McFadden Pulley letter, so she knew nothing about that. She informs me she cannot face the prospect of living in India the rest of her life. I must go home to England, where brother John can guarantee me a good job with an M.P. subsidiary run by the people who own – used to own – M.P. She begs me to come to Delhi to discuss it. She's a nice girl, Max. Very nice. If you can call a woman of twenty-nine a girl. I suppose so. Unfortunately, I don't love her.'

'Don't say it!' Max cried. 'Go to Delhi and talk to her. It'll be all right.'

'I doubt it,' Rodney said, grinning. 'It took me time to get over Victoria Jones, the Anglo-Indian girl I met in Bhowani in '46, during the K. P. Roy affair. That was probably an attempt to avoid expulsion from India, the psychologists would say. There was an earlier love, which I shall never get over. Now I've spent a year of chastity for the sake of Frances, who is a very decent young woman – but nice, don't forget that. Today, looking at Sumitra got me by

45

the balls, and I'm sure I could love her if things worked out that way. But they won't . . . Meanwhile the manager of the cement works has informed me that the local harlots are superannuated, diseased, or both. He himself always sends to a little village called Pattan – it's hidden in the jungles behind Lapri – where there are a pair of beauties. I have already taken his advice. Ratanbir went with the company jeep to fetch the girls some time ago. He ought to be back any moment.'

'Ratanbir!' Max exclaimed. 'You wouldn't have . . . '

'No,' Rodney said, smiling the wolfish smile. 'I wouldn't have. I have never involved any soldier or servant or friend in anything of the kind, as far as in me lay. That is the sahib's way. I am no longer a sahib . . . I won't ask you to stay, because I know you – and I know Janaki. Thanks for coming. Good night, old boy.'

Max stopped in the doorway. 'For God's sake, Rodney, remember what I said. You're not alone.'

Rodney stood in the middle of the room, unswaying, smiling, saying nothing. Max strode heavily out and down the veranda steps. In the drive the headlights of the jeep flared on to him, half blinding him. When it had passed, slowing rapidly, he noticed two women, their saris drawn across their faces, sitting huddled together in the back seat behind the dark, stolid silhouette of Ratanbir.

Arrived back at the dak bungalow, Max felt very tired. I'm forty-four, he thought, but sometimes I feel like ninety. Perhaps it had something to do with the long fight for Independence, twenty years of being shot at from two sides, the anti-Indian British sneering at him for a Wog, the anti-British Indians sneering at him for a lackey. Rodney's reminding him of it had brought out the feeling of fatigue, of sheer exhaustion, that used to assail him. There had been days when he felt he had lost all his friends, all love, everything. Only an inner conviction that he was doing right, could indeed do no other, had supported him, and a sense that the tide must turn, and bring all to him – freedom, and respect, and love.

To his embarrassment he found Sumitra the Rani sitting in the main room with his wife. He had not had time to adjust his face, and came in showing the heavy thoughts that had weighed on his mind, as after a bloody failure in

46

Burma, and for the same reason – the inevitability, and the waste.

'What's happened? What's the matter with him?' Janaki was on her feet, her hand urgent on his sleeve.

He said, 'Quite a lot, I'm afraid.'

He sat down and told them, as briefly as he could, about Rodney's state. When he ended he looked up and saw tears glistening in his wife's lower lashes and a shining wet line down her left cheek. Sumitra's heavy, perfectly curved brows were bent down in a frown over her huge eyes. It was she who spoke first. 'A casualty of history. Just as the D.C. said.'

Janaki muttered. 'But it's dreadful. He wouldn't be a casualty if he didn't care.'

Sumitra said, 'Unfortunately, that is always true, everywhere, *nahin*?'

Her eyes shone and the frown had gone, and her face had taken back its ancient-seeming statuary beauty. She stood up, the rich sari rustling heavily over her thighs. She arranged the end of it lightly over her head, drawing it over the curve of her breast in a slow sweeping motion of great provocativeness.

'I will go to him,' she said. 'Casualties need nurses.'

After a moment of stunned inaction Max sprang to his feet. 'Sumitra. I don't think . . . he's drinking, you know. He must have put away a bottle by now. It's bound to hit him soon.'

'Perhaps I can stop him drinking,' Sumitra said, smiling slightly.

'Really,' Max mumbled, 'really, I wouldn't. I don't think you . . .'

She gazed at him steadily. 'You mean he has more than a couple of bottles to keep him company?'

'Yes,' Max mumbled. He felt acutely uncomfortable. This woman was pure Indian by blood, by manner pure foreign – French perhaps, French grande-dame, courtesan, actress, God knows what.

'You're blushing like a schoolgirl, Max. I shall go to him. No, I'd rather walk.' She spoke with finality, and, trailing her hand in a small graceful gesture, left the room.

Max blew out his cheeks in a long sigh. 'I need another drink,' he said. 'She's incredible. Rodney's got two girls from some village there – tarts. Heaven knows what they'll be

47

doing by the time Sumitra arrives . . . She's *immoral*! And yet, I don't think she's going down there for her own sake, for her own gratification, do you? . . . I suppose it's a wonderful thing to do, when you think of it, even though he has two tarts with him . . . especially if he has two tarts with him.' He found the whisky in the corner cupboard and poured out a stiff peg. 'She doesn't give a damn. Poor Dip . . . poor Rodney. I wish I knew what he was talking about, half the time. Some woman who's his ideal. They were lovers and then she left him . . . grew away. He said it was inevitable. Because she was Indian? I'm not sure he said that, but I somehow feel that's what he meant.'

He was talking to himself, revolving his glass in his hand, staring at the tabletop, trying to see in its polished teak surface the solution of Rodney's riddles and allusions, trying to bring into the framework of his common sense these mysteries of sensitivity which so many others, especially Indians, knew about while he didn't. Well, I'm a Jat, he thought. We're supposed to be as dense as buffaloes . . .

He looked up and saw his wife's head bent over the table, her hands to her face. The violence of her silent sobbing had loosened the fastenings of her hair, and already it was falling down. He stumbled to his feet, whispering, *'Kya hua, piari?'* and stretched out his hand to her. It brushed hard against her shaking head and completed the undoing of the smooth-swept hair. Her head bent farther down and her black hair swept out across the table, a shining river of light and shadow.

Max gasped, and staggered. 'Janaki!' he cried.

The hidden head nodded and the hair moved on the table, heaving and writhing and then lying again still, a dark river, frozen in motion. The hair fell back and her face came up, tear streaked, working, ugly in grief.

'Yes. Yes, it was I. All true. The love, why it came . . . and what kind. What happened afterwards . . . true . . . all so many years ago . . . I was not hurt, till now, now, when it's all been over so long. He's only hurt because he cared. And I can't do anything for him, I just can't . . . I'm your wife. I always have been.' Again her head sank, and again the heavy sobbing filled the room.

The General looked at her a long time. Hers was the flowing hair that haunted Rodney Savage's dreams. He

48

himself was the husband who had possessed, but not possessed. The same man who had saved his career had taken his honour. A surge of anger rose slowly in him and his thick fingers clenched.

Why hadn't they run away together? Why was she still here? Why had she stayed with him all these years, fourteen years since the Peshawar days? Fourteen years of love, comradeship, affliction, partings, joinings, children. The woman of Rodney's dream was Janaki, but it was also India.

The astrologer had chosen the date for his marriage, but he'd had to change it – exigency of the service. So perhaps these sorrows were inevitable, no human being to blame. It seemed to him, as the anger sank and vanished, to be replaced by a deep thankfulness, that perhaps he could never suffer, now, as Rodney and Janaki had, and would.

He walked round the table, gathered his wife gently in his arms, so that her face rested against his shoulder, and carried her to their room, murmuring to her in their own language as he went.

Chapter 4

Frances Clayton turned the page and glanced up. The three overstuffed armchairs were arranged in a group at the edge of the lawn, just in the shade of the trees. From behind the trees, beyond the low brick wall, came the hum of motor traffic and the steady clip-clop of a tonga pony's hoofs.

A sudden jangle of the tonga bell made her start. On the invisible road someone poured out a torrent of blurred, angry Hindustani. Someone else answered, other voices joined in . . . Another near miss, another argument, Indians yelling and screaming at each other. Why couldn't they settle their differences sensibly, without hysterics and bad temper? And dust everywhere even though the rains were hardly over. Frowning, she looked at the men in the other two chairs.

'I think you're mistaking Roy's character. He's not cheap. It's not *you* he's against, but all British. And you're over-estimating his influence. The men who have floated the new company are out to make money . . . '

That was her brother John speaking. A ray of sunlight streaming through the branches had landed, like a magician, on his head, making the thin blond hairs vanish and turning the head into a pink football. His long face was pale, and he seemed worried, as usual. Well, now he'd got something to worry about.

He continued: 'You don't seem to realise that you've made more money for M.P. in one year than I have in twenty – well, say thirteen, not counting the years I was in the army. That bakelite deal which you suggested has been snowballing ever since.'

'I heard it was going well. But all I did was read that this American chemical wizard was in Bombay, and go and see him.'

'Yes, but no one else did. I wouldn't have.'

No, Frances thought, you wouldn't. You wouldn't want to push in on a stranger, even though his ideas might possibly produce business. You would remember that you were in the Shipping Department and this was the Coal Department's pigeon – if it was anyone's. You wouldn't risk wasting time you might have spent with a fishing rod. Sensibly, you would have worked out that the chances were a thousand to one against, and you would have been right. Rodney was just lucky.

'The truth is,' John continued, 'I am far more likely than you are to be in the first 75 per cent sacked.'

Rodney said, 'You can count me out of the musical chairs. I wrote to Graham yesterday, resigning my . . . commission in the Imperial Army of Scottish Merchants Trading to the East Indies.'

'You did!' Frances exclaimed. She laid down her book and gave up the pretence of reading. She smiled warmly at him. Since arriving in Delhi the day before yesterday he had said nothing about her letter. She had been afraid to broach the subject. Rodney was not a man you gave ultimatums to lightly. That was one of the things she liked about him. When they were married, there would be no doubt who wore the trousers. She despised henpecked husbands.

'I did,' Rodney said. He poured himself a stiff whisky with very little soda. Frances frowned. That was his third already. It was Sunday morning, yes, but hardly half past eleven yet. He was drinking much more than he used to. That was India again. It had a terrible effect on people.

Rodney said, 'Roy or no Roy, I'm not going to work for a Marwari-owned firm. I'm not saying they'll be more corrupt than us, or less efficient. I'm just saying they'll be different, in method and outlook and thought. I'm too old to change my whole personality.'

There was silence. Now should she ask, Frances wondered, now should she ask the obvious question – what *are* you going to do? Better let John ask it, she decided. A few minutes later he did. Frances waited, her hands tensed in her lap.

Rodney answered with another question. He said, 'Do you know what kind of jobs M.P. are going to offer us in England?'

'Not exactly,' John said, 'but it's not hard to guess. Something in the City. They're connected with investment banks and shipping. I imagine we'd have to spend a year or two as glorified office boys, until we find our own level. You needn't worry.'

Rodney sat with head thrown back, staring up at the leaves. London, she thought. If he has to go to the City to work, I suppose we'd start in a semi-detached house in one of those ghastly suburbs you get to from London Bridge or Holborn Viaduct. It wouldn't take Rodney long to reach the top, though, and then they could move out to Surrey. Or perhaps Buckinghamshire. A big house that looked old but wasn't, with decent plumbing . . . a garden with a high wall round it; a tennis court; quiet, leafy roads, errand boys on bicycles, whistling, but not yelling at each other; voices that were never raised, and meat that tasted like meat; peace, and decency, and a soft light, air that did not feel as though they were rubbing sandpaper into your skin; the windows open winter and summer, no snakes or dust storms or howling monsoon rains flooding the drive and turning the lawn into a lake and carrying dead rats down the open drainage ditches . . . Her eyes slipped into focus and she found she was staring at the *mali*. He was squatting over the zinnia bed, the hose in his hand.

'Not now!' she called. '*Nahin, nahin! Pichche* . . . When the sun's off them.'

The *mali* salaamed and dragged the hose somewhere else. How often have I told him? she thought. They don't *listen*. Rodney was looking at her, frowning as though in thought. I ought to have learned better Hindustani in my time here, she thought. But I didn't want to.

Rodney said, 'Come out for a drive, Frances. We'll be back for lunch.'

She stood up at once. 'Wait a minute while I change my shoes.'

She went to her room and looked at herself in the mirror. A little more lipstick, smarter shoes, and . . . that dress looked dowdy. She changed quickly into a blue linen suit.

Rodney was waiting in the driver's seat of the huge old Bentley. That was a terrible waste of money, she thought. She hoped he wouldn't try to take it home. Besides costing a fortune in petrol it was rather flashy – not like an American car but . . . just too much. It would create a bad impression in England, especially in the kind of place they'd have to live in at first.

Rodney turned into the road and trod on the accelerator. The warm air rushed past and she put her hand to her head as her hair began to shake loose. Faster yet, the engine making a continuous burbling roar, bicyclists all over the road as usual, talking, hands on each other's shoulder, never looking where they were going, never thinking of giving a signal . . .

'Rodney!' she cried. 'Please go slower. It's not safe here in Delhi.'

Rodney whipped the Bentley round a traffic circle in a long, squealing skid, hurling gravel far out on to the grass lawns beyond. He slowed down. 'You are quite right,' he said gravely.

She tried to pat her hair back into place. 'Where are we going?'

'The Red Fort,' he said.

She felt a small twinge of unease. The Red Fort was very imposing, no one could deny that. It was not picturesque, like an English castle – it was just huge, with a gigantic wall all the way round. He would want to walk about inside it, among the formal gardens and mosques. If only he'd told her, she would have put on a pair of wedgies instead of these heels.

The car slipped noisily through the teeming traffic and soon drew up in the parking area outside the main entrance to the Fort. After helping her out Rodney stood awhile, gazing up at the Congress flag tugging gently at its staff. Then he walked on fast. She hurried to catch up with him, and laid her hand on his arm to slow him down. Sikh sentries stood stiff as ramrods, bayonets fixed on their rifles, beside the entrance. She thought Rodney would speak to the sergeant and other men standing nearby – he usually did, when he met Indian soldiers – but he passed without even looking.

Inside the arched gate they walked down the middle of a high-roofed bazaar. On either side shopkeepers called, and thrust out examples of their wares. Files of school-children scurried by, shepherded by young teachers in cheap, pretty saris. There was an overpowering smell of jasmine perfume.

Rodney said, 'You don't want to stay in India.'

She tightened her hand on his arm. What a place he'd

chosen to speak about something so terribly important. She had rehearsed, many times, what she would say when this moment came. Now she found she had to search for the words, and go very carefully. She said, 'I – honestly, Rod, I don't. I haven't been here long enough. Lots of people say you always spend your first five years hating India. I don't know enough, the way you do. It can't be *home* for either of us, of course . . . but it's been, well, a special place for you . . . Not for me.' She hesitated and then got it out in a rush: 'It can't be such a special place for you any more now, can it? Darling, I do know what you feel, but there isn't anything else we can do, now, is there?' He did not answer, and she said again, 'Is there?'

'As a matter of fact, there is,' he said. 'The question is not Can, but Will. I'm still not certain what I'm going to do. I've never felt like this before in my life. I *will* do something, I mean I will make a decision – but I don't have any idea what it will be or what will cause it.'

He looked down at her, his face suddenly inquiring and almost anxious. 'Do you love me?' he asked.

She ought to cry out, 'Of course I do, I love you, I love you!' She could not say the words. She said, 'I don't think I honestly know what love is, Rod. I've never lost my appetite, or not been able to sleep, or felt simply swept away . . . the things that are supposed to happen to people.'

They were passing under another huge arch of pink stone, walking down wide steps on to a gravelled walk between green lawns. 'I respect you,' she muttered, 'I like you, more than any man I've ever met. I know that I will come to love you . . . and surely that's the only real love, the kind that comes slowly, after years, by living together and having affection and respect and – and mutual interests?'

'No,' he said.

She cried, 'But that's why we became engaged! I never pretended. I could have!'

'No, you never pretended,' he said wearily. 'It is entirely my fault.'

I should have lied, she thought in anguish. It's no use trying to be honest with men, not even Rodney. She *would* love him, it *would* come, deep, true, real love . . . but how was she to pretend to have a 'fever', to shiver and shake and yearn, when she felt nothing of the kind – now? And the small nervous voice inside her whispered, I don't want to shiver and shake and yearn and be miserable . . .

She must be sensible . . . He didn't like cities much. He was an open-air man. He liked mountains and sea. Perhaps it was the idea of the City, and suburbia, that was weighing on him. 'You don't have to take a McFadden Pulley job in London,' she said, speaking rapidly. 'We could go to Cornwall. Or Devon. Or Somerset. Don't ex-army officers often become chief constables of counties? . . . We could have a boat in Fowey, and a cottage on Bodmin Moor. You've talked a lot about Cornwall . . . the gorse on the cliff paths, the wonderful beaches . . . Tintagel . . . '

Rodney had stopped. He was looking at a white mosque close in front of them. He said aloud, 'If there be a heaven on earth, it is here, it is here, it is here.'

She tugged at his sleeve. 'Rodney . . . '

He said, still gazing at the mosque, 'This is the Pearl Mosque, the *Moti Masjid*. Which Mogul emperor had those lines inscribed? Was it here or at Shalimar? "If there be a heaven on earth . . ." '

She cried, 'But oh, Rod, it isn't, not any more, not for you!'

Rodney began to walk round the mosque, his head up and turned, examining it. Before she could catch him or warn him he had walked into a party of Indians coming in the other direction, knocking one man down.

Rodney glanced at the man as he struggled to get up. It looked like a cold, supercilious stare, but Frances knew that really there was no emotion in it of any kind. Rodney's feeling were somewhere else. He had not yet realised that it was he standing there, he who had knocked the man down.

The man was on his feet, dusting off his dhoti and adjusting the Gandhi cap on his mane of grey hair. He was a dark-visaged man with a heavy, square face, thin lips, and deep-set eyes. He snapped, in good but accented English, 'Do you expect Indians to hurry out of your way, still? There is Independence here now, you know.'

Rodney said, 'I didn't see you.' In another second, she was sure, he would have apologised, but the Indian didn't give him time: 'Because you are drunk! I can smell the whisky on your breath from here.'

The others of the group, two men and a pretty, languid

woman, stood a little back and behind the speaker, as she stood behind Rodney.

Rodney said, 'Oh, for Christ's sake, shut up, and go away.'

One of the other men stepped forward pompously. 'Do you realise who you are insulting? This gentleman is L. P. Roy, M.L.A.'

Rodney stared at L. P. Roy, and bowed slowly. Straightening up, he said, 'And I am Rodney Savage, O.B.E., M.C.'

Frances watched, anxious yet aware of a warm glow of certainty. This must convince him.

The two men examined each other, the Indian tensed and angry, the Englishman loose, staring down, grinning with teeth bared.

Roy suddenly relaxed. He said, 'An employee of Mc-Fadden Pulley, I think. I saw your name on the list in the prospectus. Well, I am on the board to see that people like you do not continue to fatten on India.'

Rodney took her arm under his and walked away, towards the outer wall. Here, on a wide walk, marble water channels, but empty, ran under gateways of marble carved with such delicacy that they seemed to be made of lace. Rodney said, 'The women of the emperors sat here. The water flowed in the channels then, green and cool. The emperor sat on the *gaddi* on that marble bench, facing the crowd, some of them in the open and some under the pillars in the shade . . . Now, you must see how impossible it is.'

'Yes,' she said.

'I can't go. I will fight.'

She felt weak, and sat down on a bench. A passing Indian couple examined her curiously. Below her the wall dropped sheer for forty feet. The ground down there was bare and brown and dusty, covered with thorn scrub. Ragged strips of canvas spread from thorn to thorn made a little shade for a gipsy family engaged in cooking their meal. Black-and-brown goats wandered among the thorn, standing on their hind legs to pluck leaves from the higher branches. Beyond, the haze of heat enveloped the view in the grey pall that united earth and sky.

He said, 'I have asked you to marry me. But we will stay in India.'

He stood beside her, but still not looking at her. He looked out over the land, to which he seemed to be speaking.

She was desperate for a place as a married woman. She could say yes, and hope he would change his mind.

The land out there, and the sky, and the grey haze densely enveloping them both, was hot and uncomfortable, full of dust. Sun and glare, anger and lust, and starved women lying dead in the gutter. She could not do it. There was no happiness here for her.

'Just because an Indian insulted you,' she said heavily. 'You're mad, Rodney.' She gathered strength. 'What are you going to fight? The Indian Government? L. P. Roy? You can't win. They'll break you, and the longer you hang on the worse it will be . . . John bends, but you won't. You'll break.'

'Perhaps,' he said; 'there's always that chance.' He spoke as though going into a battle, acknowledging the possibility of death.

'Have you fallen in love with someone else?' she asked suddenly.

He said, 'I have loved two other women. Hopeless cases from the beginning. I have met another. A generous, curious woman. I could manage to forget her if I left India.'

'Then . . .'

'Would you arrange to forget your right eye? Leave it behind on a hilltop and walk away?'

'If it hurt enough.'

He shrugged. 'That's the eye I see beauty with, and everything that's valuable and wonderful. The other one's for earning my living, protecting myself, all the necessary, material things.'

She burst out, 'How can you ask me to marry you if you are in love with someone else?'

He said, 'You are not promising me your love, are you? Respect and affection, remember? I can give you that . . . And, I told you, I do not love her – yet. Thank God. It looks like another hopeless case. But it's possible that I shall. It won't be the first time love has grown out of sex.'

She felt cold. 'Did you . . . have her?'

He said, 'Yes. After I got your letter. She is stimulating, and independent, and her views on sexuality are original. Well, I suppose they're not really, they're just old-fashioned

– Hindu old-fashioned – but not immoral. She has no morals, of that kind.'

'Did you say . . . Is she an *Indian*?'

He turned then and looked at her. His expression was very sad. He said, 'You were on the point of saying "native", weren't you? And meaning it . . . My poor Frances, you should never have met me. Yes, she's Indian.'

Frances groaned. Indian women. Natives. Of course, she had met scores of them socially, beautifully dressed, sophisticated, charming . . . and never been able to erase from her mind the idea that they were only disguised and painted sisters of the dark dirty beggar women with the matted hair, and the brown and wrinkled sweeper witches who cleaned the filth from the streets.

Rodney said, 'If we marry I shall stay physically faithful to you. But it must be in India. I can live without physical union with this woman – and others – but I cannot live without the atmosphere wherein they exist – this air, this dust, these smells, these skies . . . We'd better go back. It's nearly lunchtime.'

'Lunch!' she cried, but she got up. An American with a funny white cap was staring at her. She walked at Rodney's side, drying her tears with the back of her hand.

So it was sex. She had known from the beginning that Rodney was supposed to be a great lady's man. When he began to pay her attention she expected an early attempt at seduction. She had been glad, and delightfully surprised, that he had made no such attempt either before or during their engagement. She would not have agreed, anyway. She was a virgin and meant to remain one until they were married; but he had not even tried. Even his kisses had always been gentle and proper. She had seen nothing of the Casanova in him . . . but it must have been there all the time, held in check by God knows what will power, if he was desperate enough to turn to Indians. Had she driven him to such a thing? He must be frantic. If they did get married, she'd have to live with and assuage this beastly, animal side of him . . . yet she could not, would not give up the idea of marriage. Marriage was her only goal in life. No one but Rodney had asked her. She was twenty-nine.

She drew a deep breath and said, 'Rod . . . we don't know each other . . .'

'Eh? I'm sorry, I didn't hear.'

She felt the hot flush covering her face and neck. She couldn't talk about it, she just couldn't. But she could do it.

She sat preoccupied, trying to conceal her trembling, during the drive back to the house at the far end of New Delhi. Before lunch she quickly downed two pink gins. John looked at her with eyebrows raised, for normally she never drank during the daytime; but Rodney did not notice. During the traditional curry and rice meal – why must we have it *every* Sunday? she thought – she drank two gin and tonics. Afterwards, still queasy at the stomach but exhilarated and determined in mind, she caught her brother's arm and muttered, 'Take a drive, John. A long one. Rod and I have to talk.'

'Oh. Oh, all right.' Now it was John who blushed and she thought crossly: the wretch! Does he think I do this all the time, that I can't wait till bedtime now that Rod's back, even after what presumably happened last night? But of course, with Rod's reputation, that's probably what he did think.

She waited, breathless, sitting in the drawing-room with a magazine, until Rodney got up and said, 'I'm going to take a nap.'

She waited again, until she heard the door of his bedroom close behind him down the passage, then went quickly, on tiptoe, to her own room, and took off her clothes, Naked, she glanced at herself in the mirror, and hurriedly averted her eyes. Her figure was all right, she supposed, but her femaleness looked terribly obvious. Coarse. She found a nightgown and slipped it on, brushed her hair and went to the door.

After a long moment of waiting, while the blood pounded in her head and her stomach felt painfully empty, so that she thought she would faint, she opened the door, ran across the passage in her bare feet, opened Rodney's door opposite, and went in.

He was lying on his back on the bed, staring at the ceiling, naked except for a sheet flung loosely across his belly and loins. Slowly the scarlet colour spread from her neck to her face, to her breasts, to her body, down her legs and up her back, to blend again at her neck. She tried to keep her head

59

high, looking at him, but it sank of its own weight until she was staring at the small Persian rug on the floor.

He sat up. 'You don't have to do this, Frances.'

'I –I want to,' she whispered.

She didn't want to. Perhaps Rod could teach her to want to, someday. Now she was only empty and afraid.

'You're a liar,' he said. 'But the real trouble is I don't want to, either.'

'Rod!' She ran the few steps to the bed and flung herself on to it, crouching beside him, turning to hold him, pressing her breasts against him. She put her mouth to his and kissed him, opening her lips as she had never done before. She moved against him, and after a moment, feeling neither shame nor fear, only desperation, she pulled the sheet away, spread her legs and straddled him.

He lay back. 'Frances, it's too late. In the beginning, if I'd tried to create this kind of thing between us, perhaps it would be different now. Perhaps I'd possess your soul and be eager to follow your body anywhere in the world . . . But I didn't. It's my fault. But it's over.'

She would not surrender.

Nothing happened, no stir of emotion in herself or in him. She began to cry.

Rodney moved her over gently and eased the pillow under her head. 'You are a good-looking woman,' he said. 'It will come out all right, with someone else . . . But, Frances, don't have a purpose for love-making. And no duty. Just love, or desire, or both.'

She lay, her eyes closed and her face pressed into the pillow so that he should not see them. She controlled herself after a long hard struggle, and sat up. She said, 'You said you had an idea, about something to do in India. What was it?'

Through the haze of the recent tears she saw him looking at her with respect. 'You're a hell of a girl, Frances. But don't think of me any more. I mean it. This is the end . . . Yes, I have an idea. I think I can make a living, and lead the kind of life I want to, and be my own master, in India. I'm going to be a white hunter. I'm going to start a *shikar* camp for rich foreigners.'

He jumped out of bed, found his cheroots, lit one, and jumped back in. She found herself noticing dispassionately that he was a lean, well-muscled man, densely covered with black hair from the navel down to the loins, the chest broad, flat, and hairless. He smiled at her and waved the cheroot. 'Every year before the war they used to extract hundreds of thousands of dollars from Americans in Kenya and Uganda and Tanganyika, and what do they have there except game? We have the game, and we have *India*, too, India! Temples, maharajahs, nautch girls, the Taj Mahal, Nehru, tall bearded Gurkhas waving their keen-edged *chilamchis*, subtle sinuous Sikhs clamouring for more muezzins . . .'

She found herself smiling. She felt tired but calm. Rodney was not going to make love to her and it was quite proper and sensible to be sitting up in his bed in a transparent nightie, listening to him talking about his plans. That was how she had first met him, only then they'd been sitting on the sofa in the drawing-room. So, after two years, she was back where she'd started, minus a few clothes. She felt like a little station on a big railway line. Rodney's train might have stopped forever here, but it hadn't. He was on his way again.

He said, 'I've got the place, too. An abandoned Forest Rest House beyond Lapri. I had a good look at it last week. The firm leased it twenty years ago for some reason and have practically never used it. It's nearly falling down but it could be fixed and I know they'll transfer the lease to me. I'll have to raise a bit of money. It will cost four or five thousand rupees just to fix the Rest House. Then I've got to buy equipment, tents, camp beds, mosquito nets, rifles to hire out to the clients . . .'

'Station wagons?' she said.

He waved his cigar energetically. 'Not a hope. The road's jeepable from the main road as far as Pattan village, but after that there are just tracks climbing on to the escarpment. Besides, it isn't going to be that sort of safari. I don't want people riding around in station wagons thinking they've seen India. They've got to get out in the jungles, on their feet.'

She said, 'If you're really going to attract the rich ones, you'll have to provide some sort of comfort, Rod.'

'Well, yes, something . . . But they must realise they're in a jungle, and in India . . . Then I have to live. There will be servants' salaries, *shikaris*, baksheesh and what not to keep the villagers of Pattan in our pocket – and, the biggest expense, advertising, publicity. The scheme will sink like a stone unless people hear about it in America, and England ... I'm going to raise the money from my friends. If I can.'

'I'm sure John will lend you some,' she said.

'I'm going to ask him,' he said. 'I think it will work, and pay a good return on the investment.'

She said, 'I'll lend you some, too.'

'My dear,' he began.

'I know ... but you can let me lend you some money can't you?'

He got up, pulled on his trousers and kissed her. 'Yes,' he said, 'out of affection, and respect. Now you'd better go.'

Chapter 5

Margaret Wood looked vexedly at the dense swirling crowd that filled Lapri from end to end. She would have to get through that somehow, unless she turned off into the fields, and that would mean scrambling through thorn fences and over irrigation ditches and beds of stinging nettles. It was too hot. The whirring sound of a small car engine made her turn her head. The car stopped beside her and she saw that it was the Deputy Commissioner of Bijoli, Mr Ranjit Singh.

He climbed out and said, 'I was just coming to pay you a call. I hope it's convenient.'

'Oh, yes,' she said. 'Please.' What's the time? she thought. About half past four. Tea with smalll cakes would be enough. If she could find anyone to prepare it. Today was the biggest day of the Hindu festival of Holi, one of the most important of the year. Whether officially Christian or not, everyone disappeared from the mission. She had to keep one of the nurses on duty by a combination of main force, threats, and bribery.

'May I give you a lift?' the Sikh said, and she cried, 'Oh, yes, please.' She waved her hand at the throng ahead. Ranjit Singh smiled. 'You should be in your oldest clothes today. I am.' She saw that his khaki shirt was splashed with violet and red spots and streaks. She suppressed a grimace of disgust. During Holi the Indians threw coloured dye over each other, over everything, and sometimes water that had been dyed pink and red and violet. Educated Hindus energetically denied it, but she had heard that the red liquid represented women's menstrual blood, and it was thrown about at this time because Holi was the feast of spring, of fertility, and lust. An extra source of disgust was that Holi always coincided closely with Easter. The actual truth of the legend didn't matter. Hindu India, in the essence, as she saw it in this buried, forgotten corner, was quite capable of such a bestiality. You only had to look at the Pattan temples to realise that the Hindus really worshipped sex and everything to do with it. Last year, during Holi, she and Henry had seen men dancing in the road at night with huge wooden phalli strapped to their waists.

They crawled forward in low gear, the little Austin worming its way through the singing, shouting, dancing crowd. Small bands blared on their side, bombs of dye burst on the closed windows, and the heat inside was stifling. A young man, laughing and happy, leaned over the bonnet and sent a long squirt of red water on to the windshield. Ranjit Singh switched on his windshield wipers and the young man laughed even harder.

She gasped, 'Look!'

There was Rodney Savage, among the crowd. A mob of men and girls surrounded him, and they were all pelting each other with powder. As she watched, a paper bag burst on his forehead, and pink liquid flowed down his face. His shirt and trousers were a motley mess of red and violet, hardly any of the original colour visible. Near him she saw his chauffeur, the Gurkha Ratanbir, in the same state.

'He's gone absolutely native,' she said, and flushed: 'I'm sorry, I didn't mean . . . '

The Sikh smiled. 'I know what you mean, Mrs Wood.'

Savage saw them in the car at that moment. He straightened, then bowed deeply.

'He's drunk,' she muttered, 'he must be.'

Ranjit Singh said, 'He may well be – but he doesn't have to be. As you said, he has identified himself with these people and does not need to be drunk to share their pleasures . . . and their pains, I suppose.'

They reached the end of the town at last, and pulled up in front of the mission bungalow.

She hurried up the steps. 'If you'll excuse me a moment . . . '

'Please . . . just a glass of water. I cannot stay long.'

They sat down on the rickety chairs on the veranda. The blare of bands came strong on the hot afternoon wind. Ranjit Singh sipped his water. His face was slightly pock-marked and he had shrewd, prominent eyes and thick, sensual lips. She had found him a pleasant visitor on the two or three occasions when he passed through Lapri on his way to visit the Pattan valley behind. But his visits had been purely social, for Lapri itself was not in India but in the princely State of Chambal. She wondered what was the purpose of this present call and why he was spending so long sipping his glass of water.

The Sikh put down the glass. 'Do you see much of your neighbour in Pattan?'

'Colonel Savage. No!'

She realised she had spoken with considerable vehemence. The Sikh fixed his prominent eyes on her. 'That seems a pity. Another Englishman, so close. He must be lonely . . . until his first batch of clients arrive.'

'He has hardly spoken ten words to me since he came last October – five months ago,' she said. 'It does not upset me, I assure you. I am not lonely, and even if I were, he would be the last person I would want to see.' She paused to gather breath and then the rest of her anger poured out, unchecked. It felt good, rushing out like a released flood. 'We used to get many villagers from Pattan and the valley coming down to the Mission. Now, since he came and started to repair the Rest House – none. He encourages them *not* to come. He wants to be a little tin god there. He encourages them in their old horrible superstitions. He even made a sacrifice.'

'Not human, I'm sure,' the D.C. said. 'I think I would have heard of that, even as far away as Bijoli.'

'No – goats and a buffalo, I heard. In October.'

The D.C. nodded. 'At the time of Dussehra. The Gurkha regiments always do it, though it's not a usual custom among other Hindus.'

She said, 'I saw him with some men from Pattan one evening, a week ago. They were carrying a sambhur doe.'

The D.C. said, 'Of course it has been a very poor winter crop and the villagers are hungry. But it seems an odd way to ensure good hunting for his clients . . . Has he annoyed or molested you in any way?'

'No,' she said at once, 'not personally. Not since . . . well, he did once, a long time ago, not here, but I have forgotten it and I don't think he even remembers. I'm not being spiteful, Mr Ranjit Singh. Only, he's giving all Europeans a bad name, and he's a bad influence. I'm sure he's setting up a little kingdom of his own. He's the only employer in Pattan, and can spread the money, which isn't even his, just as he likes. He has them eating out of his hand . . . My nurses

5   65

desert as fast as I can begin to train them. He . . . he has women. I don't know how any decent woman can even visit him, but they do. Mrs Dadhwal went, with the General, in December. The Rani of Kishanpur is there now, alone.'

'They are all old friends,' the D.C. said, 'except the Rani . . . He has a catholic taste.'

'Catholic!' she cried. 'He's just – just a lecher.'

The D.C. paused a long time before speaking again. Then he said, 'You may be right, I do not know him well. I have only met him a couple of times, and the first time he did me and the Government of India a good turn. But I think you misjudge him if you believe that is all he is. Some men who pursue many women are seeking for an ideal – and some already have an ideal, but it's unattainable. It's important not to underestimate him . . . How are your relations with Mr Faiz Mohammed and the Chambal authorities in general?'

Mr Faiz Mohammed was the administrator of the Lapri district, and so Mr Ranjit Singh's opposite number, over the border in Chambal. He represented the government of the State. She frowned in puzzlement as she began to answer. What had Mr Faiz Mohammed got to do with Rodney Savage? She said, 'Not as good as they used to be. There's been no actual trouble . . . just pinpricks. It's hard to get to see Mr Faiz Mohammed when I want to. Just after my husband died the Chambal government gave an order re-quiring foreign missions to get authority before bringing any more missionaries into the State. We applied at once, that is, our headquarters in Manchester did. They're still doubtful whether they can find anyone to come out, but even if they do – Chambal hasn't given the permission. We had been seriously thinking of moving the mission to Pattan. Henry had talked to me about taking over the old Rest House. Then we'd have been in India, instead of at the mercies of the Chambal people. They seem to be getting more fanatically Muslim every day . . . but we don't have a proper missioner, and Colonel Savage has the Rest House.'

The D.C. said, 'And I'm afraid you would not find the attitude of our government much more helpful. Who was it who said the missions too often acted like an ecclesiastical

66

branch of the I.C.S.? Ah, I remember, it was Rodney Savage.'

'It's not true!' she cried angrily.

'I know it does not apply to you,' he said hastily. 'Mrs Wood, I must explain something to you in plain words, which you may have thought out for yourself . . . As you know, when the British left this country they left it divided up into two sovereign nations – India and Pakistan – and several hundred princely states, varying in size from a few acres to thousands of square miles. Nearly all those states have since acceded to one nation or the other.'

'You invaded Hyderabad only six months ago,' she said.

The D.C. smiled. 'Our politicians use a less blunt language, but, yes, we did invade Hyderabad, the largest and richest state of all – because we are determined that these anachronistic despotisms have no place in the modern world, and we are sure that they cannot survive alone, whatever their rulers might say. *We are determined.*' He repeated the phrase with emphasis, staring at her. Then he continued: 'Half a dozen states have still not joined either us or Pakistan. They are all situated in this part of India, they are all contiguous or practically so, and the largest of them, the ringleader of the resistance, if one might call it that, is Chambal – this state. The others, such as Kishanpur and Konpara, are small and by themselves do not matter, But Chambal borders India, here, and also borders Pakistan, three hundred miles west of here, in the Sind Desert. Its ruler, the Nawab, is a Muslim. Ninety per cent of its people are Hindi.'

'You are going to take over Chambal?' she said.

He smiled carefully. 'It's not quite as easy as that. We wish to avoid violence. We suspect there is an understanding between Chambal and the smaller uncommitted states, and possibly between all of them and Pakistan, that they will act together to resist any overt action on our part. We must move carefully. But if there should be military action – this is the main gateway into Chambal from India.'

'Of course,' she muttered. 'That's why General Dadhwal was visiting in December. Mr Faiz Mohammed had three policemen waiting on the frontier to escort him whenever he stepped back into Chambal.'

The D.C. said, 'General Dadhwal was merely, ah, enjoying a shooting holiday with Colonel Savage . . . What I wish to tell you is this. After Chambal is incorporated into India, as we are determined that it shall be sooner or later, the position of the Lapri Mission will be greatly helped if it has not been identified with the Nawab's futile struggle against us. Rather, the reverse. We would appreciate any information that can be given to us about unusual activity, visits of Chambal generals, high officials, and so on. We have other means of getting information, of course, but few of them are as well placed and as . . . innocent, as you. There is a lot of tension between us now, and anything – a border incident, another speech by Mr Roy, further defiance by the Nawab – is liable to make matters worse at any moment. What are Colonel Savage's relations with Mr Faiz Mohammed? Have you noticed or heard of him meeting Chambal officials here or elsewhere?'

The abrupt questions again surprised her. She shook her head. 'I don't know . . . I haven't heard . . . Pattan is in India . . . he has no reason for dealing with Mr Faiz Mohammed.'

'Precisely,' the D.C. said. 'That's why it would be very interesting . . . and, to me, sad, if he were. I'm sorry for him.'

'Sorry?' she exclaimed, and checked herself. That was not a charitable outlook. Henry would have reproved her for that. She said, 'Is he suspected?'

The D.C. stood up. 'He has enemies,' he said enigmatically. 'Now I must run the gauntlet of the crowd again. No use washing my car, or myself, until next week. Thank you so much – and don't hesitate to call on me for any assistance I can give you. My *tehsildar* at Sabora will always forward a message. He is a very reliable man.'

She watched the little Austin drive down the road, and slow to a crawl as it reached the outskirts of the crowd. Soon it was engulfed.

Colonel Savage a sort of a spy, a secret agent of Chambal . . . It would fit what she had heard about him in the old days; but somehow it didn't fit the new Savage, dancing and singing in that crowd there, the Savage of Pattan. This man seemed to be withdrawing from power, rather than meddling with it. She had not sensed any intrigue. What annoyed her was a feeling that he exerted a secret pull, like that of a hidden magnet, back towards the jungle, and a barbaric, sensual past. It was a strong pull, and it seemed to affect everyone who could be reached by the power of his personality, or his money. It affected her.

His first batch of clients was coming any day now, she had heard. She wondered how it would go. It would certainly be nothing like the African safaris one read about . . .

She glanced at the little chapel down the road. Henry's grave was indistinguishable from those of his converts now. Sometimes there were only two people at Sunday morning prayer service. Henry had ordained her a lay preacher during his long illness, and she did her best to feel the inspiration . . . but how could she guide souls when her own floated lost and desolate, here in the jungle, unable to go, without purpose to stay?

Now they wanted her to be a spy. It sounded exciting. She would write secret messages, pay secret calls on the *tehsildar* at Sabora, creep stealthily through the jungle to Pattan and, unseen, watch Rodney Savage's intrigues. Angrily she kicked a small stone off the veranda. What would Henry have said? No one would have suggested it to him. He was incapable of doing any work but God's. The affairs of man had meant nothing to him.

The sun was setting behind the Chambal hills to the west. Soon it would be dark. Time to check the oil in the lamps, and the wicks, and see whether the buffalo milk had curdled in the pantry, and read another chapter of the Bible, and pray, and wonder, and wait.

Chapter 6

March, 1949. The intrepid white hunter strode tirelessly across the rolling hills, the topi shading his keen handsome face from the tropical sun. His clothes were well worn but, oh, so obviously the work of a West End tailor, and his fingernails were clean, for Colonel Savage, O.B.E., M.C., late of His Majesty's Indian Army, was first, last, and all the time a gentleman, and could no more be found with dirty fingernails than the Holy Roller down in Lapri could be dragged out from under a bus and, horror of horrors, have it revealed that the corpse was wearing off-white drawers. At the Colonel's heels trotted his faithful native servants, doglike devotion written all over their inscrutable Oriental faces...

I was wearing a pair of khaki shorts and Bandelkhand slippers, as a matter of fact. Chadi, Mitoo, and Ganesha wore slippers and loincloths, mere ball bags. I'd have worn the same if I'd thought we might run into the Holy Roller, but that didn't seem likely, and I prefer shorts. That woman hated me and I resented it. Hated, feared, and despised me. The unreason of it haunted me, so that I'd see her face in my imagination, wearing a number of expressions I'd never seen it wearing in real life – compassion, amusement, speculation. Very odd, in spite of her auburn hair and fine race-horse thighs.

It kept drizzling a warm rain, and I tried to think of Sumitra, to keep my mind off being tired. The sweat and rain ran salt into my mouth. My legs and chest and face were thorn-scratched and bleeding in a dozen places. My stomach felt empty as a drum, the skin drawn back from the front against my backbone by a sheer sucking emptiness, and my mouth like a pot of stale glue. Not a sight of game all day, and now we were almost home again – only about four miles to go.

Yesterday we'd done thirty-five miles, from Pattan to the Gond village of Bhughat. I'd sat up most of the night with

70

Gulu the chief, arranging to get their help in producing game for my clients. The Gonds live so close to nature that they can do almost anything with wild animals. Now we were on our way back, another thirty-five miles. And Sumitra probably arrived yesterday, expecting to find me there . . .

All this because of the weather. Six days of rain now, to ruin scent, drive the animals to shelter, reduce visibility – just before my first clients came. Weather bad, crops bad. I knew the crops had been bad, but I didn't know quite how bad until a month or so ago when I found a child, a little girl of eight, lying in the path between the Rest House and Pattan village, almost in front of the old temples. She was starving to death, and had fainted. I carried her into the Rest House and fed her up, and swore I'd eat the same as the poorest people in Pattan until I really knew what it was like to starve. I found the poorest family in the village, and for a week ate exactly what they ate, no more, no less. Then I took my rifle and started poaching game for the village to eat. It might have been more helpful to give them some money, or go and beg grain from the Holy Roller – she had a few rupees for such charity, I believe – or go and tell Ranjit the D.C. . . . but life isn't all sense, thank God. These were my people and we were going to come through it together, by our own efforts.

Chadi, Mittoo, and Ganesha were the faithful natives, trotting at my heels. Actually they were padding along in slow time, almost as dead beat as I – not quite, because they were all three typical hill-men from the Vindhyas, wiry, no surplus flesh, the skin tight on the bones but wrinkled at the joints, legs like match sticks with lengths of dark muscle cord wrapped over the bone and knotted here and there.

Chadi saw the stag first and touched my bare elbow. We all stopped. The stag was a monster, one of the best heads I've ever seen. He was feeding near the edge of the escarpment. Behind him the land dropped sharply away to the Shakkar valley, the Rest House, and the cart track from Pattan to Lapri. By then we were less than a mile from Pattan. The rain slanted gently from the northwest, not quite from the stag towards us, but diagonally. We sank down, the four of us, and stared at the stag. The three experts sniffed the air, looked at the trees, felt the earth. I

71

couldn't help thinking, what a trophy! I could leave one of the men to mark his movements, and give H. Huntington Blauvelt or Lord Hillburn a near-record head – their first day. And we would still eat the carcass. My mouth began to water and my jaw to ache. No, this was food. Pattan needed food, and I couldn't afford to risk losing it.

I wanted to shoot at once, but the beast was a good six hundred yards off, moving in and out among scrub teak and scattered bijasals. A flame-of-the-forest tree spread a kind of dull, wet-sheened scarlet light over him for a moment and my heart cried, don't fire, he lives here too, he walks these hills, and feels the earth underfoot, and the sun on his back, and smells the jungle at night, and caresses the does clustering round him. Then my jaw hurt more and saliva squirted out suddenly into the corner of my mouth and it hurt so much that I bit my tongue to avoid groaning aloud.

Chadi and Ganesha, the oldest and the youngest of the three, slipped away to the left. I understood well enough. They intended to drop over the edge of the escarpment and work along the slope below the stag until they were up-wind of him. They'd have to get pretty close, in this weather. Then he'd raise his head and start moving, more or less towards me. We must not let him turn across the wind and down towards the Rest House, which he might easily do with the scent so indecisive and occasionally distorted by rain flurries.

When the others had been gone ten minutes Mitoo slipped away from my side. He would follow in their path, but closer to the top of the escarpment. When the stag began to move, he would come up to the crest line and show himself. No, that would be too crude. He would move subtly, make a noise that might mean anything, not enough to frighten the stag, enough to puzzle him. I had to remember that their hunting methods were based on the bow and arrow, and even the spear. They had no firearms, except one old blunderbuss in the village, which the government allowed them for the watchman. Nor could they afford cartridges.

I knelt beside a pterocarpus, my body hidden behind the bole, and watched the stag. My rifle was cocked now and I kept nervously examining the sights. Suppose I had hit a rock with the foresight sometime, and not noticed it? Suppose I'd bent the backsight against a tree trunk?

The stag flung up his head and stared west, towards the edge of the escarpment. He took a couple of steps in that direction – away from me. My heart sank and my throat contracted in pain. None of the men were carrying any weapon but the long-handled hatchet.

The stag began to move along the edge of the escarpment. Now was the bad time. He was moving away from Chadi and Ganesha, but would not reach Mitoo for another couple of minutes. He only had to take a couple of steps to the right and he'd disappear over the edge. I had the sights on him, but there was no strength in my arms, and the rifle barrel wavered and swung so that sometimes I could see all of him above the foresight, sometimes the barrel blocked him out altogether, and bushes and trees kept obscuring him.

He went on, fast but not trotting, his head high, suspicion in the curve of his back and the set of his tail and the carriage of his great head. Another minute and I began to feel easier. He would be almost directly above Mitoo now.

He jerked his head sideways, stopped dead for a fraction of a second, then turned and trotted straight towards me. After a hundred yards his trot eased to a walk and he stopped, turned again. Another bad time – if he continued now in his original direction he'd disappear into a patch of thicker jungle, still nearly 500 yards away.

Mitoo appeared, rather to the left of where he must have been when he made his little sound. He stood now between the stag and the stand of dense jungle. The stag swung heavily round and broke into a full gallop. He passed me at thirty yards, and I hit him exactly behind the point of the left elbow. He dived head first on to his nose and never moved again, his head ploughing through the fallen leaves like a bulldozer, the horns remaining spread and upright.

They came, running, dancing, waving their axes in the air. I threw down my rifle and grabbed two by the waist, and we danced round the corpse, yelling. I broke it up by grabbing Ganesha's arm and shaking him. 'Run down to the village,' I shouted, 'and bring men to carry the stag. We cannot manage it by ourselves.'

Ganesha ran off, a huge grin splitting his dark narrow

73

face. The older men stopped their prancing, and we went slowly down over the edge of the escarpment towards Pattan.

We came in on a game trail that passes half a mile behind the temples, and about there met Ganesha and a dozen men carrying long bamboo poles, all trotting up the path and chanting a vigorous song: Question from Ganesha in front, 'Who saw the stag?' Response from the crowd behind, 'Who saw the stag, wah!' Then, in chorus:

> *'Chadi saw the stag, Chadi saw the stag, wah!*
> *The Gora Raja waited, the Gora Waja waited, wah!*
> *The Gora Raja fired, wah!*
> *We shall eat, we shall eat, wah!'*

Gora Raja means Pale Face King. That was me, and it was the best title, the sweetest in my ears, of any that I'd ever held. No one awarded it to me. I earned it.

We entered the village at about half past five in heavy rain. All the small boys ran out, shrieking and dancing and singing round me. I gave one of them my rifle to carry, and he put it on his shoulder and marched beside me like a body-guard. I soon had a naked little girl in each hand and another riding on my shoulders, her thin legs clasped round my neck and her fists beating a tattoo on the top of my head. Their mothers and elder sisters were running out and throwing hurriedly made garlands round my neck. Mitoo's wife hugged me, and I held her naked waist with one arm and cried to Mitoo, 'Hey, this one wants to fornicate in the street in broad daylight. No wonder you look so tired.'

Mitoo yelled, 'She is a bottomless pit! She would like to be one of the stone women at the temples!'

The Pattan temples were covered with statues of communal love-making. For some time the near-famine had been scraping layers of repression and layers of modern organisation off the villagers. The temple and the kind of communal life they portrayed was now, again, very near the actuality. There wasn't a mixture of poverty and wealth. Everyone was the same – poor. One man's poverty or starvation affected everyone, because everyone shared in it. One man's good fortune affected everyone the same way, just as they were all dancing and laughing now. It was not at all hard to see in the present excitement, caused by the prospect of eating meat, that desire also would affect everyone. It

74

only required a small step – forward or backward – for it, too, to be equally shared.

When we reached the headman's house the whole population of the village, about four hundred, was with us, except the men who had gone back up the hill. Lok Chand, the headman, came out of his little house, his wife behind him. They were both short, and usually cheerful, though they were no richer than anyone else. They both used to be fat, but had lost many pounds during the lean spell.

I called out to Lok Chand that we had killed a stag and he said, 'Do you think there is anyone here who doesn't know that? Shall I divide it?'

'The usual way,' I said. 'I do not want anything for myself.'

His wife pushed through the crowd, holding a brass jar of warm milk, and gave it to me. I drank some and passed it to Chadi, who drank and passed it to Mitoo. Everyone in Pattan was the same caste, a Sivaite sect of Sudras, except the village Brahmim. I had long ago been elected an honorary Sudra too, inasmuch as that mattered here. As the Brahmin and I had discussed several times, the Hinduism of Pattan seemed in many ways to be pre-Brahmin, Tantric and Rudric. Max had noticed it and commented on it during his visit in December.

I noticed that a couple of the older villagers who had been squatting outside the headman's house – combined hovel and byre would be a better word – were now arguing fiercely with each other, waving their arms, shaking their palms in the air, and gabbling away at high speed, though they kept their voices low. I called over the heads of the crowd, 'What is this, brothers? Should we quarrel when there is food?'

The two stopped, rather shamefaced, and the headman said, 'It is the old land dispute, sahib.'

'Are you two still quarrelling over five square yards of rock and one thornbush?' I cried. Everyone laughed. Lok Chand said, 'There is no bringing them to reason. I shall have to ask the Deputy Commissioner Sahib to settle it when he comes next.'

'The Deputy Commissioner?' I said. 'What do we in Pattan need of him? Can we not settle our affairs by ourselves? Come here, brothers.' The two men came forward.

'It's that piece of land at the southeast corner of your maize field, eh?' I said to one.

'At the southwest corner of *my* maize field,' the other said.

'My father . . . '

'My uncle . . . '

'Who were one and the same person,' I bellowed. 'Shut up! . . . Listen, will you accept my judgement? It will be either mine or the Sikh's. Make up your minds.'

The two old fools looked at each other. They spoke simultaneously. 'We will abide by your judgement, Gora Raja.'

'All right. Give me a coin, Lok Chand.' Lok Chand ran back into his house. Coinage wasn't used much in that village, where payments were made by exchange or barter or in kind. He came out with a two-anna piece. 'You,' I pointed to one of the old men, 'you will call either heads or tails when I flip this coin in the air. If you call it correct, the land will belong to you, but you will lease it to the other, without rental payment, for a period of ten years from this moment. If you call wrong, the opposite . . . Call.'

He called wrong. 'It is settled,' I said.

'It is settled,' they said gravely. Their old wives appeared from nowhere, beaming at each other – they'd been glaring and glowering like little old witches for the past three months and more. I covered my eyes with the palm of my hand and cried, 'Those eyes! Take me away before I faint from desire.' More shrieking and cackling. I could have kissed them all.

I beckoned Lok Chand. 'Come with me a little way . . . ' We walked on between the houses, the crowd still with us. It was something like those old pre-war newsreels of Hitler entering Vienna or the Prince of Wales in the Welsh coal valleys: take your pick. I'd had the little naked girl wrapped round my neck all the time, and wondered whether any previous Solon gave his judgements wearing such a becoming scarf. I lowered her, smacked her behind, and told her to go home. She ran off, laughing.

'Listen, friend,' I said to Lok Chand. 'That stag is a big one, but it will not go far among four hundred. Tomorrow, leave behind in the village all the men I shall need as beaters and *shikaris*. Take a party of the rest to Bhilghat, and fish in the lakes.'

76

Lok Chand cried, 'The Gonds will kill us, sahib!'

I said, 'No, they won't. I have their chief's promise. Once a week, until your new crops ripen, you may take two hundred pounds of fish from their lakes and rivers.'

Lok Chand said, 'Sahib, in this weather not even our best fishermen will catch anything.'

I whispered in his ear. 'Dynamite. I have it and the detonators at the Rest House. Grimoo and Maldi and Taharu have all worked at the Sabora quarries, and know something of the business.'

Lok Chand dropped back, his palms joined. He had a deep sense of responsibility for his village, and usually no means to discharge that responsibility, being as helpless as the rest of them in the face of natural calamity and hardship. He was a good man.

By then we were almost at the temples. I went up the steps on to the great platform, followed by about half the original crowd – the rest had drifted back into the village. I took off my battered little garlands, kicked off my slippers, and went into the temple with the great red phallus, and hung the garlands carefully round the head of it. Most of the others came forward after me, with flowers they'd picked along the track, and green twigs, whatever they had in their hands, and laid their offering at the base of the phallus.

Then we all looked at each other awhile, smiling in contentment, and I waved my hand and went on towards the Rest House. They, my people, turned back towards Pattan.

Sumitra was standing on the veranda when I came round the last bend in the track. She was wearing slim-cut fawn slacks of drill and a pale-blue silk blouse, with a wide belt and a big silver buckle. I went slowly up the steps to her, dirty and wet and smelling of woodsmoke and sweat. She held out a tall cold glass of lemonade. 'Congratulations. I hear it was a beauty.'

I nodded, busy drinking the lemonade.

'Too good for your clients,' she said. She laughed. 'Really, Rodney, you are impossible. Don't you have any sense of self-preservation?'

I didn't answer that, but I said, 'I'm sorry I wasn't here. Things got urgent and I had to go.'

She said, 'Don't worry. It was nice being alone for a change.'

77

It was getting dark under the rain clouds and Ratanbir had appeared to take the rifle from my hand, '*Ghusl tayyar chha,*' he said, saluting. I needed a bath more than anything just then, so I went in, with a word of apology to Sumitra.

Half an hour later, clean-scrubbed and dressed in a thin black dinner jacket and white trousers, I rejoined her. The butler brought us whisky and soda, and hot meat titbits to nibble on.

I said, 'I thought Dip was coming with you again.'

She said, 'He was. Then something turned up – a sudden visit by the Grand Wazir of Chambal. Dip had to stay.'

'Chambal?' I said. 'Oh, more bribes and threats, I suppose.'

She said, 'I suppose so . . . I had hell getting across the border yesterday, you know. The Chambal police practically turned my car, and all my luggage, inside out. It's that speech the Nawab made.'

'I know,' I said. Three days ago the Nawab of Chambal had made a fierce radio speech, all about how the great, ancient, independent, and sovereign kingdom of Chambal would take no nonsense from anyone. And that was in response to a speech by L. P. Roy in Delhi, who'd said that India's patience was not inexhaustible, that India could not stand by for ever with folded hands while the Chambal despots threw democracy-loving citizens into jail and forced Hindus to eat beef at bayonet point.

'A pox on both your houses,' I said rather irritably. It didn't require much *nous* to realise that here at Pattan, peaceably going about my business, I was nevertheless in the firing line. Max had obviously done some snooping while on his shooting trip, and doubtless even now some Chambal general, bent over a map in Chambalpur, was announcing 'We'll stop them here' – with a large forefinger covering the words 'Lapri' and 'Pattan'.

'Aren't you going to take sides?' Sumitra asked. 'Or perhaps you already have?' Outwardly she looked very un-Indian, like a sun-tanned French brunette just in from riding round the grounds of her château. But her eyes, and the particular pose she adopted, relaxed in the long chair, and the set of her head, were pure Indian. Then there was something peculiarly Sumitra, special to her, which I recognised at once even though I'd seen her only three times: her eyes were alert, examining, and set, in the way a trigger is set, ready to go *tock* and set off a propellent charge of enormous power.

I wanted that charge to go off, aimed at me, though I knew it would be dangerous. I was lonely, and, busy as I kept myself, I could not prevent Janaki and Victoria Jones coming to me in my dreams – only to look at me with the helpless, puzzled look of people who see each other out of trains in a station, and then the trains begin to move in opposite directions, leaving me more lonely, more in need.

I said, 'No, I am not going to take sides.' I added in Hindi, 'I am a poor man of Pattan. Let the mighty ones fight over my head while I cultivate the soil.'

I reached out my hand, took hers, and said, 'I hope you've come to sleep with me.'

She let her hand lie in mine, and her eyes kept on mine, but the trigger notion was not in them so strongly now, or perhaps not at all, just a mirror-like self-inquiry.

'I don't know,' she said, 'I don't think so.'

I had a right to ask her, bluntly and without a gavotte of preparation. That first night she came to the Rest House and stayed the night – she and the two girls from Pattan. If I hadn't already seen Khajuraho and the Pattan temples I would have been hard put to it to know how to comport myself in such a situation. As it was, everything fitted into place, not only physically but spiritually. By morning my body was drained clean of any animal emotion whatever – love, hate, jealousy, anxiety, what have you. This was the original design: after the orgy those medieval Hindus went thus, empty, to the temple, to understand God. And so I had gone, empty, to Delhi.

She said, 'I have never slept with a cultivator of the soil.'

'*Quelle snob!*' I said: but it had always been clear that a man's mental state, his condition of tension and effort, what one might call being strung like a bow against his fate, meant more to her than the physical side. Her way and walk of life had not brought her into contact with a cultivator in rebellion against the soil, that was all. I was no longer in rebellion, and was digging my way into Pattan and rural Indian life so fast that in a year or two there'd be nothing left of me visible above the ground.

She turned away her brilliant eyes and spoke to the night.

79

'I can see you want to fall in love. I don't wish to act as a substitute for Janaki, much as I admire her. And it wouldn't do you much good, either, would it?'

Dip Rao, her husband, was a friend of mine and always had been, though we had not seen much of each other since boyhood. In the Western world, and in the old days, twinges of guilt would have assailed me about sleeping with a close friend's wife, but Sumitra's original kindness had altered that, at least in respect of her, and life in Pattan had confirmed the change. Here, in the pattern that seemed to be modelling itself on the ancient temple statuary, you slept *only* with friends' wives. After all, it is a situation which calls for a lot of understanding, sympathy, and affection.

'You have those two girls, I suppose, for your needs?' she said.

'Kunthi and Devi? I have been teaching them what I know of hygiene, sanitation, and elementary first aid. I think the village needs something like that. But I have not had them professionally since Sabora, in spite of the Holy Roller's tales to the contrary.'

She sank her hand on mine and squeezed it. 'Oh, Rodney, you are a fool! Why do you try to hurt yourself?'

She was as sharp as a razor. However energetically I sank into the life of Pattan I could not conceal from myself that something vital was missing; and that something was a woman of intelligence and power to share my secret life and thoughts. It was a desperate lack, and because of it I could not bring myself to waste my substance, the substance of my loneliness and need, on the frivolity of sheer fornication.

'This is impossible,' she said suddenly. She pulled her hand away and got up. 'I never thought it would be as hard as this. I'm going.'

She ran into the bungalow. It was nearly seven. She had 120 miles to go to Kishanpur. Well, she could always stop the night with Max and Janaki in Bhowani. She came out carrying a small suitcase.

I got up. 'Goodbye,' she said. 'Will you promise me something, Rodney? Send for those two girls. If you're going to give up the rest of the world, do it thoroughly. Otherwise – you'll get torn in pieces . . . Oh, I passed our elephants on the road. They'll be here tomorrow morning.'

She held out her hand and I raised it to my lips. A

80

moment later she had slid behind the wheel of the Rolls shooting brake, and the lights came on, shining down the long avenue of the forest road to Lapri, and shining on the place by the stream, near the Irish bridge, where I had doused the Holy Roller with water, and then the red tail light shone dim and dimmer and she was gone.

After a long silent time, sitting slumped in the chair, I stirred myself and called for a double whisky. The rain clouds seemed to be lifting and perhaps my clients would not get soaked every day, though conditions would still be most unpromising. Tomorrow they'd arrive, Lord and Lady Poop, Mr J. Theophilus Hackenschmidt, Mr and Mrs whatever their bloody names were. My purpose in being here, my original object in becoming involved so closely with Pattan, was to prepare for them, and yet ever since the first preparations began, the clients had been taking shape in my mind as intruders.

The stretch of grass beside the Rest House, that had once been empty, was covered with big tents. Tomorrow I must move out into one of them myself. It wouldn't do for the clients to live in tents while the White Hunter, the paid servant, slept under a roof. We would use the Rest House for dining, bar, and common-room purposes. The servants' quarters and other smaller tents alongside them were full of servants. We had a Goanese butler and a Goanese cook, Carlos and Francis, respectively, and half a dozen bearers, plus sweepers and *bhistis* from Pattan. None of the men from outside was happy, and I'd had to pay vast sums to get them. The kind of servant who is at home in the jungle is apt to look primitive to the eyes of people straight from England or America – like my mother's old sweeper in Manali, who'd stride through the drawing-room while she was having a tea party, a full chamber pot in his hand, crying genially, 'Going to empty piss-paat, memsahib!' Conversely, such men as these, who knew how to handle all the complicated requirements of tourists, hated and feared the jungle. So they, even though Indians, were intruders too.

Tomorrow the rape would become final, the actual violation of Pattan. The peace would be broken, the enclosed entity shattered. I felt as though I were holding down a little girl, perhaps the naked nine-year-old who had ridden wrapped round my neck through the village just now, and

6

guiding some ignorant foreign sod into her secret place. I felt terribly lonely, and for a moment fought against a frantic desire to send for Kunthi and Devi. Then my deeper longing won, and I called instead for dinner to be served at once.

The next morning dawned well, and the elephants arrived. These were half a dozen State elephants belonging to Dip Rao. He had to use them for ceremonial processions during Holi and again in October, for Dussehra. The rest of the time he was lending them to me, free of charge – in fact he was paying for their upkeep. I had promised to pay him back when we got going properly.

Later the first clients arrived. The hired cars made the journey from Bhowani Junction, where I went to meet the mail train, with only one puncture and no mechanical break-downs. The clients rolled happily along with many Ohs! and Ahs! at the sight of the Romantic Orient. They thought the Rest House picturesque, the tents thrilling, and the servants amusing. At dinner the roast lamb was dreadful, but liberal lubrication with champagne did its work and by the end of the evening we all knew each other pretty well.

There were five of them – Lord and Lady Hillburn, Mr and Mrs Wilson, and H. Huntington Blauvelt. Hillburn was a shortish, fat fellow with a paunch and a face like a butcher's. The peeress – Cynthia, she told us to call her – was several inches taller, a natural blonde, long face, long legs, small breasts, hard blue eyes. She was obviously the boss, and the better athlete of that pair.

The Americans were the other way round. George Wilson was a rugged six-foot specimen, about forty-five, black hair cut short, an oil man from Wyoming. He assured me three times that his company had no connection whatever with teapots, and never did have. Baffled but polite, I agreed, and then he relaxed. His hunting equipment was workmanlike, and I enjoyed his manner. His weakness was an excessive fondness for his wife, Mother, as he called her. Dot Wilson was just what you'd have expected, a little plump friendly woman, totally unused to the wilds.

H. Huntington Blauvelt was the really important member of the group as far as we were concerned. Who hasn't read *The Doughboy and the Duchess*? Well, I hadn't until a month before, but apparently everyone else in the world had, certainly everyone in the U.S.A., and even I had heard of it. He wrote it in 1919, and followed it with three or four flops — (John Clayton got all this from the Indian Government and they from the consulate in New York) and then he more or less disappeared from view, though making millions writing scripts in Hollywood, until the 1930's, when he emerged as a writer on shooting. Some of these later books I had read — *King of the Icefloes, Safari, An American Hunter.* Then he'd been a war correspondent, and just a couple of years ago had written something called *Return to the Duchess . . .* He'd had numerous wives, and looked like Apollo — thirty years on. He was bald but wore a toupee, not a very good one. His skin was a peculiar grey shade, odd in a man who spent so much time out of doors. He had blurred grey-blue eyes and a fine sensitive mouth.

Then there was John Clayton, come down to assist me in dealing with this first and all-important batch of clients. Frances sent her best wishes, he said. After that we did not mention her again.

We went to bed about eleven o'clock. The clients were excited, and I was keyed up. The next day we were kicking off with a tiger hunt on elephants.

Came the dawn. I checked that the clients had been awakened with *chota hazri*, and went back to the kitchen to see that breakfast was coming along. All well. I found the chief mahout in charge of the elephants. Work in progress there.

By 7.0 a.m. we had finished breakfast, but Blauvelt hadn't appeared. I went to his tent. He was lying in the camp bed, his face greyer than ever. His mouth twisted slightly when I entered, and he motioned wearily to the bedside table, where there was a glass of water and four bottles of pills. 'I'm sorry, Colonel . . . a touch of the old fever.'

'What a shame,' I said. The place stank of whisky, and I knew, if I looked, I'd see an empty bottle under the bed.

'It always does this to me,' he said. 'Been suffering with it since '24, when I went to Uganda.'

'Damned shame,' I said. Blauvelt's eyes flicked on to mine, passed by. He knew that I knew. One observed the amenities.

'I'll probably be all right tomorrow, maybe even this afternoon. The temperature usually goes down in the afternoon,' he said.

I nodded and slipped out. I'd have to rearrange the groupings on the elephants.

The elephants appeared, swinging round the corner of the Rest House in single file. They knelt and we climbed up into the howdahs on a little stepladder. I put myself on the lead elephant, with Lady Hillburn; Hillburn and Dot Wilson on the second; George Wilson and John Clayton on the third. Two spare elephants followed. Everyone had a good heavy rifle except Dot Wilson, who said, quite rightly, that she couldn't lift it. Naturally, John and I were not going to shoot except in emergency.

We rolled off down the drive, on to the cart track, left towards Pattan. The mahouts sagged comfortably on the elephants' necks. Everyone except John and me was wearing a huge quilted sola topi. Cynthia Hillburn wore a daringly cut bush shirt and khaki slacks.

We rolled majestically past the old temples, and Cynthia looked at the carvings with a clinical sort of interest. On through Pattan, where what was left of the population (half the men were out as beaters) lined the muddy path to watch us pass. Kunthi and Devi stood in a doorway in Kunthi's parents' house, looking very sexy. Lok Chand came out, made salaam, and told me the beaters had left two hours earlier. Chadi would meet me at the rendezvous and confirm that all was in order.

We heaved on, a convoy of little ships in line in the great ocean of the jungle. We passed a small lake set among red rocks, and there was a man burning brushwood on the far side. Two pictures came together before my eyes, unconnected in time or space but superimposed now by a combination of stimuli – I saw Rifleman Jitbahadur Gurung, dead the previous evening from a tribesman's rifle bullet through the chest, lying on a rough platform of logs. Nearby the battalion Brahmin intoned a prayer. My company *subadar* squatted beside me, and the flames were beginning to rise from the pyre. That picture was from 1937. Behind and in that picture there was the water of a lake, not this one, another, but it was water, and a pale grey-green light along the horizon, and I waited with shotgun ready. Above the crackle of the logs, where Jitbahadur burned in the first picture, I heard the whirring wings of the wild duck flighting, and felt my orderly stiffen behind me, and we crouched deeper into the reeds. That was a cold-weather dawn in the Punjab – 1936 perhaps?

The elephant rolled on.

But where else had I smelled the incense burning, and rich oils on a flame? I saw a man and a woman in gorgeous clothes kneeling over a brazier, and the flames leaping up red on to his face. The girl kept her head down and her sari drawn far forward, and I saw nothing of her skin. Hand in hand, round and round the fire they went in the ceremony of marriage. Now, as before, a second picture superimposed – this time a long file of men and women struggling up a stony path, a strong cold river beside them. Where was that? Why so many old men with sticks, and old women carried on beds on the shoulders of coolies?

'Badrinath,' I cried, 'the pilgrim road to Badrinath!'

'I beg your pardon?'

The peeress was staring at me. Hard as a bar. of steel. I thought. I must make sure she got at least two good trophies, or she would see that the word went round – Savage is a fake.

I said, 'Sorry. My mind was wandering.'

'So it appeared,' she said, 'you were looking straight through me.'

'What a waste,' I said lightly, and then she smiled. I made sure we weren't touching in the howdah. No Francis Macomber stuff for me.

When we reached the rendezvous Chadi and Gulu, the Gond chief, and a dozen villagers were waiting there. We had covered four miles and were in scattered jungle near the head of the Shakkar River. Here the valley, which had been climbing gradually between the steep walls of the escarpments, spread and widened. The river was only a stream, and we looked south over a sea of waving tall brown grass, with a few trees dotted among it. It must have been an old lake bed, for it was quite flat, and nearly two miles long by a mile wide. Tigers frequently lay up in there, and it was just the country for a hunt from elephants, the only such area anywhere near Pattan.

The elephants knelt and we all got down. 'We'll have about half an hour here,' I told the clients, 'in case anyone

85

wants to stretch his legs. Only don't go forward of this line, please.' They stood in a group, lighting cigarettes and talking.

Chadi said, 'There are two in the grass, sahib, a male and a female. The other pair may be in there still, but Gulu thinks they left during the night.'

I thanked Gulu. This hunt would have been impossible without the Gonds' help . . . and that stemmed from old William Savage. I was living on the reputation of my great-great-grandfather.

We ran through the plans again. The elephants were to get into position first. That meant moving forward about a quarter of a mile, to a point where the grass sea was just wide enough to take four elephants at a proper distance from each other, about a hundred yards. The villagers would extend the line, so that the tigers would not try to escape past the ends. When we were in position Mitoo would start down the grass from the far end, in the centre of thirty beaters.

More bloody tigers, I thought, that's what I need. At least one for Hillburn, assuming that Lady Hillburn and George Wilson got these two. I would have needed another except for Blauvelt's ague. He *had* to get a tiger sometime, and a good one, even if I put it in a cage and brought it to his tent so that he could stun it with a bottle. When viceroys and globe trotting grand dukes used to hunt tiger the maharajahs would have men trapping the beasts for a month beforehand, and cart them to the area, and release them only as the beat started. But those spacious days were gone, and I just didn't have the resources.

The elephants knelt again, we mounted, and moved forward, the villagers on the flanks. At the far end of the grass I heard the heavy boom of the village blunderbuss. We reached our position and waited. The hot, spring wind blew down the sea of grass, making long, curved waves, changing the colour and the brightness. The grass stood about six feet tall, with heavy tasselled tops. The elephants grunted and moved about. None of them were trained for this sort of thing.

A tremendous roaring boom made me jump, and our elephant backed and fidgeted. There was no sign of Hillburn in his howdah. Mrs Wilson, her fingers in her ears, was yammering with terror. That elephant was dancing about and curving up her trunk. Hillburn hauled himself up into view from the bottom of the howdah. His dear lady beside me snapped, 'Charles has shot at a bird.'

I had noticed a jungle hen rocketing skyward just after the shot. Damned fool. That would alert the tigers long before they were near us.

'Sorry,' Hillburn called to the company in general, 'I slipped, trying to keep my balance, and it went off . . . I say, can't you keep this animal still?'

My heart sank. We waited another ten minutes – fifteen, thirty. The beaters were coming very slowly. Now and then I saw an arm waving above the grass, and heard the clatter of pots and pans coming closer.

Cynthia Hillburn raised the heavy rifle and swung right. 'Mine,' she called, her eye to the sight and her cheek cuddled professionally into the butt.

I saw a tigress, a good one, creeping along on her belly almost directly towards the elephant on our right, Hillburn and Dot Wilson's. It was not Cynthia's tiger by a mile, but let *them* fight that out. She fired, and the tigress sank her head to the ground and never moved.

'Good shot!' I said, and had no time for more, as I saw her swing the rifle up to her shoulder again. This time it was a big male tiger, following at a hard gallop in his mate's tracks. George Wilson must have seen that if he didn't fire at once he was going to lose this one, too, because Hillburn had not even got his rifle into his shoulder, and the peeress was clearly a lady who shot first and discussed the niceties later – if at all. He fired. The tiger bounded into the air and began clawing at the head of Hillburn's elephant. The mahout scrambled back into the howdah, the elephant screamed and turned, ready to bolt. I took a big chance and, aiming at the tiger's hind quarters, fired, and blew it off the elephant on to the ground, where Wilson dispatched it with a final shot through the heart.

I reloaded – we were all using double-barrelled rifles, as I think they are safer with dangerous game. Cynthia reloaded. 'That's going to be all,' I said, 'I don't think there are any . . .'

But, by God, the rifle was whipping up into her shoulder again, and on came a third beast, this one a real monster of an old tiger with a magnificent ruff, heading along the same trail, straight for Hillburn.

I pushed Cynthia's rifle barrel up and yelled 'Yours,' to Hillburn. He was leaning far out over the front of the how-dah. The mahout crouched underneath, lying almost flat. Blood ran from long claw stripes down the elephant's neck and forehead, and some of it had got on the mahout, who looked as though he had been mauled. From the corner of my eye I saw Cynthia's mouth set in a hard straight line. Hillburn fired both barrels at once. He dropped the tiger stone dead, but you can't fire both barrels of a big-game rifle without ill-effects. Hillburn went straight over back-wards, and out of the howdah altogether. As he fell, heavily, his lady snapped, 'Bloody fool,' put on her safety catch, and found a cigarette.

We had a picnic lunch by the lake we had passed on the way up. Everyone, except perhaps me, was in tremendous good humour, and very excited, even Cynthia in her cold-fish way. After pointing out that she knew the etiquette of shooting quite well, thank you, she indicated that I was quite a presentable male, for a colonel, Indian Army, and that she would tell me, in due course, when I was to be given the privilege of pleasuring her. George Wilson measured his trophy in every direction. Hillburn drank more champagne than he could carry, and showed us his bruises. He was turning purple-black already, all over his right shoulder. Then we went home to the Rest House, and sat up late – Blauvelt too. He talked a great deal and was very amusing, mostly at his own expense.

For the next day I had arranged a small-game beat. When we were almost ready to go – no sign of H. Huntington Blauvelt. I went to his tent and said sympathetically, 'The old trouble again?'

I don't know why I felt sympathetic. If the bastard didn't go out shooting, what could he write that would help us? But he looked grey and worn and vulnerable, and I liked him.

'No,' he said. 'A touch of dysentery, old man. Got it in Greenland, of all places, back in '38 . . . some piece of seal meat the Eskimoes gave me. Never shaken it off.' His fine mouth was twisted in disgust. The place stank of alcohol – not whisky this time, something else, coarser and sweeter. I knew it wasn't whisky, because I'd counted the bottles in the bar at bed time, and at dawn, just to find out how much he did take. He'd had about a bottle during the afternoon and evening, but had not taken any to bed with him; and he didn't have any of his own. The bearer I'd allotted to him told me that. I sighed wearily. He must be getting arrack from the village. Well, I'd find out . . . not that I could do anything about it.

'Hope you'll be better by afternoon,' I said, and left him.

We set off, myself again with Cynthia. I felt tired. After the others went to bed I'd sat up till nearly three in the morning, talking to Chadi, Mitoo, Ganesha, and Gulu about the leopard shoot planned for the next day after this. I did not expect this small-game beat to produce much. The leopard shoot had to succeed.

The beat was to be over a stretch of rolling upland jungle about half-way between Pattan, in the valley, and an even more isolated village called Dhain, on the hills to the west. The beaters – forty men from Pattan and ten from Dhain – were already in position outside Dhain. When we were ready, at nine o'clock, they'd drive towards us through the teak and sal jungle.

I spread the shooters out, giving each one a Pattan man as general factotum and helper, though none of them could speak English. I put Wilson and Cynthia Hillburn in the middle, where I expected the best game to come down a slight fold in the ground; Hillburn and John Clayton on the extreme right, where some animals might try to break past the line; and Dottie Wilson on the extreme left, with myself.

We waited. We waited a long time. You can't hurry game if you want to guide them, and the beaters had a long way to come, and they had to come slowly to make sure that no animals hid in the scrub until they had passed. Their line was long, fairly extended and the shape of an untidy crescent, the points towards us.

Hillburn got the first animal – a small lean boar. Dot Wilson had got over her initial nervousness, having found she could lift the lighter rifle, and I had left her and was standing by a tree more or less behind the centre of the line, where I could see everyone. Hillburn struggled to his feet – he had been lying down – waddled forward to inspect his trophy, kicked it, and waddled back.

Wilson fired next, about five minutes later, and got the stag out of a small herd of five chital that came straight at him at full gallop. The chital is a small and beautiful deer which I personally don't like shooting – it has white-spotted brown hide and a big white tail and a fine delicate head. Wilson dropped his cold with a single shot at about sixty yards. Dot Wilson fired at another chital, a doe, and, thank God, missed. Cynthia expertly polished off a small sambhur. Another long wait, then a bunch of weasels, rabbits, and jackals dashed out. Dot Wilson got a jackal in the hind leg, though I was calling to her not to waste her shots. I killed it as it crawled away.

By then I was kneeling behind Cynthia Hillburn. A big boar charged out, head down, and passed close by us, going like an express train. The peeress never raised her rifle. 'I have not come here to shoot pig,' she drawled.

Then we had a long pause, with nothing moving. The rattle of the pots and the clangor of the tin cans on the ends of sticks came closer and closer. There was no tiger grass here and we could see a long way through the glades of the jungle. It was very hot. I could see the beaters clearly now, their thin legs working, right, left, right, pause, raise the stick, rattle-rattle, on again. When they had closed to about two hundred yards from us, I stood up, cupped my hands, and called. 'No more shooting, please.'

I saw Wilson jerk the bolt and eject the cartridge from his rifle. At my feet Cynthia Hillburn began to do the same, when my gigantic sambhur stag broke cover dead ahead of us, and no more than sixty yards away. He was as good as the one I'd got to feed the village. Where he could have been hiding that great bulk and that superb spread of horns, in that open jungle, I don't know – but there he was, running at a gallop from right to left across our front, between us and the beaters.

Cynthia Hillburn slammed shut the bolt of her Mann-licher and in the same motion lifted it to her shoulder. As I jumped forward, she fired. I slammed the muzzle down into the ground with my foot, the sambhur leaped high in a long convulsive buck, and collapsed. It looked as if she'd got him clean through the neck, severing the spinal cord. A grunting, screaming cough from the farther trees made my hair stand on end. It broke down into a confused gobbling moan. I saw a beater writhing on the ground.

I stood over the Hillburn woman, a painful knot in my belly. If my rifle had been in my hand I would have shot her, but I'd put it down when I called to everyone to stop firing. I whispered, 'You selfish, self-indulgent bitch! You want a bayonet ramming up your gut. Now get back to the Rest House, pack, and get out, at once.'

She looked pale, but composed. It was, after all, only a peasant, and a black one at that.

I ran to the wounded man. It was Piroo, the girl Kunthi's father. The expanding bullet had gone straight through the sambhur's neck, without mushrooming much, and hit Piroo in the left shoulder, making a bloody mess of the collar bone. He was in agony and I opened my first-aid haversack and gave him a shot of morphia. Then with George Wilson's proficient help I bandaged the wound with a shell dressing and my shirt. Meanwhile one of the young men had run off as fast as he could go to the Rest House, to bring Ratanbir and the jeep to Pattan. Then a couple of strong men lifted Piroo and began to carry him down to the village. As I followed, I saw the peeress examining her trophy. Before she could stop me I snatched the Mannlicher from her hand and with a few savage swipes broke the antlers in several pieces. I don't suppose I did the rifle much good, either.

She said coldly, 'That was quite unnecessary . . . I will, of course, pay compensation to that man.'

'Our insurance covers that,' I said, 'and no compensation can pay for an act of pure, selfish murder, done to get a trophy. I told you to pack your bags and get out.'

'It was pretty bad luck,' John Clayton said awkwardly, 'I mean, the bullet going right on through. Of course Lady Hillburn shouldn't . . . ' He always thought of money, our John. Why not? He was a businessman. He wasn't stingy, but to him this was a business venture, and his money, his savings, were involved.

'Look,' I said to the peeress, 'I'm going to Lapri with Piroo now. When I get back, I don't know how long that will be, you had better be gone.' Then I ran down the slope.

When we reached the Lapri Mission nearly an hour later Piroo was dopey with the morphia, and not in so much pain. I was driving the jeep, Ratanbir following in the

Bentley. I left Kunthi and Chadi holding Piroo, and hurried into the shack that was the hospital. The Holy Roller was there, bending over a bed in the corner. She turned, and half raised one arm defensively.

'For Christ's sake!' I snapped. I recovered myself. 'I beg your pardon, Mrs Wood. I have a badly wounded man outside. Bullet through the left shoulder.'

She said, 'I am a nurse, you know, not a doctor . . . Bring him in, that door.'

We carried Piroo into the little operating room. It was small, clean, and primitive. She undid the bandages, and then began to move with decision and certainty, cleaning the wound while the rest of us held him down. She talked to herself in a low voice: 'The clavicle is fractured . . . compound . . . shoulder blade irregular in the lower part. I can feel it – pierced by the bullet . . . lacerated exit wound . . . lucky he was not wearing any clothes to be driven into the hole. He must have a tetanus injection.'

She took a needle, filled it, gave him the injection, and wrote on his forehead with some purple dye: TT 2 cc 1230 19/3.

'He must go to the general hospital in Bhowani as soon as possible,' she said. 'He must get there before shock sets in.'

'I'm ready now,' I said. 'Is he?'

She nodded. I told Chadi that I was off. Chadi looked troubled, and Piroo reached out his right arm slowly and took my hand. He whispered, 'The sahib *log* . . . the hunting . . .'

'What do they matter when . . . ?' I began. But of course Chadi and Piroo were worrying about the success of my hunting camp. For the people of Pattan it might make the difference between near-starvation and a half-way decent life. Or was it my success they were worrying about? I couldn't follow the inner causes any further. Piroo was severely wounded and I, being responsible for him, ought to take him to Bhowani and see him into hospital.

Piroo said, 'You must not come, sahib.' He tried to sit up, his face working. 'The camp! The sahib *log*!'

I turned to Margaret Wood. 'He ought to have a nurse with him on the drive. Can you go?'

'No,' she said abruptly.

92

I glared at her; then told Chadi and Kunthi to carry Piroo out to the Bentley. I told Ratanbir to drive them to Bhowani hospital, fast but not too fast. Five minutes later they were gone. Margaret Wood and I stood alone in the road outside the hospital, opposite the tiny chapel and its graveyard.

'Why couldn't you go with him?' I said. 'He might need attention on the journey – trained attention,' I added, to forestall any criticism from her. *I* ought to have gone, but I knew Piroo would fret himself into a terrible state if I did. He thought my clients would starve to death, or die of terror in the wild Indian jungles, if I left them alone for even a few hours. Perhaps the Holy Roller had recognised all that, too, because she did not try to counter-attack me. She said, 'I did not go because I cannot. I have two patients in there who need me.'

'Don't you have any other nurses trained, after all these years?' I said.

She turned on me like a panther, her dark-gold hair shaking heavy over her shoulders. 'I did have trained nurses,' she cried. 'I have trained eleven since I came here nearly two years ago. They have all gone! You have lured them away with your filthy money and your filthy life, the way you've lured back all the men.'

'Only four girls came to you from Pattan,' I said automatically. My temper rose. My nerves were throbbing and curling like a broken bridge cable. I snapped, 'And *then* came back because they don't want your damned religion rammed down their throats. They've got one of their own.'

'Organised lechery!' she cried. 'Worship of sticks and stones! But you are the real cause. Why can't you go away and leave me in peace?'

'Go away?' I said. 'I'm only starting. I'm going to be in Pattan for a long, long time. I shall be here long after you've appreciated the impudence of what you're doing, packed up and gone home, where you belong.'

I spoke with the assurance of temper. Actually I was not at all sure how the camp would go, especially after throwing out the peers in such a high-handed manner and getting no publicity from Blauvelt.

For a moment she seemed to lose all control of herself. 'I'll see that you go!' she cried. 'You wait! You're not as safe as you think you are! *I* know what you're doing!'

I felt in my pocket, fished out a handful of rupees, and threw them at her. 'For the treatment,' I said. 'Don't bother to send a receipt.'

Then I got into the jeep and drove away. In the rear-view mirror I saw her staring at the rupee notes in the road. Before I turned the corner she stooped and picked them up. I felt a sharp pang of pleasure at seeing her degrade herself; then realised that she had no choice. She needed the money for the mission, and the hospital. It was only myself I had degraded by that gesture. That did not improve my temper.

Halfway to the Rest House John Clayton passed me in his car and I saw the Hillburns in it. He waved to me, rather nervously. The Hillburns sat up straight, ignoring me.

The Wilsons were sitting out on the lawn, in the shade of the big neem tree in the corner, overlooking the stream. H. Huntington Blauvelt's spot of dysentery seemed to have gone, for he was there, too, drinking pink gin. I ordered one for myself, drank it down, and ordered another. Wilson said, 'I want you to know, Colonel, that I would have done the same thing in your place.'

'And so would I,' Blauvelt said.

I thanked them. Dot Wilson looked a little glum. Partly the sight of blood, I thought, and partly the departure of the peerage. It was she who, a little later, said, 'It's so pretty here, isn't it?' She waved her hand at the tents, the Rest House, the Irish bridge, the heavy trees. 'So pretty. And quite different from what I expected, really.'

'What did you expect?' I asked. There was an edge to my voice, and in my mind I suddenly saw John Clayton's worried face. I added in an oily tone, 'If there's anything we can do, please let me know.'

Dot spread her plump hands. 'Well, India, you know . . . the splendour and the spiritualism.' She burbled on. Yoga. Mysterious. *The Razor's Edge.* Nice maharajah, met in Lander, Wyoming, hunting antelope. *Lives of a Bengal Lancer.* H. Huntington Blauvelt was looking at me with real sympathy in his eye. He poured two gins, and thrust one into my hand. George Wilson said nothing. He liked the *shikar*, but he too had expected something different.

What they were saying, really, was that they were being cheated of India because they were being shown it by an

94

Englishman. They wanted to be seated here, or in some more Oriental equivalent, but with a maharajah in my role, deep-thinking Hindus wandering in and out, a yogi (English-speaking) at the gate, ready to expound abstruse spiritual themes. I felt tired and a little ill. No place for me even here, if this were true.

We did nothing much that afternoon. In the evening John Clayton came back. I was glad he did not speak again about the Hillburns. I suppose he had realised that, though some of his savings were at stake, my whole life was.

The following morning Wilson and I fished – poor sport, unhappily – while Dot inspected the hand-loomed cloth I'd got some of the village women to start making, in bold patterns, for outside sale. At lunchtime we heard that Piroo was out of danger, though he'd be in hospital a month or so and might never be able to raise his left arm more than a few inches. In the evening we set out to sit up for panther. Again, Gulu and his Gonds had been at work for days on my behalf, the *machans* were ready, Blauvelt had no dysentery or ague, and I felt optimistic.

Optimistic, but unsettled. During the afternoon I had a sudden terrible yearning for Sumitra, as definite as a fever, which left me trembly and full of an appalling loneliness. That was succeeded by another, this one mixed with intense curiosity – what sort of woman, what sort of human being was she, really? – and with a violent, stallion-like desire.

Long before dusk we clambered up into the howdahs and rolled off along the cart track, past the temples, through Pattan with its usual crowd of onlookers, and then directly into the jungle, going slightly west of south. After a mile we came to the first *machan*, on the bank of a small stream, and Blauvelt scrambled down, carrying his rifle very professionally in the crook of his right arm. 'I ought to be back in half an hour or less,' I called down to him. A villager was there, tying up a lusty goat.

'Fine,' he answered. We left him gazing interestedly up at the *machan* in which he and I intended to sit. A few hundred yards farther on John Clayton and Dot Wilson got up into their *machan* and, farther on still, George Wilson and Ganesha, who had excellent night vision. Each *machan* had a goat tied up underneath it. I started back.

At the first *machan* Blauvelt was sitting on the ground,

his head back against a tree trunk. He put a hand to his forehead when he saw me coming, and struggled to his feet. I climbed down. He looked grey and weary, the mouth twisted into the familiar scorn.

'A touch of the old neuralgia,' he said, 'got it at Saint-Mihiel in the trenches, in '18 . . .'

For a moment I thought I was going to lose my temper. But I couldn't, not with him. Instead, what I wanted to do came to me with great clarity and force. I wanted to get drunk with H. Huntington Blauvelt. The Wilsons were installed, there was no reason on earth why I should sit here, alone, and have my goat distract the leopards, if any, away from the Wilsons'. I untied the goat and it galloped off towards Pattan.

'I'll come back with you,' I said.

Blauvelt's eyes lit up and his face brightened. He licked his lips. Then he remembered the neuralgia. After all, he had his pride. This kind of drinking, to sodden oblivion, was better done alone. 'If my head gets any better,' he said, 'otherwise I'm afraid . . .'

'A couple of aspirins will fix that,' I said cheerfully. I felt good, bounding with vitality. We climbed back into the howdah and set out for the Rest House. On our way through Pattan I told Lok Chand to make sure that no one from the village left the houses after dark, so as not to disturb the leopards; and spoke to Gulu, who said he thought there were at least four leopards in the area, and all hungry. I felt better yet.

We rolled on. As we passed the temples Blauvelt said, 'You know, I've never had a look at those.'

'Now's the time,' I cried. 'We can see well enough. Besides, we have a lantern.'

Our elephant knelt and I lit the hurricane lantern I'd taken along. I also had a powerful flashlight. I told the head mahout to take all the elephants back to the Rest House, and warn the cook that two of us would be in for dinner, and we wanted a good one.

Blauvelt and I walked through the short grass to the platform and climbed up. Blauvelt shone the flashlight around — it was not fully dark yet, but without the light there were only vague shapes, no clear outlines. The wavering powerful beam picked up a red group towering above us on the wall of the nearest temple. 'My God!' Blauvelt muttered. It was a woman standing with right hip curved out in a pose of utter pride and joy in being a woman. Two men stood beside her, one cupping her right breast, the other pleasuring her loins. All three smiled proudly up at the night sky. Blauvelt stood transfixed, a dim insubstantial shadow-being linked by the bar of light to the real life up there in the stone. Jackals cackled in the jungle behind and Blauvelt moved the light on.

We walked slowly around, stumbling now and then, for Blauvelt held the light upwards and I too was looking up. There were many garlands and offerings on and around the base of the great phallus. When Blauvelt switched off the flashlight the more diffuse light of the hurricane lantern put us in the middle of a huge cave of darkness, peopled by these vital images of love – all kinds of love, for there were women holding babies, and couples holding hands, totally loving but not linked sexually at that moment, and an old man playing in the dust with his grandson, and children in a log frieze riding the buffaloes back to the village, as you could see them any day now if you went out to look.

After half an hour we left. 'I need a drink,' Blauvelt said. 'You shall have one,' I said. 'And so shall I. Many drinks.'

He didn't speak on the short walk to the Rest House. He didn't speak until we were sitting in the common-room, where the bar was, large brandy-and-sodas in our hands. He finished his in two gulps, and put it down with a sigh.

He looked at me. 'Colonel, you have been thinking you didn't get much value out of me, especially as I am a non-paying guest, eh?'

It was true, and I didn't attempt to deny it. 'It doesn't matter,' I said. 'After what I did to Lady Hillburn, and realising that tourists want something more exotically Indian, I don't think it's going to work anyway.'

He said, 'More exotic? Well, yes, you might fix up a bare-ass holy man or two, and a snake charmer, and maybe arrange a visit to a maharajah. You'd better do that, next time, because I shall write that you had it all *this* time. And I shall write about the near-record heads I got, thrilling days on the trail of the king of beasts, the hard comradeship of the jungle, the quiet luxury of the hunting lodge. And all of that will hinge on the central character – the tough, hard-bitten white hunter. Women swoon for him, but he doesn't give a damn. He'd as soon slap a beautiful countess's face as undress her.'

I poured myself another brandy.

'There are two kinds of truth, Colonel,' he said pontifically, 'and you know only one. I am going to write the best, most exciting piece, about you and about this place, that I've ever written. Then that will be truth for everyone who reads it, which is going to be approximately fifteen million people in the United States alone. Afterwards, when they start coming here in droves, you'll find that events will conform to what I've written, and you will conform to the character I've painted. You'll have to.'

I knew, without a moment's thought, that he was speaking the truth. That was just how it would be. The jungle recluse, dedicated to his village and his animals, the 'character' whom one had to meet . . .

'You'll have to,' he repeated bitterly. 'Once a certain image of you has been created, you have to conform to it. I know. *The Doughboy and the Duchess* was a freak. I didn't really feel at all like that. I was copying someone else, and it worked. Afterwards I tried to write the way I really wanted to . . . tender, sensitive, introspective things, about what makes men and women tick, without drama or excitement, no violence, all the action inward. They flopped. There was this enormous pressure on me to be the man who'd created that tough, sexy, the-hell-with-it bastard Bill Carden. Everyone thought it was autobiographical. Jesus, it wasn't even wish fulfilment . . . And what do you want to be?'

I couldn't answer him at once. I had wanted to be a good soldier, a good businessman, a good lover, many more or less unconnected things. Now I didn't know. Perhaps more than anything else I wanted to escape the present, and sink into Pattan. But, then, I felt lonely.

Slowly, with unusual hesitation, I tried to tell Blauvelt something of this. He listened, drinking from time to time, his sad eyes fixed intently on mine. He said at once, when I finished. 'Why haven't you got a village girl?'

I mumbled something unintelligible.

He said, 'As long as you hold aloof, it means you are not satisfied, you have not yourself accepted what you say you want. There's someone else, isn't there, and you're thinking she will come here to you . . . to complete your happiness? Well, she won't, and if she does, it won't be to sink into Pattan with you, but to drag you out . . . It happened to me, you know. I married my first wife in the full flush of fame after *Doughboy*. It seemed like the final touch of happiness – but remember, I wanted to sink into an introspective life, and she not only wanted to bring me back to the "real" outside world – she *was* that world. It failed after two years . . . I'm afraid, Rodney, you've got to marry someone who is interested in *you*, involved with *you*, not with what you *do*, or might do, or can do.'

I thought of Janaki. Yes, she had been involved in me; but now she was the other side of the wall, and would be for as long as Max lived, and, very probably, beyond that. Sumitra . . . Blauvelt's uncanny empathy had felt, through God knows how many protective layers, that her interest in all men was in their capacities and capabilities, not in them. And that this interest would not extend to a man's capacity for self-withdrawal. And, remember, he hadn't even met her.

Blauvelt said, 'You're here. You're going to stay here. Take a girl from Pattan, and settle down. This camp is going to be a success. I personally guarantee it. I'm going on to Chambalpur from here, as a guest of the Nawab – I don't know why they're inviting me, but I'm sure I'll find out soon enough what it is they want publicised . . . and I'll write the piece about you as soon as I get there. By mid-summer you'll be snowed under with applications.'

I knew why they were inviting him to Chambalpur – to put Chambal's case for independence before the world, especially the American public, in a roundabout sort of way. Well, that was the world I was trying to get away from, the world which involvement with Sumitra – or any other woman from 'civilisation' – would drag me back into.

Blauvelt stood up suddenly. 'Come on, let's send for a couple of girls. Break it up! Make up your mind. The temples, and Pattan . . . or this lady of yours, the God-damned, stinking rat race outside. I know what *I* want. I want the temples . . . right now.'

I hesitated a little longer. It was easy for him. He didn't really mean that he wanted the lost, all-loving world of the temples – he meant he wanted it tonight, as a respite from the rat race. For me, the choice was permanent.

I made up my mind, by what process or accident I do not know. 'All right,' I said. I called for Ratanbir and told him to take the jeep and fetch Devi and Kunthi. He saluted woodenly and went out. One of the things I was giving up was being a sahib, with a sahib's standards, and it came surprisingly hard. A sahib does not involve his servant with his amours, or he will upset the man's sense of values and of his own position.

Half an hour later the girls slipped in, making deep *namasti*. Kunthi had her war paint on – a diaphanous sari, made of material I'd given her, with no underclothes or bodice, her nipples painted red, reddish-blue lines drawn with face paint under the swell of her breasts to make them stand out more, and the sari itself slightly damped so that it clung to every curve and fold of her body. Devi never used those artifices. She was thin and intense, tonight looking almost demonic, her eyes huge and heavily rimmed with kohl in her small, pointed face.

I poured them drinks. Like most of the people of Pattan, they either didn't drink at all or they drank to extinction, but I hoped to keep them from passing out tonight.

I pulled Devi down on my knee. Kunthi went to Blauvelt. We fondled them and they smiled. We all drank. Blauvelt got excited. I told the girls to take their saris off, it wasn't going to make much difference. They did so, and danced a languid indecent dance, gliding round the table, bending over us and in front of us, singing softly in their high wavering voices.

We ate, off and on. Carlos the butler dropped the soup when he first came into the room, later became so uplifted that Blauvelt invited him to join us at the table. He looked nervously at me, but, as I said, this was goodbye to sahibdom, and I held him by the shoulders and forced him to sit down. Also Ratanbir. More girls appeared, and some men from Pattan.

At about two in the morning I had a great idea, the sort that often strikes at that hour. We went in a body, singing lewd songs, to the temples, and lit several bonfires on the platform. Ratanbir in the jeep brought along two or three cases of rum. No one wore any clothes, or, if so, they were peripheral and decorative rather than prurient in purpose.

Devi's mother, Piroo's wife, for instance, wore a bodice but nothing else. Most men kept on their ragged puggarees. Many women wore the red *garghara*, the short swinging skirt of the peasant women, feeling that it was more proper – as the temple carvings often showed – to lift them or have them lifted while they danced and coupled, rather than go stark-naked. Blauvelt, forgetting which particular past he was re-entering, pranced about like a long, thin Pan, blowing tunelessly on someone's wooden pipe. He also took off his toupee and threw it away. Whatever I did I kept thinking of Sumitra.

It was said afterwards that the whole village of Pattan joined in the orgy on the old temple platform. This is not true. The population of Pattan was 403 at my last count before this, and there were some too old, some ill, some shocked, many tired, some disinterested. At dawn we had about forty present and active. The number had fluctuated all night, starting low, building, decreasing, increasing again. Nor was it an orgy, but a re-creation of the time and mood of the temples themselves, most religiously exact.

I saw the dawn coming. A greenish light spread fast over the eastern trees. The soaring temple towers, lit by the jumping red light of the fires on one side, all darkening into silhouette as the day drew on, made a most impressive and moving vision.

With Kunthi, Devi, and another woman, as a last triumphal act, I was trying to get into one of the most complicated of the interlocking positions shown in the carvings. It started with my standing on my head against a temple wall. Opposite me, between Kunthi's spread legs, I could see the model we were imitating, carved in red on another temple. Then, to the side, something alien and out of tune caught my eye. Out of tune because it was fearful, and shocked. It was the white, strained face of the Holy Roller, Margaret Wood.

She stood, frozen. I overbalanced, landed right way up, and walked over to her, the three women clinging to me wherever they could get a hold. Devi was by now on the edge of extinction.

'What can I do for you, madam?' I asked. I was not far from oblivion myself.

Her lips moved, whispering. 'A jackal ... in the operating room ... It has rabies.'

The light was strong but without any forewarning of the sun, yet, Devi slid slowly down my right side and collapsed gently, smiling, on the stone, her face to the sky.

The night was over.

'And you have no rifle, or anything?' I asked.

'No,' she whispered. 'No one in Lapri would help. They wouldn't even open the doors to me. It was dark. There was no one at the Rest House.' She was sweating, her face cold and wet and white.

I jumped down from the platform and climbed into the jeep. 'Get in,' I said. Like a sleepwalker she climbed in, looking straight ahead. On the platform the music and the shouting were dying, and men and women staggering home, others lying down where they were, out to the world.

I drove off. The light struck with a jolly warmth against my eyes and my head felt full of a joyous nothing. The road curved continuously when I wasn't looking, the cunning devil, so I had to swing the jeep nose fast and keep my wits about me or it would have slipped away from me. Once it got away and I had to dash in among the trees to catch it again. Margaret Wood bit off a cry but said nothing. The jeep seemed to want to fly and once or twice we actually took off, but there wasn't enough power, or the aero-dynamics weren't quite right, and we returned to earth a few yards farther on.

The buildings of the mission were doing a cheerful fandango when I saw them, the bungalow on the left, chapel beyond, hospital on the right. 'Stop!' Her voice was sharp and full of panic.

'Whatsa matter? Jackal can't have escaped,' I said reasonably.

'Quick, behind the bungalow, *please*,' she cried.

'O.K., O.K.,' I said, and turned off.

Behind the bungalow she said, 'Stop!' and I stopped. 'Quick.' She grabbed me by the arm and dragged me up the back veranda steps, opened a door and jerked me inside.

'Jackal in here?' I asked in surprise. I knew she'd said the beast was in the hospital. But she had vanished. She came back with a pair of trousers and a shirt. "Put these on,' she said. She'd got plenty of colour by now, and she wasn't cold or sweating any more.

Whims of women, I thought, and shrugged. I put on the clothes. They didn't fit very well and I couldn't get the trousers on because the leg hole had St Vitus's Dance, and when I had finally done it, by sitting down and holding the damned hole so that it couldn't escape, I got the other leg in the same hole. She was watching, and finally gave a sort of exasperated sigh and knelt down, dragged the trousers off me, and then with a couple of expert heaves and a wiggle, pulled them on properly.

'You'd better let me take the rifle,' she said.

'There's no need to be insulting,' I said, and walked out to the jeep and got the rifle. Then I followed her across the road to the hospital. One of the patients, wrapped in a blanket, was standing at a back window, peering in. It was a woman and I was glad I had made myself presentable. I peered in through the same window, the woman respectfully making room for me. I was looking into the little room where she had bandaged Piroo's shoulder. The jackal lay on the floor, slavering and panting deeply, obviously rabid. 'He went in, moaning, about four o'clock,' Margaret said. 'I heard the patients screaming . . . I ran over and shut the doors . . . '

I knocked out one pane of glass with the rifle butt, and, leaning in, shot the jackal through the head.

'All right?' I said.

She nodded wordlessly. 'One good turn deserves another,' I said, and walked back to the jeep.

'I'll drive you back,' she said. I frowned, and she added. 'You're as drunk as you were the first time we met.'

I said, with dignity, 'Madam, we have never met,' got into the jeep and drove back to the Rest House. Carlos, wan but fully clothed, was setting the table for breakfast. Two leopards, one very respectable and one magnificent, lay on the lawn with a grinning Chadi, Ganesha, and others squatted beside them and Wilson taking photographs. The hunting camp was going to be a great success. I seemed to have found my niche at last.

Three days later Blauvelt left for Chambalpur, the Wilsons for Agra, and John Clayton for Delhi. They were all very happy. Kunthi and Devi had installed themselves in one of the servants' quarters and were obviously my property. Dot Wilson had been deliciously titillated, George man-to-man approving. By chance a wandering *bhairagi* came by the day after the saturnalia, and I offered him a tree, a leaf roof, and the devotion of Pattan if he would be our yogi. He agreed, and took up residence. I had a letter from a friend in Delhi telling me that everyone was talking about how I had smacked Lady Hillburn's face and bodily thrown her out of the Rest House. My new suit of personality seemed to be settling into an excellent fit.

In the afternoon of the 23rd I was sitting on the veranda, reading my Sanskrit grammar, when I heard the whir of a small car, and Ranjit Singh, the D.C., drove up. I went down to greet him.

'What about some tea?' I said. 'The cook's off, so Ratanbir will make it, and it will have pepper in it.'

Ranjit grimaced, but did not smile. He looked worried, almost shamefaced, as much as a Sikh can look behind that imposing curled, black beard.

We chatted about nothing in particular until Ratanbir served the tea and left us. I noticed his shirt was dirty, but what the hell, so was mine.

After sipping his tea, with the pepper, and grimacing again, Ranjit abruptly set down his cup and looked at me. 'I've got bad news, Savage. You've got to leave Pattan.'

One's instinct is to repeat inanely some word or phrase that has shocked you. I try to resist it, and this time, after a pause, said reasonably, 'Don't be silly. I've only just come. I have a long lease.'

He flushed. 'It's been cancelled.'

I thought suddenly of Margaret Wood. She had sworn she would get rid of me, and now I had given her just the evidence she wanted. The Government of India, like the rest, exercises a fierce selectivity about its own past. You get a pat on the back for bringing the glory of Indian art to the world's attention. You get an expulsion order for recreating the guiltless sensuality which made that art possible. 'The bitch!' I said aloud. 'Look, Ranjit, it's in the air here, in the people's minds, in their history and folklore.'

The D.C. stared at me with his best inscrutable I.C.S. face. I became desperate, and yet, at the edge of my mind, had a sharp realisation that Ranjit and I were playing, in reverse, a scene that had been enacted how many million times in the past century and a half – the alien consul trying to decide between two quarrelling natives – which is truth, which is invention to work off a grudge?

'She's furious because her converts and nurses leave,' I said, 'but it's nothing to do with me.'

Ranjit stroked his beard.

'She saw what she saw,' I pleaded. 'I'm not trying to deny it. I'm not trying to deny that you have to take a serious view of it. The Pandit would have a fit if it got out into world publicity. I know that. I'm only saying that it's not vice, here, but something else – tradition, love, something . . . Why are you taking sides with a damned mission, trying to convert your own people away from your own religion, against me, who's trying to bring tourists into India and gain a lot of foreign exchange for you?'

Ranjit drank tea while I paused to gather breath. He said, 'You had better tell me just what did happen.'

The wily bugger. Well, I told him. I poured out the whole story of the hunting camp from beginning to end, including some sharp comments on the government's neglect of the near-famine situation in Pattan, which had driven me to poach game to feed them; and our illegal methods of killing fish for the same purpose; and my alliance with the Gonds; the tensions of the camp; Lady Hillburn; my state of mind; Blauvelt; the choice of sinking right into Pattan, or staying alone and lonely, yearning for something I couldn't have – I told him all.

I ended: 'So you see, it's not just a simple case of Satan debauching innocent villagers.'

Without a word he handed me a long envelope. It was not sealed. The letter inside was addressed to me, and signed by the Governor of the province, Sir Chandragupta Chenur, another I.C.S. man. He informed me that under the provisions of section something or other of the Defence of India Act my lease of certain lands and buildings lying in the Pattan Reserved Forest (this meant the Rest House) was hereby terminated, as were my shooting leases over Blocks 3, 6, 7, 9, and 11. I was required to vacate the area by midnight on March 23 – three days hence.

I slammed the paper on the table. 'Christ, Ranjit, I've just been explaining!'

'Look again,' he said.

I looked again. The message said nothing new to me. But this time I noticed the date of the Governor's signature. It was March 19, the day of the leopard hunt – that is, before the affair at the temples.

Ranjit said, 'I am not required to give you any reason for the action, under the Act. *You* know that. And I have been specifically ordered – not by the Governor, by high political figures – not to say anything at all. But – ' he fingered his tie, the same Free Foresters tie he had been wearing when I first met him – 'between gentlemen there are certain decencies . . . You are too close to the frontier with Chambal. The Nawab's recent speech decided the government to remove all possible sources of danger. You have had contacts with the Chambal authorities . . .'

'About the shooting!' I shouted. 'I've got to be able to cross the line when the game does. Look, the frontier's just over there.' I pointed across the Shakkar stream at the rise of rock on the far side of the Valley, a mile away.

'I'm sure they would wish they had waited a few days,' Ranjit said, 'if they were ever to hear of this other business. That would have given them a much better case. But I suppose they never would have heard of it – nor I for that matter. You see, Savage, the real truth of the matter is that you have enemies, and the present tension allows them to act against you.'

'I have friends, too,' I said furiously. 'One word and I could have you torn in pieces, Ranjit. I could put the clock back here and in Bhilghat a long way, back to the time they killed your policeman down there! I could destroy your career, and the Governor's. I've only got to raise my finger and you'll have a thousand men in rebellion in these hills.'

He said sadly, 'You're right, I'm afraid. Which is why this order, instigated by malice though it is, is perhaps right, for India.'

I stood up. I wanted to pick up the table and smash the D.C.'s car to pulp with it. I didn't want to hit Ranjit. He was an impersonal servant, a disembodied force, pushing and shoving at me. 'I had it all settled,' I said, stammering with rage, 'I got out of your damned way. I left you to run the bloody country as best you could, and even then you had to send for me when you came across something you didn't understand. Now you're after me again, dragging me out of my hole in the ground. I didn't give a damn about Chambal. Force it in, let it join Pakistan, let it be independent, I didn't care. It wasn't my business any more. And now you, you . . . '

Ranjit stood up, too: 'I'm really sorry, Savage, and I'm deeply ashamed that it was I who had to deliver that order. But I had to, and I have . . . If there's anything I can do, now or afterwards, to help you, please tell me. I mean it.'

I did not answer. After a while, he was standing there with his hand out and I ignoring it; he turned away and got into his Austin and drove off.

I slumped back in my chair. For a time I just hated – nothing in particular, everything. But I do not have the sort of temperament that can for long scrabble and batter at an irrevocably closed door. Now where? Back farther into the jungles? There were more remote places than this, deeper jungles, bigger and less penetrable hills, peoples still farther removed from the complex meanness of the century. There were Todas in high secret valleys of the Nilgiris; tribes in the back of Orissa whom only a dozen outsiders had ever heard of; Nagas, Abors, and Mishmis of the Assamese frontier – they were hard men, too, and they would fight harder to preserve their own ways. There would be other trails to walk, other girls like Kunthi and Devi, other fires in the night, other arrack, other dancing. And even as I thought of those places and those people I saw Ranjit, wearing the impeccable Western dress and the Free Foresters tie, advancing steadily, holding a pamphlet on planned economy in one hand and a pair of trousers in the other; and behind him, the Indian Army, and behind them, the dedicated faces of Jawaharlal Nehru, and L. P. Roy, and the ranked Gandhi caps, and the whey-checked tee-totallers, the city planners, the vote getters, the speechmakers, the engineers with slide rules, the lawyers pleading *habeas corpus*, the university students carrying dingy banners – every one of them sprung from *my* mind, *my* work, *my* wounds. There was no denying that the creation of these people, this India, was the object, acknowledged or not, of my ancestors – but the wheel had turned full circle, the clock again reached twelve. They were forcing me back to the coral strand where old Jason Savage must have landed, if he ever existed – but where were the magnificent kings who had then walked the sands of Coromandel under golden umbrellas? Where were the Rajput knights who had put on their wedding silks – the same finery I had seen in one of those near-visions, beside the lake – and ridden out to die in hopeless battle against such as my ancestors? Where were their wives, who lit the pyres and leaped in, children in their arms? Where were the Madrassi sepoys who gave Clive the rice at Arcot and took only the water themselves, and yet had no knowledge of inferiority? Where now did I hear a man say, 'I have eaten your salt'? Where was the Rani of Kishanpur, splendid in steel armour, hating England and loving my great-grandfather? And the men in the stands of sugar cane along the bank of the Ravi, who gave you *gur* and milk to drink, and sat talking with you in dignity and pride and poverty at the corner of the house, in the shade? Where were the gentle lovers of Khajuraho and Pattan, and proud women who walked unveiled? Where was the splendour of India's soul, that met Jason Savage on that shore three centuries ago?

What had I done?

God damn them all. God damn them all.

Chapter 7

'Margaret Donoghue, you lazy thing, you, will you get out of bed now?'

Her mother's Londonderry brogue was strong, the voice laughing under the pretended sharpness. But Margaret couldn't get up. Her legs and arms lay like lead prolongations of a central core which had only just the strength to realise, and to hear, none to stir or lift. That's what it used to be like. Then strength would come very, very slowly as her mother clumped up the stairs and sat on the edge of the bed, and bent down to kiss her. Then the strength used to flow in, starting at the tips of her toes and the ends of her fingers.

Mother wasn't here. Rats scrabbled at the ceiling cloth. Or bats, or flying foxes, or horrible long centipedes, or scorpions, or shrews, or some of the small animals that had flitted across her path in the earliest dawn as she walked to the Rest House the night the jackal came. How long ago was that? A week. The rats would gnaw through the cloth and fall on her, helpless in the bed. She stared at the ceiling. It was a dim blur. Hard to know whether it was day or night outside. The ceiling swam into focus — no movement, no bulging and heaving, like sea waves, across from one end to the other, as the rats ran across, no squeak or gibber. The creaking continued.

She moaned, and turned her head. Wind, hot-weather wind. The window across the room was open and in the twilight she saw trees thrashing behind the empty servants' quarters. A spasm gripped her belly, she held on to herself with all her strength, leaned out of bed, fell to the floor, and crawled across the patched blue *durrie* on hands and knees to the bathroom. She grabbed the edge of the wooden toilet box, tried to pull herself up but could not, and relieved the agony where she knelt. Afterwards she hung dizzy and blind for a time to the commode seat, then crawled back into the bedroom, clutching the sheet, tried to

109

pull herself up, failed, and fell back to the floor. Floor and ceiling, heat and smell, receded on slow painful waves.

She was cold, shivering in a sleet-laden wind that slashed through her clothes and the flesh under them and the bones supporting the flesh and the marrow in the bones. She hung against a tree and screamed and screamed, alone in the forest with the swinging corpse of herself, hanged from the bough of a tree. The corpse's face – her own – was a flat white with no expression. Rain dripped from its face and chin and lay in shining oily drops in its hair. Now she recalled with perfect clarity that there had been no rain, and the corpse was not real.

It was worse than that. It was a straw-filled effigy of herself, wearing short skirt and blouse, the cardboard face painted white and wisps of reddish horse hair representing her own, the effigy dangling on a rope from the nearest tree to the chapel, on the side of the graveyard.

It was worse than that. The instant she saw the horrible thing she knew that she did not want to continue the work of the mission. She did not have the faith it needed. She had known that for a long time, but this show of hate had broken through the façade. When had she seen the effigy? In the dusk, when her bones already ached, but she was hoping the fever would pass, and had taken quinine and gone out for a breath of fresh air. How many days ago? Two, three, four?

Without faith, or purpose, why did she stay? Because she had promised Henry that she would. Not in so many words, but in her acceptance of marriage, in her comfortings during his last illness, which had said as plain as words, I will stay until another comes to replace me, however long that may be. But Henry had now become a vague figure whose face and eyes she could not recall, whose voice had vanished; and from England no other was coming, ever. They wrote, and hoped, but she knew.

She had felt totally empty, like a lake that has been steadily drained over a long period, until at last the water is gone; and after that the sun has worked in the damp earth and dried it, and there is finally neither water nor memory of water. There had been a crisis like this, in England, after the war, just before Henry came. Twenty-eight years of age passed; the war passed; two of the inevitable nurses' affairs with handsome young doctors behind her; gone also three successive suitors in whom she had seen nothing, hard as she tried, except that they were men . . . and then the crisis of emptiness. Henry arrived in the middle of it, obviously in search of a trained nurse to be his wife – not the other way round. Yet as soon as he had approached her she accepted him – and at once the lake began to refill, and she knew again a sense of purpose, of fullness, or fulfilment.

She realised that she still lay on the floor. Rested now, with a great effort she pulled herself on to the bed, and lay there panting feebly. It was night, perhaps, but not late. The fourth night. She ought to be over it soon, one way or another. The darkness slowly, firmly closed in upon her. In an infinity of weariness she surrendered to it, in silence.

It was cool again, not cold. The coolness moved in waves, as all feeling had for a long time, down from her head, through her neck, across her breasts and belly, between her legs, under her buttocks. Her head ached with a hollow pain. The hollowness kept her sane, for it enclosed the pain and made it come to her as from an immense distance, through a vacuum.

Why had the lake emptied itself again? *Because I did not love.* When had she noticed the desiccation, the dryness? At the moment of Henry's death, that was the truthful answer. It had taken half a year of loneliness after that before she could admit it to herself, and that brought her to – now. And what had made the next change, which she would never have admitted for another six months, except in the death-like honesty of this illness? What was it that brought once more a sense of life into her existence, as palpable as running water to refill the emptied, dried lake? The water was cold at first, bitter cold. She shivered at memories of anger – but anger meant life; of hate and striving – but with growing energy. Then, in the night, the night before the fever, or perhaps it was already upon her, the pulsing warm flood, her heart lifting and beating, faster and faster, her voice singing in the silence . . .

A man's head hung in a halo of light very close to her. Rodney Savage, his head a foot from hers, his eyes down, his lips slightly parted, a look of total absorption on his face. He was dressed, but very tired. The halo was a lantern on the table behind him. The blurred pink to the left, at the lower limit of her field of vision, was her own body, naked. He was sponging her down with a cold, wet sponge. The texture of substances became very clear, though distant. She was lying on one of the big, rough jail-made towels, near the outside edge of the bed. The wooden edge of the bed bit into her buttocks. Under the towel she felt the criss-cross pattern of the *newar* mattress.

She whispered, 'Do I look as you expected?'

He went on sponging, but turned his head slightly. 'Yes . . . better, as a matter of fact. Don't worry. It's only tit for tat, isn't it?'

She closed her eyes. It was intolerable that he should meet her, ask her to take her clothes off, and not even remember her, however drunk he had been. That had always annoyed her. And now, when he did see her naked, he still did not remember that first time, but only the other day, the time when frightened and lonely she had come upon that fantastic scene at the temples. Fantastic, and frighteningly wonderful.

Yet, it was a towel that she lay on. So he must have cleaned her of vomit and faeces, and taken away the sheets and clothes. She could not move her head, but the room smelled of soap and water.

'How long . . . ?' she whispered.

'Three, four hours,' he said. 'It's one o'clock in the morning. Roll over now, on your front.' His hands helped her, and she lay face down, feeling the cool sponge, hearing the tinkle of water as he wrung it out over an empty bucket, dipped it again in a full one, half-wrung it, put it to her back. 'You have a temperature of $104\frac{1}{2}$,' he said. 'What have you got? Here – ' she felt his hand slip into hers as it lay beside her – 'press my finger when I say the right word. Typhus? Malaria? Dysentery? Typhoid?' She squeezed his finger in her hand.

'Para,' she muttered into the pillow.

'Paratyphoid? Should I move you at once to Bhowani? I have the Bentley. Yes? No?' She squeezed again.

'No? You're too weak. I'm going to try to keep you warm and clean. There ought to be some glucose in the hospital, and I'll find that and give it to you. And I can

112

get some milk and boil it. Nothing else until you can tell me. Is that right?'

The last word echoed and repeated in her head . . . right-right-right-right, becoming fainter and fainter as her reserve of strength faded, rhythmically falling away in the repeated echo. She closed her hand tight on his finger and holding on to that drifted out on a heaving dark tide of sleep.

The light hurt her eyes, and someone whistling sounded like a shriek in her ears. She moved and the whistling stopped. It was daylight. She was wearing a man's pyjama coat and nothing else, and there were two blankets on the bed. She was sweating heavily.

'Something to drink,' he said.

She felt the spoon in her mouth, contracted her throat muscles and forced herself to swallow, again, again. When she could take no more she turned her head and muttered, 'Warm chicken broth . . . Pills, labelled sulfaguanidine. Twenty at a time.'

She slept. She drank warm chicken broth, and knew from the taste that some sulfaguanidine must be ground up in it. Night time. She slept again.

She awoke to a hot morning light. He took her temperature, and said, 'A hundred exactly. Feel able to talk?'

She said, 'I didn't tell the D.C. anything. I never saw you do anything suspicious, or meet anybody except Mr Faiz Mohammed once or twice, and I didn't think it worth telling them that. Nor about . . . the temples.'

He said, 'I know you didn't.'

She had to tell him now, while it was clear in her mind and he was here. At any moment he might vanish again, as he had come. 'Ranjit Singh stopped here on his way back the other day. He told me he had just given you the order cancelling your lease. I hadn't done anything, said anything, but I was pleased.' She looked at him, but he had his back turned to her. He must turn round and see her face; but he did not. She had to talk to his back as he went on mixing something in a bowl, a *degchi* of warm milk beside him on the table. 'Then that evening all the rest of the people here left. Two old women and a child left the hospital, though they were sick. Men came and carried them away. The sweeper left. The servant here.'

8

'It was nothing to do with me,' he said, still not turning.

'Oh, I know, I know – now! There was an effigy . . . '

'You saw that? I hoped you had not. I cut it down and burned it.'

Then he did turn and come towards her, a mug in his hand. Dark pouches lay under his eyes, and a black stubble round his chin and jowl. He looked murderous, the pale-blue eyes shining feverishly.

'You're sick, too,' she muttered.

'Not sick – just tired.'

In the ocean of sleep there had been islands, painful islands. She had sat on pots, bones aching, clinging convul-sively to something or someone. She had vomited, emptied her bowels, felt hot urine on her legs, drunk soup. Towels had been changed, and sheets, and blankets. Through the window now she could see blankets and towels and sheets and pyjama coats and shirts and dishcloths hanging on a clothes line. He must have washed them.

He said, when she had greedily finished the broth, sud-denly aware of violent hunger pains, 'Now, should I take you somewhere where you can be properly looked after?'

'Are you going to Delhi?'

He shook his head impatiently. 'I don't know. That's not the question. Where should *you* go?'

She turned away. 'I'm staying here,' she said flatly. 'You can leave me now. By evening I shall be able to look after myself.'

'All right,' he said. 'But I shall bring Kunthi and Devi before I go. They're two girls from Pattan, and I've already given them some first-aid and hygiene training. Their normal profession is whore, but they'll look after you as long as you want them to.'

She mumbled. 'Thank you,' into the pillow.

'Now can I leave you safely for an hour or so?'

An hour! When before dark he was going away for ever. 'Yes,' she said.

'I'm off now, then. Go back to sleep.'

'I'm hungry,' she said resentfully. Did he have no aware-ness of any of her emotions or feelings?

'I'm sure you are. But no food now. Go back to sleep.'

Sleep, she muttered, sleep, sleep, sleep. But against her will, she did. When she opened her eyes she saw a thin, dark Indian girl, her hair drawn tightly back from the high forehead, squatting on the floor near the head of the bed, her eyes fixed on her in an intense, unwinking stare. She recognised the girl at once as one who had been in his arms on the temple platform.

'What is your name?' she whispered.

'Devi,' the girl answered. 'He says you are to eat when you wake.' She stood up.

'Where is he?' she asked.

'Asleep,' she said over her shoulder as she went out towards the kitchen. 'I will awaken him.'

'No!' she cried.

'It is his order,' the voice said from the kitchen.

He did not come in until she had finished eating, and Kunthi had taken away the bowl, and also firmly made her change out of his pyjama coat into one of her own night-dresses. She sat up, pulling the sheet higher to her neck.

'Mind if I smoke a cheroot?' he said. 'I'll sit near the window.'

'Oh, please do,' she said. 'I'd like a cigarette, too.'

He found one of hers, put it in her mouth, and lit it. He puffed away at his cheroot. She saw that he had shaved and now looked a little less demonically villainous, though just as tired.

'I must go soon,' he said. 'I think you'll be all right. Kunthi and Devi will see that no harm comes to you. I've told them to tell Faiz Mohammed at once if you have a relapse . . . Don't take that effigy too hard, or your people leaving. There are all sorts of rumours flying around. The Chambal Army is going to move everyone out and dig defences against India . . . The Indian Army is coming through with guns and tanks, blasting everything before them with bombers. That's what's caused the flight, more than your excessive Christianity. . . . It did seem excessive to me.'

She said, 'I didn't feel very Christian when I lost my temper with you . . . when I tried to hate you.'

He said, 'You seemed more human to me then. Before, when I saw you, from what I heard . . . there seemed to be nothing but Christian resignation, turning the other cheek, love thine enemy. A saint in a church, palms joined, looking upward, beatific smile on the lips. Fixed beatific smiles make a woman look stupid.'

Her heart beat with a pleasant warmth. So he had thought about her! Why, oh, why, couldn't he have come earlier, when he was alone in Pattan, and discussed all this?

She said, 'I was lonely . . . afraid . . . afraid of India . . . bored . . . frustrated. I am not a missionary, I have no real faith, I was terrified my husband would find out . . . But I did not want to show it. I wanted to stick it out, to do my job to the end, without failing. Sometimes . . . sometimes I used to think, lying awake in bed at night, that it was all a preparation. Once I told him at least that much, and he smiled and said "Yes, it was, a preparation of heaven." I didn't think so, but I could not say anything.'

He had listened with a sort of curious half-attention, his eyes sometimes fixed on hers, sometimes wandering round the room, his fingers fiddling with the sheet. Now ask me what I really felt, what I thought about you, she willed him; talk, talk about us; bring it all out of me; the right word, the right look, a touch, will do it . . .

He got up listlessly. 'It's the times. Something's pushing us out of India – rejecting us.'

'Yes!' she cried. 'We're in the same boat.'

'We're both being pushed out – you for trying to change old patterns, me for trying to get back to them . . . I must be on my way.'

'Where to?' she asked quickly. 'What are you going to do?'

He said, 'I don't know. I only know that they're not going to push me out . . . I dropped in that evening to return the clothes you lent me. Your husband's, I suppose? Also to tell you that you'd won, here.'

'No, no!' she cried.

'I also meant to tell you I didn't think you'd find your victory very real. Then I saw the effigy, and I knew I wouldn't have to say anything, Except good-bye . . . We didn't really affect each other at all. We just thought so, but really it was events, and times, which caught us both up and threw us against each other. There's no need for us to part as enemies.'

She looked at him and said, 'I am not your enemy. The opposite.'

'I'm sorry,' he said simply, and there was no way of knowing whether he understood but did not care, and was sorry; or did not understand, and was sorry; and no clear understanding, in her exhausted calm, of which of the two would be worse.'

'Kunthi!' he called.

Another girl came in, the curvaceous one who had fallen down dead drunk on the platform. Margaret could see her now, more clearly than her smiling, clothed presence – her firm full breasts pointing to the sky, the legs parted, a beatific smile on her face, and every finished curve speaking of a woman's fulfilment.

Rodney spoke to her and she walked, hips swinging, into the other room, and came out with a bedding roll on her head. Rodney followed, returning with a suitcase.

'You pyjama coats!' she cried. 'I saw two on the line . . . It must be lunchtime. You must have something to eat.'

But he shook his head, and Kunthi came in with the pyjamas and in a trice they were packed away in the suit-case.

'Good-bye,' he said.

'Good-bye,' she said, 'And – and thank you.' The door closed behind him and she whispered. 'With all my heart . . . Oh, God, oh, God,' and sank her head into the pillow.

Chapter 8

'Rodney!'

I'd heard that call twenty, thirty times the past few days, since arriving in Delhi. I couldn't walk in the street, have a drink at a bar, swim at the club pool, without a voice calling me. This time I was walking down the long corridor on the ground floor of the Imperial, and it was Max. He was wearing uniform and looked fit, burly, and business-like. I had decided, long since, that he had learned about my love for Janaki, and had – sensibly and typically – realised that it had hurt me a great deal more than it could hurt him.

'What are you doing here?' he asked.

'Robbing a bank,' I said.

Max laughed. The usual conversation followed: Where was I staying? Good heavens, that flea pit! (I was staying at a small hotel of Old Delhi.) I must go and live with his cousin Hari. That, too, was as usual. Everyone invited me to stay, but I always refused. My old room was ready for me in John Clayton's bungalow, but I did not want to go there. Not that it would have been 'awkward'. The business with Frances was over and she knew it. She had already got a passage home about a month hence.

For politeness' sake I should have asked Max what he was doing in Delhi, knowing that his division was in Bhowani, but I didn't want to continue the conversation. Besides, I knew. Obviously he had been called up to discuss the increasing tension between India and Chambal. If India decided to deal with Chambal by force, Max was going to be the bullyboy.

'I've got to go,' he said finally, with a rather unconvincing look at his watch. He summoned up his courage. 'And, Rodney, old boy, you know, if there's anything I can do . . . I have lots of friends – Daulat, Rikhye, P. R. Sethi – '

'Don't worry, Max,' I said, 'I'll come round with my hat in my hand before I have to sell the Bentley.' That was a lie, but what else could you say to a man like Max?

We parted and I went on out into the street and walked aimlessly towards Connaught Circus. It was hot then, at the very end of March, and I was not wearing a hat. Out in the bustle of the crowd, the clop of tonga pony hoofs and the rustle and murmur of people in my ears, dust rising by the hawkers' stalls, students lolling in the shade on the grass under the trees, bicycles ebbing to and fro like schools of fish . . . I slipped back into the chain of thought which Max had interrupted – the morass of thought would be a better notion.

From the beginning, when the D.C. came to throw me out of Pattan, there had been interruptions, like finding Margaret Wood ill and alone at the mission, and since then, these chance meetings. I could not decide whether the interruptions prevented me from achieving an orderly thought sequence, which would solve my problems, or mercifully yanked me out of a futile nose-chasing-tail hypnosis.

In the foreground, when I trod water in my swamp, all I could see was debt. John Clayton had put a lot of money into the hunting camp, and so had Frances. It had gone – not through my fault, but all the same it had gone, and I felt I owed it back. I had also lost all but a small amount of my own savings, and now had less than 300 rupees in the world, plus my pension. I wasn't going to starve, but neither was I going to be able to repay my debts.

So – I must get a job. Here I could feel my teeth gritting together, and a voiceless repetition of the words *In India*. Daulat, Rikhye, and P. R. Sethi, whom Max mentioned, were industrialists, owners of banks, airlines, cotton mills, God knows what else. P. R. Sethi was, in addition, a hell of a good man. Any of them, plus half a dozen others I could think of, would give me a good job, and were powerful enough, and independent enough to tell L. P. Roy to go to hell if he tried to prevent it.

Also, I wanted to meet Sumitra again.

Here all forward progress stopped, and the heavy mud of the morass began to rise about my hips and waist, clasping and dragging. Try as I might, I could think of no job that I would accept. No job that I would be offered, that is. There were plenty that I would *not* be offered. For instance, I had already heard whispers of trouble between the new government and the Assam hill tribes, especially

119

the Nagas. I saw the Nagas' point of view, and I saw the government's. I know the Nagas – fought with them in the war – was an honorary Naga myself. If the government made me Special Commissioner for the Hill Tribes, and promised fifty years to me and my successors to bring the tribes into their new India – I'd go like a shot. But it was part of the problem that such a job *had* to be done by an Indian. It would make no difference if I crossed over into Pakistan, except that I could claim Pakistan citizenship by birth, having been born in Lahore. Even so, they would definitely not send me to Gilgit, Chitral, Waziristan, or any of the places where I wanted to be and where I could have done a good job. In brief, I didn't want what I could get and couldn't get what I wanted – and needed.

So, back to the money . . . By now I must have been round this circle 750 times. I wondered occasionally what Margaret Wood thought of me, when she recovered sufficiently to be aware that I was there. What I had to do in that forlorn bungalow I did in a trance. She was filthy, and I had to undress and wash her, many times. I don't suppose any man has ever had such a good-looking body under his hand and been so little aware of it. I remember briefly wishing it were Sumitra, that's all. I remember leaving with my suitcase, and I know she was saying something, but I have no idea what. I only hoped I hadn't been rude to her, unintentionally. She seemed a good, brave woman now that our troubles had got us below the squabbling level, and I didn't want to leave any bitterness.

So, back to the money . . . I saw that I was passing the Connaught Circus office of the Bombay-China Bank. I had told Max I was here to rob a bank. Well, why not? I had been thinking like a sahib. All the jobs I wanted, the jobs that no one would give me, were sahib's jobs. Such jobs had been created out of nothing by the British Raj. The Indians and Pakistanis were taking them over, using their own sahibs for the purpose – and we had created *them*, too.

There was no place for the English sahib, then. All right. Go back behind the day of the sahib, and what did you get? Merchant adventurers, soldiers of fortune, wandering mechanics . . . men who provided India with what it needed, or thought it needed, without any missionary or evangelical purpose. Translate that into today's conditions . . . There was a shortage of lipstick, whisky, perfume, the luxuries which Indians crave as much as anyone else. Cars, big American cars, high-priced shotguns and rifles, cartridges. Wireless sets, ornate radiograms. There were laws against the importation of all these things, or heavy import duties. There were currency restrictions – but if you knew the right people you could easily get round all that, what with Portuguese territory touching India in Goa, bits of Pakistan to east and west, cordial dislike between all three nations, and not enough troops or police to guard the long borders. That was the sort of thing my ancestors would have been in, up to their necks. I could just see them, in wigs and heavy with sweat, working it all out in a back room off Chowringhee with a couple of tough, smoothly obsequious Bengali moneylenders to provide the initial working capital.

I found myself passing the Bombay-China Bank again. I needed working capital, first to pay off my debts, secondly to start this or any other venture of my own. I did not know any moneylenders and did not want to have them exercise any control over me. Inside the bank the British manager sat in the far corner, at a big desk of his own. Two Indian clerks worked at the counter and three at tables behind. Outside the door the bank guard sat on a stool, a shotgun in hand and a *kukri* hung in a red sash over one shoulder. He was a Gurkha. Obviously a pensioner, probably a *naik*, I thought from his appearance and manner. Not one of ours though, at least not during my service.

I walked on. It was a large step, to think of robbing a bank, though I did gamble with 'borrowed' money once, to help Max – Janaki, I should say. But, as I strode on, heedless of the sun burning down on my head and the crowds around me, I felt a distinct lightening. The morass seemed to be less gluey. This was not a sahib's thing to do. I would at least get rid of that damned albatross, which had been hanging round my family's neck for about a hundred and fifty years now.

Ratanbir, I thought. Ratanbir can make part of the reconnaissance. I can make the rest. I might rob the Bombay-China Bank, or I might not, but if I did I was going to do it properly, when it had a lot of money on hand, and get away without a trace, and have some means of converting the money, much of which would be traceable.

I hailed a tonga, and jolting along in the back, my mind working fast and constructively, drove to Old Delhi and my hotel, which was near the main railway station. I found Ratanbir polishing my shoes, though they were as bright as day already. I told him to go to New Delhi and make friends with the guards at the Bombay-China Bank. I gave him twenty rupees, and he saluted and went out. I looked at the closed door behind him, and thought, Max would not approve of this: rob a bank, all right, a chap might have to do that, but involve a soldier! Fine, Max, but you're still a sahib. You can afford to be; I can't.

I went down to the little bar and ordered a whisky and soda, then another.

'Colonel Savage?'

I just managed to repress a groan. I raised my head and turned. It was a slender middle-aged Indian, slightly bent, with thin, greying hair and a long crooked nose. He was wearing well-cut European clothes. He said, 'Forgive the impertinence,' and passed me a card. It read, *Mr Hussein Ali*, and underneath, *Chambali Industries Ltd.* I handed the card back.

He said in a low voice, 'I wonder if we could talk in your room, Colonel?'

The barman was out somewhere and I thought, what the hell. We went up to my room on the second floor.

Mr Hussein walked to the little balcony and peered out right and left. He tapped the wall. I watched, smiling. I love cloak-and-dagger stuff. He saw me, and smiled himself, rather charmingly. 'Silly,' he said, 'but one is a fool to omit small precautions.' He spoke with almost no accent. I had heard of him of course. He was an Ismaili, one of the Aga Khan's sect of Muslims. The family had gone to Zanzibar about fifty years earlier and made a fortune. Just before the war they returned to their homeland, which happened to be the State of Chambal, and now they owned practically every industry in the State – less the compulsory 15 per cent share that belonged to the Nawab.

I indicated a chair, and myself sat on the edge of the bed. He said, 'I have come to offer you a position, Colonel.'

I said, 'I'm afraid . . .'

He raised one hand. 'Not an ordinary position, or there would be no need for these precautions. I showed you my business card just now. I am also a member of His Highness's Wizarat.'

A Wizarat is the cabinet of a Muslim maharajah. (Muslim princes, by the way, are never called maharajah – always Nawab, Mir, Amir, or the like.) It was no surprise to learn that the richest man in Chambal, and its chief industrialist, had an official position with the Nawab's government.

He said, 'In business I can offer you a great deal of money, Colonel, because I am sure that with your talents you will earn it. But I am also sure you have been offered that by many others. I am not here to offer you money – but a task, for India.'

'For India?' I said, raising an eyebrow.

Hussein Ali said, 'Yes – for the India that still lives, and strives to find expression under the mean-spirited Congress rule. For the India of splendour, of great men, of heroes, if I do not embarrass your English reserve . . . I understand that the Indian Government expelled you from the Pattan Reserved Forest and ruined your most interesting enterprise, on suspicion that you were acting as a secret agent for us?'

I nodded. It was not quite accurate, but it was near enough.

He said, 'We wish to prove the Indians right, though there will be no secrecy about it. I am authorised to offer you a post as an agent of the Wizarat. Officially we would employ you as a brigadier, and you would have advisory duties with our armed forces – very real and important duties, I should add. Your military salary will be two thousand rupees a month. In your other capacity you will receive ten thousand rupees a month, with a suitable house, servants, et cetera.'

'What makes you think I am worth that much?' I asked. I have a high opinion of myself, but this was flying pretty high.

'First, our own observation,' he said. 'Second, your attitude and background as – '

'A sahib,' I said.

'Precisely. I can see that you now reject the word. Naturally, I have resented the idea, too . . . but you cannot in a moment undo what your predecessors have done. Whether you like it or not, you command respect, for you have conquered and ruled us. You have a reputation for impartiality, incorruptibility – and decision . . . Third, we have the opinion of Mr Huntington Blauvelt.'

'My God!' I said. Blauvelt, the Wandering Minstrel, was affecting my life more than any one of a dozen people who were earnestly trying to.

Hussein nodded. 'Yes, Mr Blauvelt, who is at this moment visiting the State as a guest of His Highness. Mr Blauvelt has certain – problems, but he is a singularly acute observer, even when apparently in no condition to observe anything.'

'All right,' I said. 'Now tell me, what are you trying to do, in the State? And what is my job to be?'

He started at once to tell me, and I made an approving note. He had had the sense to realise that he must make up his mind about my reliability before approaching me at all. It would be no good hemming and hawing and fencing once he reached me.

'His Highness is determined to maintain Chambal's independence from both India and Pakistan,' he said.

All right, I thought. With luck, he might just manage it. Hyderabad, a slightly larger state, had tried, and Nehru had sent in the Indian Army. Two days – no Hyderabad. But Chambal had the enormous advantage of touching Pakistan as well as India, and so could not be treated quite so cavalierly, besides giving the Nawab the chance to play the two big nations off against each other.

'We are determined,' Hussein continued, 'to maintain the old values of India. Most of our people are Rajputs and Jats, as you know. They reject the sickly Hinduism of Bengal. They reject Congress demagoguery. They are warriors. Three centuries ago they took the oath of allegiance to His Highness's ancestor, and they are determined to uphold it. His Highness, for his part, while remaining a devout Muslim himself, rejects the intolerant spirit of Pakistan. There has never been any penalisation of Hindus in Chambal, and there never will be.'

'There'd better not be,' I said, Rajputs and Jats were not people who took kindly to oppression.

'We reject democracy, bureaucracy, socialism, and communism,' Hussein said. 'Chambal has always been ruled by a sovereign, respectfully advised by the Wizarat. Under that rule there has been peace and plenty, and as much freedom as a reasonable man might ask. If a man wants to have a say in our government, let him rise by his own efforts until he sits in the seats of power – as Faiz Mohammed rose, from a butcher's son, to be Subadar of Lapri – and as a score of others so rose, whom I can name. If a man has not that ability, let him keep his mouth shut, till his soil, and obey the orders of those who have proved themselves his betters . . . We will advance materially, but through the enterprise of our own leaders, not on the plans of clerks sitting in Delhi – or Karachi.'

And you, doubtless, will make your tenth or twentieth million, pounds sterling, I thought. That did not bother me. I knew a good deal about Chambali Industries Ltd. Yes, they made money – but it all went back into new enterprises, certainly as well chosen as any government could do, and backed by a single man's drive and determination.

'That is what we are going to achieve,' Hussein said. 'We have a hard struggle ahead of us. You will have heard of our preparations to put our case to the United Nations, if need be. Other political and financial arrangements I will not bother you with now, though you will have to learn about them in due course. One political matter, though, will fall in your province – that is, the winning of the uncommitted states of Bandelkhand to our side. Their rulers all have the same point of view as His Highness. They too wish to preserve a way of life more suited to India than this cheap democracy. If they allow India to absorb them, not only will they themselves become landless paupers but their kingdoms will vanish, losing the identity of a thousand years – sometimes much more, as with Kanpara – to become so much more raw material for Nehru's socialist experiments. . . . We believe you can exert great influence on the ruler of Kishanpur at least, perhaps also the Rajah of Konpara, through your family connections and your own personality. We want you to persuade them to join Chambal.'

'Why should they?' I asked.

Hussein stretched out his hands, turning them palms upward in a very Indian gesture, which I was pleased and reassured to see. He was, otherwise, so cosmopolitan, so much the international financier, that he could have been a Rothschild or a Morgan or a Baring, discussing some steel merger in Belgium. He said, 'In Chambal we already have twelve rajahs happy to admit the Nawab's suzerainty, and

125

all those twelve and their ancestors have ruled their lands without interference for a long time, subject only to the orders of His Highness on matters of common concern . . . I think it should not be hard to persuade Dip Rao Rawan that it is better to become the thirteenth rajah, than to disappear totally.'

I agreed, while thinking privately that those small states like Kishanpur and Konpara were probably expendable, in the Chambal view. If they could be persuaded to join Chambal, or to try to do so, the Indian Government would certainly not permit them; but it would have to turn its efforts to bringing them back into the fold and would find it hard to deal with Chambal at the same time. Of course, if the mergers *could* be managed, so much the better . . . If I had to deal with Kishanpur, I would meet Sumitra.

Hussein stood up. 'I have nothing more to say, Colonel. I shall leave you to think it over, and would ask for a reply within forty-eight hours. I am at Chambal House, in New Delhi.'

He looked straight at me, and the small, piercing dark eyes almost glittered. 'I think you are a man who has an ideal for this country, as I have. I am offering you a post as important for the future as any you have ever had in the past. Work of value to the spirit. Something you can fight for. And afterwards, when we have achieved our independence, there will be a secure place for you, and even higher rewards – in business or government, as you wish. We shall need you.'

He went out. I had controlled my feelings during his stay, but now I let them go. The first thing I noticed was that the morass had vanished. My legs were free. Then my eyes were focused. I had something to do, somewhere to go. Then, my heart was warm – someone needed me. Then, I felt a thrill of satisfied revenge. The bloody Indians had harried me from pillar to post, thinking I was helpless and harmless. They would regret it.

I stood up, and exhilaration flowed in, replacing all other emotions. I thought of what was to be achieved. Was this not precisely the sum of my thoughts that dreadful day at the Pattan Rest House when I asked myself what we had done, to destroy the old India which my ancestors had found, and hand it over to the worst sort of mediocrity? I was

126

being given a chance to start again, to create and preserve instead of destroy.

After a few minutes I came back to the actual question, almost as an afterthought. There was no doubt in my mind at all. I would take the task and do all that I could to make Chambal free, independent, and, above all, Indian. And I would meet Sumitra.

I was fast asleep when Ratanbir returned at midnight, drunk. He stood wavering and teetering and saluting, telling me that he had got to know the bank guards. The man on duty during the evening was a Burathoki, the same sub-tribe as himself; they were even distantly related; and he had been a *naik* in the 8th Gurkhas. 'He's an honest man,' he said, belching, 'but he drinks . . . weak head. It won't be difficult.'

I told him to go to bed. Perhaps I should have told him I'd never meant to rob the bank, that such an idea was degrading for both of us – but I was too tired and too involved in other thoughts, and I didn't.

The next day at once I went to Chambal House. After a short wait I was ushered up a flight of carpeted stairs, along a tiled passage, and into Hussein Ali's expensively simple suite. I told him I would accept his offer. He said, 'Good,' and, opening a drawer, handed me a long envelope, marked 'Brigadier Savage, expenses (not accountable).' He said, 'Please report to me in Chambalpur within the week.'

I said, 'O.K.,' and that was that. One thousand rupees.

I took a tonga to the Imperial and sat down to lunch. Before I was through the first course the *khidmatgar* handed me a note. I looked up quickly. 'Who gave you this?'

'A man,' he said, 'a *desi admi* – a native. He went away.'

I opened the envelope, which was properly addressed to me, including my decorations. The note inside read, 'Be so good as to call on me in my office, Secretariat Buildings, any time after three o'clock this afternoon. L. P. Roy.'

I finished my lunch, chewing carefully and trying to avoid excessive thought. I might be able to work out what L. P. Roy wanted of me, then again I might not. I might reach a conclusion, but find later that it was quite wrong. It is better to have a blank mind than a mind full of misconceptions.

After lunch I read the *Statesman* and then set out for the

Secretariat. A *chuprassy* told me that Roy Sahib's office was close to Sardar Patel's. A few minutes later I was announced.

Roy's office was not large and what with piles of books and papers, another visitor sitting in a cane chair across the table from him, and a secretary bending over Roy's shoulder, it seemed crowded. Roy said politely, 'Be so good as to wait one moment, please, Colonel.' I sat down on another chair, in the only corner free from furniture, reflecting how universally and truly Eastern is the custom of doing business in public.

They talked in the wonderful and fantastic mixture of Hindi, Urdu, and English which had already become the lingua franca of bureacratic India. The subject was some mines that had been willed by one petty (and deposed) rajah to another. I listened with joy to such remarks as '*Lekin yeh* joint royalties *aur* overriding commission *ke* arrangement *hai*' and '*Agar Ram Singh apne* collateral descendants *ke lie* life interest *dena chahta*' and 'Legal aspect *bilkul* clear *hai, magar* . . . '

Roy finished his business with dispatch, and when he gave the decision there was no argument. A moment later we were alone, and Roy got up and closed the door. He was wearing the same clothes he had worn in the Red Fort, the clothes he wore, as far as I knew, all day and every day – a spotlessly white dhoti and shirt, bare feet tucked into sandals. His square face somehow managed, without the Gandhi cap, to look lean and ascetic, and his mop of grey hair stood out like a halo from his head.

He said, 'I have a short temper, which I cannot control. It is a grievous fault. I apologise for my words when we last met, near the Moti Masjid.'

'I was equally at fault,' I said, 'my mind was elsewhere.'

He nodded. 'Good . . . I have, naturally, held a prejudice against you because you killed my brother. But I am told by many whose judgement I trust that you are, in your way, a friend of India.'

I said, 'Of India? Yes, I think so.'

He said, 'You must not take the appointment you have been offered in Chambal, whatever it is.'

'Why?'

'It would be wrong. How could you then be a friend of India?'

'Perhaps not a friend of your government, or of Mr Patel's plans.'

'An enemy of ours is an enemy of India,' Roy said.

I began to feel that peculiar throbbing behind the temples, with a tightening of the chest, which my ancestors must have experienced when they first came to grips with the Brahmin mentality: the calm arrogance; the cold contempt for anyone else's opinions; the belief that the Brahmin is in direct communion with God, is in fact a part of God, and can do no wrong. It is fortunate that in those early meetings the Brahmins came across perhaps the only other people in the world with the same colossal self-conceit and set in much the same terms. Of course Roy was not technically a Brahmin – but that did not matter. The attitude had been inherited by the new rulers of India.

I controlled myself, and said, 'That is a matter of opinion.'

'Not a bit of it,' he said. 'There can be no matter of opinion about it. The so-called princely states are a part of India – like Goa and the Portuguese colonies – and we are going to have them.'

'Regardless of what the people concerned say or feel?'

'They are ignorant,' he said. 'Some have been oppressed, some misled, all exploited . . . I believe Dip Rao, Rajah of Kishanpur, is a friend of yours?'

I nodded.

'I imagine that your new employers, if you are misguided enough to go to them, will use you to try to influence the Rajah's future course of action. I should advise you, if you really are a friend of his, that we will treat any collusion between him and Chambal as treason on his part and will punish him accordingly.'

'Treason!' I burst out. 'How can a sovereign ruler commit treason? Until 1947 Dip and all the other rajahs acknowledged England as the Paramount Power and surrendered to it all rights in foreign affairs and defence. But we – England – abrogated paramountcy when we left, and told the states they were free to work out their own relationships with the new Government of India – as sovereign entities.'

'We shall regard it as treason if any ruler acts against the best interest of his people – and that means any action

9   129

which does not guide the people back to the arms of free, independent Mother India.'

'Oh yeah?' I snapped. 'You think that Hari Singh did the right thing then, in handing over to India a people 90 per cent Muslim, who would certainly have wanted to join Pakistan – and still would – if you allowed a free vote?'

'Certainly. Besides, he was a sovereign ruler and had the constitutional right to do as he wished. We merely accepted his decision.'

'But the Maharajah of Junagadh wasn't a sovereign ruler when he tried to join Pakistan and you sent the army in? And the Nizam of Hyderabad wasn't when he wanted to be independent?'

'They were wrong, and wicked,' Roy said. 'They were enemies of India.'

'How's your non-violence going these days?' I asked.

'We shall never resort to violence to resolve our problems,' he said. 'It is the sacred teaching of the Mahatma, often repeated by Panditji.'

'Kashmir and Hyderabad were fought with feather dusters, then?'

'They were in the wrong. They were the aggressors.'

'You mean, your bottomless patience was exhausted?'

'Yes – precisely.'

'I wonder where I've heard that phrase before? . . . You don't agree, perhaps, that aggression might be a matter of opinion, subject even to evidence, factual evidence?'

He waved his hand. 'That's a waste of time. We are a peaceful state, therefore how *can* we commit aggression?'

I longed to possess, for just half an hour, the power my ancestors had used to solve just such impasses as this . . . There was the Brahmin found with the dead body in his courtyard and a knife in his hand. *Yes, I killed him.* That's murder, then. *Oh, no, because, you see, I am a Brahmin; murder is wrong, but Brahmins can do no wrong, therefore I cannot commit murder, and if I cannot, obviously I have not.* Then how did this man here die? *It was the course of events.* I see; well, I'll tell you, the course of events now is that you're going to die, too . . . And in marches a squad of soldiers, the gallows are set up, and amid anguished wails and howls and the thunderstruck disbelief of the populace, the Brahmin is hanged.

130

But I did not possess the power. The attitude with which I was now faced, the strong belief in its own total virtue, was the attitude of the new India, and it – not I – had that power.

Roy said, 'You interest me. Tell me, why do you wish to serve the Nawab of Chambal, who, as you must know, is a bigoted and suspicious despot?'

Just so must old William, my great-great-grandfather, have sent for the other Brahmins, after he'd shown he could hang one of them just as easily as the next man, and said, 'Tell me now, what makes you tick?' And just so, after days and years and centuries, would there stand an opaque wall between true understandings, however clear the paintings each of us put on the surface of the wall, in an attempt to communicate.

I said, 'These states are in many ways anachronisms. I do not think that any one man ought to have the powers and privileges of the rajahs, unless they have been freely voted to him. It is wrong that the people should have no say in their own government – '

'You were not saying that very loudly a few years ago, here,' Roy interrupted.

'Who's sitting behind that desk – you or I? . . . It is also wrong that in a huge country like this, with so many different ways of thought, so many religions, so many backgrounds, so many manners of living, that one party, one group, one viewpoint, should impose itself on the rest by force. The Nawab of Chambal, for all his faults, wants to make a country which is anti-socialist, more individual, more closely linked with the past, with tradition, than you believe in. I believe he has the right to do so, and I'm going to help all I can . . . because I believe in that sort of India, too.'

Roy's face grew suddenly red with anger. 'You wish to preserve your economic stranglehold!' he shouted. 'Economic imperialism! You wish to preserve an India subject to your exploitation. You will sell Chambal anything – guns, aeroplanes, whisky, big American cars, stupid luxuries . . . '

'And are those, any of them, un-Indian?' I asked.

'Yes,' he shouted. 'They are wrong, wicked. Gross materialism . . . exploitation of baser nature . . . '

I let him rave on. Like several other prominent Indian

131

politicians, he was a fanatic. When any of them climbed on to his pet hobby horse, whatever it happened to be – whisky, spinning wheels, the wonder of the Hindi language, economic exploitation – it was impossible to talk to them – as impossible as to talk to the sort of Englishman who claimed that the course of history showed God's guiding hand over England's destiny; or, more accurately, the sort of German who yelled that all his country's troubles were due to the Treaty of Versailles.

When he ran out of breath I stood up and said, 'If that will be all, sahib, perhaps you will permit me to take my leave.'

'Sit down, sit down,' he said. He did not make any apology for his outburst. How could he? He was in the right. He sat very still at his desk, looking at me out of his hot, black eyes. He had a great capacity for stillness. He began to speak, slowly. 'I am sorry for you, Savage . . . You are ready to fight for your ideals. But it is not human beings that you will be fighting against. It is a great river called History. This river sweeps away all who struggle against it. Nor can anyone stand aside, in neutrality, and hope to let it pass undisturbed, because it undermines the foundations and causes the silent collapse of the place on which he stands. By its existence it changes the climate of the time, causing orchards to grow where there was desert, putting a blight on groves where there used to be palaces.'

'True,' I said softly, for I felt close to Roy at that moment, 'but it is not necessary for those riding the crest of the river, downstream, to don garments of unctuous virtue, still less necessary for them to crow over the flood's senseless destruction of much that is beautiful and valuable.'

'It is!' Roy said. 'Cast your mind back a couple of centuries. Did your ancestors, when they overthrew the old India, wait and beat their breasts? Did they not proclaim, rather, the merit and rightness, even invoking God's will, of what they were doing?'

I nodded. It was a good point. I said, 'You are probably right . . . But you agree, then, that at that time you were the ones trying to fight against the river?'

'Yes.'

'And did that knowledge stop you from fighting?'

'No.'

'So?'

'Ah. Perhaps those people did not recognise the course of history. They were, after all, ignorant of the world outside India. You are in a different position ... Do you know how *I* would look for the course of history, these days? I would think of you, someone like you. You have been floating down on the current, now I notice that you are swimming upstream. Your ideals have not changed, nor has the course of events changed, yet their relation to each other has changed. This is very strange, and only your Einstein or our mystical sages can explain it. Yet one thing is sure, and I feel it in my bones – that you are doomed, like the Flying Dutchman, to swim and sail against overpowering headwinds and currents. So – I can be sure my course is correct if I merely go in the opposite direction from you, eh?'

I said, 'I see. You remind me of a story – by Somerset Maugham, I think – about a naval officer who gets into desperate financial trouble and goes to Monte Carlo, to an old man whose life he had once saved. This old man was always amazingly successful at the gaming tables and the officer begged him to tell him his system. The old man offered to give him whatever he needed, but the officer's pride wouldn't accept that, he only asked for the system so that he would win for himself. The old man said the system would do *him* no good, but the officer kept pressing and pleading, until finally the old man said, "My system is simple. I bet against those who *must* win. They never do." '

Roy stood up. 'I am the old man, Savage. I am offering you the equivalent of the money. Do not let your pride refuse it.'

I was standing, too. 'I'm sorry. I don't agree that history has a course of its own. I think it is influenced by men who are not afraid of it. I don't believe in systems, either. Sometimes you win, sometimes you lose – but you've got to play.'

Roy's voice became hard. 'Very well. Do not expect any preferential treatment when the time comes to settle the Chambal affair. You will pay the full price for whatever you have staked.'

I said, 'That will be the lot, sahib. The whole lot.'

133

Chapter 9

Three months to the day after I reached Chambalpur I was sitting in my office one morning, wondering what to do next. Wondering is too serene a word, since it gives a picture of a man sitting back in calm debate with himself. It was never like that in Chambal. I had no one job but was involved in everything. I had been imported to bring to Chambal the sahib's direct approach, executive efficiency, the sense of what is to be done and then the going out and doing it. But the affairs of Chambal were run on the system of the *Arabian Nights*, with one grand wazir receiving one set of orders, and another, and another, and both knowing that they were *really* supposed to do something else entirely. Above all, the ruling principle of government in Chambal was not justice, or right, or even autocracy – it was suspicion. Everyone was suspicious of everyone else, and, usually, with good reason.

There was excessive secrecy. The atmosphere was heavy with mistrust and intrigue. Whispered rumours flew around: 'X is in secret touch with India.' 'Y is ready to turn his private troops against the Nawab.' 'Z is sending money out to Swiss banks under an assumed name.' Everyone was an amateur spy – except when they were professional. I was trusted, but not therefore liked or followed. There were intrigues against me by officers who suspected that I was responsible for having them removed from important posts. There were financiers who wanted to nullify my influence in the awarding of military contracts, so that they could deal more amicably with someone else. I was permanently in a bad temper, curt and ruder than I needed to be, because I felt that the air was tainted by noxious gases.

So when I said that I sat wondering, what I mean is that I sat and glared at the wall map, while angry thoughts crowded for preference in my mind. If A didn't report soon that he had paid the guerrillas now being trained in the north, I would go and shoot him. But it was more urgent to see that the mechanical engineers were actually installing the new machine tools in the tank repair shops and not selling them to factories in the city. But it was more urgent still to see that B was fired at once from command of his brigade as he was a hopeless alcoholic; but to achieve that I would have to put him into a position where he would insult either the corps commander or the commander-in-chief – or, of course, the Nawab. They already knew he was inefficient, but that was not enough, not in Chambal. It had to be an insult, and B was too easygoing to become rude, even when boiled as an owl.

I had expected to be employed in negotiations with Kishanpur, but so far that had not been mentioned and after the first week or two I understood why. They did not trust me yet. My office was in Army Headquarters and a wooden plate on the door announced in gold-leaf letters, in English and Urdu, that I was Brigadier R. Savage, Assistant Military Secretary to His Highness the Nawab. I had a *babu* clerk, a telephone, a typewriter, and a water *chatty* in the corner. A few doors down the passage was the office of the commander-in-chief, General Prince Afif Khan Bokhari, a cousin of the Nawab. He was a dear old boy, seventy-eight years old.

Just as I had decided to take a trip to Digra and have a look at the port defences, an agitated *chuprassy* in full dress gold and green dashed in. 'Sahib,' he said breathlessly, 'His Highness is waiting.'

'Where?'

'Outside, in the car.'

I hurried down the stairs, in and out of courtyards full of dozing servants and sweeper women. I had a telephone, and His Highness could have indicated his intentions well in advance; but that wasn't the way things were done in Chambal.

Sir Mohammed Akbar Bokhari, G.C.B., G.C.S.I., G.C.I.E., etc., Nawab of Chambal, was sitting bolt upright in the back seat of one of the twelve State Rolls-Royces, a vast Phantom III drophead coupé with gold fittings, the top down, and a liveried chauffeur at the wheel. I got in. His Highness was sixty-five, clean shaven, gaunt, pale brown. Still, after four hundred years you could detect a faint trace of the Mongolian fold in the corners of his eyes. His family

135

had come from Bokhara in Central Asia with Baber, the first Mogul emperor, hence the family name, Bokhari. He wore pince-nez and was a simple man, in that he knew what he wanted: he wanted to keep all real power in his own hands. He was wearing, as usual, tight trousers, slippers with turned-up toes, a plain black achkhan reaching down to his knees and buttoned up to a high collar, with two jewelled stars on the left breast, the Order of the Bath and the Order of Chambral.

We drove off without a word. Chambalpur was a complete epitome of India, in romance, in fable, and in actuality. The old city stood around a mile-square lake. The Nawab's rose-red palace soared sheer from the water on one side, hanging like a vivid dream against the blue sky and the sharply etched backdrop of sand-coloured hills. Other palaces and mansions surrounded the lake – among them Army Headquarters, which was mid-Victorian icing cake. On the other side of the lake an inordinately ugly factory belched foul-smelling smoke from three tall tin chimneys. In the city there were narrow alleys where time seemed to have stood still for ten centuries, and others, nearby, where the squalor was not patriarchal but modern. And there were real slums, and tin cans piled in the offal dumps, and chemicals running down the open sewers from hidden shops and factories.

We passed under one of the immense city gates, with hardly room to squeeze through; and on among the jumble of shacks that had long since spread outside the walls. Near the point where the shacks finally died away and the empty semi-desert spread out in front of us, the Nawab spoke a single word to the driver. The Rolls stopped. The Nawab pointed. 'What is your opinion of that?'

About fifty yards in front of us a deep ditch crossed the road. Concrete anti-tank pillars made a line a hundred yards broad in front of the ditch. An immense amount of work had gone into it.

I said, 'The concrete is up to specification, I know. I have checked it myself.'

He said, 'So have I.'

I had a brief vision of the second richest man in India, perhaps in the world, banging away with a hammer in the

136

dead of night, taking the chip back, bending over a test tube . . .

The anti-tank defences, taken by themselves, were fine, but they were in the wrong place by about eighty miles. They should have been put in the Lapri Gorge or just where it debouched on to the plain; and Lapri was eighty-five miles east.

On the other hand, I had to work with General Gokal Singh, who had chosen the site.

I said, 'The defences look very good, Your Highness. But I know that General Gokal Singh is planning to supplement them by another system nearer the border – at Lapri or Sakti.'

The Nawab grunted. 'Drive on.'

We drove to the main airfield. It was one of the only three all-weather fields in Chambal capable of taking the heaviest planes – and it lay forward of the anti-tank defences. Someone must have seen the Nawab coming, for we were greeted by an Air Force guard, and by the air marshal himself. I followed the Nawab, and said little. This felt much better. There were about fifty P-47 Thunderbolts dispersed around the field, and the Air Marshal – a Chambali prince and ex-playboy – knew his stuff and seemed to have an excellent relationship with the motley crowd of Australians, Austrians, Americans, and Italians who were flying the planes. Also, he had accumulated large stocks of high-octane petrol, and spare parts for the planes. India had already cut off all supply through her ports.

My heart missed a beat when the Nawab said, 'You have been spending a great deal of money on petrol, Air Marshal. Are you sure you need that much?'

The air marshal made the point I had just been thinking about – building up a reserve. The Nawab said, 'You do not need a large reserve. It is just a waste of money.'

I kept my face wooden, though the air marshal caught my eye as he began to defend his expenses. The Nawab grunted and moved on. I wanted to talk to the air marshal about the progress he had made in training supply-dropping teams, but I had to trail along behind the Nawab and only had time to make an appointment with the air marshal. Supply dropping was a vital part of my plans for guerrilla war against the flanks of any Indian advance.

We drove on, round the outside of the city, towards the main barracks. Here, 'by chance', we met Lieutenant-General Gokal Singh, the deputy commander-in-chief, and also commander of the striking force. He turned his car and followed. He wasn't going to let the Nawab wander about unobserved, especially in company with me. Gokal was a Rajput, thirty-three years of age, a very bright and clever young man, sharp as a knife. With experience he might have been a great soldier. As it was, he thought he was much better than the facts indicated.

At the barracks Gokal shot out of his car and reached ours in time to open the Nawab's door with one hand and salute with the other. The Nawab stared at the dozen Sherman tanks rumbling back and forth across the sandy parade ground. After five minutes he said, 'Why is it flying a yellow flag?'

Gokal said, 'That is the troop leader's pennant, Your Highness. Each troop has a different colour, and – '

'They should all be green,' the Nawab said, and climbed back into the Rolls. I saluted Gokal punctiliously, and followed. The old bigot wanted all his tanks flying the Muslim green. The majority of his soldiers were Hindus. I wasn't thinking about that, but about the waste of track mileage. Tanks can go only so far before their tracks and engines need major overhaul or replacement. The tank commanders were wasting mileage because the exercise they were carrying out here should have been done in a classroom. I pulled out my notebook and made a note. Somehow I'd got to persuade Gokal that his tactical brilliance would do him no good if his tanks wouldn't run.

The Nawab said, 'Is he loyal?'

'General Gokal Singh, sir?' I said, startled.

The Nawab said, 'He is a Rajput. No family. I made him what he is, raised him up from nothing, so that I would have a man who owed everything to me. He ought to be loyal. But I can trust no one.'

I didn't answer, because doubts about Gokal had entered my own mind. I had rejected them, feeling that I must not allow myself to be trained by the universal suspiciousness. If we could not trust our chief battlefield commander, then we did not deserve to stand.

The Nawab dropped me off at Army Headquarters and

drove on. I looked at my watch. Another morning wasted. Now I couldn't set out for Digra until the next day.

But I could not afford to waste the day. I went up into Headquarters and looked for the chief of intelligence. I wanted to find out how the corps of observers and spies I had organised along the borders was working. The chief of intelligence had gone to lunch. Tried to find the commander-in-chief, to discuss a training programme for senior officers. He had not left his mansion today, and could not be disturbed. Looked for the commander of the city garrison, to check progress on plans for the protection of radio and power stations against sabotage. He had gone north to his son's wedding. Went disgustedly to my own office, stared at the wall, and wondered how I could make Lieutenant-General Gokal Singh understand that he was not Rommel. Worried about the guerrilla plans for Lapri and Bhilghat . . . Sent for the armoured brigade tank history sheets and studied them; situation bad, as I thought; engine replacements due for about 20 per cent already, and the political affairs with India like a keg of dynamite. Wrote all afternoon, went to my house weary and ill at ease.

And so on . . . I only give a typical day during the period when my duties were solely military. Then, about another two months later, when I had been in Chambal five months, Hussein Ali sent for me and told me the time had come to use me in the political manoeuvrings designed to bring Kishanpur and smaller uncommitted states into some sort of alliance with Chambal.

My waning enthusiasm rekindled. I needed Dip and his sensible, modern outlook here. Whatever the terms Chambal offered to him, they would have to include a measure of power in the affairs of the new country, and Dip had good ideas.

I do not want to give the impression that life in Chambal was all bad. I was tired, and if there had been nothing but the medieval intrigues of the court and government, I would have given up within a month and crept back to England with my tail between my legs – or perhaps even gone back to Roy. But the thing that I believed in did exist, and you only had to leave the capital to feel it, as real and as wonderful as a dove in the hand. The peasants greeted you outside their hovels, standing upright against a poverty

139

that would have caused many to bow and wail. There were
country gentlemen living on their estates, where every man
for five miles around behaved and was treated like a member
of the aristocrat's family; and on the squire's white-washed
wall hung a sword that had been carried at First Panipat
against Baber the Mogul in 1526, and at Laswari against
Lord Lake, and finally been broken on a Sikh skull at
Chilianwala. There were old men with long white beards,
who sat under the village tree and talked not of economic
exploitation or democracy or colonialism but of honour and
right and obligation. There were women with bright shards
of mirror glass let into their swinging red skirts, who primly
hung the sari over their heads when I passed; but if I went
to the well and stood nearby, and talked to Ratanbir about
the kind of woman we would like to marry, looking at them
as we talked, then they would begin to laugh and giggle and,
not looking at us, would throw out tangential comments of
wonderful earthiness.

Every time I escaped from Chambalpur my conviction
that all this was worth preserving – not the poverty but the
simple dignity – became recharged. At the same time I
became more sure that Chambal's hope lay in diplomacy
rather than fighting, so I was delighted when Hussein gave
me the orders that would, for a time at least, take me away
from the charming old historical monument called the
commander-in-chief, the Renaissance *condottieri* disguised
as twentieth-century generals, and all the other animated
museum pieces of the Chambal military establishment.

Dip had long since, in August, invited me to Kishanpur
for the Dussehra celebrations, so there was no need to invent
a reason for my visit. Then, a few days before I was due to
go he wired that the Indian Government had summoned
him to Delhi and he had thought it expedient to obey. I
arranged to pick him up at Bhowani Junction on his way
back, and so, in a beautiful dawn early in October, I set out
in the Bentley, Ratanbir beside me and the suitcases and
bedding rolls thrown into the back seat.

Chapter 10

I was in excellent humour by the time Dip's train whistled
for the station. First, I had escaped from Chambalpur.
Second, I would see Sumitra again, and as a new man. I
had a feeling that she had slept with me, and later visited
me, out of compassion, which galled my pride. Now we
could start afresh. Third, I had had time to reflect that Dip,
after his visit to Delhi, would probably be in a receptive
mood for my proposals. Roy might have frightened him
with his threats: the method of getting the states into the
Indian Union was quite simple – the iron hand in the iron
glove – but it was more likely that Dip would be annoyed
at the bullying. Fourth, while buying some matches in the
Bhowani bazaar I had run into Tilakbahadur, the *subadar*
major of the 1/13th Gurkhas, my own old battalion. He
insisted that I bring Dip to the head cutting, always a very
moving ceremony to me. Fifth, and last, the news that I was
in Bhowani had then filtered rapidly from Tilakbahadur
up to Max, who had invited us to have tea at Flagstaff
House before setting out for Kishanpur.

So I was feeling happy and almost young again as I
scanned the windows of the incoming train, looking for Dip.
Blue smoke and the smell of hot steel from the brakes filtered
up from the grinding wheels. They stopped, and Dip opened
a door, opposite where I waited.

He looked cross, and I understood why when another
man stepped down after him, and Dip curtly introduced
him: 'Mr Mehta, of the C.I.D. Mr Mehta, this is one of my
oldest friends – Colonel Rodney Savage.' The C.I.D. man's
jaw dropped, and he licked his lips. It was obvious that he
had been lecturing Dip all the way down from Delhi;
equally obvious that he had specifically warned Dip to be
on his guard against the dangerous Chambal agent, Savage.

He had a large padlocked briefcase in one hand. I leaped
forward obligingly. 'Can I help, Mr Mehta? Allow me to
carry that briefcase for you.'

Mehta clutched the briefcase tightly to his breast, and snapped, 'No! . . . Thank you.'

'Just as you wish,' I said affably. 'Come on, Dip. I've got the car outside and we're going straight to the lines. Good-bye, Mr Mehta.'

We left the station, shuffling slowly out among the mob of travellers, Dip's servant and two coolies following behind with his suitcases. Dip muttered, 'Bloody man. What right does he have to tell me what *my* duty is? . . . The lines, did you say? What lines?'

I told him about the head cutting, and he said, 'Really, I ought to get home, Rodney,' but I saw that he did not mean it, and, being also certain that the change of atmos-phere would do him good, I had no difficulty in persuading him.

We sent the servant straight to Max's with Dip's kit and, ourselves, headed for cantonments. Ten minutes later we passed a Gurkha sentry at the roadside, and turned up a gravelled road leading towards a row of long barrack build-ings. As the car stopped, a dozen officers in jungle green came forward, followed by Gurkhas loaded with garlands. Dip joined his palms and bent his head. 'Marigolds,' he muttered. 'Marigolds and zinnias. Don't you wish people would sometimes use flowers with a less cloying-sweet smell?'

I introduced him round. 'His Highness of Kishanpur, Colonel Mahadev, in command. Major Harbans Singh, Captain Lal . . . I don't know you. What's your name?' I stopped in front of a burly young man with second lieuten-ant's badges and a fierce moustache. 'Govind Singh Badh-war, sir. I have your old company, A.'

'Any relation to Hari, of Hodson's Horse?'

'He is my uncle, sir.'

'Good . . . He's a great man, and a good man. Don't let him sell you any ponies, though. He may be your uncle, but he's a damned horsecoper at heart. Have you still got that *gad* head, the one Rifleman Khagu shot in the middle of a battle in '37?'

'Yes, sir. We always keep it in the champion platoon barrack room now. One of the eyes is missing.'

I smiled and turned to the colonel. 'Is General Max com-ing, Jai?'

'No, sir. He's with the 1/4th this afternoon.'

'Oh, are they in the division too? Well, Dip, the colonel now proposes to hand us over to the *subadar* major . . . Tilakbahadur Gurung, *Sardar Bahadur*, O.B.I, I.O.M., M.C.'

Tilakbahadur was about forty-five, grizzled and powerful. His grip crushed Dip's fingers. I spoke aside to Tilakbahadur in Gurkhali, and Dip said, 'What have you been telling him? To spike my drinks?'

'Just the opposite. I was reminding him that we had a date with the general after this, and then we have to drive forty-seven miles – so would he please see that the drinks are kept at a reasonable size.'

Dip grinned, the *subadar* major saluted. We all drifted to the edge of the parade ground, and sat down at tables set out there under awnings. Huge glasses full of orange-tinted sweet rum appeared at our elbows. The *subadar* major sat on Dip's right, and an alert young *subadar* on my left.

I sighed and settled back. So did Dip. This was the Indian Army. This was a Gurkha battalion celebrating the great Hindu festival of Dussehra. Tomorrow and the next day, in Kishanpur, Dip would preside over more formal celebrations of this same festival. It would be quite different, but it would have something of the same atmosphere as here – a very different atmosphere from the miasma prevailing in New Delhi.

All the battalion's arms were massed in hollow square to our right. Flowers stuck out of the rifle muzzles and garlands hung from the machine-gun barrels. This was the festival of the god of war, and good luck with sacrifices would mean good luck in all the battalion's endeavours during the coming year. Though there was no shrine or image on the parade ground, the spectre of Kali the Destroyer, the necklace of skulls round her neck and her protruding tongue red with blood, towered over our imaginations. If we did not pay her homage correctly, it was we whom she would destroy.

Tension mounted as a group of soldiers sang Gurkhali hymns. Others dragged a big male buffalo on to the parade ground and tied its head to a post set in the earth. A squad stood ready to fire a salute, rifles raised. A single man stepped forward, in white shorts and undershirt. He raised the heavy sacrificial *kukri*. The blade flashed in the sun

143

and the buffalo's head flew off into the dust. Quickly the Brahmin bent and placed a live coal on the dead forehead. A smell of burning hair, and blood, drifted into our nostrils. Dip looked shocked. I shouted, 'Well done!' Everyone cheered and clapped and stomped. The squad fired three volleys.

The soldier who had done the sacrifice came forward and bowed his head. Colonel Mahadev stood ready, a white cloth in his hand. I whispered to Dip that the colonel would wind the cloth round the man's head, like a puggaree, as a reward and a mark.

But Mahadev turned to me, and said, 'This was your battalion, sir. You made it what it is. We would be honoured if you would tie the puggaree.'

For a moment I thought I would cry. My eyes hurt, but I managed to look up and take the cloth. 'For the last time, then,' I said. '*Ai-ja, choro.*' The man stepped forward, straightened in salute, then bowed his powerful shoulders. I tied the cloth round his head. As I wound the cloth I said aloud, 'You have done your duty cleanly and well. Do it so always.'

More men dragged on more buffaloes. There was more singing, and more blood; more horned heads joined the row in the dust. Small boys strutted out on to the ground, and with their fathers' heavy swords cut cucumbers in two. The rum was strong, Dip had settled into drowsy relaxation. 'A barbaric spectacle,' he said, 'but in keeping with certain aspects of the religion. Very Indian, somehow. You won't see any sacrifices in Kishanpur, only processions, with the State elephants parading the streets and me in the Rawan jewels and the big hat – and my soldiers – all fifty of them – in yellow coats and pikes. A waste of money, but great fun, and a great annual event. I wonder how much longer it will go on ... '

Soon it was time to leave. All the officers and Gurkha officers saw us off, and we were hung with more garlands until I wondered how Dip was able to see over the top of them, and I could hardly drive. Just before we started Ratanbir ran up and bundled himself into the back seat. I told him it looked as though the *havildars* had been generous with their rum. He grinned amiably but said nothing. We drove away through the dusk, among cheering soldiers, and

I had a big lump in my throat and a pain in my chest.

At Flagstaff House the sentry at the gate saluted, examined us, and let us pass. A large table, spread with a white cloth, was set up on the far side of the lawn. Pressure lamps hung from trees nearby and turned the grass into a brilliant, translucent green carpet. Janaki Dadhwal came out on to the veranda, petite and beautiful in a white sari faintly patterned with green. I went slowly up the steps, took her hand and kissed it. Max came out, rubbing his cheek with his hand. 'Phew!' he said. 'Those damned bun-faces of yours are going to wear me out, Rodney. And there's a nautch later tonight. Two more parties, a parade, and another nautch tomorrow . . . Whisky, Dip?'

Dip held up his hand. 'Orange juice, please,' he said, 'and blotting paper.' He helped himself to a curried titbit.

Max said, 'Rodney, have you got any time to spare for a look at the Caves of Konpara? Janaki and I thought of going over next weekend – to recover from Dussehra. Or have you seen them?'

I said, 'They're worth seeing a hundred times, but sorry. I'm booked up.'

Conversation flowed gently round the table. I told them about a ruined Rajput fort I'd found in the southern part of Chambal, and the wonders which I thought a proper exca-vation would reveal. Janaki brought out some paintings she'd bought, done by a Punjabi artist just coming to prominence.

Someone mentioned Gonds, and Dip said he had a prob-lem with a small tribe of them living in the southern part of his State. They would have to be moved because a new dam and reservoir would flood their land. He didn't know what to do about them.

I said, 'Talk to the D.C. of Bijoli – Ranjit Singh. Sumitra knows him, so does Janaki here. Get him to fetch the Gond chief up from Bhilghat, old Gulu, and send him down to your Gonds. Gulu has enormous influence, and he's learned to adjust his thinking to the new times better than most. But, whatever he says to do, do it, or you'll be in worse trouble than ever – and so will the D.C. Gulu doesn't like to have his advice ignored.'

Janaki said, 'Is there anything you don't know about this country, Rodney? It seems such a . . .'

She did not finish, but sat, looking helplessly at me. Such a waste – I finished the sentence for her in my own mind. I felt like that, too. India's time for freedom had come, and I didn't want it otherwise, but why did I have to be thrown on the rubbish heap? Was it inherent in the situation, or only in my character?

A visitor wearing sandals, dhoti, and Gandhi cap came across the lawn, his hands joined in a perfunctory *namasti*, the sentry trailing anxiously behind him. It was L. P. Roy. Max stood up, a look of alarm on his face.

'Oh, please sit down,' Roy said. 'General, I am sorry to upset you at such a time, but there is an important matter . . .'

He glanced round the group at the table. Janaki, as the hostess, had risen and was making *namasti*. Dip and I made the same gesture where we sat.

Roy stared at me. 'You!' he said. 'Colonel Rodney Savage!'

I said, 'No, sahib. Brigadier Rodney Savage, O.B.E., M.C.'

For a moment I thought Roy was going to lose his volatile temper, but he controlled himself and turned instead to Max. 'I did not expect to see this enemy of India at *your* house, General.'

Max said heavily, 'He is an old friend, and a guest.'

'Where did those come from?' Roy indicated the garlands lying piled on the grass beside my chair.

I began to say, 'That is none of your business,' but Max interrupted: 'They were given to him by the officers and men of his old regiment, the 13th Gurkha Rifles.'

'Ah,' Roy said. 'He has been visiting military installations? A Chambal officer, visiting Indian military installations. At your invitation?'

Max lowered his heavy head. He looked like a bull being goaded by a bull terrier. He said. 'Not at my invitation. At the invitation of the colonel commanding the battalion, but with my full permission and approval . . . It's an act of common courtesy.'

'You put courtesy before proper military caution?' Roy snapped.

Max said, 'I put it before anything, sahib . . . Not courtesy, I mean – doing what an Indian gentleman ought to do, or any other kind of gentleman . . . what he *has* to do.'

146

'I see,' Roy said, pressing the tips of his fingers together and raising himself lightly up and down on the balls of his feet. 'I see.'

Max was beginning to lose his heavy Jat temper. He growled, 'Colonel Savage and others like him taught our army to do its duty, at all times. It was not he who tried to subvert the loyalty of Indian troops for political purposes.'

'For political purposes, General? Can you refer to our efforts to attain the independence of our nation?'

Max did not answer, and I thought sadly, Roy's too clever, too intense for him. Still, they were such *bloody* fools. Casting aspersions on Max's loyalty to India was like accusing Nehru of selling out to the British . . . and I'd heard that said, too.

Roy said, 'Well, I did not come here to meet Colonel Savage . . . or even His Highness of Kishanpur.' He bowed perfunctorily to Dip. 'I have some important matters to discuss with you, in private.'

'Excuse me,' Max said and, at Roy's side, crossed the lawn towards the bungalow.

No one spoke. Roy's job was to take all necessary political action, create all necessary political pressure, which would force Chambal and the smaller Indian states into the Indian Union. He had paid one official visit to Dip in Kishanpur, but was in constant secret correspondence with the leaders of the Kishanpur Progressive party. The party contained about a thousand members and everyone knew that their role was to riot for union with India on the signal from Roy – thus giving India an excuse to send in her troops to restore order. To send in Max, in fact.

I caught Dip's eye and stood up. 'I think we'd better be on our way, Janaki.' As though at a secret signal, Dip's servant slipped out of the darkness behind his chair and murmured, 'The Presence's bags are loaded into the car.' Ratanbir was there, saluting.

I did not speak until we were ten miles out on the road to Kishanpur. Dust hung under the double avenue of trees, for bullock carts swung slowly along the wide unpaved verges or in the middle of the road, sometimes with the drivers dozing on the cart. The Bentley's headlights bored a short wide tunnel, which shaded away from white to a dense green-shadowed brown as the dust reflected back the rays. Bullocks, and carts, and occasionally a man on foot loomed suddenly out of it, and once the leaping orange flames of a fire at the edge of a mango grove, where a family prepared to sleep.

The familiar, appalling sense of home, of love that could not be returned, settled in me. There was no sense of time when that mood came, only place – India. I knew that a Roman legion would not come out of that dust ahead – that would be ridiculous, though I'd often expected to see one march out of a fog on the Wiltshire downs . . . but Aurangzeb might come, sick and old, carried in a litter, reading the Holy Koran, remembering all the people, all the beauty, he had destroyed in order to preserve the Faith, and knowing at the last that he had preserved nothing – only destroyed. British infantry might come, with fife and drum, Kipling's infantry, the green flag with the bull, and Kim, and Mulvaney, Learoyd and Ortheris, and Danny Deever in the middle, a rope round his neck and the Pioneer Sergeant on his right with apron and axe . . . Or the Mahrattas, Dip's ancestors. *Can you hear the light horses neighing and the muffled pad of the hoofs in the dust, round shields and steel helmets shining in the light there, and the spears slanting back on their shoulders, and the smell of blood as they canter endlessly past? . . .*

I shook my head violently, shaking away the dream. I said, 'Do you realise that that is the man – L. P. Roy – who will take over rule of your State, Dip?'

Dip made a half-motion, touching my arm and at the same time indicating that Ratanbir and his own servant were in the back. The atmosphere in New Delhi had made him nervous and suspicious. I said, 'A Gurkha *havildar* and the body servant of a Rajah of Kishanpur are to be trusted, totally. When the time comes that such men cannot be trusted, then there will be no need or place for a Rajah of Kishanpur, or for Rodney Savage – or for Max.'

Dip said, 'I don't know what to do.'

We remained silent for some miles. At length I said, 'Feel that you're in a swamp? I've been there . . . There's not much more I can say about the political side which others haven't told you before, a dozen times, a hundred times, I expect – from both sides.'

'Two hundred,' Dip said bitterly.

'Yes. Well, I'd like to stress another aspect. You know the Indian Government, besides taking away your powers, will also take over the State revenues and give you an allowance instead, decreasing it for your children –'

'I don't have any.'

'Perhaps you will, later . . . There's a lot of money in these states, much of it in gold bullion and jewels . . . '

'I have a couple of million pounds' worth in the castle vaults,' Dip said.

'I know. And there's plenty more under your money-lenders' beds. That money is doing nothing. It ought to be hiring international lawyers for us, to put our case to The Hague, and the UN. It ought to be employing public relations experts for us. It ought to be buying more fighters and bombers, so that we'll be too strong for Nehru to take the high hand he took with Hyderabad. I say "us", and I mean "us". If we don't hang together we'll hang separately. Even if you don't want to come in with Chambal afterwards, you're mad not to join us in a mutual defence pact. India suspects that we've got such a pact already – and another between all of us and Pakistan. That's the only thing that's prevented them sending Max in months ago. And what do you think they're waiting for now?'

'Kashmir,' Dip said.

'Of course. As soon as that's settled, or at least put on the shelf – you've had it.'

Dip groaned aloud. 'I know, Rodney, I know! But . . . however much I hate them individually, however much I dislike some of their ideas, however hard I try, I can't finally see any practical alternative.'

'The new Chambal Federation is the only answer . . . Tomorrow I'll give you a long secret letter from the Nawab, written in his own hand, in Urdu so high-flown that no one can understand it – but there is a typewritten English version. It is in three parts: the terms of incorporation into Chambal, the details of a mutual defence pact, and the details of a loan programme, at enormous rates of interest to you. We need money.'

'But I thought the Nawab had all the money in the world, now that the Nizam's out,' Dip said.

'He did,' I said, 'but we really mean to be independent. I'll tell you something that Mr Roy does not know yet. He

149

will tomorrow morning. We have bought a six-inch-gun cruiser and two destroyers from a certain South American country. They will be delivered tonight, at Digra, complete with Italian crews.'

'My God,' Dip said, appalled. 'There'll be war.'

'Not just yet,' I said. 'But I want you to stop thinking we're all helpless, that we're in the grip of something bigger than we can cope with. India is not all-powerful.'

Then Dip said almost exactly what Roy had once said, 'No, but history is.' And I sat silent, half in fear, half in anger.

The Bentley rolled out on to a long bridge. As we always did at this point, we looked upstream. The black bulk of Kishanpur Fort towered above the right bank of the placid river, silhouetted against the lighter southern sky. The smooth water reflected lights from the fort windows, and a thousand lights pricked the darkness from the city huddled to the left of the fort.

'Home,' Dip said.

'For how long?' I said.

I turned the Bentley carefully through the narrow, double-angled entrance to the Fort. An old man in yellow livery made a deep obeisance. The servants appeared under distant arches, running,

Dip climbed out. 'Sumitra's come down to greet us,' he said. 'She doesn't often do that.'

I watched Sumitra sweep forward with the smooth, swinging motion that sent a tremor through my loins the first time I saw her.

She had heard what Dip said. She was smiling, her hand extended. 'Of course I came down when the watchman telephoned. I'm the chatelaine, aren't I? How are you, Rodney?'

She looked stunning – a slim white silk cocktail dress, high heels, a single rope of rubies. As I greeted her I wondered again whether Dip knew of our affair. She had come alone to Pattan once, and Dip knew it was hard for any man to resist her if she set out to seduce him. But that was the time she returned two days earlier than he expected – so perhaps he would believe that I *had* resisted her. I'm afraid it didn't matter very much to me. Whatever the basis of their marriage, sexual jealousy certainly didn't form part of it or Dip would have committed suicide or murder ten years ago. I thought he loved her, and her waywardness hurt him only because he could not himself provide, could not himself become, whatever it was that she needed – and that was much more than a stallion. I was surprised that he hadn't long since decided it would be a kindness to everyone to divorce her and take a new wife. Probably he had thought so, but couldn't do it. He was like me. He just had to go on the way he was going, and take what came.

We went up into the Fort.

Chapter 11

'You are not very exciting company tonight, Rodney.'

Sumitra touched my arm as she spoke. We were leaning over the upper battlements of the Fort, watching the procession forming in the courtyard below.

I said, 'Sorry.'

I was dead-beat. Five days had passed since Dip and I drove in that night. Every day had added up to exhaustion – long, wrestling conferences with Dip; colourful, noisy public processions; fireworks; nautches; State dinners. Dip was as tired as I. I saw his head nodding forward under the big sail hat down there in the caparisoned howdah far below me, and I saw the chamberlain nudge him respectfully. Dip started awake, and sat up. The elephants rolled out towards the lights and the yelling crowds and the rockets already soaring up into the night.

I would not have been tired if I had won. I had lost. Before dinner this night Dip finally told me he would not join Chambal, would not sign a mutual defence pact, would not lend us any of his gold. He was in terrible distress to have to say it to me, and he still did not know what he *was* going to do – only what he was not. I had been plodding round and round in his personal morass with him for so long that I was almost glad to get out of it, even though in the wrong direction.

I had lost. If only L. P. Roy had come, fanatical and threatening, it might have swung the trick. If only Max had moved his troops menacingly closer to the frontier. He hadn't (but his division had been reinforced by an armoured brigade of Sherman tanks, I learned). I had lost. And if Kishanpur kept out, Konpara and the smaller states would certainly follow suit. They had no choice. Without Kishanpur they would be politically and geographically isolated.

I looked at Sumitra. She twitched the blue chinchilla cape a little more closely round her shoulders and stared back at me. The starlight showed the clear outline of her face against the distant violet blur of the night horizon. I was wearing a dinner jacket, the coat buttoned against the chill from the river, and a white silk scarf thrown round my neck. I was smoking one of my cheap strong cheroots. She was wearing black diamanté sandals and a slim three-quarter-length black evening dress. Her manner towards me these five days had been warm, but until now no natural opportunity had come to be alone with her, and I had created none. My whole being was concentrated on Dip and my task. Nor had Sumitra made any advance; only watched me with increasing concentration and, it seemed, puzzlement. I had been very much aware of her. There were moments when a purely animal lust stalked upon me like a lion out of its cage. Desperately I wanted to feel those satiny thighs wrap round me; but before the desire could become frenzy, a thought would come about the business in hand – some point I had not fully explained to Dip, some new angle from which I could exert pressure on him . . . and lust would slink back to its lair.

As the tail of Dip's procession left the courtyard I said, 'That's that.' I turned to her, dropped my cheroot, and took her in my arms. After a moment's resistance she responded eagerly, and at once my exhaustion left me. In a trice we were locked in one of those bellypressing, leg-twining, rocking, helpless clinches which can only have one proper end. I could feel her sliding down, going limp in my arms, and at the same time becoming muscularly and rhythmically alive. It would finish on the stone roof there, and that would be right. That's that, I had said, and now the lovely beast was out of its cage for good. I moved my hand and slid it up under her dress.

With a tremendous and unexpected effort she fell away from me and stumbled across the roof towards the far parapet, overlooking the river. I ran after her, and caught her shoulders as she leaned over. She resisted the pressure of my hands, as I tried to turn her round to face me. 'Sumitra,' I whispered in her ear. 'For God's sake! We have so little time. In a couple of days I've got to be back to Chambal, and then . . .'

And then we'd be cut apart for as long as my mind could imagine. Win or lose, there was soon going to be no chance for me to revisit India or for her to come to Chambal. I

153

pulled more urgently at her shoulder.

She half turned. 'Wait . . . ' she began.

I caught her and kissed her again. Again, for a moment, she gave herself up, and was swept to me by the same violent physical need that made me tug and pull at her dress until it was up over her waist.

'*Rodney!*' she gasped, turning her lips away from mine. '*Wait!*'

I stood back a pace, breathing deep, trembling, utterly aroused, my eyes fixed on her loins, where the high-riding dress hung like a theatre curtain over the remembered dark triangle of hair and the strong curve and countercurve of thigh and groin and mount of Venus.

She recovered some of her breath. 'There can . . . be more . . . time . . . for us . . . ' She got the words out slowly, in bursts.

One side of the dress slipped down of its own, covering half her loins. I made a move to her but she held up her hand. 'I can come to Chambal . . . '

The other side of the dress slipped down over her hips and, gracefully, the whole fell in a slow draping until it hung as before, feminine and civilised, covering the female animal.

She said. 'Give me a puff of one of those awful things.'

I lit another cheroot and when it was going well handed it to her. She drew on it two or three times, coughed once and gave it back to me. 'That's better . . . Dip has made up his mind against you.'

She was leaning back against the battlements, the stone pressing into the small of her back. I said nothing. We had never mentioned politics in front of her and she had never showed any sign, now or before, of taking the slightest interest in it.

She said, 'Dip hasn't said a word. But it's obvious. I am not a fool, and I do have interests outside *Kinder, Küche, Kirche* – perhaps because I am a childless atheist with a good cook . . . What would you do if I told you that I did not agree with Dip? That I thought Kishanpur should join Chambal?'

'I don't know what I would do,' I said slowly, 'but I know you couldn't do anything . . . short of poisoning Dip, announcing yourself as rani-regent, and issuing a proclamation. But the days for that kind of thing are past.'

'What about money?' she said. 'Don't you need money?'

I found myself saying 'Yes,' though our financial manoeuvrings were covered in as much secrecy as our military preparations. (When the news of our cruiser broke, the Indians ordered their biggest ships up to Bombay, which is less than two hundred miles steaming from the Chambal port of Digra. Pakistan promptly sent its tiny fleet to sea, on manoeuvres. What annoyed the Indian Government most was that our cruiser hit headlines all over the world. Their interest was always to sweep the whole business under the rug and keep the world ignorant not only of the issues but of the fact that there was a problem at all.)

'I could give you half a million pounds,' she said.

I stared at her in astonishment. Six million rupees was a lot of money. She might have saved a lakh or so, but Kishan-pur was not a very rich state. The gold in the vaults had been collected over centuries. Dip had never been in a position to give her a really big allowance, nor had she picked up exclusively with multimillionaires on the Riviera.

'You're serious, aren't you, in this Chambal business?' she asked.

There was something about the tone of her voice, something about the steady, penetrating look in her huge eyes, that made me pause before answering. I began to speak slowly. Yes, I was serious. I had never been so serious in my life. I tried to tell her. I tried to tell her about an Indian land where there could be dignity as well as progress, splendour as well as justice.

'And you think you can attain it?' she asked. 'I mean you, yourself. Or are you fighting for the sake of fighting?'

'I think we can attain it,' I said. 'Myself . . . I feel that I have been given a second chance. For all the time we English have been here, certainly for the past fifty years, we seem to have been heading the wrong way. Now I've been given an opportunity to put that right. At the moment it's a matter of fighting, or being prepared to fight, like Israel. But I suppose Israel has an idea beyond self-defence, something it means to become – and so do we . . . Why aren't people like Max and P. R. Sethi in public life? They and hundreds of thousands like them, some who speak English, plenty who don't. I mean *decent* people, people everyone respects and

155

trusts. Why? . . . Because they won't lie and stoop and fawn. What is right is not always popular – it's practically *never* popular . . . We left the democratic process here, but we did not leave England's real secret – mutual respect among people, tolerance, independence of thought . . . '

My cheroot tasted foul and I threw it far out over the battlements, so that the red spark fell in a long curve down to the river.

'I, too,' she said slowly, 'I, too, have been given a second chance. India was mine. What could I not have achieved with this name, this position – Sumitra, Rani of Kishanpur? I rejected everything. I don't know why. Perhaps because everything seemed so settled. I do not like to have my fate cut out for me. This is a custom-bound country, and Dip is more deeply held by it than you would think. I would obviously have no say in the running of the State, so I never tried. I should have looked further, but I didn't. I went to Europe, and found men I could influence, men who were making something of themselves, against odds. Men like you.' I put out my hand, but she only touched it delicately, then went on speaking. 'I never thought of the British leaving India. I never expected to feel involved in the fate of peoples, only in the fate of people, singly . . . Now I do. I am involved, deeply. I will come to Chambal.'

I felt a little dizzy. If the Rani of Kishanpur came to Chambal, openly announcing her support of our position, it would be a tremendous coup; and it would give us more publicity. No other rani would have served that purpose so well, because the European and American press knew her, and her name and picture meant something outside India. On the other hand, the old Nawab would look on her with deep distrust, suspecting more Hindu trickery. Perhaps not. Who was it said there is nothing so persuasive as a million dollars? She was offering more than that.

'Where is the money coming from?' I asked her. I still could not quite convince myself that all this was not a crazy joke.

She said, 'The Rawan jewels. Tomorrow evening Dip and I will be wearing all that we can carry of them, and the rest will be in the vaults. I can hand the whole lot to you any time in the night. They fill two suitcases.'

The Rawan jewels were very well known. They were a

fabulous collection of gems, brooches, tiaras, rings, neck-laces, and other Hindu ornaments, such as anklets, and nose jewels, made up at various times over the past thousand years. One or two pieces were valuable simply because they were old, others because of the size of the gems, others again because of the artistic genius that had gone into the shaping of them. The whole collection was priceless in the sense that Ajanta or the Konpara sculptures or Nanda Devi or the Ganges is priceless. They were part of India's heritage. They were part of the whole complex that *is* India.

Earlier this evening Dip had rejected that heritage. Though I understood his reasons, I despised him. If a man will not fight for what is his when the chance is given to him, he does not deserve to keep it. He himself might wish to knuckle under to India, but he could not complain if Sumitra had the courage to fight. It was also peculiarly fitting that she should bring with her not bearer bonds or Swiss francs but jewels. It was very right, and very Indian, that ancient jewels should be used to preserve an ancient dignity.

I would have to devise a plan to smuggle the jewels out of Kishanpur. I had the Bentley. I had Ratanbir. I could . . . But tomorrow was another day. Tomorrow would be time enough for that.

Full realisation of Sumitra's meaning flooded into me. 'You will come to Chambal – with me?'

I could say no more. It would not be quite truthful to say that I loved her. Yearning for her body, longing to learn what made her tick, fascination with her personality, these did not yet amount to love. Perhaps it was an element of self-protection that had prevented me going quite over the edge while she had seemed so inaccessible. I could hardly stand another hopeless love, such as I had given in the past to Janaki and Victoria Jones. But the sudden revelation of her ideals and sense of purpose; recognition of the depths below the narcissistic surface; appreciation of her courage in taking this tremendous step – these set off a trigger, which ignited a charge, which would, I knew, lead now inevitably to love.

I took her hands.

'Wait!' she said again, with a terrible sharpness. 'Rodney, it's no use pretending I don't find you exciting. But I didn't

157

say I would come to Chambal with you. I said, I will come to Chambal . . . Think, Rodney. Remember what I said to you at Pattan. I cannot promise to fall in love, as you will. I cannot promise not to betray you, as I am betraying Dip. There is a woman in me who is not subject to any rules of behaviour, or decency, or obligation. When this woman starts to move me, I go.'

I took her hands and lifted them and put them round my neck. I leaned forward and kissed her on the lips, my arms round her. Her hands tightened, her head turned away. She whispered, 'I warn you, Rodney, I warn you!'

I found her lips again and slowly, resisting, they opened to me, and she gave a long sigh against my mouth, and I led her across the rooftop, she leaning against me and walking with dragging drowsy steps, and I took her down to her room, and locked the door and undressed her, and as she lay naked on the bed I looked long into her eyes, which had grown dull and wide and feverish, and, having lost all frenzy in the knowledge that this was a beginning, not an end, I kissed and stroked and made love to every part of her body, and finally locked myself into and upon her in a passion of love that seemed to have no end, but went on outside time, in the motion and countermotion of a liquid eternity, until a long bar of duck-egg green light shining on the ceiling told us it was dawn.

Chapter 12

Sumitra came to Chambalpur five days after my own return there. My first day Hussein and the Nawab and the council of state kept me so busy I hardly had time to think. I told them first about my failure with Dip. The Nawab questioned me sharply. My enemies hinted that the failure was my fault. I would have found it easy to lose my temper if I had not been thinking of Sumitra. Hussein protected me from the more foolish insinuations by letting out that the mission had been regarded as hopeless from the first. Of course, I thought. How could I have believed that they would let *me* get the credit, if they had expected any credit to be going?

Then I told them about Sumitra. After a few moments of thunderstruck silence, enthusiasm became general. The public relations expert embraced me. The Nawab looked suspicious – but he always did; and even he smiled when I told them about the six million rupees.

The second day I waited with increasing anxiety for Ratanbir. We had left Kishanpur together at dawn the day before in the Bentley, with the suitcases containing the jewels just thrown into the back seat under our own. Five miles outside the city the car I had hired was waiting for us. Ratanbir transferred to it, and they set off southward on a by-road, while I continued west. I drove slowly, and a little later spent an hour sitting in a jungle clearing, the Bentley concealed. Near Bhowani, when over the border, the Indian police stopped me. That was interesting because it showed that Dip had decided to bring them into the matter; which in turn meant his total surrender, because the Indian Government had already announced that they regarded State and crown jewels as the property of the people, hence *their* property.

It also showed that the theft had been discovered early. Sumitra had warned me she could not give me more than an hour's grace, and I was prepared.

While I was at the police *thana*, after they had searched

the car and found nothing, the inspector telephoned Kishanpur. Since the Indian telephone system was primitive, and
since I was in the next room, I heard every shouted word.
The inspector was speaking to Dip himself. He said that he
had found nothing. Nevertheless, he could arrest and hold
me under Emergency Regulations if His Highness wished.
A long silence. No, His Highness did not wish. Then Dip
must have asked to speak to me. The inspector called to me,
but I shouted, 'I have nothing to say to His Highness.'

I felt no qualm of conscience about the jewels. If he was
willing to allow India's claim to them he could hardly treat
it as a personal theft for personal gain, which of course it
wasn't. I would have liked to tell him, before it happened,
that Sumitra was leaving him, but she wanted to tell him that
herself. I would have liked to say I was sorry it turned out
that she was leaving him for me, because in spite of everything I liked him; but Sumitra was going to leave him sooner
or later, everyone had known that for years, and in truth I
was not sorry. I was delirious with happiness and expectation.

A little later the inspector let me go. By then I reckoned
Ratanbir should be thoroughly lost to view on dirt roads and
jungle cart tracks in the south. He should have entered
Chambal territory the same night, and reached the capital
this second day.

He did not. The third day he did not come. The fourth
day I left Chambalpur at dawn, drove to the southeast
corner of the State, and spent the day inquiring of police
officials, guerrillas, and military outposts whether they had
seen such and such a car, or such and such a man, whether
they had heard of an accident. Nothing. I reached Chambalpur again at three in the morning, and slept fitfully and
unhappily.

At noon Sumitra arrived. The propaganda people had
arranged a huge press campaign to tell the world about the
accession of the Rani of Kishanpur to our side. I was waiting
at the Nawab's palace when she drove up in a big Chambali
Cadillac with her maid and the Grand Wazir. A hundred
photographers and journalists milled about the reception-
room like a racecourse crowd. Flash bulbs exploded, cameras
clicked, women scribbled, men shouted questions.

Standing with her on a dais the Nawab looked old and
disgusted. He hated publicity of all kinds and could never

160

unbend. Sumitra made a little speech about freedom and self-determination. She was very beautiful. Someone asked her whether the rumour was true that she had brought the Rawan jewels with her. Dip and the Indians had tried to keep that quiet, but something had leaked. Sumitra said she knew nothing about them.

Two hours later they drove her to one of the Nawab's large houses by the edge of the lake, and the press finally left her alone. I was already living in another wing of that house. The fact would doubtless be mentioned by some of the journalists when they wrote up their stories. I did not care.

She came to me as soon as she had bathed and changed. We fell greedily into each other's arms and assuaged our physical hunger. Afterwards, her face again made up, we talked business. I told her that Hussein Ali was coming round after dinner for a formal discussion of her role here. Then she ran through the names of the principal men of the State, their positions, characters, and influence. She knew an amazing amount about them and I had little occasion to correct her.

'And now you'd better give me the jewels, darling, so that I can give them to Hussein,' she said. 'That's the price of admission, after all.'

I said miserably, 'They're not here yet.'

Watching her arrival, making love to her, talking to her, had enabled me to forget my worry, but now it was back. She looked at me with her big eyes, which were momentarily cold.

'Ratanbir hasn't arrived,' I said. I walked up and down the room, beating my fist in my hand. 'I don't know what the hell can have happened to him, but something has. Suppose he was caught and arrested while passing through India . . . I don't think so. There must have been an accident. The poor little devil's lying injured in some hut miles from anywhere . . . '

She got up and put her arm round me. 'My poor Rodney . . . He's all right. The car may have broken down. He would have had to use some pretty bad roads, wouldn't he?'

'Yes,' I said. 'He was crossing India through Bhilghat. The road's awful.'

'Don't worry,' she said, 'he'll turn up soon . . . I can

find some other way of convincing the Nawab of my value to the cause . . . though he'd much prefer to have the jewels. What was he going to do with them, by the way?'

'Sell them in Europe,' I said. 'There are ways. We would have raised about half their real value . . . The Indians are watching every road now. Ratanbir may have had to leave the car miles back and come on by bullock cart. I sent a message to the Gonds to look out for him . . . '

'The Bhilghat Gonds?' she said. 'But they're in India.'

'Yes,' I said, 'but they're working secretly for me. They will be ready to rise when the time comes.'

Later, the meeting with Hussein went off well. He advised her to introduce herself to the ladies of the Nawab's household, and the household of all the leading council members and generals. She was to keep her ears open, particularly about the strength of the ladies' attachment to the Chambal cause. She was to visit hospitals and run fund-raising bazaars, and do anything else that would get her picture in the papers.

'Can I not organise women's battalions, for labour and clerical work, nursing, even fighting?' she asked.

Hussein looked a little unhappy. 'That is against the Nawab's policy. Woman's place is in the home.'

I had a twinge there. This was feudalism, but I could not complain. You have to take people's bad ideas as well as their good ones, and do the best you can to teach them.

Hussein took an opportunity to speak to me alone the next day. He warned me to tell Sumitra nothing that was not necessary for her to know. I was indignant. 'What is the point of having her if we don't trust her?' I asked.

'We do,' he said, 'but in another sense, we trust nobody. You, after all, do not know exactly what I am always doing, do you? Because I tell you only what you need to know.'

'How can you mistrust someone who's giving half a crore's worth of jewels to the cause?' I said heatedly.

'She hasn't, yet,' he said, smiling.

'But damn it, I've told you, that's nothing to do with her. If it's anyone's fault, it's mine.'

I began to tell him that this universal suspicion was the curse of Chambal, but soon gave up. Hussein could not abolish it any more than I could. I turned to my work.

It felt better, more worthwhile now.

Sumitra made the difference, sweeping through my existence like a current of fresh air. It helped her that she shared a house with me, because none of the high Chambal ladies – and they were as suspicious and secretive as a nibble of weasels – could think that she was after their husbands. In two days she had got to know a dozen of the most important women in the State, and became so busy I hardly saw her until late at night.

So I was surprised when she came to my study about teatime on her fifth day in Chambal. I was working on a master plan for the defence of the Lapri Gorge. I pushed the maps away and stood up. She was smiling, her arms out. She hugged me tight, and kissed my face and neck and arms. 'Oh, Rodney, I'm so glad!'

'What's happened?' I asked.

She gave me a letter. It was from Dip to her. He thanked her for seeing that the jewels were returned to Kishanpur. He told her that he had paid Ratanbir the reward. He hoped that she was well. Signed. 'P.S. I shall always love you. Do remember that, wherever you go.'

'Of course, I had nothing to do with getting the jewels back,' I heard her say.

I read the letter three times. I threw it down on the floor. 'It's not true!' I shouted.

She looked at me. Her smile had become sad.

'It's a bloody lie,' I shouted. 'The Indians caught him and handed back the jewels. Ratanbir had nothing to with it.'

She held my arm. 'Rodney, is it so impossible? He knew that you and I stole them. Didn't you tell me, the other night, that you once had him making preparations to rob a bank in Delhi? You're not Colonel Savage of the 13th Gurkha Rifles any more. You haven't been for a long time. Is it so dreadful that he should not be Havildar Ratanbir any more? That he should have learned these other attitudes from you, in the same way that he learned to shoot and march?'

I could not speak. I could not accept what she said. If it were true, I could trust no one. I could not trust her.

She said, 'It doesn't matter. I'm so glad! I thought you had taken them for yourself.' She caught my look. 'What else was I to think? It didn't seem so very terrible, to me. And you must admit that you are a mass of contradictions.

163

How am I to know when you are going to think like a sahib and when you're going to think like – like one of your merchant-pirate ancestors?'

She hugged me and kissed me again, but I felt miserable. The more miserable I felt the more she warmed towards me. 'What about that P.S.?' I asked. 'Do you still love Dip?'

She said, 'I never did. This Chambal cause has given me the incentive to end a farce. He ought to marry again. I like him, that's all. It's finished.' And she hugged and crooned over me.

Two days later she came in, again at teatime, and began to hug me with a warmth and affection quite distinct from sensual passion. 'What now?' I asked.

'Dwarkanath and the bribe,' she said, looking fondly at me.

'Oh,' I said. Dwarkanath was a man who'd landed a contract for building barracks down at Digra, the port. I had flown down, found the work far below specifications and was even then writing a report to Hussein Ali. Dwarkanath had offered me twenty thousand rupees to keep quiet. I had refused with vehemence and abuse.

'You realise this will put So-and-so against you,' she said, naming three generals and a minister who owed a great deal to Dwarkanath, and vice versa.

'I don't care,' I said. 'I'm fighting for tradition – but not this one.'

'Yes,' she said slowly. 'You are an idealist, after all.' That night, after the love-making, which was as long and as detailed as the night at Kishanpur, she whispered in my ear, 'I love you, Rodney.'

Then she burst into tears, and for an hour I held her against me, while she sobbed quietly and whispered over and over again, 'But I love you, I love you.'

I felt that I had mounted the steed Pegasus. She lifted me out and above the poison gas of Chambal politics. I went at my work with a new vigour and came back at night refreshed and alert, to be transported by the magic of her love and affection to new, more vivid clouds.

I needed all the energy and élan I could muster. India began an economic blockade against us, and it became harder and harder to keep the army and the civilian populace content. Our three Constellations flew in from

164

Europe, via Karachi, as fast as they could make the round trip, bringing in arms and supplies, but it was a drop in the bucket against our needs. Chartered ships plied in and out of Digra at enormous cost. There the cruiser H.M.S. *Chambal* lay to her moorings, conserving oil, while the Italian crew played cards and suffered from *le cafard*. Our puny railroad system began to fall to pieces. We were fast reaching the point where we must force India to act. If we did not, we would collapse of our own weight.

I poured out my thoughts to Sumitra. She soothed me, her hand on my brow. I said, 'There are times when I feel there can be no building until we pull everything up by the roots, His Obstinate Highness included, and start again from scratch . . .'

'That's what the Indians are trying to do,' she said. She took my hand and held it tight. 'And, Rodney darling . . .' she began.

I interrupted. 'But I've eaten the old bugger's salt and, by God. I'm going to earn it.' I jumped up and poured myself a stiff drink. Sumitra sighed, and I mentioned that the Nawab mistrusted her, as he mistrusted everybody. 'I expected it,' she said. 'Perhaps he'll feel different tomorrow. I've unearthed an Indian agent – quite an important one. Ram Lubhaya.'

'My God,' I said. 'Are you sure?'

Lubhaya was No. 2 in the Communications Department.

'Yes,' she said, 'I heard something, and told the secret police yesterday. Today they searched his house and found incriminating letters from L.P. Roy. He's in jail now.'

'That ought to show them about you,' I said.

She said, 'Yes. I think it will.'

Two weeks later I went down to Lapri to run a training exercise for the local guerrillas. I had been to Lapri many times during my time in Chambal, for the gorge and the Sakti plain behind were the keys to any military defence of Chambal. Twice I had seen Margaret Wood. She was looking more composed, though wan and tired. The loneliness must have been getting her down because she gave me tea and obviously tried to keep me, talking about nothing, until I had to break away.

Now here I was again, this time standing in thin trees near the edge of the slope, about halfway between Dhain and Lapri, looking down on the gorge road from India. The little village of Gidha nestled halfway up the farther slope. A motley gang of local men surrounded me and I examined them carefully. This was the kind of thing the American magazines would love, if only I could afford to let them take photographs here. I could see the captions now . . . *Jungle Natives Fight for freedom! Intrepid Guerrillas Prepare to Defend Homeland against Armed Might of India! . . . Tall hawk-faced ratmouthed Savage (see cut) English mystery man prepares secret hideout.* In my mind's eye I picked out the men who would make the most fierce photographs.

I sighed regretfully. To work . . . I had twenty men from Lapri, Dhain, Gidha, and other villages farther west. Five had modern rifles, and all knew how to use them. I had personally given them a course, back in the jungles, earlier in the day. That was a waste of my time – any *lance naik* could have done it – but Gokal Singh had protested his inability to spare me even a *lance naik*, so I did it myself.

The men were mostly ignorant and raw, but most had a spark of patriotic feeling, and one or two some basic knowledge of the problem. I had just appointed a wizened old bird from Dhain as the over-all commander. Age is always important in India, and he was a skilled *shikari* and poacher, though getting a little creaky in the joints. I called him the Marquess, as he looked like Reading, the ex-Viceroy.

Now I gathered them all closer, made them squat down, and began to talk. 'This is where you have to work, when the time comes,' I said, pointing down at the gorge. 'The Indian soldiers will have to use that road for their tanks and trucks, and for the men who march. They cannot defend every inch of it – it is too long, the jungle is too thick. On the other hand, you can't stop them. They are too strong and you are too weak . . . '

A few faces showed a glimmer of understanding. The rest stared down in wooden puzzlement, mixed with alarm. I told them they must organise into groups of three or four. They must hit and run away – snipe a single man here, blow up a culvert there. They must prepare several caches in the jungle, where they could hide ammunition, rifles, and also wounded men. I told the Marquess that each group was to know only the site of its own cache, so that they could not even by accident betray the others. (Or under pressure, I added to myself.) The Marquess raised one wrinkled and hooded eyelid, like a sardonic cobra. The object was to delay the Indians, and to force them to use more and more soldiers on guarding their communications, so that there would be fewer when they debouched on the plain, where our own army would meet them.

More . . . we wanted information about little-known tracks through the hills south of Dhain, and north of the northern escarpment. We must know which paths the Indians used, how many men, how fast, any tanks or vehicles. I would set up an army post at Sakti, ten miles west. All information must be sent there by the quickest means.

We began a series of small exercises. I pointed out a tree or a rock as a pair of Indian sentries. The Marquess divided the men into groups, and I watched while group after group did a quick stalk and pretended to kill and escape. I showed them how to cover each other, so that men in hiding protected the man in motion. We examined various sites for caches and discussed their advantages and disadvantages.

Finally, I arranged a practical ambush. A broken stream bed ran steeply down the hill in a north-easterly direction, from somewhat below Dhain towards the Pattan Rest House and the Shakkar. It was a steepish run of rock, in step and fall, not very wide. I would wait at the top, and after half an hour begin to walk down it, alert. I was supposed to represent a patrol of six men. The guerrillas, acting in concert under the Marquess, were to ambush me before I reached the jeep road at the foot of the hill. They went off down the nullah and I lit a cheroot.

It was time Sumitra and I got married. There were still mysteries and depths in her which I could not get at, and, I felt, never would until marriage gave her full confidence. I suppose there has never been a mistress who is not always aware of the relationship's impermanence, and therefore holds back something vital, which she can salvage from the wreck. I had also come to appreciate the depth of her involvement with her native soil (and mine, incidentally). Her years in Europe and America had passed like a shallow stream, and, except for the occasions when she still wore Western clothes, might never have existed. I ground my teeth on the cigar. We'd *got* to win our fight for Chambal's independence. Otherwise we would both be in exile, for ever ... if I did not end in front of a firing squad.

I glanced at my watch, stubbed out the cheroot, and started down the nullah. I kept my eyes open, but not unnaturally so. Let's see, I thought, a section would come down here with two men in front, one on each side of the nullah and as high up as they could get; then would come the section commander and the Bren gun team; and two more men would follow thirty yards or so behind. The ambush must take account of all those. They'd probably forget to allow for the dispersion, rush in on the front men, and get caught by the two at the back ...

A slight change of light, from a reddish matt of rock to a darker sheen, caught my eye a little right and ahead of me. Now, would I have seen that? Before I had made up my mind whether to start pretending firing, a man materialised from the shadows, a rifle in his hand. I was Chadi, my old *shikari* from Pattan. A sound behind me made me turn my head and I saw Mitoo and young Ganesha. Both were armed.

'Chadi!' I said. 'My friends! Is the village hungry again? And I see you have rifles. A little old, but good.' They were of a obsolete mark, obviously from Indian arsenal stocks. I smiled.

Chadi did not smile. He said, 'Sahib, you are on Indian soil.'

'Well,' I said, 'we'd probably have to get a map and a surveyor's instrument to make sure of that, wouldn't we?'

The border between Chambal and India ran due north and south here, across this very hill. I realised about now that the three had not seen or heard the Marquess. How could that be? Ah, the cunning old Marquess, really in the spirit of our game, had moved his party downhill off to the side, so that there would be no footmarks or crushed leaves in the nullah to attract the attention of the 'Indian patrol'. Was he within earshot? Probably not, because if he could hear us, these three could certainly have heard him getting into position.

Chadi said, 'We shall have to take you down to Pattan to the head constable.'

I was wearing Chambal uniform, and carry a long thumb stick. Otherwise I had no weapon. It would be awkward to be dragged off prisoner into India, whatever the legality of

168

the matter, which would be impossible to prove one way or the other. Here, possession would be all ten points of the law.

I had not expected this. I had an organisation among the Bhilghat Gonds, under Gulu, but nothing in Pattan. It seemed to me that the Indians, knowing my close connection with the place, would be too much on the lookout there. but this . . . that *they* should have organised guerrillas, and from my own people! I felt cold, and murderous, but held my face under control.

I said reproachfully, 'Is this how you repay what I did for you?' I looked at Mitoo and Ganesha.

Ganesha was young, and I had been a great hero to him. He muttered, 'Surely we can let the Gora-Raja go?'

Chadi felt the strain, but life in these hills is hard, as I had learned for myself. For a time I had led them towards a dream. The dream had collapsed. Chadi had to live. He'd taken a new allegiance.

'I am sorry, sahib,' he said quietly. 'We have promised.'

I shrugged. 'Let us go down then. Or would you prefer to shoot me here and save yourselves trouble?'

'Don't speak like that, sahib,' Mitoo wailed, 'we have promised . . .'

I started down the nullah, hoping we would get far enough down for the Marquess to hear us before Chadi headed out and east, directly towards Pattan, which now lay almost behind our right shoulders. I hadn't gone ten paces when he said, 'This way, sahib.'

He was as sharp as a razor, Chadi. He had realised that I knew perfectly well where Pattan was. Therefore, if I was heading on down the nullah, I must have a reason for it.

We climbed up out of the nullah, and at the top the Marquess was waiting with his rifle aimed at Chadi's heart. 'Don't raise your guns,' he said in a hungry voice. 'I am not alone.' We heard the rest pounding up the hill then.

The Marquess said, 'You were late, sahib. I came up to see . . . and saw . . . and went back and told them to come . . . and hurried up myself. I know you, Chadi of Pattan. What are you doing on the earth of Chambal?'

Chadi did not answer. The three were surrounded now. 'Take their rifles,' I ordered. Grinning, my guerrillas did so. They were wildly excited, their eyes shining. The boring

169

game had turned into reality. I looked at the three prisoners. It would be best if they did not return home. Nothing would more discourage the people of Pattan and other villages from doing police and scouting work for the Indians than to have it leak out that three of the best *shikaris* in the district had mysteriously disappeared.

The Marquess was carrying the universal long-handled small-bladed axe, tucked now through his loincloth. He handed his rifle to another man and drew the axe. I stared at the three men. Young Ganesha was quaking with terror, though silent. These bloody people had betrayed me. They'd all better learn that the day of the pukka sahib was over. The day of Hodson and Edwardes and Nicholson was coming back, the day of the hard men of total power, instant decision, and no remorse.

I remembered the warmth of Mitoo's wife's arms round my neck. These people had given me something, too. We'd shared everything, during time that could not be measured, and it wasn't their fault that that time had ended. It was the shape of the continuum at that point in history.

The Marquess looked expectantly at me. I said, 'Take them to the jail at Sakti. They are to reach there alive and well. Understand? From there I will have them moved to Chambalpur as soon as possible.'

I would have them thrown into the dungeons, to join others. The effect, of total disappearance, would be the same; but sooner or later they'd get back to their families. If the Indians won, they'd be released. If we won, I'd see that they were let out. The bastards ought to be thankful for their lives.

The Marquess looked disgruntled and still hungry, and I said sharply, 'Remember what I said! Without discipline we are lost before we begin.'

Ganesha fell to his knees. 'Thank you, Gora-Raja . . . Raja, Gulu has been arrested.'

'Silence!' Chadi snapped. The Marquess hit him hard on the side of the head with the axe handle and he stumbled, and groaned, but recovered himself.

Ganesha gabbled on, 'Yesterday, sahib. He and a dozen others in Bhilghat. The police went. Another man is to answer messages in his name, pretending . . .'

170

'Thank you,' I said. I motioned to the Marquess. 'Take them away, by the hill roads.'

We split up, the others going back up the nullah towards Dhain and I going on down alone. My mind raced and caught.

Gulu arrested. The whole of my guerrilla organisation among the Gonds wrecked. They must have had an eye on Gulu, after I'd given the D.C. a practical demonstration of my special position with Gonds; but this was more definite. They had something on him. As he kept no papers, couldn't read, in fact, it was something else. I had met Gulu twice since coming to Chambal, once on the border near Bhilghat, once outside Lapri . . . and that time, by pure chance, Margaret Wood had passed, walking alone along a deserted path miles from anywhere. She'd seen us. Jesus Christ, the bloody bitch had told the Indians . . .

I reached the road and strode fast along it towards Lapri and the mission. I'd fix her for good and all this time. His Suspicious Highness was right after all – trust nobody, nobody at all.

At the mission bungalow I ran up the steps and knocked on the door. She came out smiling, an envelope in her hand. 'I saw you coming,' she said. She gave me the envelope and I took it automatically. 'Do come in and . . . '

I snapped, 'You are to evacuate this mission in forty-eight hours. If you are not out of Chambal territory within that time you will be arrested and taken to the concentration camp. You will receive confirmation of these orders, in writing, before – ' I looked at my watch, it was five o'clock '– before six.'

I turned and went down the steps. I heard her crying behind me, 'What is the matter?' I heard her footsteps running down the veranda, felt her hand on my arm. 'Rodney! Colonel . . . Brigadier . . . what's happened? What have I done?'

I soon outdistanced her and in Lapri stood over Faiz Mohammed while he wrote out the order. The Nawab had long since given senior civil and military officials authority to put any suspicious or traitorous people into a concentration camp, without inquiry or trial. I watched him walk down the road to the mission bungalow to deliver it. Then I got into the Bentley and drove back to Chambalpur.

171

There I had a dozen people to tell, a dozen moves to make to counteract the effects of the action against Gulu. It was very serious indeed, because I had counted on the Gonds, with their jungle craft, posing a real threat to the Indians' southern flank. Good quiescence would release at least two more Indian battalions to come against us. And there was an air of urgency liberated by the act, because the Indians would not have moved until they were on the point of major action. Otherwise they'd merely be giving us time to start all over again.

I did not reach the house until midnight, and only then remembered the letter Margaret Wood had given me. It was dated from Bhowani the day before. It was from Max. It began: *My dear Rodney, Some friends and I got together a week ago, and agreed that your tremendous talents are being wasted in your present job . . .*

The letter went on to offer me any one of five jobs: secretary of a club in Calcutta, another in Bombay; secretary of a racecourse somewhere else; top executive positions with two big industrial firms. It continued:

We have a good deal of influence, and can assure you not only that the jobs mentioned are all available and held for you, but that we can ensure that any previous misunderstandings between you and the Government of India will be forgotten.

In view of that last paragraph, Max must have got on to some of my I.C.S. friends. Senior Indians of the I.C.S. were quite indispensable, and the government knew it. Swallowing my peccadilloes, if the I.C.S. demanded it, would be no trouble at all.

The letter ended. *We – all your friends – do most sincerely urge you to accept one of these offers, and as soon as possible.*

Sumitra came in while I was reading, and leaned over my shoulder. When I had finished I put the letter back in its envelope, and burned it carefully in the grate, where a small fire sputtered – it was winter now, and cold at night. Sumitra said, 'Why do you burn the letter? Don't you want to keep it, for later . . . in case?'

I said, 'Max has to be protected against his own better nature. He could get into a lot of trouble, writing letters like that to English adventurers in the pay of the Muslim despot . . .'

I thought what a damned *good* man Max was. Max, my enemy. Max, the cuckold. Max, too big to think of that, only that I had shared a love for all that he loved, and I had lost. Max, oh, Max, I thought, what a God-damned bloody tragedy.

'What sort of a day did you have?' Sumitra asked. I leaned back and she gently rubbed her fingers through my hair, massaging my scalp, leaning over the back of the chair, her breasts warm and firm against my head. I thought, she talks as if I'd just come back from the City on the 5.06. And what have I done? Crawled about the jungles, nearly had three men executed, thrown a woman out of her house. I began to tell her, and when it was over, drowsily, lovingly, we went to bed. Got to ask her to marry me, I told myself sleepily. This must go on for ever.

Chapter 13

The daily bus left Lapri at seven in the morning, reaching
the capital four hours later. Margaret Wood, huddled among
the zenana passengers in the back, was grateful that she was
a woman, for the lightly drawn curtains, shielding the ladies
from the public gaze, also gave some protection against the
bitter chill of the upland morning. Later, exhaust fumes
filtering up through the floorboards, and the swaying of the
bus on the many corners beyond Sakti, made two of the
women sick, and she had a hard time holding down her own
queasiness. Usually, on these buses, the women chattered like
magpies all the way and she would be asked innumerable
questions about her family and children; but the tension of
the past months had seeped into the people's hearts. Few
talked, and they in low tones.

When the bus reached the alley which was its terminal
in Chambalpur, she climbed down and walked stiffly out into
the bustling street. There she stopped. Men passed her,
gaping inquisitively. The dark eyes of women examined her
through the mesh of *barqas*. She stood like a rock, awash
in a half-tide.

She realised that during her sleepless night she had decided
to come to Chambalpur to protest her banishment from
Lapri, but she had not thought whom she was going to
protest to. The government? Yes, but who in the government? The only man Henry had known was the Home
Minister, and she could not remember his name. Two or
three home ministers might have come and gone since Henry
died. The army then. It was an army order that Faiz
Mohammed had handed her. No, it was the Nawab's own
order, but given 'on account of the military emergency'.

Rodney himself had done it, and she bowed her head in
the street, remembering the sickening blow, like a kick in
the stomach. She had hurried out warm and expectant, and
seen his face, cold and harsh . . . He was a brigadier, and

worked in Army Headquarters. It was him she must face, whatever the pain.

She beckoned to a passing tonga and told the man to take her to Army Headquarters. Sentries stopped the tonga at the gate and she filled out a form, and a *chuprassy* shuffled off with it. She waited. Half an hour passed and the *Chuprassy* returned.

'*Nahin hai*,' he said, twisting his hand, palm upwards. Where had he gone, where could she find him? The man said something in Urdu which she could not understand. She asked him to repeat it and he said, in English, '*Millitairy see-crut*,' and grinned tremendously.

The tonga driver, who had been dozing in his seat, the tonga parked under a tree, called out, 'Who does she want to see?'

'The English brigadier sahib.'

'I know where he lives. I can take you to his house. He may be there.'

She climbed back into the tonga and the driver lashed the gaunt pony into movement. Rodney was living with that woman, the Rani of Kishanpur. The Indian papers had said so openly at the time she first went to Chambalpur. Margaret had no wish to meet her again. They had met once, exchanging a few polite words when she and her husband passed through Lapri on the way to Pattan. When she went through later, alone, Margaret had only seen her pass. Well, it was Rodney she had to talk to. The Rani would hardly force herself into such an interview.

The tonga stopped in front of a big house facing the lake. She paid off the driver and walked up the steps. A servant came, took her name, and left her on the wide veranda. The front doors were open, the tatty screen pulled up, and she looked into a marble hall hung with Bakhara rugs and aglitter with brass ornaments. The *chuprassy* returned at once, but stopped inside the hall, holding back a curtain. The Rani of Kishanpur glided through the doorway and towards her. Her violet sari made Margaret's own khaki shirt and white blouse seem sordid.

'Mrs Wood . . . Rodney is not in Chambalpur and won't be back until evening, I'm afraid. Can I help you?' She smiled pleasantly.

175

Margaret said stiffly, 'It is Brigadier Savage I wish to speak to, Your Highness.'

The Rani said, 'It's about the order to leave Lapri, I suppose? I know something about that. I can't promise to be able to help, I'm afraid . . . but won't you please come in? You look pale. You must have come up by bus. That's an experience to upset anyone.'

'I didn't think *you* would have travelled much by bus,' Margaret heard herself saying and knew that her face was still set in frozen dislike.

The Rani smiled again. 'Not much – but enough. I have taken many bus rides since coming here. You hear a lot, in buses, if you are hidden under an old *burqa* and let the other woman talk, as they're only too pleased to do . . . Please, Mrs Wood, let us be sensible. You have nowhere to go, you look hungry. Rodney won't be back till six at the earliest. Please come in.'

Margaret finally managed to say it: 'Thank you.' She followed the other woman into the hall, through the curtain again held back by the bowing servant, and into a big drawing-room. A voice was speaking in Urdu from a radio in the corner and the Rani listened to it a moment before switching it off. 'Mr Roy again,' she said, 'giving me another personal mention, too. I sometimes wonder whether the propaganda value of my coming here has not been out-weighed by India's ability to focus people's dislike on me as a personal symbol of treachery to the cause – their cause. Me and Rodney – the Traitress and the Foreigner . . . The rather ornate furnishings are not *my* taste,' she added with a gesture. 'This is one of the Nawab's guest houses. Make yourself comfortable. I'll get us something to drink.'

She walked out of the room, her hips swaying, and Margaret heard her voice, faint, from farther along the airy house.

The pictures on the walls were dreadful Italian oleos, and a huge imitation-Rubens nude hung over the fireplace. There was a low coffee table, and a Buhl cabinet that clashed with everything else in the room, some chairs and sofas, the radio, and a locked roll-top desk. And on the desk a big picture of Rodney in a silver frame. She stood in front of it. It was recently taken, an enlargement of a candid camera shot of him in his Chambal brigadier's uniform, smiling at someone off the picture to the left, his hair wind-blown and the clear mark of sun tan in the light values of his face. He looked wonderful, there, and so happy, but too thin round the jaw and cheeks, as though he were not eating enough and working too hard. This woman did not feed him properly.

She did not hear the soft glide of the Rani's returning footsteps and did not know how long she had been standing there, in the door. The first that Margaret knew was her voice: 'He is a man.' The voice was sad.

Are you going to get married? Do you love him? Aren't you ashamed of leaving your husband? Why don't you go back to him? A hundred accusing questions flew to the tip of Margaret's tongue; but she said only, 'Yes.'

The Rani changed her tone. 'Do you know why Rodney gave you that order so suddenly?' she asked matter-of-factly.

Margaret sank on to a sofa. 'I have no idea,' she began formally. Then the memory returned, the cold dislike on his face, the ice in her heart, spreading so that she thought she would never be able to move again. The words poured out: 'I don't, I don't! Once, months ago, I said I'd fix him, but that was when he was in Pattan and I . . . I didn't understand him, I didn't *know* him. He was so different from anyone I'd met, and Henry only just dead. But I *didn't* try to fix him, I didn't do anything. I explained all that when I was ill and he saved my life, and . . . '

'He saved your life?' the Rani said.

'Didn't he tell you about it?'

She could not believe that those days of her illness had meant so little to him.

'He saved my life,' she repeated. Her hands weaved and knotted on her handkerchief. 'I suppose he doesn't remember, but he did, and I did explain it to him and I thought he believed me, and then . . . and then . . . '

'Here, my dear, have a drink.' The Rani poured out a small glass of whisky from a decanter that had appeared on the table. Had the servant come and gone while she was talking, and she had seen nothing? She could see nothing now, except the Rani's face, and feel nothing except the whisky burning her throat.

The Rani said, 'He gave the order because he believed you had betrayed Gulu.'

'Gulu?' she said. 'Who's Gulu? I've never heard of him.'

'I don't think you would have. He's a Gond chief, from the Indian side of the border. He was working with Rodney to prepare the Gonds to rise against the Indians when the time came. Rodney had just heard that the Indians have arrested him.'

'Is he a small very black old man, wrinkled skin and . . . ? He must be the man I saw once with Rodney, near a jungle footpath up the hill behind Lapri. But I never said a word to anyone!'

'I know you didn't,' the Rani said sadly, 'but Rodney believes you did . . . I wouldn't worry too much if I were you. I think the clash between Chambal and India is going to come very soon, and then everything will be different. If India wins, it won't do you any harm to have it believed that you did give the information . . .'

'But I didn't,' she cried. 'And I don't care what the Indians believe if *he* believes that I was spying on him.' She collected herself. 'Another missionary is coming from England, at last. He is due in Bombay the beginning of next month. I only have to last out that long, and then . . .'

'And then what?' the Rani asked.

'The mission will . . .'

'No – what about you?'

Margaret wound and unwound her handkerchief. 'I . . . I don't know. I was just waiting, staying.'

'And you were as near him as you could get?'

'Yes!' She looked up quickly, but the other woman's face held no gleam of triumph or discovery. It was as unhappy as her own.

The Rani said, 'You are a trained nurse. How would you like to run a nurses' school?'

Her professional interest was touched. She said, 'You can't start a school, just like that. It has to be part of a hospital.'

'There would be no difficulty in getting you a post as senior matron of a hospital, and all the facilities you wanted to turn it into a first-class teaching hospital for nurses as well.'

'Where? Here?'

The Rani hesitated. 'In Chambal – yes. If India succeeds

. . . my direct influence will be nothing, but I can still manage that for you, anywhere.'

Margaret burst out, 'But what will happen to him, if Chambal loses? India is so strong. Mr Roy has openly threatened him, he has so many enemies, he has done so many things against India – oh, they're all in the papers, even more than he *has* done, probably. Where can he go?'

The Rani said, 'I'm afraid he will not live to be worried by that question. He is going to fight, to the end. If he does not die under Indian guns – *Indian* guns, O God! – he will die by a knife wound – someone here stabbing him in the back . . . And there are many kinds of knife wounds.'

'It's your fault,' Margaret whispered. 'If it weren't for you, he wouldn't be here, fighting this hopeless battle.'

The Rani's huge eyes burned with a dry flame. 'Some think that it was the other way round – that he brought me here, Mrs Wood. That if it were not for him, I would still be with my husband, and, through him, attached to the Indian cause . . . You love him. Don't attempt to deny it, please. I saw your face looking at the picture there.'

Margaret said. 'Yes. For a long time now I've known that Rodney is all I have to live for. All I have to live *in*.'

'What are you waiting for? Me to die? My God, you are like a vulture sitting on a tree.'

'I do not think you will stay with him. As you did not with the others, in Europe. I think, soon, that he will be alone again, and lonely.'

Sumitra gasped, then said slowly, 'I suppose that is deserved. I can see you will have him, if he lives. You have the tenacity . . . '

Margaret said, 'I told you. I have nothing else to live for. But he does not love me. He is not aware of me, except that I betrayed his friend. I know him well enough to know that he will never forgive a betrayal.'

Sumitra's hand trembled so that the jewelled wristlet shivered and clinked on her wrist. Her breathing came in gasps.

Margaret said, 'I will stay here until I see him. He must know that I did not betray him.'

'You must go,' Sumitra cried, jumping to her feet. 'About Gulu – I shall tell him myself. Yes, yes, I promise. What is it to me? Within a week it will be settled, one way or the other. He will be dead . . . he will be mine for ever . . . or he will never be mine, and this petty nothing about you and Gulu will be buried, forgotten. . . . I shall order your lunch now, and afterwards the chauffeur will drive you back to Lapri in my car. You will receive an order to Faiz Mohammed delaying your eviction for a week . . . Goodbye.'

She stood well away, and briefly joined her palms, then turned and ran out of the room, her sari rustling like a dying wind in the trees.

Chapter 14

'First, we will hear syndicate solutions to the problem. Then Brigadier Savage will bring out the main lessons, and I will sum up.'

General Gokal Singh sat down and I stood up, leaning on my pointer staff. We were running a cloth-model study based on an Indian attack up the Lapri Gorge. I had thirty senior officers of the Chambal Army there, divided into six syndicates. The cloth model, set out on the floor of a huge room that had been a reception hall, was about 30 by 60 feet and gave a very fair representation of the ground between Lapri and Sakti. After explaining the locations of our own troops, and two different versions of what the enemy might be doing, and putting out various flags and toys on the model to represent the troops. I posed the problem: How and where to engage the enemy? An hour later General Gokal made his little speech and I called on Colonel Nazr Ahmed to begin.

After the first two sentences I knew I didn't have to listen to *him*. My mind could run about among its numberless worries. Mid-January and our affairs fast coming to a head. The Indians were ostentatiously strengthening their garrisons along our northern borders. Prince Afif and I were convinced it was a feint. There was too much desert up there, too many miles of nothing, all open to our excellent air force. Gokal Singh, in command of the corps which was our only striking force, wasn't so sure, and we were having a hard time preventing him moving the armour and part of the infantry northward. I said flatly that the Indians would not come from the north. Gokal said with pointed politeness that the responsibility was not mine. I ground my teeth.

Our defence forces were standing by, some at thirty minutes' notice, the rest at four hours'. The morning cold was like a razor these days, until the sun rose. Then the shadows retreated fast, withdrawing like an army across the empty courtyards, leaving the bare stones bathed in dry golden light.

Two more syndicates spoke – unimaginative nothings. I called on the next. A young Rajput major stood up. 'Our object,' he said, 'is to draw the enemy's armour into battle piecemeal against our own armour, concentrated, and supported by all our anti-tank guns.'

I glanced up. This fellow had the idea. I made a brief note on my pad. The young major went on. He was good, at least on the theory of it.

The other syndicates followed. My opinion had been better expressed by Churchill: 'The answer is in the plural, and they bounce.'

. . . One of the fealty rajahs in the northern part of the State had refused to move his private army unless the Nawab agreed to transfer a few thousand acres of desert from a neighbouring barony to his. That quarrel had been going on for three centuries and now he saw his chance. The Nawab had flown up to beg his rajahs to be reasonable; or, possibly, to throw them both into the dungeons.

L. P. Roy had been on the radio, swearing that India would never use force in the solution of its problems. Nevertheless, India's patience was exhausted. Chambal's provovocation, Chambal's suppression of its people, Chambal's aggression . . .

Margaret Wood was still at Lapri, saved by Sumitra's soft heart. Gulu was still in an Indian jail.

The last syndicate gave its solution. I made a few more notes and began to dissect what had been said.

The vital point was obviously that Max had to get his armour out of the Lapri Gorge and up on to the Sakti Plain, by one steep, twisting road, in rocky jungle-covered hills. Numerically, our armour about equalled his. If we could attack him, with all our armour, at the moment when the leading half of his tanks had come out into the plain and the rest were still in the gorge, we would stand an excellent chance of destroying him completely – because he would either have to retreat or push forward the rest of his armour and let us destroy that in its turn. Max was no bloody fool, and there were many manoeuvres he could pull to circumvent us . . .

I won't go into any more detail. Of the six syndicates only one, the young major's, had produced a sound plan, because only he really understood what we were trying to do. Few syndicates had thought to use our air forces at all, and only two had used them properly.

My suppressed anger carried me into some harsh words. Why hadn't all these matters been studied for the past weeks and months? Because Gokal Singh insisted that secrets would leak out, plans become known. Yes, but there were ways round that, and anything would have been better than to leave these semi-trained officers in any doubt of their exact objective.

When I had finished a brigadier stood up, his face taut with spleen. 'My opinions are entitled to more respect than you have given them,' he said. 'I have twenty-eight years' service . . . '

'So had Frederick the Great's mule,' I snapped. The brigadier turned pale, and I expected Gokal to rebuke me. He certainly should have; and I would have accepted it and apologised. He did not and I thought, even in my fury, he *wants* dissension.

A second cousin of the Nawab got up. Oh, God, here it comes! 'Since I am of the Blood Royal, I *must* be right . . . ' It wasn't as bad as that. He wanted to know why I had not given the place of honour to the horsed cavalry squadron of the Nawab's Bodyguard.

Gokal summed up. He played both sides against the middle in a masterly appraisal in which he supported my solution in every particular, but ended by pointing out that the battle might not be fought anywhere near the Sakti Plain. Once again I suffered a sharp spasm of doubt, of suspicion. If we didn't fight on the Sakti Plain we would not fight at all. The Chambal Army had its virtues, but it definitely did not have the training or the confidence to fight after a long withdrawal.

I thanked General Gokal profusely and hurried out. I was meeting him again in fifteen minutes at the C-in-C's office. I had to rush upstairs and collect a secret file from my safe. The lock had been tampered with, and I swore, and congratulated myself on keeping all really important papers in the safe at home. Besides, this was very unlikely to be the work of an enemy agent. It was a henchman of the Nawab's, or of Gokal's, sent to learn what I had said to one about the other, and vice versa.

In his office the old C-in-C, General Prince Afif, was

squatting on cushions on the carpet, being fanned by a pretty girl and smoking an ornate hookah. The girl was some sort of slave. Oh, yes, slavery had been officially outlawed in Chambal a century earlier, to please Queen Victoria, but it still flourished.

Afif was a delightful old man and the soul of courtesy. He had made his battle plan: he was going to drive out to fight in his Rolls-Royce, the Rolls drawing a horsebox containing his favourite charger. He would wear the full war costume of the Bokharis, and would charge waving his scimitar. At the funeral a *mullah* would recite the appropriate chapter from the Holy Koran.

The business at hand was unfortunately more complicated. Gokal and I squatted on the carpet, facing the Prince. The old boy passed round the mouthpiece of the hookah.

I began the negotiating. I've forgotten now what the problem was, except that it ought to have been solved three months ago by a junior captain. Now a general, a lieutenant-general, and a brigadier thrashed it like a dog, for an hour.

We wrangled and fiddled on, the cloud of hookah smoke thickening and fine perspiration beading the girl's bare torso. Next we had to appoint a new paymaster for the guerrillas. X wouldn't do because he was already responsible for meat procurements – a lucrative post. Y had trodden on the Nawab's great-uncle's cousin's mother's nephew's toe at a reception in 1898. Not *him*, Allah forfend! . . . The centuries surrounded me, not in succession but all at the same time, in a frightening jumble. I was De Boigne, teeth set, trying to convince Scindia that if he didn't patch up his feud with Holkar, both of them would be swallowed by the Peshwa. I was Dupleix, listening while two maharajahs squabbled over precedence and Clive marched. I was a lone Amir of Sind, shouting, 'The English, they come!' to a tent-ful of torpid despots while Napier brought his troops into the battle line. The disciplined combination of intrigue, diplomacy, and brute force was on the other side, down there with Max and Roy and Nehru. *They* were Warren Hastings, Stringer Lawrence, and Eyre Coote; I, squatting on this carpet, was the old, free, chaotic India . . .

We agreed on a name. Next problem.

Poor old Afif closed his eyes in pain. We were giving him a headache.

Gokal stated his case. I stated mine . . . Wrangle, wrangle, wrangle. I had, in effect, won on the first problem, and I knew the C-in-C would rule for Gokal this time, and he did.

Military police to control traffic. There weren't enough. There ought to be. Something must be done . . . What?

Two hours later Gokal and I stood up. Afif remained squatting, looking very much his age. A *chuprassy* sidled in with a signal form, and handed it to him. He fumbled around for his spectacles. The girl found them and gave them to him. He put them on. He read the signal. He read it again, aloud. ' "Tanks, trucks and infantry moving from Bhowani towards Bijoli . . . Deciphered at 11.30 a.m." . . . Why wasn't this given to me sooner?' he said querulously.

'Prince,' the *chuprassy* whined, 'you were in conference. Your orders . . . '

It was a strict rule, true enough. No one could disturb the Prince when he had the girl and the hookah in there. It was now two o'clock and I was ready to die of hunger.

'You will move your troops, then?' the Prince said.

Gokal scratched his chin. 'Perhaps we should first inform His Highness . . . ?'

'We can't reach him till evening,' I broke in. 'He's spending the day out hunting with the Rajah at Maragan. We have his signature, approving this movement as soon as we get this information.'

Gokal said, 'It is a big decision to make without His Highness's knowledge. Action might precipitate war.'

I said, 'Sir, inaction might precipitate some executions.' I saluted, and went out.

In my office I told the *chuprassy* to get me food, quickly. The C-in-C sent me a note, telling me that he had ordered the troop movements, in writing, and I felt a little better. After eating I drove out to the barracks and found remarkable little turmoil. I was congratulating the Chambal Army, in my mind, on a higher state of training than I had thought it possessed, when I stopped behind a group of officers, under the brigadier who had been so angry at the cloth model. I found that they were conducting an exercise. It had only just begun, and they were doing it with live tanks. I counted forty of them out in the plain a couple of miles away.

I took the brigadier aside, saluting punctiliously and using 'sir' every other word, and asked him whether he had yet received the order to move. 'Yes,' he said, his eyes glinting nastily, 'but we are to finish this exercise first. After all, remember Drake finishing his game of bowls . . . '

'Yes, sir,' I said, 'but I understand that the C.-in-C gave definite orders for the move to begin at once.' By God, over an hour had passed since the order went out. The leading troops should have been ten miles out.

The brigadier became ugly. 'This is my business, Savage.'

I said, 'Sir, I assure you that Prince Afif has given his personal and most stringent orders to move at once, according to Plan Panipat. Any disobedience is likely to be punished by death.'

'That's very funny,' the brigadier said, with a wolfish grin. 'General Gokal told me personally, ten minutes ago, to continue my exercise.'

That's when I became positive that Gokal was on the other side. The commander of our striking force!

It was a moment of doubt and indecision. All at once the full weight of the situation came upon my shoulders. What was I doing, involved with these bunglers and traitors and idiots? How was it possible that I stood here, prepared to fight and kill Max, my friend, to whom I had handed my Colours, my country, my love? What possible hope of success was there, and even if we won, what possible hope of improvement, of progress? From all that I had seen, an independent Chambal, loosened from the stringent supervision of England, would go back to those jolly days when a Nawab could burn a couple of dancing girls alive for some minor peccadillo. (It was undoubtedly his right, since he was sovereign – but that had not prevented the viceroy of the time from summarily removing him from the *gaddi* and appointing his son instead.)

I should leave this bloody mess at once, go to Sumitra and ask her what was to be done. Hold a council of war with her, and Hayden, and the few other Englishmen in Chambal . . .

I remembered that all this had happened before: to Clive in the mango grove before Plassey. If Clive, the boldest man India ever knew, had had his moment of doubt, surely I could be allowed mine?

The thought of Gokal and his friends winning their victory exactly as they planned, from inertia, was too much for me. What a laugh they'd have, in the years to come, over how they'd hoodwinked the stupid Englishman!

I drove furiously into the barrack area. Gokal had vanished – east towards Sakti, it was said. I found two dozen tank transporters drawn up on the polo field, waiting. I told the major in command to take his transporters out to Brigadier Narain Singh and say, as from the C-in-C, 'Load! Move!' Then I went to the C-in-C's house and got him to send a personal order to the brigadier – to all officers of the corps – to get going. Then I drove back out to the barracks and watched for two hours while the order was obeyed. At five o'clock the movement was in full swing. Where now? Where was the focal point?

As far as I knew there'd been no diplomatic démarche, no ultimatum from India. We must get hold of the Nawab and bring him back to the capital. We must expect news that Indian troops were also advancing closer to our northern border. I must prevent the Nawab or the C-in-C detaching any part of our armour to face that threat. I decided that my place, for the moment, was here in Chambalpur.

I went to the palace and found Hayden, the ex-I.C.S. Englishman the Nawab had hired as constitutional adviser. There was some commotion in the streets and an unusual number of police about. I was not surprised to hear that half an hour earlier the Indian National Congress had issued a proclamation, calling on the people of Chambal to resist the Nawab's tyranny. Hayden had somehow contacted the Nawab, who was already on his way back.

Hayden said, '*Five* minutes ago the Home Minister ordered the arrest of Dunawal and all his crowd.'

Dunawal was head of the pro-Indian Congress group in Chambal. We had refrained from arresting him, thus far, in order to avoid provoking India.

Hayden said, 'All India Radio announced the arrest *twenty* minutes ago . . . It was all fixed in December. He was to take out an illegal procession, and force us to arrest him, on such-and-such a signal. He got it, he did it, we arrested him.'

'What now?' I asked.

He indicated a mass of paper on his table. 'Preparing this cable to the United Nations. It'll go off as soon as the Nawab arrives.'

'And what will the UN do?'

He shrugged. 'Just what they did in Kashmir.'

'Pakistan?' I asked.

He lit a cigarette. 'On the edge of bankruptcy. Their only real use was as a threat. Bluff, if you like. Nehru is calling it. Look, you go and get a good night's rest. I'll see that you are told if anything happens or they try to do something silly with the army.'

I drove home.

When I walked up the steps into the house the doors were open, and I left them like that, as I usually did. Sumitra was waiting for me in the hall, and the first thing she did even before kissing me was to go and close them. At once it became quieter in the house, and the load on my back began to lighten. I leaned on her, my hand on her shoulder, and she guided me like a sick man to the drawing-room. As we entered the room she left me and walked over to the radio. Someone was making an angry speech, and probably the speech piled more fuel around us, ready for the spark that invisible demons were even then carrying down from Indra's Abode of the Thunderbolt. At that moment I could not care. As the voice hiccuped into silence in the middle of a sentence I sank back into a chair and closed my eyes.

It took me all the early part of the evening merely to return to a full awareness of myself as a human being with ten fingers, ten toes, one nose, two ears, and the rest. I bathed and changed, I know. I ate, I know, but did not record it until afterwards when the sense of well-being that surrounded me included, I noted, a well-filled belly and a glass of liqueur brandy on the coffee table. I noted, properly then, the closed doors and the turned-off radio. For this night she and I would be alone. Let it be so.

Later we walked together to my bedroom, she now leaning against me, my arm round her waist and under her breast, her legs languid and her pace voluptuous. In the bedroom, having undressed myself, I unfastened the knot of her sari and she stood like Niobe, her eyes slightly averted and downcast, while the heavy silk slid slowly down the coppery satin of her thighs. I loosened her *choli*, and she extended her arms slightly so that I might the more easily draw it off them.

There are many degrees of love and sometimes it is easy to know what degree you are experiencing at a particular moment – as when the slim column of a woman's neck is all tenderness, all beauty, nothing else; as when the rough texture of her bush and the slippery passage between, contrasted with the daintiness of the underclothes she may still be wearing, jolts you with the electricity of desire; as when tired hands work for you, tired eyes search for the aches that they can soothe in body or soul, and you know only the dependence of love; as when, standing together against sorrow, there is only the dignity of love.

This was not such a moment, classifiable into its category, but one of the others, rare and so total that there is no experience like it except probably death, when all the degrees and kinds are fused into one, when you are overwhelmed by the simultaneous flooding over of every channel of your being. I saw her eye, large, the lashes curled upwards, brimming with the Madonna's bliss. I felt, pouring into me from her brain, her deep respect for me. Her generous spirit overflowed with no more and no less of grandeur than overflowed the secretions of her loins, soaking the rose petals between. The twin awareness of shared danger and affection thrust into my heart no less and no more than did the rigid, extended nipples crowning her full breasts. I could not tell, when I poured the liquid essence of my love into her, whether it was the commonplace of animal husbandry, the thing every bull has done to every cow since the world began, or whether it really was my life that I was giving her, all that I am, spiritual as well as physical. I know only that I was immeasurably increased – just as Christ said – by giving away all that I had. We did not make love, we were love.

When finally, this state of unearthly union having continued several hours, we could bear to separate the bodies that had served so well as the vehicles of emotions far larger than they could in themselves contain. I laid my hand upon hers and said, 'Will you marry me?'

I thought it sacrilegious to mention marriage after what we had shared, but in a material sense I wanted to weld the link, to let her know that I never would wish to escape from this mutual bondage.

She must have felt the same, for she said, after a time, 'My darling, is it necessary to decide that now? What more can life possibly give us, whether you put a ring on my finger or take me by the hand and lead me round the sacred fire? We have just been living *in* it.'

But now I was obstinately decided that the inward miracle should wear the conventional label for all to see and wonder at. 'Please,' I said, 'I love you.'

'I love you,' she said, and relapsed into silence.

After a time she said, 'Would you want to take me to England?'

'No!' I said violently. 'Here, here . . . Do you *want* to go to England?'

'No,' she said, 'but if you did, terribly badly . . . or if you had to . . . I could not go with you. At least, I didn't think I could before tonight. Now, I don't know. Could you ask me . . . in the middle?'

Neither of us could tell when such a miracle would happen again. And, no, I could not ask her anything 'in the middle'. Nothing existed, during the miracle, outside of it — so how could I refer to some exterior thought or event?

'Why England?' I said. 'We are here. We have work to do here. There is a sink of corruption to be cleaned up before the genuine ideals of the Chambal people can be realised. Who knows, perhaps our son will be prime minister, and finish what we begin.'

She took my hand and placed the fingers to her lips, and kissed them sweetly. 'I can't answer you now,' she said. 'I can say neither yes nor no. There is nothing left of my will or thought except you, and the knowledge that I touch you and lie beside you. Good night, sweet prince.'

I lay on my side, propped on one elbow, for a long time, examining the beauty that seemed to grow more troubled as the body that fed it sank into sleep, so that gradually the exhausted calm of the face began to ebb, the warm, wet lips to move without sound, the rounded thighs to twitch against me, and hair-fine creases to mar the broad forehead. Deeply stirred, and fearful, I thought I would never sleep, but sleep came upon me with so sudden and powerful an assault that I knew nothing until I awoke, tense and alert, in the house before dawn.

Where was the Nawab? What was Gokal doing down at Sakti and Lapri? Why did I dream our cruiser had opened fire on an Indian submarine? Had Max's boys crossed the frontier? What was Prince Afif doing? Birds chattered, and it was dark, one window wide open. A thin cold mist from

190

the lake filled the world and our room, so that neither eyes nor any other sense could find the line of demarcation between the mist and the night, or between them and humanity – we were all one, beings with no defined limit, Sumitra, and the mist, and I, and the lake.

I thought of Ratanbir. Where was the poor devil now, what thinking? How was he finding it, to live with wealth stolen from my trust? That hurt too much and I turned to curl up against Sumitra's back. In that instant I heard the heavy, dull crash of distant bombs, and the tearing roar of aircraft's multiple machine guns.

Sumitra sprang out of bed in one motion and crouched naked, staring out the window. The first light of dawn was coming, and the mist clearing. The crash and crash of bombs came from the northeast, about five miles away. Two Spitfires flew low over the city and I saw the Indian Air Force roundels on their sides.

I switched on the bedside radio and began to pull on the first clothes that came to hand – the shirt and dinner jacket I had worn last night. The radio was in the middle of an announcement, but it had nothing to do with the air raid. It was the Nawab's own voice, speaking in his classical Urdu. He repeated his announcement: 'We, Mohammed Akbar Bokhari, Nawab of Chambal, being independent of all earthly powers, by the Grace of God, being encumbered by no treaty or other hindrance, do hereby declare ourselves King of Chambral, to be known from this moment on as His Majesty King Mohammed I. In the name of Allah the compassionate, the merciful! There is no God but God, and Mohammed is the prophet of God.'

Then an announcer said it again, in Hindi, Gurjrati, and English, with a note that the announcement would be repeated throughout the day.

'Good!' I said. 'The old boy's showing his mettle.' That definitely committed us to break with India, even more perhaps than the air raid, still in progress. For the Nawab there was no turning back now, no chance of accepting a compromise. The proclamation definitely divided us into the sheep and the goats.

The announcer said, 'Attention!' This time it was about the air raid. Indian aircraft, without warning or shadow of justification, were attacking the peaceful inhabitants of

Chambal. Naked aggression – resistance to the utmost – keep off the streets – take cover – persons spreading rumours will be shot – victory.

Sumitra had dressed while I did, she also in the unsuitable finery of the evening before. She looked pale and frightened. 'Don't worry,' I said, hugging her. 'They're not attacking the city, and they won't, except perhaps with leaflets. They're making a surprise raid on the airfield – but most of our fighters aren't there . . . This is it, at last.'

'I'm not frightened,' she said, 'I'm afraid . . . '

'What's the difference?' I began.

Knock knock knock on the door. Who's there? Servant. A man to see you, sahib. He says it is very urgent. What kind of a man? A village man. The voice of the fat servant trembled with terror. Well, at least he hadn't run away, yet.

'He says his name is the Marquess.'

The Marquess came in, very tired, but his old eyes gleaming. He said, 'At ten o'clock last night, sahib, while I and another were hiding on the escarpment a little east of Dhain, a man came past, moving hurriedly and secretly. We hit him with our axes and he died. He was carrying this.'

He held out his hand and I took the envelope. It was addressed to Lieutenant General Gokal Singh in English.

'I cannot read English,' the Marquess said, 'but the other with me has worked with the cement factory, and he could. He read it. So I brought it to you.'

He was wearing only a loincloth and the high-backed slippers, his legs grey with the patina of age and the dust of travel.

The letter was from L. P. Roy. The text was short and clear: *My dear General, We agree with your proposal to keep your tanks on the south side of the Sakti Plain. Circumstances where a surrender would be proper will probably occur about 12 noon. If you will place yourself somewhere near the Sakti dak bungalow at that hour, bloodshed can be more rapidly brought to an end. We hope that shooting can be kept to an absolute minimum even before then. Sincerely.*

I folded the letter carefully and put it away in my trouser pocket. The old man had brought it eighty miles, through the night. God knows what feats of persuasion and bribery he had performed to get here, probably on returning supply trucks from Gokal's corps.

'All right,' I said slowly. 'Wait down in the servants' quarters. Tell them from me to give you food and drink. Be quick.'

He said, 'I must get back, sahib. There is fighting.'

I wheeled round, 'Fighting? Where? When?'

He said, 'The news has not reached you? . . . At midnight Indian soldiers left the gorge below Lapri on the north side and began to move west. They crossed the border there, and our men from Gidha ambushed some, killing two. I heard a machine gun just after we killed the messenger. The news of the Indian advance reached the post at Sakti, I know.'

I said, 'Eat fast, then, I shall take you back with me.'

He made a perfunctory salaam and left the room. Sumitra and I were alone, the sound of aircraft faint and far now. The click of the closing latch was like a trigger to my mind.

I said to Sumitra, 'What are you afraid of?'

She stood taller, her back straightening and her head coming up.

'Tell me,' I repeated, 'what are you afraid of?'

A hundred incidents dropped into their proper slots, like the latch, click click click, so fast that there was no sense of progression, rather of a whole pattern falling into place at once. There had been hints, careless words, inexplicable actions. She had not been careful, rather the opposite. Love is blind. Whom the gods wish to destroy they first make mad. There are a dozen proverbs to meet the case.

'You know,' she said.

Yes, I knew.

Once, wounded by bullets, I saw my blood flowing out of me on to the ground, staining it a dark red, and knew that at an uncertain moment the continuing outpour of blood would relieve me of consciousness, which I would welcome because my wounds then hurt severely. While I lay temporarily bereft of awareness and pain the blood would still flow out on to the ground, and after another time I would be relieved of life, and neither awareness nor pain would ever come back.

So it was now with the spirit, the soul, the whatever one calls it, however one defines it, which makes us human. That spirit, which had overflowed in love a few hours earlier, now flowed out of me on to the carpet, staining the whole world a pale grey. This time there could be no doctor, no comrade, no shell dressing to stanch the flow. The sharer and giver of love stood opposite me, the knife still in her hand. She did right to be afraid, but perhaps she did not then realise just why. It was not love for her that was draining out of me, it was my capacity for any love.

She broke down first, and flung herself to the carpet, clasping me round the knees. 'Rodney, my darling. I tried to show you, to let you know, so that you could send me away, at least protect yourself. I do believe in the new India. I know Chambal cannot survive alone. I know it cannot achieve what you believe in, because the Nawab, these men here, don't want it to! Your ideals are not theirs – but that doesn't matter. It's all over, and we can go now. I'll go anywhere with you, do anything for you. I can protect you against Roy, anyone. I have the Prime Minister's own word.'

It was she who had betrayed Gulu and the Gonds of Bhilghat, and allowed the blame to fall on Margaret Wood. She who had kept Gokal in touch with Roy. She who had caused Indian agents, their names given to her by Roy, to be thrown into jail, so that her own loyalty should be above suspicion. She . . . the list was too long. I felt strong, strong enough to strangle her with one hand. The flowing wound still hurt, but already I could feel the waning capacity for feeling. Unconsciousness, sleep of the spirit, would come soon, and then, while it slept, its death. Cauterisation might help. I must get to the fight, at once.

I said, 'I am going to keep my promises. Remember, sometimes, what might have come to us if you had kept yours. When they bow down and worship you, the heroine, the lady minister, the ambassador – remember. When you are lonely and alone – remember.'

'Rodney!' she cried. 'I have a car ready. We can go, we can hide in any one of a dozen places and they'll never find us. The Indian Army will be here tomorrow. Then you'll know how hopeless it all was from the beginning, how everybody here tricked you and used you and betrayed you, far worse than I have.'

I said, 'I don't want to know and, with luck, I shall not.'

She clung harder to me. Without deliberate effort, I threw her across the room. She crashed against the wall, fell to the floor by the window, and lay there, pulling herself up on her arms, weeping, her hair in the disarray of the night, after love.

I strapped on my automatic and its belt, went out, locked the door behind me, and called the servant. I told him the Rani was under arrest, on the King's order, and was on no account to be let out, or allowed to pass any messages to anyone. I telephoned Hayden, and after a delay got through, and told him. I tried to ring the commander-in-chief, but was told he had left the house in his car, with an aide-de-camp, a groom, and his charger in the horse box.

I found the Marquess eating cold chicken, left over from our dinner last night, watched by no one. Most of the servants were out on the lawn, staring at the sky. Some held leaflets in their hands. I took one and saw that it was an official notification from the Government of India, in three languages. In response to public demand, in answer to intolerable provocation, and to end the misrule of the Nawab the Government of India was temporarily taking over the administration of the State. Everyone was to keep calm, stay at home, and take no part in any fighting which the foolish Nawab and his wicked advisers might cause.

The Bentley's tank was full. I backed her out of the garage at high speed, pulled her round, and waiting only for the Marquess to clamber in beside me, rammed her out into the road. It was about eight o'clock. I gunned her along the boulevard round the lake as fast as the cold engine would take. Beside me the grim, fearless old man shook with terror. I patted him on the bare knee and shouted, 'Relax, father! If death comes to us today, it won't be in this machine.' He closed his eyes and held on tight.

There were no police about, and very few people, just one or two huddled inside doorways, staring upwards or reading the leaflets. I went through the winding streets of the city more carefully, and at the far end passed through the Bhowani Gate and out into the open country.

I pressed the accelerator against the floor boards and snugged down in the bucket seat, ready to drive as I'd never done. I saw a khaki staff car racing towards me under a cloud of dust. I recognised it as the air marshal's, just in time, skidded to a stop across the road and jumped out. I ran to his car, saluted (though hatless – a serious military crime) and said, 'What's happened, sir?'

'Lost three on the ground,' he said. 'Shot down one, chased the rest back. What's happening at Sakti?'

'I don't know,' I said, 'but Gokal's in Indian pay.'

He swore. 'That explains . . . He's just sent me a message —nothing to report. We have another raid reported coming in from the north and I've sent one squadron off to intercept it.'

I had been calculating and interpreting ever since the old guerrilla gave me the time and place of the earliest clashes. 'I'm going to Sakti, sir,' I said. 'I don't think anything serious can happen until near noon, perhaps eleven. Then we'll need every plane you can put over.'

'All right,' he said, 'I'll do my best . . . but the Nawab – the King – just called, ordering me to send *all* my planes north. I'm going in to protest.'

I saluted, got the Bentley out of the way, and we passed. I rammed my foot down, jammed the gears through the box without using the clutch. We had foreseen all this – the Indian feint attacks by land and air to draw our air force away from Sakti. Was the King trying to cut his own throat now? No, probably some bloody tinpot rajahling up north had telephoned that he'd go over to the Indians unless he was protected. Nothing more I could do about it.

The yellow sun climbed straight ahead over the hills. The air rushed past cool and solid, the tyres whined and even that old slow-breathing monster of an engine began to roar. After a minute the blower cut in and we went east behind a banshee shriek that sent chickens and children diving into the ditch and bullocks lumbering away across the fields. We left the Chambalpur plain, and the white stones marking the edges of the road flashed by. Bridges passed, the exhaust wavering against the pillars like running a stick along a railing . . . A dak bungalow, white under a red roof, set back in a clearing, whitewashed stones leading to the round arches of the veranda, two men staring at us. I could observe, but not feel. Past, present, and future blended, the material and the immaterial, as in the dawn.

That was the bungalow in the Dun where at dusk I brought back a thirty-pound mahseeer after a four-hour fight, knee-deep in the river. Twelve years ago? Ten? I remembered utter exhaustion, and exhilaration, but could feel neither.

One, two, five, six, fifteen bullock carts in file, steep hill, swinging down in the whining shriek of the tyres, past, behind. Army trucks, soldiers standing up in the back, staring up at the sky, blare of the old klaxon, past, behind. Tank transporter broken down, overturned, the tank upside down lower on the hill, men squatting round it, smoking, past. Another plain, open her full out again, and again the rising whine of the supercharger. Maize in the fields, women at the well, men with sickles, infantry marching in the slow dust column that infantry carry with them always, like the packs on their backs.

These are the fields, five hundred miles away, I marched through with the two stars of a lieutenant on my shoulders and not a care in the world, a field company of purple-black Madrasi sappers and miners in front of me. They couldn't speak a word of Hindustani, only Tamil and English, and I had to translate their occasional shouted comments to the pert girl children running and leaping beside them, pointing at their black faces. Tall stovepipe khaki hats and names like Coomaramangaladamaswami that made them all address each other by their numbers, very polite, 'Please, '498, adjust my left packstrap, for it is aching into my back.'

Rise of trees and jungle and the sun hot as fire against my eyeballs. Hills and rocks and the whitewashed stones again, dulled under dust, more soldiers, a long reach of scrub and a deer transfixed beside the road, monkeys crashing away in yellow green of the bushes. Down and around, this was the last hill line, the last gap, the plain of Sakti beginning to spread out, seen small, gradually larger through the trees as the road swung, tilting, fading, foreshortening as we reached the foot of the slope. Open land, rocks, almost desert, soldiers waiting in a dry nullah.

Dogras they'd been, a platoon of them under a jemadar, as soft spoken as the Madrasis, but high-caste pale-skinned Hindus, always decorous and well-mannered, escorting fifteen Mahsud prisoners back to the Political Officer after a North-West Frontier fight. Hardly prisoners, just men found wandering about the hills in their baggy cotton, with or without rifles, unable to account for themselves. I rode past with the Dogra colonel, him nearest the prisoners in the narrow nullah. One of them sprang out of the ruck and up at him, dragged him off his horse, a knife flashed, Colonel Dougherty struggling and kicking, both of them practically

197

*under the horse. The nearest Dogra ran his bayonet through
the Mahsud. Then no one gave an order, and I was bending
over the colonel, pulling him to his feet and holding both
horses' bridles with the other hand, and hardly realised what
was happening until I looked up. By then only two of the
prisoners were still alive, and the shy, quiet Dogras were
cleaning their bayonets. A sepoy methodically ran the last
two through the stomach. Then they set the colonel on his
horse, asked politely whether I was sure I had suffered no
hurt, and marched on.*

Tanks moving, far to the right, the south. If there was
firing, I could not have heard it. Many trucks jammed
together at the foot of the hill and the empty road running
straight as an arrow across the plain, to the clustered houses
of Sakti, and, on the near side, by itself, the white dot of
the dak bungalow. In the distance the line of hills, and the
cleft marking the top of the Lapri Gorge.

Many transporters were parked off the road. I stopped
the Bentley and called to the worried-looking major,
'Where's General Gokal Singh?'

He pointed up the road. 'At the Sakti dak bungalow, sir.
He's holding an orders conference, I think.'

'Thank you. Have you got a car to spare?'

'For a few minutes, I think,' he said doubtfully.

'This man is the leader of the local guerrillas, and must
get as far forward as possible, quickly. Send him up, will you?'

I explained quickly to the Marquess. He clambered out
of the Bentley, his legs trembled so much that he nearly
fell down. We shook hands.

Then I went on. I stopped the Bentley off the main road,
and walked down the driveway, between the inevitable
whitewashed stones, towards the dak bungalow. Staff cars
and jeeps lined the drive, nearly all flying pennants showing
the commands of their owners. A company of infantry was
waiting about in the compound, more or less at the alert.

Two sepoys with tommy guns and a *naik* with a pistol
stood on sentry at the foot of the veranda steps. The *naik*
held up his hand. I said, 'I carry a message from His
Majesty to General Gokal Singh. It is most urgent and
important.' I showed him the intercepted letter, trusting
that he could not read English. He saluted and stood aside.

As I walked up the steps I had no idea what I was going

to do. But on the top step I distinctly saw the Dogra who had saved Colonel Dougherty's life in 1937, his face unemotional, thrusting his bayonet forward in the long point just as though he were practising it on the drill ground. I quietly pushed open the double doors which, in bungalows like this all over India, lead into a central hall.

I knew exactly where everything would be. Sure enough, the hall was full of officers. Maps, map cases, and map boards covered the table and hung over the backs of chairs. A larger map was tacked to the far wall. General Gokal Singh, his back to me, was saying in Urdu: 'There is no need – ' It was a quarter past nine.

I drew my automatic as I went in, and shot him three times in the back of the head. He jerked, spewed a stream of bright blood across the maps, then lay still, sprawled on the table.

I said, 'He was a traitor. There's the proof.' I flung the letter on the table and swung round. The sentries burst in. They were Muslims. Holding the automatic on the *naik* I said, 'Wait. The Hindu general was betraying us. I act on His Majesty's own orders.'

They hung back, perplexed and doubtful. A brigadier began to read the letter out loud. 'It's true,' he said at the end. He motioned to the sentries and they backed out.

A colonel retched noisily in a corner. The rest, though they may have been listening with some part of their attention while the brigadier read the letter, stared at the mess on the table. Their faces were an unpleasant grey colour under the varying shades of brown, and, if I'd had to do this earlier, say the day before, mine would have been, too. Gokal's head was twisted sideways, revealing that the bullets had come out mushroomed, blowing half his face, one eye and a mess of blood, brains, and mucus on to the table. Sumitra would not have looked different.

I took back the letter and put it into my pocket. I hesitated a moment, and that moment of standing there, staring at them, may have had important effects later. They must have thought I had come out hotfoot, direct from the King, with orders to execute a traitor; and, obviously, to appoint someone in his place. But for a few moments I did not know what to do.

I could take over the corps myself. Then my credentials

might be queried, my authority demanded. Being super-seded in command was far more serious to most of these clots than losing a war. Certainly there would be frantic jealousy, and the consequences of that might be worse than the normal and to-be-expected incompetence. Some of the men in that room must also be in the plot to sell out to the Indians – but which? At that instant, not knowing who might have talked, or how much, someone was quaking in his boots, someone was wondering how to put me out of the way.

I made up my mind. I must work through the senior officer. I turned to the major-general commanding the infantry division, and – 'Sir, His Majesty charges you with the command, and appoints you to the rank of lieutenant-general . . . May I have a word with you in private?'

The major-general, Sher Khan, called for the sentries to come in. No one spoke while they lifted the corpse and half carried, half dragged it outside. Sher Khan said, 'The rest of you – get the mess cleaned up. Wait here.'

Then he and I went into one of the bedrooms. He bolted the door. 'There must be other traitors. Who are they?' he asked. 'I need to know. Otherwise I may entrust one of them with some vital job.'

He looked haggard and very old, though he was hardly fifty. You're probably on the edge of the plot yourself, I thought. I said, 'His Majesty did not reveal that to me, sir . . . Can you tell me briefly what is happening?'

Sher Khan stared down at the bed, his hands shaking. He pulled himself together with a visible effort and began to talk.

The Indians were advancing on a broad front – up the gorge itself astride the main road, and wide round both north and south flanks. None of the dispositions we had planned had been made. 'Gokal's orders,' he said miserably. 'He said – '

I interrupted him. What Gokal had said or done no longer mattered. He was dead. 'Have you had any identifications of units yet?' I asked.

'Yes,' he said. 'The 1/13th Gurkha Rifles on the north, and the 3/5th Mahratta Light Infantry on the south.'

'In the centre?'

He said, 'Tanks of the Central India Horse, and infantry 2/18th Royal Garwhal Rifles . . . They're going to have us surrounded if we don't pull back.'

I said, 'All those are in different brigades. My God, it can't be possible!'

Max and I, both commanding battalions, served in Burma together under a flatulent genius who had read too much American Civil War history and had a cold contempt for men whose skins weren't white. Inspired by this combination, he had launched us not once, nor twice, but three times, on grandiose double encirclements, like a boxer trying to hit his enemy on both ears at the same time. Needless to say, the despised yellowbellies had counterpunched straight back down the middle, smashed the pivot, overrun guns and headquarters, and left Max and me to get our battalions back as best we could, without ammunition, food, or medical help. It seemed incredible that Max was doing the same now. If all three of his brigades, and the armour, were in the line he had no reserve to speak of.

We sent for the intelligence officer and he gave us more identifications, more reports from spies and guerrillas. There could be no doubt about it. Max was committing a cardinal sin.

I talked rapidly to Sher Khan. A great victory lay to hand. His eyes began to gleam. Every soldier dreams of the laurels, of the people in the street saying, 'That's him, the man who won the Famous Victoree.' Sher Khan may have been on the edge of treason and he was not the most intelligent man in the world, but he could see this clearly enough. There were some technical points to be agreed, where to put the anti-tank guns, and when and where to commit the tanks – but the outline was plain enough. 'It only needs energy and decision, sir,' I said, 'and the will to fight.'

He was eager to go on, then. 'One moment, sir,' I said, 'I have another message for the officers, from His Majesty.'

The grey look returned to his face, but he nodded and we went through to the hall. The murmur of nervous conversation ceased. I stood there, suddenly aware of my dinner jacket. I took it off, for the day had become warm now. The white shirt and black bow tie did not seem so odd. I gathered their eyes to me. I began.

'Gentlemen, officers of His Majesty . . . General Sher Khan sees the prospect of a great victory before us. In a moment he will give us his orders to bring it about . . . We

201

have only to do our duty. His Majesty reminds you that you are fighting for the honour of your names as well as his. He repeats that we are fighting for our future as free men, for the right to rule ourselves in our own way, and not by the dictate of *babus* in Delhi. If we fail in our duty none of us will ever be able to stand straight and look another man in the eye. *We have eaten His Majesty's salt.*'

I watched them as I spoke. Some kept their eyes downcast and did not look at me. In others, a spark of spirit began to glow. I am no Churchill and there was little emotion in my words, for I could find none. But there was agate hardness, and ruthless determination.

I ended: 'I have one final message from His Majesty . . . ' I looked slowly round the room, trying not to load my glance too heavily with menace; I didn't want to *drive* anyone to desperation. 'It is this. His Majesty knows that this treason was not confined to General Gokal Singh alone. The action he will later take depends not on words or thoughts but on deeds – on what is done today.'

I saluted Sher Khan, left the room, and sat down exhausted on the veranda steps. Gokal Singh's body lay on the grass, covered by a blanket. No one went near it.

And the will to fight. Those were the key words. I knew why Max was coming on like an amateur. I had seen that formation many times before – in the military history books, in the diagrams showing the methods used in our old battles against petty rajahs, nizams, amirs, shahs, and mandarins, from Suez to Peking. I could quote the text, written about 1870: 'Against an Oriental opponent, too much manoeuvring is a waste of time and can lead to disorganisation. It is usually best to go straight for him, confident that a determined assault, pressed home, will cause his febrile enthusiasm, unbacked by discipline, to evaporate. A few scattered groups, led by individual brave men, may fight with desperation, and cause considerable damage, while the rest flee, but even this serves in the end only to destroy the enemy's leadership and break his cohesion . . . '

Max was treating us just as the old Indian Army had treated his ancestors. For 'Oriental' substitute 'old-fashioned', 'non-progressive', 'reactionary', or any of the other labels the Indian radio had been tying on to us for the past six months, and you had Max's tactical doctrine.

I got up, went back into the hall, and listened to the last part of Sher Khan's orders. The colonels and brigadiers hurried off. I checked with Sher Khan to make sure I knew what was planned. Then I got into the Bentley. Now my real job began – to force the commanders to fight.

I drove south across the plain, on rutted cart tracks, found a brigadier, and listened while he gave his orders. I went up to the battalion in contact and heard the sharpening of the fire, so much so that the Indian artillery, which had been very quiet, opened fire. But our men held them. Returning to brigade headquarters I saw an other battalion marching off post-haste to enter the general reserve for the great blow.

At twelve I ran back to the Bentley and drove to the main road. Max was getting annoyed, and now his medium artillery began to fire. The heavy shells whined overhead with an angry roar, and burst far back where the road came out on to the plain, where the transporters were parked. Other guns began to fire on the Sakti dak bungalow, since the heavier fighting had now made it obvious that there would be no rendezvous with Gokal Singh, no agreed surrender there. I found our tanks, concealed in scrub jungle, the men resting, the junior commanders studying their maps.

At two I went forward to the leading battalion on the main road, near the entrance to the Lapri Gorge. Here the shelling was heavy and the raw troops looked nervous as men were hit and trenches destroyed. The brigadier came round with me and I thought his men would hold long enough. They were due to pull back in half an hour. Behind them engineers worked with frantic haste to lay a minefield, on to which we would draw Max's armour when this lot retreated. I visited the anti-tank guns, which were concealed as carefully as possible – not very well, but one or two of our own fighters were always in the air, and the Indians had not attempted to come over.

Going back, on my circuitous way to the northern flank, I found the commander-in-chief's Rolls parked in a grove beside a small stream that crossed the road there. The old Prince, dressed in a magnificent Mogul costume of green and gold silk, was eating lunch off silver plates laid round him on the grass. His chauffeur was preparing a hookah, and the groom was currycombing the grey charger tethered to a tree.

He invited me cordially to share his lunch with him,

but I refused. He had no idea what the battle plan was and begged me not to tell him. He was sure it was good, but much too complicated for him to understand. One of the young colonels would come to him when the climactic moment was at hand. He looked very calm and sure, and before I left I knelt quickly before him, and placed my hands between his. He squeezed them and said, 'God be with you, Savage. You are a good man, a real sahib.'

Over to the north flank: the same situation as on the south – one of our battalions holding two or three of theirs, the rest gone into the central reserve. I drove back to the main road, begged food off the headquarters of a regiment of field artillery, and ate it quickly.

Crash! On the stroke of four o'clock Max's artillery opened up all along the front. He had stopped fooling, and begun his attack. Calls for defensive fire began to increase until they came in like a flood. From them, and the occasional situation reports, I could tell what was happening. On the south our men were pulling back, drawing the enemy farther along the slope. Over there I saw shells bursting in the distance, and clouds of dust rising on the ridge. To the north the same, but our men were retreating faster than they should. In the middle, reports of enemy tanks advancing under heavy covering fire. Our anti-tank guns in action. Two Indian tanks on fire, three . . .

Now was the moment. We had them trapped, just as we had planned – half his tanks on the plain, half in the gorge, and no reserve to counter ours. A heavy attack by our fighter bombers had been called for. The anti-tank guns and forward infantry only had to stand firm for half an hour behind the minefield while our own tanks moved up, with the reserve . . . They were on the way now.

The artillery colonel turned to me, his face anxious. 'The planes aren't coming.'

'Why?' I said.

'No reason given.'

Who'd ordered that, I raged. But perhaps it wasn't an order. Perhaps the Indians had raided the fields Perhaps . . .

'Call for SOS fire on A.36,' the gunner colonel said. I looked at his map. SOS A.36 was right in the middle of one of our forward positions. 'They've vacated it,' the gunner said.

SOS on B.7, also in the centre, also where the men were

supposed to be standing fast. The line was crumbling at the one point where it *had* to stand firm. Who was giving these orders? Where was the treachery now? The automatic itched against my side.

'Our tanks ceased their advance. Halted at 403621. That's a mile over there, on the north.'

Prince Afif rode by alone, on his charger, his scimitar on his shoulder. I jumped into the Bentley and tore up the road. Smoke and dust and bitter explosive fumes from bursting shells lashed at me. If I could reach the armour – if I could get to them, shoot the man who had ordered the halt, take command myself, find the young major, someone, anyone who had a fire in his belly . . . I rammed the Bentley along a cart track, turned right, raced it across country.

I knew what had happened: Max was right, the old textbooks were right – that was all. But there was still a chance. If I could just get to the armoured brigade . . . surely someone would stand fast over there, in the centre, when they saw their old Prince riding forward alone? Surely, just for a few minutes . . . ?

The rock outcrops concealed a sunken road. I bounced into it and turned left. The sound of aircraft distracted my attention and, looking up, I saw Indian Spitfires overhead. When I lowered my eyes I found myself motoring at fifty miles an hour straight at the dark-green hulk of a tank – a Sherman tank of the Indian Army. I stood on the brakes, and dived out while the Bentley was still moving. I heard the roar of the tank's '75, and felt the blast of the explosion as the shell ripped into the Bentley's engine. She exploded in flames but by then I was out of the sunken road and running across bare ground. There were other tanks behind the first and their co-axial Brownings tore the air into noisy strips about my ears. I saw a sort of depression near a low bush, and as I dived for it a mad mule kicked me in the back and hurled me into it.

I felt no pain then, only suffocation, and my breath trying to come in heavy groans. My shirt was getting wet.

Three or four co-axes were tearing up the earth by my head, like pneumatic drills, deafening me. They stopped, and a colossal explosion showered me with dirt. That was a turret gun again. One more of those would blast me to pieces. I staggered to my feet, wondering whether they'd bother to stop firing, whether they could. Someone might have his finger on the trigger as I rose.

I stood there a long time, one hand on my belly, blood pouring out over my fingers, hurting badly now, seeing nothing in the low glare of the sun. I thought I was in water, and swimming. Everything was silent. The tank engines must have been running but I didn't hear them. One of the tanks glided close to me and I tried to focus. Someone was leaning out of the turret.

'*Salaam*, sahib,' a familiar voice said. '*Ap kaise hain?*'

My head cleared with miraculous suddenness. The pain grew steadily worse, but I could see and understand very clearly. It was Rissaldar Rikirao Purohit, of the Bombay Lancers. I knew him well, because we had fought in Burma together. Also because he had shown me his family's most treasured possession, a faded letter commending Daffadar Rikirao Purohit of the Bombay Lancers for good work against a Thug gang. The letter was dated March 27, 1826, and signed by William Savage. His great-great-grandfather, and mine.

'*Salaam, rissaldar* sahib,' I said. '*Ap kaise hain?*'

One must observe the decencies. The rissaldar-sahib had asked me how I was, I had asked him how he was. Next must come a formal invitation to be seated, to have a cigarette.

'*Tashrif rakhiye,*' I said. '*Sigrit pijiye.*'

He said, 'Thank you, sahib. I regret I have to be going.' He ducked down inside the turret. On the sunken road the Bentley burned with an orange flame and dense black smoke. The man leaning out of the next tank I had also known in Burma and I saw that he was now a *daffadar*. I congratulated him on his promotion. 'Thank you, sahib,' he said, smiling from ear to ear.

Rikirao's head popped back up out of the turret. 'We have been ordered to stay where we are,' he said. 'There is perhaps a cease-fire. I think the enemy have surrendered.'

Agile as a cat he climbed out of the turret and ran to me. 'Your wound, sahib,' he said, 'it is serious. Does it hurt badly?'

'Only when I laugh, *rissaldar* sahib,' I said, and fainted.

When I came round I was sitting up beside the main road. I don't know how I got there. Rikirao was supporting me in his arms, my shirt was raised, and there were a couple of shell dressings over my wound. My nostrils reeked of iodine and it hurt worse than ever. My *daffadar* friend jabbed a needle into my arm. A group of soldiers were brewing up tea in a desert cooker – an old kerosene oil can filled with earth and soused with gasoline. A few minutes later a young *sowar* brought me tea in a mess-tin, but Rikirao said sharply, 'Not with a belly wound, O outwitted yokel. Are you trying to kill the sahib?'

Dimly I heard other voices. A staff car had stopped on the road. Max and L. P. Roy were walking towards me. Everyone saluted, and I managed to raise my hand to my forehead.

Max dropped to one knee. 'Rodney, are you all right?'

'My pistol went off by accident,' I said, 'while I was cleaning it.'

A high proportion of belly wounds are fatal. Internal bleeding would show its effect soon enough and then I'd go out. I didn't care.

Roy's voice said, 'Colonel Savage!'

'O-B-E-M-C,' I mumbled.

It was getting hard to talk straight, the morphia taking affect but the wound still raging, but one has to keep the natives in their place.

'Armed, in action, wearing civilian clothes,' Roy said. 'I warned you.'

'General Gokal . . . invitation to breakfast,' I got out. 'Said, come as you are.'

'And we have half a dozen witnesses to prove that you murdered General Gokal Singh!' Roy shouted. He was furious again.

Max interrupted roughly. 'That can be settled later, sahib.' He rattled off orders: 'Get up the jeep ambulance. Take him direct to the C.C.S. You, go with him.'

Roy said, 'I shall hold you personally responsible for his safe custody, General.'

Rikirao said, 'I'll take him back myself, sahib.'

'Only when I laugh,' I mumbled, seeing no one any more, trying to shout it against the encroaching darkness. 'Only when I laugh . . . only when . . . ' I lost consciousness, my last thought being a certain knowledge that whether this dark slope led immediately to death or not I would never laugh again.

Chapter 15

Major-General Ran Singh Dadhwal, comfortably settled in the canvas chair in his office tent, slowly filled his pipe. Through the open end of the tent he looked out over the plain of Sakti, dull in the twilight. The single bulb, hanging from the ridgepole by its cord, came on, gave out a wavering light, and faded. The general frowned, listening with half an ear for the kick and the throb of the generator to start again. When it did, he noted that the current was still unsteady. He took a notebook from his pocket and wrote briefly.

A chill wind blew round the group of headquarters tents and trucks scattered among the trees at the eastern edge of the plain. The sun had just set and an even violet light spread across the sky. A burned-out-tank stood like a ruined monument in the plain, about a mile away. Farther off, the village of Sakti lay under the blue haze of its cooking fires. It was the third day after the battle.

The general finished filling his pipe and methodically found his matches. He kept them always in his right-hand tunic pocket. He lit one and held it over the bowl. With the second match the pipe began to draw well. The general blew out each match in turn, held it until he could break it, then dropped the halves into the ash tray on the table beside him. The second time, he noticed a small hole in the green baize laid over the table. He pulled out his notebook and wrote: *Camp Comdt, hole in my baize.*

Behind him, on another table in the far corner of the tent, flowers and offerings of *gur* lay at the feet of a small statue of the monkey-god Hanuman, his own personal avatar. Beside the statue, on one side, stood portraits of Mahatma Gandhi and Jawaharlal Nehru; on the other a portable bookcase, containing the *Mahabharta, King's Regulations,* the *Ramayana,* the *Indian Army List,* the *Bhagavad Gita,* the *Life of Robert Clive, Memoirs of the Emperor Baber,* and Wavell on *Leadership.*

The general heard a discreet cough outside the tent and

saw the tips of a pair of brown shoes. A voice said, 'Sir . . . it is Major Gupta. You sent for me?'

'Yes. Come in.'

A small dark fat man sidled apologetically in, saluted, and stood at attention just inside the tent flap. The general said, 'I wanted to ask how your patient is . . . Colonel Savage.'

The fat major said, 'The A.D.M.S. saw him again this afternoon, sir. Of course we cannot be sure, but bullet seems to have made clean passage without puncturing intestine or wital organs. He has been suffering from obvious shock, but owing to good general condition he is making rapid recovery from that. He is somewhat weak, naturally. Temperature 101.1, pulse 95, poor wolume, and increased rate of breathing. Unless A.D.M.S. diagnosis is wrong though, and it is confirmed by X-rays, he should recover after suitable period in base hospital.'

'Is he ready to be moved?'

The major said: 'If moved carefully, yes. He has excellent powers of resistance . . . I found him out of bed just now, sir, standing by exit. When I insisted he must get back he said he was looking for nurses' quarters. He needed a woman and told me to send him a nurse at once.'

'And doubtless you told him sexual intercourse was contra-indicated until his wound has healed properly?'

'Yes, sir. Of course! I explained the effect on the walls of the stomach tissue and the drawing away of blood, the general strain on muscle. Besides, I said his request was impossible, as there are no nurses with a field ambulance. Besides . . . '

'It's against Army Instructions, India, to have sexual intercourse with nurses.'

'Precisely, sir. Also . . . '

'Also, it is not a nice thing to suggest, being insulting to Indian womanhood. No, for God's sake, don't agree with me . . . I want to talk to him. He has important information I need. Could you bring him here?'

The major said doubtfully, 'I think so, sir. Of course, in absence of military necessity, on medical grounds alone, it is not to be recommended, but . . . '

'Bring him now. Wait – I suppose he has no clothes?'

'No, sir. What he was wearing was evening dress, mufti, without coat, and in wery poor condition, quite u/s. I have made out destruction certificate . . . '

'I'm sure. Give him these. I think they're about the right size.' He got up and handed the doctor a small roll done up in a faded blue *durrie.*

'Yes, sir. Thank you, sir.' The major saluted and backed away.

The general sat down again. Bloody silly little man. With a fellow like that in charge, perhaps it wasn't really necessary to make any special arrangements. Rodney was more than capable of dealing with him. But at any moment they'd send him back to the main military hospital in Bhowani, and that would be different.

Why did so many of the new generation take themselves so seriously? It wasn't like that in the old days. Look at Brigadier Moti Yasurvedan, Moti the Menace, with his monocle and his hackin' jacket down to his knees, motoring off to take over the pacification of Chambalpur. Moti's command car was always followed, at a respectful distance, by a three-ton truck with armchairs, sofas, silver, linen, a small four-poster bed, and a portable bar. Moti, when on outpost duty on the Frontier just before the war, had left his squadron to his *rissaldar,* with a thousand copies of his signature, and flown to Paris. And would have got away with it if he hadn't run into his colonel in Maxim's . . .

The general chuckled and wondered how much longer the teams playing cricket on the plain could continue in the rapidly failing light. With the pitch as rough as an obstacle course, they must have been playing by radar even half an hour ago.

A steady crunching of boots on the dry leaves made him turn his head to the left. He saw his A.D.C. striding through the trees, shotgun on shoulder and English pointer quietly at heel. He called out, 'Any luck, Chop?'

'Not a bloody thing, sir. The birds must have been frightened by the noise the other day. They've probably reached Cape Comorin by now.'

The young captain disappeared. The general relit his pipe. There were good ones in the younger crowd. And certainly the British had plenty of bad ones. All the same there was a loneliness . . . it took a lot of effort to combat it. He missed them – even Talbot, even Byrne, whom he'd fought to earn his nickname. What a narrow-minded blighter

Byrne was – wonder what he's doing now? Never got very far, retired as a lieutenant-colonel right after the war, probably pig farming in Essex. He was a blighter, all right. But no one ever had to tell him when to blow his nose, what attitude to adopt. He made up his own mind, and never asked anyone's permission. No one had to give him lectures about *esprit de corps* or work to convince him that he was the best in the world. He knew it.

That was it – confidence. Very unpleasant when it led to kicking Indians out of first-class compartments and yelling about Wog music, but, oddly enough, it hadn't cut them off as much as you'd expect. They never shouted at *sowar* or sepoy. Their manners to the V.C.O.s were wonderful. Say a word against Dogra or Mahratta or Garwali – whichever *they* happened to be serving with – and it was worse than imputing sodomy to the King. Their viceroys lived and moved like monarchs – wasn't it Edward P. who said he never really knew how royalty lived until he stayed at Viceregal Lodge? – but the rest didn't give a damn for the Viceroy, and not much more for the commander-in-chief. Ride hard, play hard, don't ask questions, never doubt yourself or your regiment . . . The gap they created was between themselves and the Indian upper-middle class – his own. He'd never seen an Englishman until he left the little village where his father owned land to go to school. Now they'd gone – and everything about him breathed of them, and again the laurels of victory crowned the Colours they had devised and set up as symbols, and now given into his hands.

He went out and beckoned to the Sikh military policeman sitting on a bench ten yards away. The Sikh leaped to attention, saluted, and ran up. The general said, 'Have the *jawans* eaten?'

'Not yet, sahib. We are eating by turns.'

'The war is over. You can all eat together tonight. Go now, and get your tot of rum. You needn't come back until ten. Enjoy yourselves. *Sat sri akkal!*'

'*Sat sri akkal!*' the soldier replied, saluting with a broad smile.

The general looked at his jeep, parked behind his tent, and called, 'Harnam Singh!'

Another Sikh popped out from inside the guard tent. 'You, too. Off you go.'

When the driver had followed the military policeman, the general took his red divisional flag off the jeep's fender, rolled it into its khaki cloth cover, and carried it back into the tent.

Another jeep puttered up. Major Gupta and a medical orderly helped Rodney down from the seat beside the driver. Rodney came forward, leaning heavily against the doctor. Max noticed that the khaki sweater, green trousers, and woollen shirt he had sent fitted him perfectly. About the boots he couldn't be sure, but they looked all right. He saw by a bulge at Rodney's pocket that he had the beret tucked away there. That was important. The M.P.s were demons on correct dress – as he'd insisted they should be.

The general pulled forward another canvas-seated chair and Rodney lowered himself into it. The general said, 'All right, Gupta. You can go now. I'll call you when I'm finished . . . Are you comfortable, Rodney?'

'Yes, thanks.'

'Excuse me a moment.' He picked up the field telephone on the table and said, 'C.I.E.M.E., please . . . Divisional commander. Are you ready to talk about the tank recovery state yet? . . . Good. No, give me a ring here in . . . twenty minutes.'

He put down the handset and smiled at his friend. 'Sorry, I don't have any of your awful cheroots. How are you, really?'

'Not bad. A little weak, but not as weak as Gupta thinks . . . That field ambulance is a bit of a mess, Max. Anwar's a good doctor and so's Gupta, but they've got no idea of administration. The orderlies play cards all day, the jerries aren't emptied, they keep running out of rations . . .'

Max said, 'I've had my eye on it for some time. Thanks . . . Rodney, I don't want to be melodramatic, but you're in danger. Roy got a dispatch out – I had to end military censorship as soon as they surrendered – and now the press and the government know all about you. Did you have to shoot Gokal?'

Rodney said, 'Either that or lie down. I told you I'd fight, one day.'

'I didn't like him myself . . . You can go home without feeling you've failed, Rodney. I was thinking, before you came – so much that I see and touch and feel is yours. You're

212

leaving something pretty good, at least I think so, and a few hundred thousand others like me. And you're taking a lot with you, too. You can't leave your memories behind.'

Rodney held out his hands slowly. 'Empty-handed,' he said quietly. 'Beaten . . . how did the 1/13th do?'

'Very well. Forty casualties. I don't suppose they'd have had any, except for you.'

'One does what one has to.'

The general sighed. 'I know . . . Look, there's no time to waste. In a day or two, even by tomorrow perhaps, you will be on your way, put into the machine. To the C.I.M.H. in Bhowani. Then – to Delhi jail, I suppose. Is there anyone you want me to tell? Your father . . . ' As soon as he had said the words he remembered, but it was too late.

Rodney said, 'My father is dead. He was killed during Partition, on a very appropriate date as a matter of fact – August 14, 1947, the day before Independence.'

Max said, 'I'm sorry.'

Rodney was looking down at the table. 'I should have been up there with him, with Pete Rees on the Boundary Force. I wasn't. I was in Bombay, seeing about getting a job with McFadden Pulley. Perhaps I would have been killed up there, too. And then we would have all come to an end tidily, no loose ends, exactly on Glamorous Dickie's schedule . . . It's rather wonderful to think of Attlee and the Admiral, with about three months' knowledge of India between them, breaking up in half a year what it took us two centuries to build. Not only that, but getting the whole damned lot loaded on to ships, pushed under the carpet, or at least disposed of somehow. Only they moved too fast for me. I got left over, me and five hundred rajahs. They, poor simple-minded saps, went round waving the treaties in which the Noble British Government guaranteed them their independence. They actually thought the Honest British Sailor would concern himself to see that those silly scraps of paper were honoured. I didn't *have* a piece of paper . . . You had no business to accept the partition of India, Max. No business to ride over the princes like a gang of Nazis. You only had to wait a few years, and do it honourably, even if it meant having us around that much longer. Twenty years from now this won't be the army you knew – you're brutalising yourselves, and India.'

213

Max said, 'I don't know . . . I feel a bit dirty, in a way . . . But we'd waited a long time already. Time seems different from inside a jail, even though you think the jailer has tremendous qualities. And I suppose there comes a time when you have to tear down something, so that you can start to rebuild. The princes really were out of date, a sort of political slum, somebody called them . . . Janaki's in Bhowani, at Flagstaff House. There's no sentry at the back where that lane runs along the garden hedge.'

The telephone rang. 'Divisional commander . . . Yes, it is urgent, as a matter of fact, and I want to see that damaged gun for myself. I'll be right over.'

He stood up, and picked up his red-banded hat. 'I have to go to the C.I.E.M.E. I'll be back in half an hour.'

Rodney said, 'All right. By the way, you'll find three men of Pattan in the Chambalpur dungeons. Their names are Chadi, Mitoo, and Ganesha. They probably ought to get a medal. Better still, give them some cash from the imprest before you have to go back to peace accounting.'

The general made a note in his little pad. 'Thanks,' he said. 'I'm glad about them. Roy had an idea that we might be able to add them to the charges against you, if we searched hard enough in the jungles.' He went out, glancing back once. His friend was sitting with his head in his hands, staring down at the table. He looked ill and tired and bitter. The general turned back, and said in a low voice, 'For God's sake, Rodney, no more violence.'

The man at the table nodded without looking up. The general went out and walked quickly and quietly through the trees towards a cluster of lights a hundred yards away to the east.

He had hardly reached it, greeted the waiting colonel, sat down inside a tent similar to his own, and begun to examine the chart spread out before him, when the telephone rang. The colonel picked it up.

'C.I.E.M.E. . . . Yes, he's here, sir.' He turned to the general. 'It's L. P. Roy, sir. He's on his way through from Chambalpur and wants to speak to you. He's in your tent.'

The general swore silently. 'Tell him I'll be right over.' he said. 'This will have to wait.'

He walked slowly back to his headquarters. His jeep was

still standing behind his tent. A government car with a civilian driver sitting behind the wheel was parked close by. Sheer, rotten luck! Rodney had looked fit enough to drive eighty miles, and, dressed as a sepoy, with his command of Hindi and no M.P. likely to stop him, he ought to have got through to Bhowani without trouble in a couple of hours. Trying to escape on foot, through, in his state . . .

L. P. Roy was seated in his chair and the general felt a small stir of resentment. Why did the damned man have to keep emphasising his superiority over the military? They'd done what they were told, hadn't they?

Roy spoke in English. 'Good evening, General. All is quite well in Chambalpur. We have installed Dunawal as temporary chief minister, and he hopes to form a provisional government by tomorrow. I am on the way back to Delhi to report of the Prime Minister. I am going to catch the night train at Bhowani. I would be glad if you could give me something to eat.'

'Delighted.'

'Thank you. While we are waiting, I would like to see the prisoner, Savage.'

'All right,' the general said. 'Would you care for a drink?'

Roy waved his arm. 'I do not drink, as I think you know, General. In fact, I recall advising you that the alcohol habit was un-Indian and a relic of British imperialism.' He stood up. 'Let us go and see the prisoner now.' He looked fanatical and bitter – as bitter as Rodney, Max thought. What did *he* have to be bitter about? He wished he had the Prime Minister to talk to, to explain to, instead of this hot-tempered, bigoted politician. Nehru had his faults, but ungenerosity was not one of them – and he was a gentleman.

He thought slowly, now what's the best way of holding Roy off for a little? He had promised Rodney half an hour. So far only twenty minutes had passed. Of course, Rodney wouldn't need the time so much, going on foot. He could be anywhere, whereas in the jeep he could only be up or down the road.

'Let us go,' Mr Roy repeated impatiently. His white Gandhi cap sat straight on top of his thick hair, and his dhoti was spotlessly white.

'Sir . . . General Dadhwal . . . ' The fat doctor peered into the tent, saluting. 'Sir, it is my medical duty to adwise

215

you that the patient should return to the hospital now. He has been here nearly forty-five minutes, and that . . . ' He peered round the tent. His face took on a comical expression of surprise, then fear.

Max thought of saying he'd sent Rodney back to the hospital. Then they'd all go and look for him there – but Gupta had just come from the hospital and could say he hadn't arrived. Besides, Roy was sharp as a knife, and it was too late.

'You left the prisoner here,' Roy snapped, 'with General Dadhwal?'

'Yes, sir,' the doctor stammered, 'forty-five minutes ago. I . . .'

Roy waved a hand. 'Go, go!'

He turned coldly on Max. 'We will hold you responsible for this, General! I promised Savage that he would pay dearly if he opposed us. You will face a court-martial, and it will not be packed by your friends. There are some generals who understand there has been a change in India!'

Max said nothing. The longer Roy spoke the longer it would be before he would have to give any effective orders to recapture Rodney. 'I was going to recommend you for a high order, and promotion, for your good work in this affair,' Roy snapped. 'Now I will withdraw those recommendations. Unless Savage is found, at once!'

Max said, 'You must do whatever you think fit. We all must. Personally, I think you are being petty.'

Roy was not really a bad or petty man, just a product of his nature and the political history of the past thirty years. But he was famous for two things: his fanatical hatred of the British and his short temper. Max hoped to stir the latter into further time-wasting fulminations. He succeeded.

Roy raised one shaking hand and waved it in the air, stabbing and slicing. 'Watch out, General! Watch out, you and your Sandhurst friends! We have had enough of this Sandhurst spirit. You are servants of the people now. We don't want your polo ponies and English tweed coats while the people starve! What did you do in our fight for freedom, but toady to the English!'

Max said, 'I was taught to stand by my obligations, Mr Roy, at first in my home, by my father, and also, later, at Sandhurst. I was taught to obey constitutionally given orders whether I agreed with them or not. I took the English government's arms, and their training, and if I had betrayed them, how do you know I wouldn't betray you? I have an armoured brigade and an infantry division here. General Usman has a corps in Kashmir. General Rajbir has a corps in the south. Would you like any of us to forget what we were taught?'

'That would be treason,' Roy said. 'You are under oath to defend the constitution.'

'You are wrong, sahib. I am not under oath. The British never made me swear an oath, nor has our own government since Independence. What really matters cannot be put in writing, or sworn to by oaths. That's why you are safe, and that is why my friend Rodney Savage, an officer of the Indian Army, will have at least one more half hour before any attempt is made to find him. Some Indian traditions have to be sacrificed for the future of India, but not personal loyalty. At least, not by me. *I have eaten his salt* . . . If you wish to report the matter to the Prime Minister, I shall be pleased to accompany you to Delhi. Now I am going to have a drink.'

He turned his back, opened a drawer in the table, and pulled out a bottle of whisky and one glass.

'Have you got another glass?'

The woman's voice was low and tired. Roy and the general turned. Sumitra, Rani of Kishanpur, stood in the entrance to the tent, leaning against the pole, her palms joined in *namasti*.

Roy hurried forward. 'Your Highness!' He seized a chair and pushed it forward. Sumitra sat. 'I searched everywhere for you in Chambalpur, but could not find you.'

'I was . . . in retreat,' she said.

'India owes you a great debt. I have messages for you from New Delhi . . . You did not know, General, that Her Highness was our chief agent inside Chambalpur?'

'I did not,' Max said curtly. 'Until the All India Radio announced it after the surrender.'

Sutmitra looked up, her hands spread pleadingly. 'I believed in the policy, Max. I made up my mind to do all that I could, months before Rodney came to Kishanpur that time . . . as soon as I really understood that India was free and there was work for me in shaping and building it.' Max

217

continued to look at her, his face stern and sad. She threw out a hand towards him. 'My God, Max, I tried to warn him, but in the end I was caught, just as much as he . . . Where is he? In hospital here, still? I've got to see him. Perhaps he feels better now. He did his best. No one could have done more, and he must see now that what he wanted to achieve was hopeless from the beginning. If only I could have persuaded him of that, before we went to Chambal.'

'Then he would not have gone, or taken the Nawab's pay,' Max said coldly.

She drank the whisky. Roy stood behind her chair, listening, surprise growing in his face. 'But you did not really care for him, Your Highness!' he cried. 'He is an enemy of India!'

Sumitra ignored him, and spoke to Max. 'I wouldn't do it again, if I could start at the beginning . . . It wasn't worth it, but how could I know? Anything seemed worth it, for the new India.'

'It is,' Roy said emphatically.

Max said, 'Murder? Deceiving people who love and trust you? Turning in your own mother to the police? If you think those are worthwhile, for India, it isn't a new India you'll create but a new Soviet, a new Nazi Germany . . . Rodney has escaped. Sri Roy and I were just discussing the best method of recapturing him.'

The Rani's head sank into her hands. Max saw that she was weeping. 'Alone,' she whispered, 'alone again, in the jungle, wounded. If only I'd come earlier!'

'He wouldn't have listened to you,' Max said. 'Here, have another drink.' He patted her shoulders awkwardly. 'I'm sorry I spoke like that just now. I didn't know you had . . . I didn't know.'

Roy's face was unexpectedly gentle. He had got over his temper. 'I am sorry for both of you, but I, too, have my duty to do – a larger duty than either of yours, if you will excuse me. I shall give the necessary orders myself.'

Max called after him, 'No one will obey you. Just wait a bit, please.'

Sumitra raised her tear-stained face. 'Has he gone?'

'Yes.'

'I couldn't bear the look in your eyes, Max. My father and mother are dead. There's got to be someone in the world who knows. I'm going to have his child. He doesn't know.

Only you. Not Janaki, nor Dip, nor anyone else at all yet. Only you. So that there'll be one human being's eyes that will look at me with sympathy.'

She rose unsteadily, and Max, silent and appalled, helped her into the open air.

Chapter 16

Margaret Wood pushed the falling hair back out of her eyes and began on the second shelf of the *almirah* in the corner. *Almirah* was the Hindustani word for 'wardrobe', but to be a true *almirah* it had to be this kind of wardrobe – rickety, creaky, liable to fall over on you if you tugged too hard at the door, the wood warped by forty hot weathers and forty monsoons.

One, two, three . . . four pairs of sheets for the double bed, all of them patched and frayed at the hem from the vigorous beating the *dhobi* gave them on the flat stones by the river below Lapri. She didn't need double-bed sheets. She could cut them in half. But that would make eight pairs – more than she'd need. She glanced down at the wooden, iron-banded trunk on the floor. Everything had to get into that, and one suitcase.

She took two pairs of sheets from the *almirah*, folded them and packed them in the trunk. The others she laid on a pile of linen and clothes in the corner.

Pillow cases . . . face towels . . . bath towels . . . The same insoluble problem every time – no space to pack all that she would need, no money to buy more when she reached wherever she was going.

She was folding the towels too small now, so that they made a needless bulk. They'd go better with only one fold. She knew that quite well. Henry used to say she was a wonderful packer, a wonderful, efficient woman. Where had all that gone? Vanished, with the sense of purpose. Could an aimless, unhappy woman pack well? This khaki shirts, four. She'd better take two and wash them herself, like her underclothes. She held up a petticoat in disgust, and threw it on the pile in the corner.

She heard the fast-approaching roar, easily recognisable, of a jeep, and glanced at her watch. Eleven o'clock. She'd have to stop soon or she'd fall asleep over the trunk. The jeep engine stopped outside and she raised her head. Nailed boots ran up the front veranda steps, knuckles beat on the door. She climbed to her feet and opened the door. The light from the narrow hall where she was packing shone on the face of a young Indian lieutenant.

He saluted energetically. 'Mrs Wood?'

She nodded. The jeep headlights shone across the weeds of the lawn towards the chapel and the gravestones. She saw the dim shapes of two soldiers with cradled rifles in the jeep, behind the glare of the lights.

He said, 'A prisoner of war has escaped from hospital up the road. He is on foot, and armed, and we are warning all villages to be on the lookout for him. There is a reward of five thousand rupees for any information leading to his capture.' He looked embarrassed, and his glance turned away from her. 'He's an Englishman, about five feet ten, very sunburned, blue eyes – Colonel Rodney Savage.'

'From the hospital!' she cried. 'He's hurt? But All India Radio said yesterday that he was in jail! If I'd known . . .'

The lieutenant said, 'I suppose they wanted to keep it secret, until they really had got him to jail . . . You know him? He was wounded in the stomach, quite badly, but he was recovering well until he escaped.' He looked full at her. 'It's Mr Roy who has ordered the reward . . . My orders are to advise anyone living alone, like this, to keep the house locked, and to take every means to inform us as soon as possible if they see or hear of him . . . ' He glanced past her. 'You're not going anywhere tonight, are you? I don't think Colonel Savage would harm you, or anyone else – but he might give you an awful fright if you ran across him, and . . . '

'Not tonight,' she said. 'The new missionary is due tomorrow.'

The lieutenant saluted again, ran down the steps, and jumped into the jeep. The engine kicked into life, the headlights swung round and away, along the narrow cart road towards the old Rest Home and Pattan.

Rodney, wounded! When she heard that he was in jail, charged with murder and treason, a wave of absolute lassitude, and exhausted failure, overcame her. She had hardly stirred herself, even to eat or drink, until she began to pack early this afternoon. He was in jail – but where? He needed a lawyer. She knew nothing of lawyers, and had no money to hire one. He was behind brick walls and iron bars, and she had no strength to climb, no weapons to blast open. She did not know where he was, and she did not have the money to go to him.

She stood at the open door, her mind lifting like a boat on a rising wave. He was wounded, and free, and she was a nurse. Now, if she could find him, she could at last do something to give him an inkling of her love. Later she would give him her body, which he had once asked for and she had refused; and once she had offered, wrapped in her soul, and he had rejected, through indifference more than hate.

She turned to go into the bungalow. The shadow came up the steps almost beside her. She had her hand on the door when she realised, and his voice said, 'Inside, and close the door behind me.' He followed her in, she closed the door, and with one hand he locked it and pushed the bolt across. In his other hand a blue-black automatic pistol pointed at the pit of her stomach.

'Into the bedroom,' he said. She walked down the passage and he stopped at the door, in the shadows. 'Draw the curtains, tight. Lock and bolt the back door. Now the door out of the *ghuslkhana.*'

'It's all right,' she said. 'They won't come in again.'

He stood in the middle of the bedroom, swaying like a poplar tree in a gusty wind. His face was a greenish grey under the fierce tan, and the blue eyes swam in and out of focus in time with his swaying, so that now they were sharp and cold, now dim and blurred.

'Lie down on the bed,' she said, trying to keep her voice calm. 'You're ill.'

His mouth twisted. 'Lie, sit – *prang*, I've had it. Then five thousand chips for you. Didn't they – pay enough for Gulu? Sorry, that wasn't you, was it? What's the difference?'

She drew a deep breath. 'Rodney, the difference is that I love you. I've had no way of showing you, when you so obviously didn't care. You don't care now, and I can't make you in a minute. I only want to tell you, so that you'll know. I never want anything or anybody else but you.'

'That's what – she said – in the end.' His eyes flickered on and off her face. 'They want me,' he mumbled. 'Murder. Listen radio. Killed three Indian babies. Ate them, apple sauce.' He twisted slowly and began to fall.

She had been waiting for it and from long experience was able to judge to the moment when and how it would come. She caught him, feeling her arms strong enough to hold him for ever, and eased him on to the bed. She lifted up his legs and unfastened his boots. In the stomach, the lieutenant had said. She undid the buttons of his shirt and unfastened the buckle of his web belt – Indian Army uniform, she noticed, and practically new, though stained and scratched where he had fallen and stumbled. Six miles, in the hills, at night, from the edge of the Sakti Plain. He lay on his back, his right arm dangling over the edge of the bed, the pistol in his hand. She knelt and gently tried to disengage it, but his grip was like steel and she could not move it.

She eased down his trousers. The exit wound was in the left anterior section of the abdominal wall, two inches from the navel. No granulation yet. Wound lacerated and about two inches square. Some recent bleeding and exudation of serum. The bandage had worked loose and hung round his loins. They seemed to be teaching the Indian Army the Evans Over-Cross Tie for abdominal wounds. The bullet couldn't have damaged any viscera or organ in its passage, or there would have been tubing in him, or signs of an operation. She turned him over gently. Entry wound small, one inch left of the spine at the sixth thoracic vertebra, barely missing the left kidney. Granulation tissue forming. Some recent bleeding beginning to clot. Temperature 101, pulse 108.

Systematically she began her preparations, her hands working with detached, unfumbling efficiency at their tasks; her heart soaring in dizzy ascent, singing like a lark towards the sun. He had come to her. This time she must not let go.

He groaned, stirred, and tried to sit up. She reached his side before he could move, and laid her hand on his forehead. The eyes looked long at her, but dim and blank, and the pistol did not fall from his hand. The kettle boiled. Quickly she made tea, stirred in plenty of sugar and milk, and two aspirins, and held the bowl to his lips. He drank deeply, and when he had finished the first bowl, whispered, 'More.' She made him another, and crooned over him as he drank, his head so close to her breast that there was a contraction in her womb and a swelling of her breasts. Later, in his sleep, he will wet the bed, she thought. She hoped he

223

would, that she could wash and clean him and do, out of the
fullness of love, all and more than he had done for her out
of indifferent duty.

She cleaned his wounds with antiseptic and retied the
bandage. His head fell back on the pillow, and he slept on
the instant, but his grip never loosened on the pistol. The
sound of the jeep engine, returning from Pattan, grew in the
west. She crouched over him, glaring at the door; but the
jeep did not pause this time, and in a minute the sound
died.

She pulled up a chair and sat beside the bed, staring
down at the drawn face. The thin lips fluttered with each
rapid, noisy breath, the chest rose and fell in an uneven
rhythm and both hands sometimes trembled, the left shaking the top of the sheet, the right causing the pistol to make a
rapid drumming rattle on the wood floor.

After half an hour the movements began to quieten and
slow, and finally to cease altogether. She took his wrist.
Pulse 80, temperature about 99.5.

He said in a low distinct voice, 'O.K., Harry, let's go
down to the ford.' Then he spoke longer, in a language she
did not understand. Then he laughed, a low happy chuckle,
and said, *'Hut teri ma!'* That she knew. It was soldiers'
language, meaning 'Up thy mother's!' He was smiling, and
she smiled with him.

He said, 'There's cloud on the pass but we ought to . . .
Barf, choro, barf. Snow, my son, snow . . .'

The voice changed again. Now it was sharp, yet deep with
a tremendous yearning. 'We've got to try. How many of you
are going to die in the next ten minutes?' Then edged and
confident, *'Achchi bat, choro-haru, advance garnu parchha.
Tayyar chhan? Jaun!'* He winced, his jaw set.

It took a long time for him to recover the original calm.
Then he whispered. 'Janaki, Janaki, how can your legs be so
slim and so strong?'

She looked anxiously over her shoulder, and about the
room. The lamp burned steadily on the table. The curtains
were drawn. She should not be hearing this, eavesdropping
on his soul, until he trusted her. Smiling, he mumbled in a
strong Anglo-Indian accent, 'Oah, Vickee, come in out of
thee sun, you will get all brown!'

The minutes floated by, into half hours, into hours. Like a

slowly revolving wheel his life passed. After a time she waited to hear him speak of his mother, of his father; of school in England, of green fields and cricket. He never did. Sometimes he spoke in Hindi, which she could understand a little, sometimes in the other language where only a word that was the same as Hindi came through. The sentences fell separate and disconnected from the fluttering lips, but formed a single world, a single life. Snow glittered on mountain peaks, and men climbed a long slope towards them. Indian girls danced in a closed room, very hot, and she heard the chinking of their bangles and saw his amused eyes fixed on their lascivious bellies. Rain fell, and he lit a cheroot and swore at the cook. There was a battle, and she heard orders given and taken, and the rumble of tanks under his suddenly raised voice. He danced, holding the women desirously in sardonic flirtations, and then suddenly, so that she imagined him still in his dinner jacket, he was striding fast through light jungle, and the sambhur stag was feeding beside the river.

She waited for the anger she knew so well, for the bitterness. Surely he must have hated? All his life seemed to be lust and violence and war. But there was none. A hundred names he spoke, and every one of them, English and Indian, brought a faint smile and a subtle change to the voice, an ache of love which was the same whether he spoke of mountains or of the satin heaviness of a woman's breast.

Yet there is bitterness, she thought, a bitterness too deep for words. Sumitra's name he never spoke, and for the rest, all was of the past. *This* had been. For the future – nothing; except the pistol held tight in his thin fingers.

Her head began to bow of its own weight, as though someone were pressing it gently down against her breast, and she felt a tear fall on her blouse, then another.

He awoke at four, an hour before dawn. The first sign was the clatter of the pistol falling from his hand as his muscles relaxed. She stooped quickly to pick it up, but he was quicker. He grabbed it, transferred it to his left hand and unflexed the muscles of his right. 'Mustn't lose Max's pistol,' he said. His voice was strong, his eyes unnaturally bright.

She sat down again and tried to smile, but the tears rushed up to the very brink, and she looked away until she had recovered her composure.

'I want something to eat. Quickly, please. And I'll take whatever other food you have away with me.' He swung his legs out of the bed, turned pale, and hung on to the bed with both hands.

'Let me!' she cried.

'Cook, woman,' he said, summoning the wide sardonic grin. He bent and began to put on his boots. She saw beads of sweat bursting out on his forehead. She went to the kitchen and quickly lit the fire. She heard him moving about the house. Fifteen minutes later he came through to her, and she saw that he was wearing khaki trousers and a shirt that had belonged to her husband. 'I found these,' he said, 'also a small haversack, full of bottles and bandages. I've thrown them out.'

She made tea, poached eggs, and buttered bread, and put out a pot of jam. He set it all on the mantelpiece in the living-room and ate hungrily, standing. 'Sitting hurts,' he said.

She said, 'Don't go now, Rodney. Hide in the attic. The new missionary is coming in the taxi from Bhowani, and I'm sure we'll be able to smuggle you out in it somehow, if we pay the man enough. There'll be room in the boot.'

He smiled, his mouth full. 'Me, locked in the boot of a car, with five thousand rupees on my head!'

'You must trust me,' she cried. 'You were helpless all night. Besides . . . '

'I know you,' he said suddenly. 'You were wearing a light-blue linen frock, very plain. There were some dark rain spots on it, and you were worried and frightened. I asked you to take your clothes off and you ran away.'

She said, 'I knew you'd remember, one day! It was Independence Day. You were drunk.'

'Yes,' he said. 'And they'd just given me an O.B.E. That's enough to drive any man to drink.'

'And your father had been killed.'

He gulped down the rest of the tea and said abruptly, 'I'm going. Where's the rest of the food?'

She showed him, and he stuffed it all into the first-aid haversack, a loaf of bread, some butter, a piece of cold mutton, half an uncooked chicken, a pound of sugar, a can of bully beef, the pot of jam.

'Money?' he said.

226

She emptied her purse into his hand – 108 rupees. He gave her back five, and turned towards the door. She stepped in front of him.

'Where are you going?'

He examined her. 'I don't know.'

'Are you going to try to reach Bombay? I can speak to Sir Andrew Graham. They'll arrange to get you out of India secretly. Where can I wait for you in Bombay? I'll have everything fixed.'

'No,' he snarled. 'I'm not leaving India. Now, get out of the way.'

She stood aside. 'I love you, Rodney.'

He stared at her in passing. 'That's too bloody bad,' he said.

She fell on the bed, too exhausted to feel pain, and slept.

The sound of knocking on the outer door awakened her. Ten o'clock. He'd had four hours. Drawing back the curtains she saw three sepoys, and a pair of thin, loinclothed peasants wandering round the back of the house. One of the peasants was pointing at the ground as he walked. She called, 'Wait,' washed her face, combed her hair, and opened the front door. The same lieutenant who had come in the jeep was there. He too looked tired. He saluted carefully. 'Did Colonel Savage come here, Mrs Wood?'

'No,' she said.

He said, 'Mr Roy put a couple of *shikaris* on to tracking him. They have followed him as far as this. They say he spent some hours inside, and then went on east.'

'Can they follow his trail farther, from here?' she asked quickly.

The young man said, 'He wasn't so tired when he moved again. He got into the stream over there, and they don't think they'll be able to pick it up again . . . He took me into my first battle. I was terrified, a brand-new second-lieutenant commanding a company attached to the 1/13th Gurkhas for the operation. He was . . . '

'I know,' she said. 'If he came here, I didn't see him. I know nothing about it.'

The lieutenant smiled at her. 'I'll report to headquarters.' He ran down the steps and leaned over the back of a truck parked on the road, radio antennae sticking up from it. The sepoys and the *shikaris* squatted among the weeds at the foot of the veranda.

The lieutenant returned. 'General Dadhwal would like to speak to you, ma'am. He would come down if he could, but he can't leave his headquarters. Would you mind . . . ?'

She climbed into the truck. She sat silent for the short ride, while the driver slammed the truck confidently round the hairpin bends, under the red-rock cliffs and the tall trees. At the summit, where the walls of the gorge fell back and the plain opened out, he turned right down a narrow track recently cut through the trees. General Dadhwal stepped out of his tent before the truck stopped, saluted, and helped her down.

Inside the tent, when they were seated across from each other at the green-baize table, he said, 'You know, Mr Roy can make it very unpleasant for you when he hears the evidence of the *shikaris*. Accessory after the fact, and so on. You'd better leave at once. I don't think he'll bother to have you arrested after that. Especially as I can persuade him that you won't change your story. You won't, I presume?'

'No,' she said, 'I won't.'

'Mind if I smoke?' He shifted his body and found his pipe and matches. His tunic was faded but spotlessly clean, the brass buttons glittering, the double row of medal ribbons bright on the dull khaki. There was a good deal of grey at his temples and along the sides of his heavy head. Like everyone else today, he looked tired.

He said, 'I thought . . . I understood, that you were no friend of his.'

'In the beginning,' she said. She laid her hands flat on the table. 'General, I love him. I must find where he's trying to go, what he's trying to do.'

The general muttered, 'Christ! . . . I am sorry, ma'am. Forgive me . . . ' She gestured impatiently. The general got up and paced the little tent. After a few minutes he seemed to make up his mind. He stopped opposite her. 'He's got to leave India, and everything that India has meant, every-thing he's done. He's got to leave it all behind . . . *all*. He's got to start again somewhere – England, Canada, Kenya, it doesn't matter.'

'That's the only thing he said. What he was not going

to do. He's going to stay in India.'

The general again muttered under his breath and sucked noisily at his pipe. He sat down. 'Mrs Wood,' he said, his brown eyes steady on hers, 'Rodney Savage and I have had a special sort of relationship for a long time. He is not just England, he is England-in-India. And I am not just Indian, but a special sort of Indian. I wish that much of what has happened between us had not happened – not just the imperialism and the rest, other things as well. They're all too tied together to explain, even if I wanted to and had the gift of the gab. What matters now is that I will not help you, even if I could, unless I am sure that you can give Rodney what he needs. Something different from what other women are ready to give him. *How* do you love him? Why? Tell me.'

She remembered that Janaki, whose thighs had held Rodney in the night, was the general's wife. She was sure that the general knew. There was a love almost as great as her own here. She had no cause to be embarrassed. She said, 'I came out here thinking I loved my husband, thinking I had religious faith to be a missionary. After he died I found that I had been lying to myself. I did not love him – I respected and admired him. I did not have faith – I only wanted to be a good and loyal wife. The first time I saw Rodney he wanted me to take my clothes off. I hated him and I couldn't forget him . . . But what is the difference between wanting me as a woman and wanting me as a nurse? Which is more insulting? . . . In the middle of that desert where I was, frightened and alone, there was no one in sight but him. He was there for me to hate, to despise, to fear. Then I fell ill, and if he had not come by I would have died. In the weakness and the delirium and the fear – I was very much afraid that I was going to die – my intense feelings about him simply changed round. Or I gave up the struggle of trying to pretend the opposite of the truth. I gave up trying to be loyal to Henry's ghost. I don't know much about psychology, but whatever the reason is, the thing's happened often enough before. Don't they say you only have to worry when the person you love doesn't care, one way or the other? . . . Hate became love, despisal became respect, fear became worship. He felt nothing. He was thinking of Sumitra, if of any woman. Now she's destroyed him, and he feels nothing for anyone, or anything.'

229

'How can you change that?' the general asked in a low voice.

'I don't know,' she said. 'I only know that there's nothing else but him, for me, in life. Surely, somehow, if I can only show him that, he can begin again.'

The general relit his pipe, drew a sheet of paper towards him and wrote carefully. After five minutes he folded the note into an envelope and gave it to her, unaddressed. 'That is for my wife in Bhowani,' he said. 'She's at Flagstaff House. I don't know what Rodney will do, where he will go . . . but I think it quite likely that he will turn up there for help of some kind. You can stay as long as Janaki is there . . . It is also possible that the Rani of Kishanpur may arrive, for the same purpose as yourself. I know how you feel about her – but, if you can, try not to hate her. She has been as badly hurt as you. Perhaps more, because she did have in her grasp everything she wanted – and threw it away.'

'He will go back to her,' she said miserably. 'She is so beautiful. They have shared so much.'

'It is possible,' the general said. 'I hope not . . . Now, I'm going to send you straight to Bhowani in my staff car with my A.D.C. Just stop off to collect your things. You're packed? Good.' He held out his big hand. 'Good-bye, Mrs Wood.'

'Good-bye . . . Did you say something about Mrs Dadhwal's leaving Bhowani?'

He smiled grimly. 'I have been posted to an obscure command in the farther wilds of Assam – a non-family station. Mr Roy is very angry with me. But I have a week or two yet. Janaki will come up to see me off from Chambalpur airfield. Soon after, she'll go to her mother's house in Bombay. I don't suppose you and I will meet again. I won't say "good luck". It sounds cheap. I will pray for you.'

He ushered her out of the tent.

Chapter 17

After leaving the distraught Margaret Wood and the mission bungalow I crossed the road and a ragged field, rolled up my trousers, and entered the shallow Shakkar stream. While night lasted I had to go carefully and very slowly. I could not afford a sprained ankle, and I couldn't afford to scatter water on stones which would normally be dry. They would be after me soon.

When light came I had covered a quarter of a mile. After that I went comparatively fast for half an hour, then turned up a side stream, which came in from the east, and for a time followed the bed of that. It was a torrent that fell down the high escarpment between the old Rest House and Sabora, and I knew that the linked pools of still water only reached the foot of the slope. Before they ended I sat on a rock in the water and took off my boots and socks. I wrung out my socks, spread one over each shoulder and waited for them to dry. The old Rest House, from which the hidden manoeuvrings of politics had ejected me, lay due south of me and less than a mile away. The morning was cold, not bitter-sharp like mornings on the high desert of Chambal, but raw. My wound ached and a mist as pervasive and chilly as the caresses of a drowned army surrounded me. I shivered the whole time I sat there. I could not see more than a hundred yards at ground level, then the trees became blurs and at last vanished in the mist. Above, their tops made cold patterns against the lightening pale-blue sky.

An airplane droned over, east bound, and I froze where I sat, turning my head down, before I realised from that first glance that it was a DC-3, the Indian Air Force's regular mail and V.I.P. passenger run from Chambalpur to Bhowani and Delhi, which had passed over every morning at this time while I was in the C.C.S., after the surrender.

When it had gone below the trees, and I could hardly hear the soft throb of the engines, I picked my way to the bank, barefoot on the stones, carefully put on socks and boots, and began to climb fast up the face of the escarpment. Most of the trees were bare of leaves in that season, and I felt all the time, as I climbed up that westward-facing slope, that someone was watching me from the opposite slope, below Dhain. If they saw me, at that distance of about two miles more or less, they could not hit me. But they had cars, and could get round to Sabora in half an hour, to Pattan in less, and from there converge across my path – any path. My only chance was speed.

I climbed up, a little to the right of the line where smooth red stone and long black streaks showed how the stream, in the monsoon, rushed down this face in a heavy waterfall. A long nerve in my stomach pulled all the way from my thigh to my chest at every step. There was no strength in my legs, and my breath came in short wheezing gasps – I, who had once run up and down this slope three times in an hour with young Ganesha.

I reached the top, threw myself down and vomited. A painful spasm in my stomach made me think that my wound had reopened, perhaps forcing out part of my guts. I dared not stop to look. The vomit spattered the giant teak leaves under my face, and after a few minutes I struggled to my feet and went on eastward. Just here I had killed the sambhur stag and fed the people of Pattan when they were starving. By that pterocarpus I had waited, and there by that patch of heavier jungle I had shot him . . . On, east, the leaves roaring under my feet, earth and rock as dry as splintered bone and the low sun clear and yellow in my eyes.

After two hours I knew that I had passed the first danger line. Sabora was behind my left shoulder by two miles, and Pattan six miles behind my right. I had crossed the main footpath from one to the other, which was the obvious and best place for them to cut me off. The forest ocean rolled away in all directions now, and I stopped under a tree, leaning back against the rough bark and staring all round. Where to go? Bhilghat lay south-east about twenty-five miles. I could not reach it today, but tomorrow I could. There I could find shelter, and old Gond women with pre-historic remedies for wounds, and I could lie in the hut while Gulu's grand-daughters fed me and cared for me until I was fit again.

Gulu was in jail, the settlement full of police, school-

232

masters, and probably soldiers. I could not go there. I could not go back to Pattan. I could not use roads or well-travelled paths. Where, then?

I began to walk again. There was no answer to the question, but nor could I stand still. Sometimes problems resolve best by staying in one place and thinking. Sometimes, as when I was in the morass in Delhi, holding the body still produces the same result on the mind – nothing.

Sabora, the McFadden Pulley quarries, and the metalled road to Bijoli and Bhowani were on my left, Bhilghat on my right. I walked between, allowing the sun to climb past my right shoulder . . . On through the long morning. Sleep in a dense thicket in the early afternoon. Awaken groaning with thirst, my throat gummed, and on again in the growing cool of the evening. An hour before sunset I came to the dirt road from Sabora to Bhilghat, the same I had driven along with Ranjit Singh and Max, in the beginning. Heavy military tyre treads marked the dust, with the traces of bare feet and goat hoofs. I took off my boots and crossed in my socks, carefully brushing the ground behind me with a bunch of leaves. On the far side I put on my boots and went on east.

A footpath joined my course at a diagonal. Stooping to examine it, I saw that it had once been used, but not for some months. It led east, so I followed it for twenty minutes, drawing quickly behind a tree when I caught a glimpse of stone, glowing red in the filtered rays of the setting sun. I went forward cautiously. It was a shrine, ruined and deserted, giant creepers climbing up the lone standing wall, stones fallen on one another, and a chipped and weatherworn statue of Shiva Nataraja against the inner face of the standing wall. Faded flowers lay on a stone slab below the dancing god, but when I went forward I saw that they had been lying there a long time and were now all but crumbled to dust. That explained the state of the path. This was a shrine to which the people of some neighbouring village – five or fifteen miles away – came to worship once a year. Water lay in a kind of stone urn. I stooped over it and drank. It was black and bitter and tasted of leaves, but it slaked my thirst.

It would have been safer in the jungle, but the shrine

233

attracted me and I sat down on the stone slab, sweeping the dried flowers to the ground, and leaned back against the wall, my head against Shiva's balancing right foot. There I opened my haversack and ate.

As I ate the banked red fires died down in the stone, the sun set, and the surrounding forest began to creak and move, awakening slowly to its life of the darkness. The stone turned cold under me, the daytime world of colour and texture dissolved into the night world of pattern and mass. The bats began to swoop down the dark alleys of the jungle, and I carefully refastened the straps of the haversack.

The direction of the wind changed and in the huge silence I heard the barking of dogs. There was a village nearby then, hardly a mile from me. It was to the south, but I would have to go carefully when I started out in the morning.

Who could I turn to now? I thought of Victoria Jones, the Anglo-Indian girl who had married Taylor the railwayman. She had loved me once. Taylor had got a job on the mineral railway after being dismissed from the Delhi Deccan, and they were living in Bijoli, only forty miles north-east. Suppose I went there. Victoria owed me at least shelter, money, help.

I turned angrily. She owed me nothing, nor I her. Taylor would hand me over to the police, to ingratiate himself with the Indians he despised.

I lay down, put the haversack with its sharp-edged contents under my head, and tried to go to sleep. Jackals began to howl their insane chorus, rushing aimlessly through the trees in the dark. Far in the north I heard the cough of a leopard. The dogs of the village were silent. Such shrines as this are usually the home of cobras, and I thought I heard the slithering of a big snake over the stones as I lay on my back, staring through closed eyes at the darkness, but I was not afraid and did nothing to investigate . . .

Our campfires blossomed like potted geraniums under the trees and Charlie, Beetle, and I were sharing a big bowl of rice against the temple wall. The desolation of the ruins, twenty miles from anywhere, long forgotten even by the villagers, only emphasised the comradeship of our own company. The beat of madals *throbbed up from the far end of the camp, where a sluggish stream ran under a low rock bank. Nearby the colonel was writing a letter to his wife.*

*We ate rice and dal, and sat back, at peace, in our sweaty
clothes. Tomorrow we would march to Telaghat, the day
after to Charria, the day after . . . on always to the day after,
the same, and the petals of the gold mohur falling in an
orange shower over the stone phallus in the courtyard . . .*

*I smelled hot steel and oil, heard a locomotive breathing in
the dusty twilight of an April evening, the metal scorched
from its hours in the sun, from its rushing passage through
the still, hot jungles, and rock ovens of the Vindhya hills,
over the rumbling iron bridges, along the metalled track cut
like a sword through the trees, the dust whirling in plumes
alongside the wheels. Victoria stood beside me. I smelled the
cheap perfume she used to wear, a touchingly innocent perfume trying in vain to counteract the unambiguous femaleness of a ripened woman at the end of a hot day. I smelled
my own sweat, strong and male, and, in all, the drifting invisible presence of coal smoke. Then she went and I was
alone.*

Early in the morning, the light vague and tentative, I
awoke suddenly, in my ears the dying tones of what had
awakened me – an exclamation in a human voice. I sat
up quickly and made out a dark figure below me, crouching
on the earth at the foot of the slab where I was. I heard a
low mumbling.

He raised his head and I saw that he was an old man,
wearing only loincloth and puggaree. I put my pistol back in
its holster. He quavered, '*Guru-ji*, you have come back?'
With a convulsive gesture he spread his hand. A bunch of
fresh flowers fell in my lap, then again he bowed his head to
the ground.

I did not remember ever being in this place before, though
in plenty like it, as in my dream. *Guru-ji,* the title he gave
me, means 'teacher'.

He said, '*Guru-ji*, this time you will stay? After sixty years,
the village needs you.'

Sixty years? The old man was in a state of shock, or
trance. He was not much more than seventy himself. The
dawnlight was growing and spreading fast over the world
and I saw him clearly, saw his thin eager face and hungry
eyes. I remembered that I had not shaved for three days,
that my clothes were torn and filthy, and I myself sunburned and weathered like any Indian. But boots and trousers

235

were surely out of place, whatever 'teacher' he thought I was. He was just not seeing them, any more than he was seeing my age. Time did not exist for the teacher of the shrine, whoever he had been.

The old man said, 'Good morning, Briju. Good-bye, Briju. Be good to your mother. Thank you.'

'Who taught you English?' I asked amazed.

He said, 'You spoke such words to me so many times that I learned them by heart, to please you. Don't you remember? . . . We never told anyone you were here. Not once, all those three years, no one outside the village ever knew. You asked for peace and we gave it to you, didn't we? We have told no one since . . . You are hungry, *guru-ji*? I will bring food for you! Everything will again be as it was when I was a boy, and we came to you and you talked with us, and sometimes being children we played jokes on you. We were afraid – at first because you were an English sahib, later because we knew we were committing sacrilege against an elect of God, but you only laughed with us. And do you remember my sister – aihh, long since gone! – coming with gifts because you gave her a blessing that got her with child? But you laughed again and said it was her husband's love that had done it. And the days the elders came to sit at your feet when the crops failed, or the deer ate the young corn, or there was bad blood between families, and we boys and girls hid in the jungle close there, lying on our stomachs, listening. It will all be the same!'

A picture of the past came clear. A man, an Englishman, had come here sixty years or so ago, about 1890. He had taken up residence in this shrine – perhaps it had a roof then. He had asked the villagers not to tell anyone. Whether he was a fugitive from the police, or from the world in general, from his own people, or from some particular person, I would never find out. But he had stayed three years as the village's *guru*, the resident spirit of the shrine. The old man's eyes beseeched me – you have returned, stay!

My head swam with hunger, and a lifting of material problems which had seemed reality. Why not? In Pattan I had destroyed my vision by mixing into it a desire for power. I no longer wanted power, or responsibility. I no longer wanted women. I no longer *wanted* anything. I could not be an Indian, they would not let me live as an Englishman – but a tree, a stone I could be, in this soil which had made me.

I sat cross-legged and raised my hand to bless the old man . . .

'Grandfather? Grandfather?'

The old man stood up. 'It is my grandson. Wait till he sees!'

A young man of about twenty-five came through the trees on a path from the south, which I had not noticed the evening before. He wore trousers, a shirt, a grey homespun cap and spectacles and I could tell at once that he had some education.

He was saying, 'You did not come back and my mother sent . . .' He stopped, astonished. 'Who is this?'

'It is he,' the old man crowed. 'Our *guru*, came back to us. Ah, I knew you thought we old men were dreaming when we talked of him!'

The young man's eyes were round and his mouth agape. 'I did not know,' he whispered. 'Is it really you? . . . It is such a long time.'

'Is there death, or age, for such as these?' the old man cried.

The young man dropped to his knees. Education had eroded the edges of his simple faith, such as the old man possessed, but the core was still there. He was not a town man, just a young village man with a little education. 'You will stay, *guru-ji*?' he asked.

I made up my mind. 'I will stay,' I said.

The old man wrung his hands in an agony of happiness and tears streamed down his cheeks.

The young man's eyes shone like beacons behind the cheap lenses. He cried, 'Now we will have a *guru* of our own! We will be famous all over Bandelkhand and Chambal! All over India! No other village has an English *guru*.'

I said, 'No one must know. I want peace, total peace.'

The young man's face fell. 'No one?' He brightened. 'But someone will have to know, *guru-ji* . . . for the government census. The officials are in the next village now, but they will reach us today. The question is, are you in our village of Chahar or in the village of Lihur? The *subtehsil* boundary runs close, but it has never been settled whether the shrine is . . .'

237

'Leave me out of the census,' I cried, 'I do not exist!'

Now it was the old man who looked worried. 'But there is the smallpox vaccination, *guru-ji*,' he said. 'Everyone must have it.'

The young man chimed in: 'And in *our* district the officials are making a *pilot surwey* – ' he spoke the words in English – 'showing exact details of land use, number of dwellings, number of inhabitants per dwelling, agricultural and home-industry production per head. It will be *pilot surwey* for all India, so you see – '

'We will discuss that later,' I interrupted, controlling my voice. 'I am hungry. Bring me food. Be sure to enter it in the proper column in the printed paper.'

'Oh, there is no record of that,' the young man began, but I waved, 'Go go!'

As soon as they had disappeared down the path I grabbed up my haversack and hurried east through the jungle. After two hours, when I thought I would die of melancholy, I lay down and tried to relieve my misery by tears. No tears came and after a time I went on again.

It was a day without purpose, except movement. I walked, saw no one, nothing, only two vultures very high in the blue sky, who watched me until dark. I walked east all day except for an hour, when I got up after a rest and walked west, and did not know it until I fell down a low rock cliff. In the pain and shock of the moment I realised that it was the same cliff I had scrambled up, in the opposite direction, an hour before my rest.

I do not know where I lay down for the night. It was, like the day, a nothing place, non-existent, and the night the same except that it contained aimless stillness instead of aimless motion.

The third morning, after vomiting, I felt better and ate most of the rest of my food, and it stayed down. I would have to use Max's pistol – I had stolen it from the *yakdan* in his office just before I heard Roy's car arriving – to kill some food. That would be easy, but dangerous.

I went on east. Near ten o'clock in the morning, the sun bright and a fresh breeze blowing through the jungle, myself feeling weak but not in pain, I heard the sharp crack of breaking wood somewhere close ahead, followed by a scream and a crash. I was going downhill towards a river, seen once through the trees from the ridge crest. I knew the river must be the upper Harpal. I stopped. I heard a woman crying urgently, but could not make out her meaning. I hurried down among the trees and came in a few seconds to the edge of the river. It ran about fifty feet wide there, between red-laterite cliffs twenty feet high. A wooden cart bridge had spanned the river from this bank to the village crowding the far cliff. Now the rickety structure, a hundred times half-repaired, had broken. Part hung down from the farther side, where a woman shrieked and shrieked, calling up to the village. Part swirled round and round in the pool below the bridge, where I saw too the floating red skirt and hair of another woman.

I hesitated. Some men were running down from the village, others along the cliff to the right, but there was no way down the cliff there for at least a hundred yards. The pool where the woman floated was a whirlpool, but the current very slow. Even a little effort would have taken her to the bank, or to the shallows. Perhaps she had been stunned by the fall of the rest of the bridge on top of her. Perhaps she was already dead.

Cursing my luck, I jumped over the cliff. When I came up the woman was close to me. I caught her and turned her face up. Blood stained the water from a gash in her forehead. I took her under the armpits and dragged her to the strip of sand.

My tiredness had gone in the shock and excitement of action. I stretched her at once on to her stomach, tore off her *choli* and began artificial respiration. Villagers called down to me from the clifftop, others ran up the narrow bank of sand and stones from the washing place downstream. When these arrived I was very tired again, and the particular motions of artificial respiration could not have been worse for my wound. I called to the first arrival, an agitated young man who might have been the husband, 'Watch me, watch!'

'Yes, sahib,' he gabbled, 'I see.'

'Come here.' He knelt beside me. 'Do it with me. . . there . . . there . . . there . . . Now go on doing that . . .'

I stood up and spoke to another man. 'You, watch him. When he is tired, do the same. Let there be no stopping of the work, even for a breath.'

From the cliff above an old grandmother wailed. 'She

239

is dead! *Aiiih*, my daughter is dead!'

I said nothing. Three minutes later, to my surprise, the woman groaned and retched. 'My head,' she moaned. I turned away. It was clear that the blow on the head had been her main trouble. She had not swallowed much water, and would soon be all right.

An old gentleman in clean white dhoti, shirt, and puggaree made a deep salaam. 'I am the headman, sahib . . . She whom you saved has five children. How can we ever thank you?'

I found myself swaying. 'I am hungry,' I heard myself say. 'Is there anything to eat?'

'Of course, sahib. Only our poor *desi* food, I fear, but . . . '

'Let me eat,' I said.

The old man led down the bank to the place where the path went up to the village. Twenty huddled women, who had been washing clothes, smiled at me. We went up the path in a great crowd, all the people chattering like magpies.

A policeman came running out of the village adjusting his puggaree as he ran. 'What happened? Is she dead?' he cried.

'She is alive,' the headman said. 'No thanks to you. What were *you* doing? Sleeping under the peepul as usual? The sahib *bahadur* here leaped into the river and saved her. I saw it.'

The policeman saluted me. Then his eyes widened. He cried, 'This is . . . this the sahib who did the murder! We have captured him!'

'What do you mean?' the headman said irritably. 'He has saved the life of Nathu's woman.'

I edged sideways through the mob, my hand on my pistol. The women crowded towards the policeman, shouting and waving their fists. 'Murder, fool? He saved her life! He is a hero! A sahib *bahadur*!'

Then the policeman spoke the fateful words. 'Five thousand rupees reward!' he said. 'Five thousand rupees.'

I pushed the nearest woman into him and ran. As soon as I was clear of them I drew my pistol and shouted, 'Keep back!' The policeman was unarmed, and they all fell back.

I heard the grumble and murmur of their voices. They weren't saying save him. They weren't saying, he saved her life. They weren't saying, Murder. They were saying, five thousand rupees.

I backed into the woods and when I could only just see them, gathered there staring after me, I fired a shot over their heads. Then I turned and ran. I heard the collective rising yell: 'After him! Five thousand rupees!'

I ran down the valley for a time, then turned up through the trees, and stopped. A young man was coming fast up the slope after me, with two companions. They were young and fit and I hated them. I aimed carefully at the centre of the young man's chest and fired. My hand shook so from fatigue and hate I did not kill him as I had intended. The bullet hit him high in the shoulder. He screamed, fell, picked himself up, and stumbled and fell back down the hill, screaming in pain. His two companions were by then well ahead of him. They vanished and I turned again.

On, over the brow of the slope. On, down the other side. On, miles across a shadeless flat volcanic plateau covered by stunted thorn bushes and spear grass, the sun high and every part of my body aching. On, through the afternoon. On, to the side of a main road, just in time to edge back as a truck passed full of police armed with rifles. On, across the road in the dust cloud behind the truck. On, east, over hill and valley, stream and marsh and plateau and ridge and scrub and field. On, until my legs gave way and I fell in the middle of the game trail I had been following. I crawled under a thornbush to the side, pulled up my legs tight under me and passed away, whether in faint, sleep or death, I did not know.

It was a long straight road on the outskirts of the old Hira Mandi bazaar in Lahore. Inside there is a narrow lane, stone paved, between wooden houses whose upper balconies almost meet overhead. At street level the whores sit in open-fronted booths, and a dense crowd of men walk up and down the alley jostling and staring at the women, who stare back over their heads, impersonal and impervious. Christ came out of the old city gate below that alley, but it was in daylight, and we were standing to arms at the crossroads, a platoon of Gurkhas and my company headquarters. There had been a week of rioting between Sikhs and Muslims already, over the destruction of a Muslim mosque; and that over the encroachment of a Sikh gurdwara; and that over the building of a Muslim slaughterhouse, where cows were killed; and that ... We had nothing to do with the quarrels but as soon as we came to stop it, of course, we had. The Sikhs took out a procession against the Commissioner's order. They advanced on us out of the old bazaar and down the wide road, waving banners in Gurmukhi. The banners called for Muslim blood, but it was not the Muslims barring their path, it was us. He was their leader, Christ. He had a long, saintly face, very fair of skin, and he had not tied his puggaree, so that his black hair fell over his sholders in a wave almost to his waist, like the pictures of Christ in old Bibles, only they made Him a blond. The Assistant with us gabbled through the formalities of the Riot Act. After that the responsibility was mine. Christ walked slowly on, calling out to the Gurkhas kneeling in the road that they had no business here. Were they not Hindus? He was on his way to throw the moneychangers out of the temple.

I pointed him out to Rifle Manraj. Manraj jerked his bolt, putting one round in the magazine. I called to the crowd, but spoke to Christ: 'If you pass that chalk line in the road, we fire.'

He did not bother to look down, but came on. When his front foot passed the chalk line I tapped Manraj on the shoulder. Manraj fired, hitting Christ in the left eye. He fell backward and the rest of the crowd dropped their banners, turned and ran. He did not die for a few seconds, but died in my arms as I ran forward. He could not speak but his other eye was open, staring up at me, wonderingly.

The Governor commended the battalion for quelling the riots with so little loss of life – one man killed; after they had already killed nearly two hundred of each other. One man, I thought, that's the trouble with figures, and in the last resort, with democracy. I'd rather have killed two hundred more, but not that man ...

In the morning, that nowhere under the bush in nowhere became a hillside of stones and brown grass, thinly sown with bushes, and the lowing of cattle not far off. My mind was sharp with hunger and my wounds hurt with a dry pain, like a scab almost healed that is torn open. I was making it too easy for them, plodding on east as though one dawn I hoped to catch the sun rising from its forge and hurl myself into that burning abyss. I must have been seen half a dozen times yesterday after the episode of the drowning woman.

I started off south-westward. When I saw a village I watched it from cover, resting to re-gather my nervous strength – there was not much of any kind left – wondering whether to invite a little attention to myself, and whether it could be done without causing my immediate capture. Three times I decided against it – because there was no nearby jungle – because I saw an old bus parked – because natural obstacles would channel my flight in a certain, obvious direction.

The fourth time, I saw that it could be done with only a reasonable risk, and, after preparing myself, I walked past the village on the south, skirting small fields and thorn fences well within sight of the backs of the houses. An old woman emptying pots outside her hut saw me, and later two men. They stared, but did not come closer, nor did they run for cover as they would have if they had suspected I was an armed and dangerous criminal. Yet it was enough; they would talk; the gossip would reach the ears of some busybody; the message would go out.

Three hours later I came to another jungle village, this one reached by a telephone line. A telephone line in those hills usually meant a police *thana*, and so I presumed there was one, and again skirted the village in such a manner that I would be seen – but first I cut the telephone line. This was a long and hard business for me, since I had to find a big stick, and climb a tree, then batter at the line passing six feet off. I did it, and then skirted the village much as before, fairly close and keeping my eyes sharply open. This time two small boys saw me. After a long moment of staring under shaded eyes at me across the field, they darted back into the houses. I broke into a run, hurrying over the ploughed earth by the thorn fences until I reached the jungle. Then I ran along a westward path and, after an hour, eased off on to the leaves and lay down behind a rock, waiting. I was only just in time. Two policemen, wildly excited and calling to each other as though it were only a jackal they were pursuing, came panting up the path, their noses down. Three boys and an older man followed. One of the policemen carried a slung rifle. I watched them, my pistol ready, until they disappeared westward. Then I started south and, going with extreme caution so as not to be seen at all, by anyone, at dusk found a place to lie, and lay down and tried to sleep.

I did not sleep more than an hour or two all night, from hunger, but my body got a rest, at least.

Before dawn, listening to the sounds of the jungle, I knew that I must get some food today or I would not be able to go any farther. I ought to do it at once, rather than look for it while on the move. The human mind has difficulty in real concentration on two things at once, and if I was looking for food I might forget other dangers.

After two hours of daylight searching I had found nothing, and set off eastward once more. The denser jungles and lakes of the Bhilghat area, and the tangled hills along the southern part of the India-Chambal border, now lay behind me. It was reasonable to assume that the hunters, having twice seen me heading towards them, would suppose that they were my destination – especially as the area formed a near-perfect refuge, and had been used as such often enough in the old days – by hunted Thugs fleeing from my great-grandfather; by Pindaris broken in Lake's campaigns of extermination against them; by Mahratta horsemen shattered at the Third Battle of Panipat; by all the defeated and the hopeless, starting with the Gonds four or six thousand years earlier.

In the afternoon I came to a stream, where I drank, and then a road. I lay down and observed it carefully from the edge. I saw bicycle tracks in the dust, but not fresh. Seeing no one, I crossed it with all precautions, and soon after fainted on an open hillside where my body as it lay must have been visible for half a mile in all directions. The relentless sun brought me round with a trip-hammer headache and a return of nausea, but I had nothing to vomit now, and after a time I crawled into the nearest shade, and lay down. A lizard appeared and my jaws ached painfully. Two hours later, when it was crawling about on the rock under my hand and I had not moved a muscle, a sudden spasm of effort brought it into my fingers. I broke its neck and ate it raw. At dusk a crow settled in the top of the tree ten yards from me, and cocked its eye, examining me. I shot it, it fell down through the boughs with a thump to the ground. I grabbed it and went on east as fast as I could, for the road I had crossed was close behind me, certainly within sound of that shot, and it was a time of day when many people besides police might be travelling along it.

In a thicket, two miles farther on, I lit a tiny fire, scraped open the crow's belly with a sharp stone, gutted it, and grilled it whole, burning off the feathers, and ate it, and then stumbled on another mile through pitch darkness before lying down to sleep.

At the edge of the wood, by a dusty road, two peacocks displayed before a hen. I had gone out to shoot peafowl and beside me Manparsad chattered with excitement, but I could not shoot. The cocks were grave and voluptuous in their appalling male beauty, and the hen crouched and waited so tenderly that I put my finger to my lips, and we crept away, back through the forest. We reached the road near a small village where women bent over the well and brass pots shone in the dusty sunlight. A cow had died there and forty vultures crowded the boughs of the gnarled tree overhanging her body, and ten more hissed and trampled, with wings arched into black and white canopies, to plunge their heads into her anus and vulva, dragging out long strips of bright meat. The vultures on the tree flew away when Manparsad and I appeared, and those on the ground tried to, but it took them a long time, like a modern jet, slow hop-hop and gradual run across the field, their wings dragging along the ground and raising dust as they tried to flap, at last they just got off the ground, but for another thirty yards made so little altitude that the wing tips still touched the ground and stirred the dust. I raised my gun to shoot one of the gorged despoilers – then lowered it. The peacock is sacred to some in India: the vulture to all. Without them, death would overwhelm life. Manparsad and I went back to camp empty-handed, but we had walked twelve miles in the forest, and seen the peacocks and the vultures and the dead cow and the women at the well . . .

The next day I stole a chicken from a village and got away without being seen except by the pariah dogs, which bark at everything and so are not much heeded. Again I cooked it, this time by a small lake, and drank well, and was strong enough afterwards to go ten hours, resting only twice. I did not go fast but estimated that I had covered about twenty miles. There was no more food that day, or the next, and in the late afternoon I came suddenly and unexpectedly upon the railway line. It was single track, broad gauge, the

245

rails shimmering in the sun, and no one in sight north or south. This must be the main line from Bhowani to Itarsi and Bombay. I travelled this line often during the troubles of 1946 but could not recognise this exact spot.

I did not cross it, but lay in the shade staring at it. The heat of the pursuit was for the moment far behind me, somewhere in those hills which had disappeared into the haze. When I had rested, should I cross the line and head on towards the rising sun – like yellow-dog dingo, running and running across the endless plain of Australia – like the kudu of Africa, or the sambhur of this very land, pursued relentlessly by packs of dogs, relay replacing relay always yapping and snapping at their heels until, bleeding from fifty bites in the tendons, they turn to fight, and die?

No, I would not cross it. I would jump a freight train during the night, and at last get away from this arena where they pursued me.

The first train was a passenger, going south. It came fast in the twilight, the red carriages hurtling past with a long rhythmic clatter, lights shining out from some windows, others dark and shuttered. If I tried I knew I could remember something wonderful about that train, and someone who had loved me and whom I had been able to give something to. But I could not remember, because my mind, like a baulking horse, came to a point and shied off violently, hurling me, its rider, to the painful stones.

The next train, two hours later, also was a passenger, going the other way, still fast but not nearly so fast. My time in Bhowani in '46 had taught me something about loco-motives and I knew from the beat of the exhaust that this last train was going uphill. There were only a few carriages and the powerful engine could still maintain 30 or 35 miles an hour up the slope – too fast for me.

Between one and three in the morning two freight trains passed, southbound, both going fast. At ten past three I heard in the south the laboured roar of an engine coming up the hill with a heavy load. At last the searchlight swung round the distant curve, two miles away, and laid a band of light along the rails. The thunder grew and I crept close to the track, lying among the trees ten yards from the edge of the ballast. She came on up, groaning through the night in heavy labour, towering sparks just visible high above, where the searchlight had lost its intensity. The engine and tender passed, and at once I scrambled forward and stood close to the clanking, creaking wagons. First came ten or more box-cars, tight-closed and locked; then open wagons. After letting two pass to gauge the speed and see exactly where the steps and platforms were, I ran alongside, caught a step and swung myself up. My wound shot a bolt of pain through my stomach, but I hung on and by slow, careful effort climbed over the edge of the wagon and fell in a heap down inside. It was empty, and smelled of crushed stone.

I lay there for two hours, while the locomotive up ahead worked north under blazing stars. Near five in the morning the wagon began to clatter over points and switches. I climbed up and, looking past the red glare of the engine's firebox I saw the lights of houses and the square silhouette of others, very black in that moment before dawn. Signal lights shone green and red among the fading lower stars, another track branched out beside us, more jerk and rattle of switches. I climbed down to the outer step and waited. We came up under the first approach gantry, past the bungalows of the railway colony, and from the engine I heard the hiss of escaping steam and felt the first grind of the brakes. I stepped off into the black grit of Bhowani Junction yards. So, I had come here, where Janaki was, whom I had loved, who had rejected me. I would give myself up to her – give her the final satisfaction of handing me over to the new lords of my country.

Twenty minutes later I walked along the side of Flagstaff House and passed through the back hedge. The house was dark, but the french windows on the right, facing this garden, were open. I went in there, and at once a low voice whispered 'Rodney?' It was Margaret Wood. My eyes, accustomed to the night, could see that she was sitting up on a camp bed in that room, which was ordinarily Max's study.

I sat down slowly, very slowly, in the chair by the desk. 'Food,' I said, and could say no more.

She was out of bed, hurrying into a dressing-gown, kicking her feet into bedroom slippers, closing the windows behind me. 'Don't put on the light,' she whispered, 'Janaki thinks the house is being watched. I have something ready for you.'

247

'Wha'?'

'I have, every night,' she said. 'Wait. I'll tell Janaki, and Sumitra.'

The sound of that name sent a worse pain than any physical one through me and I gasped with it. It was the first time for ten days, which seemed like a thousand years, that any thought of her, even to her name or perfume or the sound of her voice, had come into my consciousness.

Chapter 18

A log on the fire starts to burn with a light, leaping flame as the bark catches. During its maturity it burns more steadily but with a greater warmth. At the very end, often, it flares up again, and again light flames dance along it, and jets of fire, fed by the last reserves of its stored fuel, hiss out against the grate.

Four days and nights they hid me in an attic of Flagstaff House. I lay on a thin mattress on the plank floor, asleep most of the nights and all the days. I saw, the first night, a high valley of Lahoul, the main snow peaks of the Himalaya beyond, and a grey monastery set in a stony wilderness. The monks wore orange robes and tall red hats. The night I reached that place they danced the devil dance in the monastery courtyard. Ten-foot horns of copper and silver rested on the shoulders of acolyte boys, they and the trumpeters standing on a flat roof high above the courtyard. Long flags whipped in the never-ending violence of the dry Central Asian wind, gold and brass gleamed in the shadows of the pillars, and behind smoking oil lamps grotesque statues, carved in butter, loomed out of the echoing corners. Inside – the dark red and swirling yellow of the dancers in the courtyard; outside – one step – the beginning of eternity, of cold and wind, stone and snow ...

The second night I saw the Bengal famine of 1943. I passed through in a train on my way to the Burma front. Women and children lay dead beside the track as the train clanked through the hot-weather afternoon. Men lay in the fields, fallen where they had been trying to grub a leaf from a dead plant. In Calcutta corpses littered the gutter. I saw soldiers giving bread to children with matchstick legs and arms and huge staring-eyed heads. The children crumbled it listlessly in their hands – only cooked rice was food to them, bread wasn't. Later their heads sank and they too lay down in the gutter. Etched on the copper sky over the train, over the city, kites circled, vultures waited ...

The third night I revisited an orange grove near Nagpur. The time was early February – the same as now. (Often during my flight from Lapri it had come to my mind that in Nagpur and Chhindwara the oranges were ripe and sweet on the trees; and I had to swallow the aching saliva and think only of the stones under my feet.) A caravan of gypsies were camped in the orange groves. They were a criminal tribe on the move, and a couple of policemen travelled with them, to see that they did not steal the oranges from the landlord's trees; but otherwise the policemen turned a blind eye, and all night long men slipped out of the town a mile down the road, and came to the camp, to sit by the leaping fires under the golden Hesperidean apples. Here bears danced on the end of short chains. A blind man played a *sitar* with haunting beauty. Women lay on their backs under the hedge with customers. Their husbands, sons, and fathers picked pockets, danced, beat drums, sold arrack, and escorted more men in from the town . . .

On the fourth and last night it was a beach of sand, pale pink in colour under an early sun. Palm trees leaned over the sand from the landward rim, and the sea broke in long waves, alternately blue and white. I did not know where that scene came from in my past, but there it was – just that, the empty sand, the sea, and the trade wind. That was the last vision.

Janaki's servants were old and loyal, and knew me. No one came up to me during daylight, for it involved placing a ladder in the middle of Janaki's bedroom floor. The ladder would have been too difficult to hide or explain away in case of a sudden visit. Janaki came up that first night, with Margaret Wood. Margaret Wood spent a long time on my bandages, almost weeping over what I had done to myself since she last tied them. The second night she came alone, telling me that Janaki had gone to Chambalpur to say good-bye to Max before he finally left for his new posting in the wilds. She was going to have a last couple of days up there with him. I wished I could have at least felt sorry for him. The third and fourth nights it was Margaret Wood alone, twice each night, after dusk and before dawn, working on my wound and bandages, emptying the pot, feeding me, filling the water jug, leaving food for the daytime. I wished I could have at least felt sorry for her.

The fifth night, when the hurricane lantern rising like a will-o'-the-wisp through the trap door awakened me, I saw that it was Sumitra. A physical shock, like a bullet wound, set my head spinning. She saw that I was awake and came on up, but did not look at me again. For a time she set about her business, handing down the pot to an unseen sweeper waiting below, handing down the water jug, waiting for it to be returned full, taking up the tray of food, setting it on the floor beside me. I watched her, and waited. At last she squatted on her heels at the foot of my bed, and said gently, 'Eat, Rodney . . . Margaret had to go to the chemist's.'

I ate. She sat silent, her face averted. When I had finished she handed the tray down the trap door, and returned to her place. 'Have you nothing to say to me, Rodney?' she muttered.

All the time my head had ached, the plates had wavered in front of my sight.

'Come here,' I said. She began to get up, and my hands flexed. The throbbing in my head turned to sharp stabs of agony.

We both heard the creaking of the ladder, then Margaret Wood's head appeared, followed by Janaki's. The pain left my head and my eyes focused. They glanced quickly from Sumitra to me. Sumitra stared at her feet. Janaki said, 'I'm just back . . . I have to leave this house tomorrow, Rodney. The new general is moving in the day after. Sumitra's going to friends in Bombay, and I to my mother. We will take you with us. You must leave India as soon as possible. Margaret is sure she can arrange with Sir Andrew Graham to smuggle you out on a McFadden Pulley ship. If that fails, P. R. Sethi has promised to fly you to Pakistan, from there it will be easy to go on wherever you want to. Max saw Hussein Ali in jail in Chambalpur yesterday – he's being let out any day now – and he has promised to put ten thousand rupees into a Swiss bank for you. You must see that there is no other way, nothing else to be done now.'

I said, 'How do we get to Bombay?'

She stared at me, surprised. 'Well . . . that's wonderful . . . I didn't expect, somehow . . . we will leave early in the morning in the Ford station wagon, Margaret, Sumitra, and I. You will be hidden under the bedding rolls in the back. "Chop" Wazeer, Max's A.D.C., will drive for the first ten miles, and that far we'll be travelling with an artillery regiment going down to the Babina ranges. There is a police post on the road but I don't think they'll search us very carefully, if at all, in the circumstances. After that, you will be our chauffeur, an Anglo-Indian perhaps . . . '

'George D'Souza,' I said. 'All right. Get me some clothes and thin, cheap shoes.'

'I've done that,' Margaret Wood cut in; 'everything's ready. You get to sleep now.'

'The head of the regiment is passing the house at seven in the morning,' Janaki said. 'We must be ready to go by then.'

'All right,' I said.

The three women left the attic, and again I was alone, in the dark.

'Slower, Rodney, please!'

Janaki's voice was sharp. I realised I was doing over seventy, and eased my foot on the accelerator pedal. The old Ford slowed. It was a pre-war V-8 station wagon, much the worse for wear, the springs gone, the body rattling, and a hurricane of dust swirling around inside so that the two Indian women had the ends of their saris drawn tight across mouth and nostrils. Margaret Wood was in front with me.

'You really must drive slower,' Janaki said, not quite so sharply, realising that I wasn't altogether with them. 'The police will stop us.'

There were no police on that southward road from Bhowani, after the post we had passed, without incident, at the edge of town, but I tried to keep it down. Obviously I could not get away from Sumitra by driving like a maniac, when she was in the back seat of the same car.

I drove all morning. Near Itarsi Janaki bought food and brought it to the car while I had the tank filled. We ate later, by the roadside in thin jungle. I drove all afternoon, and at dusk we reached the place Janaki had chosen for the day's destination. I didn't know it, but she had driven this road many times. It was a dak bungalow on a side road which had been by-passed by more modern construction. A faded signpost pointed to *Gonaghar Dak Bungalow, 3 miles*, and soon there it was, standing back in calm decay in a clearing off the deserted road. Even the bullock carts used the new tarmac

252

now. The ancient *chowkidar* staggered out from one of the servants' quarters, and made a low salaam. 'Will you be staying the night, presences?'

Janaki said, 'Yes,' and the old man's eyes lit up. It must have been a year since anyone had stopped there, except a district commissioner or a forest officer, on tour. Perhaps not even one of them. Those bungalows were built for men who travelled on horseback. For years they'd been declining as everyone dashed past in cars.

I got out and opened the doors for the women. Then in three trips I carried their suitcases and bedding rolls into the bungalow. Every time I went near Sumitra I felt dizzy. When I returned for the cheap cardboard case they had given me, I started automatically for the bungalow again. Janaki nudged me, glancing towards the servants' quarters, and I headed back there.

The *chowkidar* lived in the quarter nearest the bungalow. He had no woman. I took the quarter farthest from him. It was the usual cell, about nine feet by five, containing a string charpoy and a string chair, both in advanced disrepair. Outside, on a small brick platform, there was a standpipe and a brass tap. I washed my hands and face and went back into the cell. The walls might have been whitewashed ten years ago, but now were cracked and peeling and kicked away at the bottom, showing the dusty brick underneath. The floor was of broken and pitted cement. A door hung on one hinge. There was no window.

Now, in my role, I should drag my bed out into the dusk, and squat on it, smoking a *bidi*. Soon the old man would come down from fussing about the bungalow, installing the ladies, and pull his bed close to mine, and sit on it. We would pass the *bidis* back and forth, holding them in our cupped hands between the outer fingers, sucking in the smoke so that our lips never touched the end. We would discuss our employers, the government, the crops, and the weather. I could not face it, and walked away.

The servants' quarters backed on a mango grove. In the dusk the formal dark-green leaves shone with an oily smoothness, and the boles marched away into outer darkness like a parade of soldiers waiting for some ceremony to begin. Yellow lights shone out of the dak bungalow's windows as the *chowkidar* lit the lamps, giving the impression of lights in a temple. It struck my fancy that the parade and the lights were for a funeral ceremony, the funeral of the Last Sahib. The *chowkidar* would be pleased if he knew he had spoken to a real sahib, a *vilayeti* sahib. It wouldn't disturb him much to realise that it was a funeral he was officiating at. After all, the play's the thing, and if it happens to be a tragedy, it's a tragedy.

The Last Sahib at the Last Dak Bungalow. I looked with a bitter longing at the ramshackle bungalow, the faded whitewash, the warm yellow of the lamps in the windows. These were mine, these and the mango grove, the jungle behind, the invisible hills beyond, and the abandoned road.

The *chowkidar*'s voice called me: '*Ohé*, driver, food is ready!' I went back to the servants' quarters and we ate rice and dal off neem leaves. The old man said I reminded him of Golightly Sahib, the Forest Officer. Golightly Sahib stayed here often. In 1906 and '07. Perhaps he was hinting that I might be this Golightly's son, but I repeated that I came from Goa and after we had finished eating he shuffled off to carry their dinner up to the ladies.

After an hour's silent smoking I dragged the charpoy back into the cell, leaving the door open, lay down, and tried to get to sleep. The long dusty day's drive had worn me out, and I did sleep, a sleep absolutely blank of thought, dream, memory, or expectation.

I awoke with a hand gently shaking my shoulder, and a voice saying softly, 'Rodney.' I recognised her voice, but even if I hadn't, the dizziness and the stabbing pain in my skull would have told me. I opened my eyes and vaguely sensed her shape beside me. 'It is I, Sumitra,' she said.

She squatted down on her heels against the wall, her face on a level with mine. She said, 'I must speak. I cannot make you listen. I only beg you to, for your own sake as well as mine . . . Margaret and Janaki have made me promise never to go near you alone, but I must . . . I have had three weeks now to think of what I did, and what I must do. I love you, Rodney. I did wrong in deceiving you, and I ask you to forgive me. I have learned that there is nothing more valuable than love . . . For the future, I must go into politics. India needs women leaders more than men. Our future depends on the women. I ask you to come with me. At first you are bound to be under my shelter. There is no way of avoiding

254

it. [*The probing needles in my head were without pity.*] Soon, though, it will be the other way round. Your mind is stronger than mine, and you know the real India better than I do, in spite of my blood. You will be the brain and the will, and I the hand. There isn't a decent politician in the country who wouldn't like to find, somehow, a way to use you and all that you represent. I ask you to be my lord, my husband.'

My wound gave me a slow long stab of pain, her blurred shape twisted and writhed, though I knew she did not move. Inside my head, I could stand no more.

'Come here,' I whispered.

She knelt forward and leaned over me. The trembling lake was the wet sheen in her huge eyes. 'Oh, Rodney . . .'

I put up my hands and grasped her round the throat. For ten long seconds, while my fingers tightened and cut off her breathing, she knelt absolutely still. Then her hands began to jerk, and she beat frantically at my wrists. I released my grip a little, just enough, and heard her croak, 'Must live . . . not for my sake . . . let me . . .'

I squeezed tight again, and said, 'Beside you. On the chair.' My head was clear, without pain.

Her right hand, reaching urgently, found the chair, and the pistol lying loaded on it. When she had it in her hand, I locked my grip and waited. There was no fear in me, no pain, no emotion of any kind. As soon as I saw this faded dak bungalow by its empty clearing in a forgotten jungle I recognised it as the end of the road. The pistol jabbed and wavered against my forehead now, but she was losing her strength. Another few seconds and she would not be able to pull the trigger. I released my grip, let her draw four wheezing breaths, and squeezed again.

Her head bowed forward, her arms lowered, and the pistol dropped with a heavy clatter to the cement. Her struggles ceased. But it was not the failure of her strength, it was the victory of her will. She had made up her mind that I should not die by her hand.

For a moment longer the power flowed into my wrists, then, as suddenly as the turning off of a tap, it failed – just vanished, leaving my arms and fingers and body full of a chill, trembling water. Even the final gesture, even the forlorn hope, had failed.

I heard her slump to the floor. Her breathing was strangulated, loud, and groaning. Gradually it settled into a painful but steady inhalation. Then I heard the rustle of her clothes as she rose to her feet, heard her stand up, move to the door, one hand slithering along the wall for support, heard her go out. All sound died, and that was the end, the absolute end.

Chapter 19

Margaret Wood watched stiffly as Sumitra stumbled out of the quarters. Sumitra did not raise her head when Margaret put one arm around her waist and under her shoulders and, thus supporting her, helped her up to the bungalow. Still she did not speak while Margaret guided her into her room, eased her on to the bed, and lit the lamp. She lay on the bed, looking up at the ceiling cloth, her eyes wide, while Margaret sponged her blotched face, and her neck with its livid finger marks.

When she had done all that she could, Margaret said, 'Do you have any sleeping pills, or shall I give you some of mine? I got them for him.'

Sumitra said, 'I have some. That bottle on the table.' She drank the water, swallowed two pills, and lay back. 'You followed me? You were there the whole time? Outside?'

Margaret said, 'Yes. Yes. Yes.'

'You didn't want to save me? Or him?'

Margaret said, 'You – no, except for the trouble it would have caused. Him – I couldn't interfere. It was between him and you.'

'I see,' Sumitra said slowly. 'You hate me?'

Margaret said, 'I try not to. Now will you go away and leave him alone?'

The woman on the bed said, 'Yes . . . You can't really mend a broken jar, can you? What would you have done if it had ended differently tonight? Would *you* have gone away?'

Margaret said, 'No. I have no politics to turn to, no power, no position, no money. You would have betrayed him again, sooner or later . . . What did you mean, when you said it wasn't for your sake, that he should let you live?'

Sumitra's congested, bloodshot eyes turned slowly up to her. 'Nothing. Leave me now, please.'

Margaret turned and left the room. Outside Janaki's door she hesitated. But Janaki must be told, and she was a woman to be trusted. She entered quietly, whispering, 'Janaki?' The other awoke and Margaret sat on the edge of the bed and told her quickly what she had seen. Janaki muttered, 'Is he all right? Will he try to do it again tomorrow? Or kill us all in the car?'

Margaret said, 'No. It's finished.'

Then she went to her own room, and, knowing that she would have no need of tablets, being utterly spent, fell into bed and asleep.

In the morning after breakfast Rodney came, pale and contained, to load their baggage into the car. By eight o'clock they were on their way again through the awakening spring of a warm February day. The hours passed in almost total silence. Sometimes Sumitra talked in a low voice with Janaki in the back seat – Margaret noticed she made no attempt to hide the marks at her neck – but her talk was of nothing, things seen by the roadside, comments on people known, small bursts of human sound that broke up the inhuman silence in the car. She herself spoke occasionally to Rodney, searching for half an hour to find something to say, then saying it. Rodney answered monosyllabically, his voice dry. The Ford raced on, driven fast but safely.

Late in the evening they entered the outskirts of Bombay. At half past eleven, when passing slowly down a raucous street near Victoria Station, Rodney pulled in to the kerb.

Janaki sat up, yawning. 'Where are we? Why are we stopping here?'

Rodney did not answer but went round to the back, opened the door and pulled out his suitcase. 'I am leaving you here,' he said. 'I do not need help any more. It will also be dangerous for you. Thank you for everything you've done.'

Margaret tried to pull open her door, but he was leaning against it. His cold, dead glance turned momentarily on her, and he said, 'Stay there, please. I do not want your help, either.' He walked up to a taxi parked a little in front, and got in. The taxi drove away.

The three women sat without motion for a minute. Then Sumitra said, 'I'll drive. Your grandmother's house is on Douglas Road, isn't it?'

She slipped behind the wheel, and they went on without another word. At the big house they all got out and a horde of women, children, and servants ran down the steps.

Sumitra said, 'Would you mind calling a taxi for me?'

Once again, there was no argument, no talk. They waited in the drive, and in a few moments a taxi came. The servants transferred Sumitra's baggage into it, she climbed in with a final 'thank you', the taxi drove away.

Then Janaki introduced Margaret to the people crowding round: her sister; the sister's husband, a banker in the city; two female cousins; a fat aunt; a dozen assorted children, shy, wide-eyed, but yawning, for it was long past their usual bedtime; her mother, a widow for twenty years; and her mother's mother, a widow for forty years and the head of the household – a frail, thin-skinned old lady with piercing black eyes and a plain white sari, who said, as she held out her thin arms, 'Welcome, child . . . you are the first English person to enter any house of mine.'

The mother led Margaret to an upstairs room with the smell of the sea blowing in through open windows, escorted by the whole family so that she felt she was in a football crowd at home. For five minutes they all wandered round, each little boy and girl proudly pointing out a light switch, a cupboard, the table where she could have *chota hazri*, until at last Janaki cried, smiling, 'Leave the lady in peace. We have had a long day.'

Then they crowded out with profuse expressions of apology, and Margaret sat down on the bed, Janaki remained standing. 'What are we going to do now?'

'We?' Margaret said listlessly. 'He isn't your problem any more.'

Janaki said gently, 'I loved him myself, once . . . We are tired, and there's nothing we can do now, unless we call the police.'

Margaret sprang up, crying, 'No!'

Janaki smiled faintly. 'You are like a tigress . . . Of course we cannot. In the morning we will talk, eh? Now, go to sleep.'

In the morning, after the servant brought the *chotra hazri*, Margaret got up and looked out the window. Between palms standing stiff in the airless morning, through the heavy sea-laden atmosphere, she could see a corner of the Indian Ocean, and a ship on it, gliding out of Bombay harbour four miles to the south round the curve of the reclaimed land, drawing a trail of strong black smoke across the blue-sheened

259

water. The ship was going west, towards Aden, the Red Sea, and England. She watched it a long time, until only the smudge of its smoke hung above the sea line, then turned back into the room and began to dress.

As she had asked, they brought her breakfast to the room, and at ten o'clock Janaki came.

They sat in high hard chairs by the window, looking out across the Indian Ocean. Janaki came to the point at once. 'Margaret, is it any use suggesting that you should go back to England, now? He doesn't seem to care for you. Excuse me being frank, but it would be foolish to ruin your life out of an illusion. The worry, the strain, are making you ill.'

'Do I look ill?' Margaret interposed.

Janaki said, 'Thinner . . . feverish. You look now the way I always expected missionaries to look, but you never did, the few times we met when you *were* a missionary – twice, wasn't it?' Janaki threw out her palm. 'I am not speaking the truth. You do look feverish, but it suits you. You are more beautiful than you have ever been.'

Margaret said, 'Now I really am a missionary, with faith, and a cause I believe in, and love – the love Henry wanted me to have for Jesus. I suppose it's blasphemous, but I can't help it.'

'So many women go the other way,' Janaki said, 'turn from men to God. No, it's not blasphemous, not to a Hindu, at least . . . I knew it was no use arguing with you. I only wanted to be sure that you understood what a long, hard road you have chosen. What do you want to do?'

'Find Rodney,' Margaret said promptly. That was all. That filled the whole of her thought.

'And then?' Janaki's voice was gentle but insistent.

Margaret gestured impatiently. 'Work for him, look after him, feed him, love him. Sumitra killed him. I must bring him back to life. I don't care what he does. He can beat me, steal from me, make me go on the streets, have other women in my bed, I don't care.'

Janaki sighed. 'Very well. Now, how are we going to find him?'

Margaret could not answer. They sat in silence, staring out at the flat blue sea.

'Private detectives?' Janaki said. 'They are terribly expensive, but . . .'

'I'll get the money somehow,' Margaret said. 'I have eight hundred rupees in the bank, and passage back to England that the mission gave me. I can get a refund on that. I can work, too.'

'Yes,' Janaki said, 'you can make a lot of money, with your training, particularly in private nursing.'

'That wouldn't give me enough time, and they usually want you to live in.'

'What about the Wadalia Hospital, then? It's run by the Parsees. It's very good – and they pay decent wages.'

'If only we could reach him with a message,' Margaret muttered.

Janaki's voice had a thin edge. 'What message? That you want him? He knows that. What can you say in a newspaper advertisement that would make him come out?'

'A newspaper advertisement,' Margaret said, 'I hadn't thought of that. Will he read the papers?'

'Not for a bit, probably. Even if he does, what are you going to say?'

Margaret got up. 'I'll think of something. Now, how do I find a private detective agency?'

It was Janaki's turn to be without an answer. At last she said, 'I don't even know if there are any.'

'There must be!' Margaret cried. 'They have divorces here, too, don't they? And cashiers they don't trust? I'll go to Sir Andrew Graham and ask him. And then, if you'll give me his name, to the chairman of that hospital.'

Ten minutes later Margaret left the house in a taxi, sitting impatiently on the edge of the seat all the way to McFadden Pulley's head office in the business district. That was the last taxi she took for a week. That was the beginning of an endless time when every day contained too few hours for the fulfilment of her restless desire for action, and every night too many . . .

Sir Andrew Graham ushered her personally into his office. Although she never said it out plain, he understood the situation clearly, and tried to warn her against banking too much on a man of Rodney Savage's proven instability and violence. She shook off his warnings, and then he answered her question. Yes, he knew of a reliable private investigation agency. Yes, he would be happy to lend her money, over and above what he would give as a small contribution.

'And when I do find him,' Margaret said, 'if he agrees to leave India, will you smuggle him out of the country in one of your ships?'

Sir Andrew fingered his heavy jowls and his Scots accent became more noticeable. 'They are not my ships any more, Mrs Wood. They belong to the new McFadden Pulley, of which I am not a partner, merely the managing director, and that for only a few months more.'

'The ships' officers are still English, aren't they,' she said emphatically, 'even in the coasting steamers?'

'It's a dangerous business for us to get involved in,' he said.

'You owe it to him!' she cried. 'What were you doing when he was being wounded in Burma?'

Sir Andrew held up his hand. 'I will see what might be possible, if the situation arises. I doubt that it will arise.' He walked with her to the door. Just before opening it he said with a half-smile, 'I was sitting at that desk during *this* war, Mrs Wood. But in 1917 I was lying wounded and frozen in a trench with a hundred corpses, at a place called Passchendaele.'

'I'm sorry,' she said.

'Good luck, ma'am. I only hope he turns out worthy of you.'

On to the address he had given her, hurrying on foot through the crowds in the lazily growing heat. A guarded talk with two small dark men in European clothes. Ah, Colonel Rodney Savage. Did Madam realise that if they learned anything about that gentleman they were in duty bound under the terms of their licence to report it to the police? The gentleman had a criminal as opposed to a civil suit pending against him. This was a special case! Yes, indeed, precisely. In the circumstances, provided it was only information, not leading to a situation where their agents could be said to have made actual contact, as in serving papers or the like . . . Aah, nothing of the sort. Precisely. In that case . . .

On, to the office of Milkwalla and Company Ltd. Wait in the outer office, cautiously scrutinised by fat gentlemen in tall hats through glass partitions. Guided into the presence of Sir Ramatoola Milkwalla, a stern old man in traditional

Parsee robes; in the corner, at another big desk, a young man with a huge R.A.F. moustache and hacking jacket. The old man reads Janaki's note, mumbling politely to himself. At the end: 'Mrs Wood, if your qualifications are as stated, I am sure the hospital will be only too glad to employ you ... but for how long? It upsets the routine of the hospital to employ nurses, especially senior ones, who come for a few weeks and when their, ah, purpose is served, leave. How long a contract of service will you sign?'

No more lies, anywhere. She lifted her chin. 'I am here looking for a man – Colonel Savage. When I find him I will leave the hospital, if he wants me to.'

The young man in the corner turned. 'Rodney Savage? The chap who rubbed out that clot Gokal Singh in Chambal?'

'Yes,' she said.

'I knew him in Burma. Came to our squadron mess once, and broke all our plates. Great binge! Next day I flew him over Homalin in a Harvard. Flack everywhere, no joy. Pranged on landing. Kersplat! No gore.'

'Murder?' the old man said. 'Do I understand, madam, that you are associated ... ?'

The young man said, 'Come into the other office for a moment, Dad.'

They left her alone. When they returned the young man said, 'A piece of cake. I'll ring old Merchant and he'll give you the job. Savage was one of the best brown jobs I ever came across.'

On to the hospital, a large brick building half a mile back from the docks. Crowds of all races waiting under the trees outside, and in the corridors. Interview with Dr Merchant, a tired, over-worked man. Talk about Dr Pallister at the Royal Mersey. She got the job, as senior night sister, medical wards. The matron did not ask her why she wanted night duty, but was only too glad to agree. Start tomorrow, to give her time to get her uniform cleaned and laundered. She would wear the Royal Mersey cap and cape, of course? Of course.

On, back to Janaki's, to eat. Out, working like a hound through crowded streets, staring at every face, until an Anglo-Indian police officer barred her way. His voice was hard: 'How long have you been on the street? I don't recognise you.'

She shook her head, a tired hound coming out of water. The street lamps glowed, her feet burned. She stared at the man. 'Where am I?'

His voice changed. 'Are you all right, ma'am?'

'Yes, yes.'

She turned and hurried away. Must get a street map of the city tomorrow, mark it out in sectors, search each sector thoroughly. Must sleep. After she started work, how many hours a day could she walk, search? Must remember to visit the detective agency every day, too . . .

On through the night, the next day. The first night at the hospital, the routines coming back to her hand so that she did automatically what had to be done, and between watched the dawdling circles of the clock until she could go home. Sleep, hurry to the agency, lean over the two dark men. Any news? No, ma'am, we must exert patience . . . .Out on to the streets.

One morning hurrying up the stairs at Janaki's at eight o'clock on her way to bed, a hand on her elbow detained her. She tried to shrug it off but it held more firmly, and a voice said, 'Margaret, *stop*!'

She stopped. Janaki linked her arm in hers and walked up to the bedroom, forcing her to go at her own slow pace. Inside the room Janaki said, 'Sit down in the chair . . . You've been running for a week now. Now you really do look ill. Do you want to get sacked from the hospital? Do you want to make some terrible mistake there and kill a patient? Do you want Rodney to think an old witch is after him, if you do find him? When's your night off?'

'Tonight, but I volunteered to give it up.'

'Oh, no, you don't. I shall ring Dr Merchant and cancel that. We haven't seen you for days, your food is hardly touched . . . '

'I've got to find him,' Margaret said sullenly. This happily married woman did not understand.

Janaki said, 'See, you're so tired you're getting bad tempered . . . Max suggested an idea, in his last letter.'

'What?'

'He said that the only hope of getting Rodney out of hiding was to find what he cares about, and appeal to that. He thinks Rodney still worries about that Gurkha driver who disappeared. Remember Sumitra telling us about him, one evening in Bhowani, a day or two before Rodney came?'

Margaret nodded. She remembered, and remembered the Gurkha's face, too. He used to drive often past the mission bungalow when Rodney was at Pattan, and he drove the wounded man to Bhowani, the man Lady Hillburn shot. She said, 'But he stole the jewels, didn't he? For the reward that Rajah Dip Rao was giving. Rodney must hate him. He was the first to betray him.'

Janaki said, 'Perhaps. But Max suggests you put an advertisement into the paper, pretending you're Ratanbir. If Rodney doesn't respond, you're no worse off. But Max thinks Rodney will want to see him again, to find out the truth. He thinks that Rodney doesn't really believe he did it. He believes, or wants to believe, that it was somehow a machination of Sumitra's and L. P. Roy's . . . '

'What will he say, if it does work, and he finds it isn't Ratanbir, but me?'

Janaki said, 'That is a risk you have to take. You can't do anything for him until you find him.'

Margaret made up her mind. 'Very well. I will.'

Janaki said, 'Max said, don't use Ratanbir's name, as the police will know of the connection and it's a distinctively Gurkha name, which would be noticed in a Bombay paper. His old army number was 2588. So many Gurkhas have the same name that the officers often speak to them by the last two figures of their numbers. You may have heard Rodney call him *atharsi* – that's 88.'

'The meeting place would have to be in code. I mean, some place that Ratanbir and Rodney would know, but would not be clear from the text.'

'Yes. Suppose you say, round the corner outside the place where he used to work. Rodney would know that was McFadden Pulley's. There's a café there, a sort of teahouse among a lot of small shops, bookstalls, and so on . . . We'll have to insert the ad. several times, in several papers . . . Would you rather I sent a servant to the rendezvous? We could describe Rodney to him, and he could follow him, and tell us where he lives. Better still, tell the detective agency.'

'No, I'll go myself,' she said. 'Where's a pencil and paper?'

When she went to bed an hour later the advertisement was

already on its way by messenger to the newspaper offices. The message, to run a week in all newspapers, was: *Waiting five p.m. every day one hour in teashop round corner from place you used to work* – 88.

That evening, from five to six, she sat in the dingy teashop, waiting. It was a worrying, anxious time, and full of problems, some of which she had not foreseen. She had foreseen that she must not sit too much in view, or he could recognise her from a distance, realise the deception, and again vanish, this time for ever. On the other hand, she must sit far enough forward so that she could see him when he did enter the teashop. She had foreseen that, sitting alone for an hour in such a place, she would be the object of curiosity and perhaps worse, and so had armed herself with a book, and also ordered a quantity of the teashop's sickly sweetmeats, so that she appeared to be taking a peculiar sort of supper.

She had not foreseen the denseness of the crowds, nor their St Vitus's Dance of purposeless motion. For minutes at a time she could see nothing but jiggling legs, waving shirt-sleeves, dark, animated faces. The teashop jerked with them. On the street outside they hurried in opposing streams, met in tide rips of animation, broke into circling groups, rushed off in different directions. After half an hour her head ached and her left eye, catching the restlessness, developed a tic.

She had not foreseen the bugs. Just when the concentrated effort to pick out his face amid the frenzy was becoming nervously oppressive, she felt a bug crawling up the inside of her thigh. Instinctively she jumped to her feet, meaning to ask the man at the counter where the lavatory was. Then she sat down again. She dared not leave even for a minute. A couple of young men standing jammed together close to her table stared at her in amused astonishment, and she bent her head over her book. But he did not come.

The next evening she doused her underclothes with bug powder. As she sat down at the same table, and opened her book, she could not help a smile, quickly concealed, at the typically Indian mixture of high tragedy and low comedy. The powerful smell of the bug powder crept out from under her skirt to mingle with the subtly expensive perfume she had bought that afternoon. The men jammed round the tea urns looking about, and at each other, and sniffing. But he did not come.

The next day, fifteen minutes after the appointed time, he came – a stoop-shouldered figure in dirty white trousers and shirt, a newspaper in one hand, at battered topi on his head, dark stubble on chin and jowl – a middle-aged Anglo-Indian, down on his luck. For a moment she did not recognise him, and obviously he had no eyes for her because after staring round the teashop, he turned and left. She half rose, fighting to hold back her tears. The men stared at her as she put money on the table, grabbed her book, and hurried out. She saw his topi above the puggarees and the bare heads, and walked faster. At the next corner, when the snarling, ill-tempered traffic held him up, she caught him. She touched his arm, 'Rodney,' she said in a low voice.

The traffic cleared and he walked on, turning his head. His eyes were dull on hers. He said, 'Oh. It was you, was it?'

'I must talk to you.'

He stopped. 'Well?'

She looked nervously up and down the crowded street. 'Not here. It's not safe.'

He opened the newspaper in his hand, and gave it to her. On the front page a two-column headline announced *Amnesty in Chambal*. The story explained that with the setting up of a democratic Congress ministry in the province of Chambal, and in order to eradicate all previous bitterness, the government had declared an amnesty in respect of acts done during the troubles. A brief editorial comment noted that this closed the cases of half a dozen men – they were listed – now in hiding or in jail awaiting trial. Rodney's name was on the list.

'It's an evening paper,' she said, 'I left the house at three and didn't see anything . . . Oh, Rodney, that's wonderful!'

He took back the paper. 'Well?'

'Please let me come with you.'

'I can't stop you,' he said.

He walked on. She walked beside him, wishing she were not so conspicuously clean, so fastidiously dressed beside him, so that men turned their heads and women stared at her.

'Can you smell the bug powder on me?' she asked, forcing a smile. 'That teashop's crawling with the beasts. My panties are full of powder. Yesterday a bug practically went to earth up there before I could catch him.'

He said, 'I can smell it.'

After fifteen minutes' walk through increasingly squalid streets, he turned into a row of mean houses on a mean street. Garbage, offal, and filth overflowed the gutters, the street lamps shone on broken glass and chipped brick, on women leaning out of windows and washing hung from lines strung across the street.

She followed him up one flight of stairs, along a passage smelling of urine, and into a small back room, its bare walls streaked with damp, the wooden floor bristling with splinters. She saw his suitcase and a chamber pot under the bed, and, thrown into the corner, half a dozen newspapers. A single electric light bulb hung from the ceiling.

'As you've got bug powder on, you can sit on the bed,' he said. 'I have to go to work in an hour.'

'Me, too,' she said. She wanted to ask him what his work was, but she had better wait. She said, 'First, is your wound healed properly?'

'It hasn't bothered me.'

'May I look at it?'

He unfastened his shirt and opened his fly buttons without a word. His trousers dropped and she leaned forward. The exit wound was still slightly inflamed. 'Turn round,' she said. The entry wound in his back was clean and healthy, faintly pink, light scar tissue well formed. 'Turn round again, please. You ought to keep that well covered, and protected with sulpha powder until it heals properly. You haven't seen any signs of blood in your urine or stool?'

'I haven't looked,' he said.

Her professional detachment vanished. She became intensely aware of the ridge of hair running down from his navel into the dense forest of his loins, of the muscled columns of his thighs, the unequivocal statement of his male formation.

A tiny movement in the hairs caught her eye. Her arms went out, holding him tightly by the buttocks. This she knew only too well, from her profession.

'Oh, Rodney,' she wailed, her voice breaking, 'you've got crabs. And you're covered with bug bites. You must have lice, too.'

'Probably,' he said. He pulled up his trousers, so that she had to take her hands away.

'For God's sake, leave India,' she cried. 'Sir Andrew Graham will give you a passage. There's nothing for you here now, nothing at all.'

She waited, pleading silently for an answer. What there had been for him, what had been offered so generously, he had refused. What he had tried to keep had been taken from him, and broken before his eyes. There was nothing.

'Go?' he said slowly. 'I can't go. I'd be ashamed.'

'Ashamed of what?' she cried.

He held out his empty hands and stared at them, turning them over slowly. He said, 'Nothing. Having nothing. Being nothing. I can only do that here.'

She drew a deep breath. 'Let me look after you, then. I have a night job, too, nursing at the Wadalia Memorial. I don't ask anything else. I won't get in your way. I don't ask you to speak to me even, but . . . I can't bear it!' Tears welled up in her eyes.

He said, 'I have nothing to give you.'

She cried, 'I don't want anything.'

He didn't speak for a long time. Then she heard his distant voice: 'I suppose nothing else will teach you. All right.'

She leaped to her feet, her arms out. In the face of his silent indifference she let them fall to her sides. 'We'll have to get a better room,' she said, 'where I can cook.'

'I'm staying here, he said. 'The room next door's empty, and there's a gas ring and a cold water tap in it.'

For a moment she felt chilled; but then at once thought, It's better not to crowd too closely on him until he asks me. She said, 'I'll take it now, and move in tomorrow morning' – she found another smile – 'with a gallon of disinfectant and five pounds of bug powder.'

'All right,' he said.

Chapter 20

February: the fresh light pouring a clean Aegean-colour
wash over the filth of the city and shading the smoke to
pastel. By the end of the month, twice daily scrubbing walls
and floors of the two rooms with soap and water, with
carbolic acid, with Jeyes Fluid, with potassium permanga-
nate, she had conquered the bugs. By taking beds and chairs
into the street, unwinding the *newar*, dousing the frames in
kerosene and setting fire to them, she burned the bugs out of
the cracks and joints. By soaking his head and her own in
kerosene, by shaving and blue ointment and vigilance she
freed him and herself of lice, nits and crabs. By miserly
scraping and clearing of rats, and cockroaches. The landlord,
a fat Muslim living in terror of his Hindu neighbours ever
since the partition massacres, at first treated her as a mad-
woman, but now with a grudging respect.

Rodney was clean, and free of parasites, because she kept
him free. Otherwise he had not altered one jot. Every
evening he left the house, walked to the Central Station, and
took an electric train three stops up the line to the cotton
mill where he was employed as night watchman. He had
originally given the name of D'Souza when applying for
the job, and saw no reason to change it. Every morning he
returned, ate the supper she had prepared, then went to bed.
At three in the afternoon he awoke, ate breakfast. She washed
up and cleaned. He lay on his bed until the time came to go
to work.

March: the heat gradually increasing in a double progression, each morning a little hotter, a little closer, than
the day before, each afternoon a little hotter, a little closer,
than the morning, a blanket-like drugging sea heat, far
different from the sword thrusts of the northern sun.

At the hospital she made the mistake Janaki had warned
her she would. In consequence a sick Parsee woman spent a
night in the oxygen tent, and Dr Merchant spoke in sad
warning to her. The hospital could not afford such mistakes,

let alone the patients. She grew distraught, snappish, and distant. For a time her job teetered on the brink. But too much depended on it: decent food for Rodney, decent clothes, good sheets, gay curtains, all that could remind him of another world outside the rat-ridden tenement and the overcrowded train to the factory. After a bitter night, knowing that it needed only a touch of his hand, the graze of his cheek on hers, in love, to cure her, and knowing he had no desire to make the gestures, and no love to charge them with meaning, she mastered herself. After that she wiped Rodney out of her mind at the moment she entered the hospital grounds, by a deliberate act of will, like cleaning a slate with a wet cloth; and took him back the moment she walked into the street again in the morning.

In Rodney – no change. He slept in the steamy heat as well, or as badly, as in the Mediterranean beauty of February. Watching him narrowly, trying to learn more about him, she noticed how un-Indian he was. There was nothing strange about his face or his clothes, but people always looked at him with surprise as he passed, even those living in the same block, who saw him every day. It was his manner, she decided. He was a dead-beat, a down-and-out. But those were Western words carrying the notion that he had once been something else, and, but for his own character, might be again. There was no resignation in him, only despair, for he was not in the grip of an all-powerful fate, like the Indian poor around him, but in the grip of his own nature.

She noticed also his absolute lack of possessions. Where were his medals, his uniforms? Most of his civilian clothes he had lost in Chambal, and the rest when he was wounded. When he arrived that dawn in Bhowani after his flight he carried nothing of the past but a wrist-watch, and somewhere even that had gone. She believed it was a presentation watch, perhaps with his name engraved on the back, and he had thrown it away before leaving Bhowani as their chauffeur. In becoming the chauffeur he had lost the clothes she had given him. Now, apart from the suitcase and the minimum of necessary clothes, he owned nothing at all.

April: heavy clouds beginning to move up in dense formations from the Arabian Sea, so that at noon the city lay dark in the stifling embrace of heat, and the sun's rays, grey and hardly visible, poured out from the stone walls, up from the oiled streets, down from the trees. The fecundity of India, which she had once scorned and feared, now twisted her bowels every time she went out. There were always two or three pregnant women squatting outside the house, always a dozen naked brown babies playing in the gutter. In the afternoon she heard wailing and cooing from every window and doorway. Wherever she turned, women squatted with choli loosened, sari negligently half covering one breast, a baby ecstatically kneading and sucking at the other.

Rodney had not changed, not a degree.

May: a sudden increase in heat and humidity, though she had thought both were impossible. A short violent dust storm, followed by heavy rain, struck on the first of the month, when the Communists marched through the streets waving the clenched fist, banners flying until the wind shredded them and the rain drove marchers and spectators alike off the streets, and ten palm trees blew down in the park. The Alfonso mangoes came in season now, yellow, juicy, firm-fleshed, and sweet as nuts. She bought four, carefully wrapped in ice, gave him two for breakfast, and waited expectantly for comment. In vain: he said nothing.

She almost lost her temper with him then, but controlled herself, and when he had gone, wondered whether in fact he ever tasted anything. His taste buds could not have been physically destroyed, but perhaps the nerves that transmitted the sense to the brain were out of action, like those others that instigated interest, pity, hate. Later, she decided it must be so, for in the middle of the month they were walking together to the end of the block, where he would turn left and she right, when a careening truck swung round the corner and ran over a two-year-old child in front of its mother. The child was half squashed, like a beetle, no longer a human being but an animal dying in pain, gobbling and writhing in blood and crushed flesh. The mother ran out, shrieking. Rodney glanced at it, and walked on, saying nothing. Later that day, punctually in schedule, May 15, the monsoon broke. She discovered a leak in the wall of Rodney's room, the plaster began to flake off her own ceiling, the rats came into the house for shelter from the flooded sewers, and a few nights later she killed two of them in her room with the frying pan.

June: the rains falling in their cyclic pattern, rain every night, clearing a little by dawn; mid-morning rain, clear in the afternoon; rain starting in the evening when she set out for the hospital. Mould forming in the shoes she ranged against the wall, in a single day. The temperature hovering around 90 every day, 88 every night. No change in Rodney . . . A subtle, growing change in herself. She saw a cockroach, and made no attempt to kill it. Half-way to the hospital she would remember she had left the dishes unwashed on the table. Or she would look in the mirror in the nurses' common room, and see that she had forgotten to put on lipstick.

July: July 1, the monsoon broke out into one of its sudden spells of violence. Lightning sizzled across the roofs of tenement and factory, and outlined the ships in harbour with violet fire. Thunder rattled the bedside tables in the wards and the lights flickered off, once for a few seconds in the middle of an important operation and later for ten minutes. The patients grew more nervous and jittery. Lightning struck a tall, old building opposite. The building cracked with a sound like a dynamite explosion, and then caught fire internally. In two of the wards the patients' collective nerve cracked, and hysteria exploded. In the morning she walked back to the tenement through a battered, shell-torn city in the rain, fell into bed, and asleep.

She awoke early, her nerves on edge . . . As soon as she had dressed she opened the cupboard and took out the bottle of whisky she kept there. She poured herself a stiff dram, drank it in a couple of gulps, and began to prepare the tea, bread, vegetables, and lamb chops for their 'breakfast'.

Rodney came in and she indicated the bottle. 'Have some. Have a lot . . . Look at it!' She waved a free hand at the small window. The rain streamed down the panes, and seeped in over the sill with the driving wind. Thunder growled in the distance, clouds hung low over the rooftops, and there was no sign of the sun.

Rodney poured himself a drink. Nowadays he did not drink anything like as much as he used to. As with pain, and with taste, there was nothing there. If she offered him the bottle, he drank. If she didn't, he didn't. Once, trying to stir him to show *some* kind of emotion, she had given

18   273

him half a dozen pegs in quick succession. Nothing changed, neither in his manner, nor in his speech, nor in his silence.

When they had eaten she pushed the plates aside – to wash them she had to take them down to the drain in the tiny back yard – and poured herself another whisky. Rodney rose, but she said, 'Sit down. Have another whisky. There's nothing else to do today. Pheew, it's close.'

The whisky burned like a small coal fire in the pit of her stomach. How long, how long? The memory of the night crowded in upon her and she felt a hysterical desire to be held tight against fear, fear of loneliness, fear of the dark, fear of the vast and heedless universe. The muscles of her wrist trembled and the tic returned to her eye. In all these weeks she had held herself back from a physical contact she needed as a flower needs water. She had thought, once, that his sheer maleness must sooner or later break out at the provocative glimpses he had of her: half dressed; bending to put on a shoe; standing with one leg on a chair to fasten garters; brushing her hair in front of the mirror – situations which she had not deliberately created because she had not needed to. Living so close, they happened. She had hoped, at first almost subconsciously, later with acknowledged hunger, that animal rut would bring him upon her. Once in her arms he *must* feel the melting totality of her love. From lust she could lead him to tenderness, to hope of a future, to . . .

He never made a move, and she never caught in his eye any glint of interest, nor heard any tremor of invitation in his voice. These, and the gradually deepening loss of confidence, had held her from a more direct approach, so that, although their hands occasionally brushed, and, in those confined spaces, more often, their bodies, that had been all. Besides, she was a woman and knew without having to remind herself that if her permanent availability and her obvious love did not move him, certainly no assault would.

But there come moments of desperation when one must do the thing that is bound to fail, because it is there in one's nature and cannot be for ever suppressed. As she stood up, her eyelid quivering, she thought of Rodney himself, rushing out in the dawn from Chambalpur to the hopeless battle . . .

She went to him, carefully lifted the whisky out of harm's way, and sat on his lap. She muttered, 'Rodney,' and snuggled close against him, her arms round him and her mouth pressed to his cheek. The long-withheld fact of physical pressure went off like a bomb in her, but not specifically in her sexual desires or in their seat. She clung and whispered, kissed and caressed in an agony of love, willing the cold body to come to life, trying to squeeze out her own life into him, so that she could lie at last dead at his feet, if only he could live, to look down on her with the love she was giving him. 'Oh, my darling, my darling,' she mumbled, 'oh, my darling, my darling, I love you, I love you.'

Thus for a long time, which she could not measure, just a long time, until he took her by the shoulders and pushed her away.

The intensity of her emotion again exploded, this time in quick-burning fuses of anger leading from all parts of her body to her head and pouring in fire from her smarting eyes. She stooped and tugged and kicked out of her under-pants, jerked up her skirt until she held it above her waist, and thrust her loins into his face. 'There!' she screamed. '*There*! Don't you even want *that*! Forget about *me*. Think of *that*! You're a man, aren't you?'

He said coldly, 'We had a louse inspection the day before yesterday. Pull your skirt down . . . The purpose of making love is to have children.'

She pushed down her skirt, her heart pounding. She said, 'There's nothing . . . '

'When you *can* have children, you can forget that they're the object. You can take sex as lust, as affection, as anything you like. When you can't – you can't.'

She cried, 'Rodney, I would die with happiness if you would . . . '

He said, 'No one can have my child, or will.'

'I will,' she said.

He said, 'No, you won't.' He met her eyes coldly. She knew that nothing of her passion, her desire, her love had communicated itself to him. He was, at least in regard to her, impotent.

She sat down and poured herself a whisky. 'What would you do if you had a child?' she asked.

He said, 'I'd take her away with me.' His hands came forward, not outspread and empty now, but slightly curled, carefully holding the invisible shape of a small baby. 'I'd

275

raise her and love her and think my life had been worthwhile. I could go then, and begin again, because I'd have
something to begin with. But, as you see – I shall not have a
child.'

'I could have your baby,' she said carefully. 'There are
modern ways. One's called artificial insemination. You
wouldn't have to make love to me.'

He said, 'A child that came out of love, of its own accord,
not planned for any purpose.'

She sat, with head bowed over the table. After a while
she said, 'It's time we both had a holiday. I need one badly,
and so do you.'

'I don't want a holiday,' he said.

'We could go up to Mahabaleshwar,' she said, 'we could
go to Ajanta . . . a rest house in the jungle somewhere. We've
got to get out of this.'

Rodney said, 'There's nothing to stop you going.'

'Without you? I'd be miserable,' she said.

As soon as she said it she knew she was lying. At this
moment, her head aching from the thunder, her nerves
jangling from the night's hysteria and the screaming patients,
the lightning flashing through the darkened wards, her body
quivering with frustrated love, she knew that she would
give anything to be away from this silent, dead corpse to
which she had tied herself.

She said, 'Then, if we aren't going to have a holiday, we
must live better. There's no need for you to work as a
chowkidar any more. Last month young Khussroo Milkwallah came to the hospital, and asked after you. I told
him what you were doing and he said, "That's a bit of a
bind, isn't it? What's the point?" He's right. Yesterday he
was in again, and told me they'd be happy to appoint you
assistant administrative officer there. The administrative
officer is no more than a glorified *babu*, and they want a
different type of man, anyway, someone who can deal with
the doctors as an equal, but take the administrative load –
the actual buying of supplies, the laundry, the catering –
off their hands. The *babu*'s going to retire in six months, and
by then you'll be ready to take over, at a much better
salary, too . . . There was no chance to tell you about it
yesterday.'

Rodney had given no appearance of listening, and again,

for a moment, the furious outburst against him hovered in her throat and in the aching tips of her fingers. Just as she leaned forward to shout at him, he said, 'There's no place for me in that world.'

'There is, if you'd just take it,' she said: 'whatever purgatory you've sentenced yourself to, you've had enough. And it's not only yourself you're punishing.'

He said. 'I didn't ask you to share my life. I told you that perhaps trying it would be the only thing to convince you. Why don't you go away?'

She jumped to her feet. 'I will! I can't stand any more.' She ran to the door, sobbing in pain and anger. He sat at the table, his head bent over the dirty plates.

She ran back and threw herself to her knees beside him. She put her arms round him and laid her head on his lap. 'I'm just going out, darling. I had an awful night and can't sleep . . . I'll be back, always.'

He said nothing. She rose to her feet, kissed the top of his head, and slipped out of the room. For an hour she walked in the thinning rain, picking her way over the wreckage of the storm, water gurgling all the while in her ears. She walked aimlessly, seeking a way of escape from a situation which would soon destroy her. Then she would be no use to him. Or perhaps, she thought, only then will I be of use to him, two derelicts together – but the idea repelled her, and she could not think of it as union – the slow sinking through turbid water of two corpses, tied together, even though one was male and one female.

She found herself outside Janaki's house and walked in. Janaki hurried to her, arms outstretched. 'My dear! Why haven't you come before? Why haven't you brought Rodney? . . . I've heard something from Khussroo Milkwallah . . . You look awful, Margaret, really awful.'

'Give me a whisky,' Margaret said sullenly, 'please.'

'At this time? Three o'clock? . . . Sit down . . . There . . . There's no reason why *you* shouldn't have come to see me, though I understand about Rodney. Surely you need a rest sometimes?'

'Not if he doesn't take one with me,' she said. She gulped the whisky. 'Why didn't you marry him, if you loved him?'

'I was married already,' Janaki said.

'Then why did you lead him on? You're the only person

277

he's ever loved. You were the one he dreamed about. It was only when you threw him over that he went to all those other women. You could have given him everything . . . but you just wanted him for a thrill.'

Janaki got up and closed the door. Agitatedly she kneaded her small, soft hands. She said, 'You must understand, Margaret. He overwhelmed me, the same way his people overwhelmed my country. I was mesmerised by his confidence, by his power. I remember the night . . . we became lovers. I'd been out in his car, and we had to come back through Pabbi. There was rioting all over the province then and Pabbi's the worst town in the country. A big crowd of Pathan roughs stopped us, surrounded the car, waving knives, yelling. I was so terrified I almost fainted – I, a Hindu woman among those raving fanatical Muslims. Rodney raised his hand and said in Pushtu, "Gentlemen, you may not have my balls until I've used them properly. Go away, and send your women to me. All of them." For a moment there was an awful silence, then the whole mob burst into shrieking laughter. We had to stay till midnight, eating an enormous *pilao* with them. When we got back to Peshawar – Max was out on manoeuvres – he looked at me, and . . . I couldn't help it, any more than the Pathans at Pabbi . . . I just keeled over. I tried to tell myself it was a reward for saving my life, but really I was helpless. He could do anything he liked with me . . . I fawned on him. I hated him. I loved him. I despised myself – never him. I had been taught never to speak to an Englishman until India was free. You have met my mother and grandmother. Of course I had to meet them when I married Max, but I never had one into our house. At that time I might have gone away with Rodney – he didn't ask me. We were both very young. He had his career. Later, when I knew that he really loved me, Max had got the same confidence. I saw that all the things which had once annoyed me in Max – his slowness, his acceptance of the British, of insults, his ox-like good temper – were really the signs of a man who had as much strength as Rodney . . . and he was my husband. I fell in love with him . . . What could I do?'

Margaret's head sank. 'What am *I* going to do? I can't get him to live, to think, anything. He won't move . . . Is one of your children his?'

278

Janaki exclaimed, 'Margaret!'

'Well?'

Janaki said, 'No. Both my children are Max's, though you are right. I was foolish to object to the question.'

'What about that Anglo-Indian you mentioned, the one who was in love with him in '46 and married the railwayman? Did she have a baby?'

'Victoria Taylor? She had no children. But – '

Margaret looked up sharply. 'But what?'

Janaki went to the window and stared out. 'Nothing. I think you ought to . . .'

Margaret jumped to her feet, knocking over the whisky glass. 'Sumitra!' she gasped. 'She's going to have his baby! That's what she meant when she said it wasn't for herself alone, the night he tried to strangle her! That's why she looked so pale in the mornings . . . Oh, what a fool I've been, blind, blind idiot! Where is she?' The whisky dripped loudly on to the tiled floor.

Janaki sighed. 'Yes, Sumitra is pregnant. Her baby's due early in September. It must be Rodney's.'

'Unless she was sleeping with other men at the same time,' Margaret said viciously.

'You know that's not true.'

'Where is she?'

'What are you going to do?'

'See her . . . I don't know . . . This has gone on long enough. He talked about a child this morning. Something's got to be done, and done now. I love him too much to see him fall to pieces before my eyes. Where is she?'

Again Janaki hesitated. Margaret got up. 'I shall find out.'

Janaki said, 'You will never find out.'

Margaret flared. 'Perhaps not now – but the child's going to be born. She's not going to keep it locked in a cupboard for ever. If she doesn't bring it up herself she's not going to give it to just anyone. It'll go to someone who knows and loves Rodney. I'll find out, however long I have to work. This is Rodney's baby!'

Janaki sat down. 'You are implacable, Margaret. Don't you understand? Sumitra said that Rodney must never know. She made me swear.'

'In case he felt it his duty to marry her? She can say no, can't she?'

Janaki said, 'What should I do? What would Max do? ... It is Rodney's baby. She's in a flat, at 78 Reclamation Road, fourth floor. She sent for her old ayah from her home, who lives with her and does all the shopping and cooking. Sumitra never leaves the flat, and sees no one.'

Margaret said, 'Thank you,' and hurried out of the house.

Chapter 21

She paid off the taxi driver and stepped out into the rain. She had meant to stand outside the building for a time, while she had a look at it and rehearsed once more what she would say. But the slanting rain beat on her cheek and she ran across the sidewalk, into the hall, and straight up the stairs. There were only two apartments on each floor. At the fourth, panting heavily, she looked at the two doors and wondered which was Sumitra's. One of those apartments would face the sea and the other the city. Sumitra would have the sea. She rang the right-hand bell.

No one answered. After waiting a full minute, she rang again, long and firmly. This time a cracked old voice from immediately behind the door said, '*Kaun hai?*'

She said, 'Wood Memsahib. Give my salaams to the Rani Sahiba.'

'There's no Rani here.'

It was a new building, cheaply constructed. She could hear the old ayah plainly through the door. Sumitra must be within earshot. Raising her voice she said clearly, 'Sumitra, this is Margaret Wood. I intend to see you if I have to stay here a week, or call the police.'

Ten seconds later the door swung suddenly open. Sumitra stood there. She said curtly, 'Come in.'

She turned and walked ahead of Margaret into the apartment, and sat down on a comfortable sofa by the window. Just over seven months, Margaret had worked out. She was showing it more than most primigravidae at this stage, the bulge of pregnancy heavy under the sari. Her enormous eyes looked even bigger in the thin pallor of her face, and were further accentuated by the deep, dark circles under them. She wore a dark sari and a pearl necklace, and her hair hung to her shoulders, loosely gathered by a silver cord at the back of her head. She said, 'Well, now you have seen for yourself ... Is he dead? Is that why you've come?'

Margaret said, 'No. I forced Janaki to tell me. Don't blame her.'

'Are you going to tell him?'

'That's what I've come about.'

'I shall have to leave then. This time no one will find me.'

'And after you've had the baby? Are you going to bring her up yourself?'

'I don't know. Sometimes I feel that I shall die of misery, whether . . . What's it got to do with you?'

'Everything. Answer me, please.'

Sumitra shot her a defiant look; but she needed to talk. Somewhere in the background, from the kitchenette, Margaret heard the breathing and shuffling of the old ayah. Sumitra had seen no other human being for five months.

Sumitra said, 'It's the old question, and there's still no answer. I talked to you about it that day you came up to Chambalpur, but you didn't understand then. What *am* I, a mother or a political leader? What kind of mother? It would be no problem for you. It would be none for me if . . . if I hadn't done what I did to Rodney. But even that would be no problem for you. You would have betrayed England for him, wouldn't you?'

'Yes.'

'Without a husband or a home I can't be a mother. I can't raise the child and give him –'

'Her . . . Rodney always says "her".'

'He knows already?'

'No – just talking about babies.'

'Him, her, I daren't think that far . . . I can't give her a home, I can't bring her up, if I am to travel round the country organising the women of India, as the Prime Minister wants me to. Without a husband I love, why should I stay in one place? I couldn't do it for Dip. For Rodney, yes . . . but I finished that.'

Margaret waited till the other woman turned her head slightly to meet her eye. Then she said, 'Come to Rodney. Show him yourself, and his child. I've lived with him for nearly five months and I know that nothing else can save him.'

Sumitra laughed rather unpleasantly. 'Has he thrown

you over, too? And you want to see him finish me off properly this time?'

Margaret said, 'You still love him, don't you? Don't you? You owe me the truth ... *Don't you?*'

Sumitra shouted, 'Yes! ... But – '

'Come to him then. He doesn't know about the baby. But it means so much to him that he may ask you to marry him. If he does, you've got to say yes. On any terms. Even if you have to give up politics, and power, and independence, and just be a woman like the rest of us.'

Sumitra's eyes darkened. 'Would ... do you think he'll speak to me?'

'I don't know. All I can do is put you in the same room, alone, with him. I know he won't do you any physical harm. I know that that' – she indicated the other's generous belly – 'will move him as nothing has been able to ever since you betrayed him.'

'What are you doing this for? What's the trick?'

'I've told you once. I love him ... Come with me, now.'

'Now? No, no. I look dreadful. Tomorrow, perhaps, when ... '

'No. Now.'

She put out her hand and slowly pulled Sumitra to her feet. 'All right,' Sumitra said, and again, 'all right ... Will you call a taxi? 11904.' Margaret made the call and then watched as Sumitra slipped into a pair of low-heeled sandals, touched up her lipstick and applied a *tika* in the middle of her forehead. The woman moved with an ungainly heaviness, and her muscles were in poor condition. What else did she expect, shutting herself up here so long? There were exercises she must and could do, even if she refused to go out.

Margaret led the way carefully downstairs, and after a short wait in the hall the taxi came.

At the corner where they lived the driver turned with a look of astonished disgust. 'Here?'

'Yes, here. Number 27, on the right ... Wait here.'

The rain had paused and half a dozen women peered at them from doors and windows up the street. Three naked children stared up from the gutter. Sumitra whispered, 'I'm trembling ... What shall I say?'

'That's up to you. You know what you want, don't you?'

They climbed the narrow, creaking stair. Rodney's door

was shut and she tapped on it. 'Rodney?'

His voice answered, 'Yes.'

She heard Sumitra's sharp intake of breath beside her. Through the door she called, 'There's a visitor for you.' He might be lying naked on his bed. What did it matter? She opened the door and slowly Sumitra stepped forward. She could not see Rodney, and closed the door.

In her own room the dirty plates from breakfast cried out accusingly at her. She swept them up, hurried down to the filthy square of black gravel below, washed them, and ran back upstairs. She tidied up her bed, removed the table-cloth, and scrubbed the tiny table. Then she sat down.

Five minutes. She heard the mumble of voices through the wall. It was hard to tell but most of it sounded like a woman's. Ten minutes. She wondered that her eyes were dry, but they were, dry as dust and beginning to scratch so that she had to rub them with a damp handkerchief, then wash them carefully. Still they hurt.

After fifteen minutes she heard the squeak of Rodney's door hinge and tensed in her chair. A man's footsteps came along the passage, but these were fast steps, unlike Rodney's slack near-shuffle. Through the open door she saw him pass. There was a cold set to his face and jaw, and pinched lines round his nose, and his lips were thin and tight locked. His footsteps receded quickly down the stairs. She hurried to his room.

Sumitra was sitting on the bed, head down. She looked up, her face hardening from its expression of utter misery to a cold stare. 'Well,' she said, 'whatever it was you were trying to do, you did it.'

'What happened?'

'At first I don't think he saw me. Only this,' She put her hand on her belly. 'He touched me. He felt it kicking. For a moment I thought everything was going to be all right. Then he realised it was I carrying it. He looked as if he would rip me open to take it away from me . . . I asked him if he would marry me. He said no. I begged and pleaded and promised. He said no. At the end he said a marriage had to have love and he did not love me, and never could. He told me never to come near him again . . . So you showed him his child, and proved that having me too is too much of

284

a price to pay. That ought to be torture enough, for both of us!'

'What are you going to do now? No, first tell me why you didn't get rid of it.'

Sumitra said, 'I have had two abortions in Europe. This was Rodney's. I couldn't.'

'And now?'

'I haven't made up my . . . Why are you tormenting me? Why do you bully me?'

'This is Rodney's. Are you going to bring her up yourself or let someone else adopt her?'

'I *can't* bring it up. Without him, I just can't . . . Three people have told me they'll bring it up as their own.'

'Who?'

Sumitra did not answer, sullenly looking out the window with pursed lips. Margaret said, 'I can guess – Max and Janaki – your husband.'

Sumitra turned her head and said bitterly, 'You do know us all well, don't you? Yes, those two, and the other. What choice would you make of it were yours – to be the foster child of a general, a rajah, or a prime minister – a prime minister's sister, to be exact.'

Margaret said, 'Give her to me.'

Sumitra stared at her for a long, long time. She said, at last, 'So that's it.'

'Of course it is!' Margaret cried. 'You must have known all the time. But I gave you every chance. I didn't cheat. I thought Rodney would forgive you, and forget, when he saw that . . . Now you know, and I know, that he can't forget, and if he can't, he's right not to marry you.'

'But you think that if you have my child he will marry *you*?'

Margaret said earnestly, 'I don't know, Sumitra. I only know that unless he has the child he will continue to sink into the earth, as you can see he has been sinking, and will soon die. But if you gave the child to him, what could he do? At best he would have to hire a nurse or housekeeper of some kind. At worst he might marry some slut. If you let *me* adopt her, though, I am responsible – and I shall never leave him.'

For five minutes Sumitra said nothing.

Margaret said, 'It was not you alone who brought him

to this state. I know that it was mainly himself. But it was you who finally stabbed him in the back. You owe him a new life.'

Sumitra burst out: 'But I hate you! Yes, you! Knowing what you want with such utter finality. Untorn by the slightest doubt about anything. Totally in love with one man, troubled by not a thought, not a worry, never thinking, what shall I do? – only, how shall I do it?'

'You want the child to be brought up in India, then? So that you can see her every time you meet Janaki, or Dip, every time you go to New Delhi? So that you can watch her growing under someone else's love?'

'Stop!' Sumitra screamed. 'You can have her, you . . . you merciless demon. You cubless vixen. You can have her, but you've got to take her out of India within a month, and never bring her back. And Rodney.'

Margaret sighed. The trembling in her body ceased, the queasy fluttering in her belly calmed. She said, 'Are you having regular prenatal inspections?'

'No. No one has seen me. No one's going to.'

'Where do you plan to have the baby? What doctor is going to deliver you?'

'In the flat. Or out in my beach hut at Pabal. No doctor. There is nothing wrong with me. I am a healthy Indian woman, and ayah will deliver me, as she delivered my mother of me. No one shall know who does not already know.'

'You are not healthy, Sumitra. You've got to start the proper exercises at once . . . Who does know?'

'Max – I told him first. Janaki. Ayah. Dip. The Prime Minister and his sister. Now you and Rodney. That's all.'

'When is the baby due?'

'I began my last period on December 24.'

Margaret had asked the question so many times that she had an obstetrical calendar in her head. She said, 'About September 24, then. Just under three months from now. You look a little later than that. You must have antenatal examinations.'

'I will not.'

'Will you let me? I am not a doctor, but I have a lot of experience. There might be some simple defect which can be easily fixed now, by medicine or exercise or dieting, but

286

could be fatal to you or the baby, or both, if we don't do something about it.'

'Oh, all right.'

'I'll bring what I need to your apartment tomorrow morning as soon as I come off work. Please have a urine specimen ready.'

'How are you going to get it tested?'

'It shall be mine,' Margaret said. 'When we get nearer the date I shall have to leave the hospital to look after you full time, and that will make a good excuse. I can pad myself out a bit.' She laughed almost gaily. 'But you must have a doctor. You really must. It's not only your life and the baby's, that depend on this, but Rodney's.'

'And yours?'

'In a way.'

'I don't care. I will not have a doctor.'

'Then I shall have to deliver you myself, with your ayah.'

'Ayah can do it without you,' Sumitra said rudely.

Margaret said calmly, 'I am sure she can, if there are no complications. But I shall be there, and I shall warn the best obstetrician in Bombay to be ready, if I have to call on him in a hurry.'

'I will not . . .'

'You may not be conscious,' Margaret said. 'The taxi's waiting.'

Two minutes later Margaret slowly climbed back up the stairs, threw herself on to her bed and burst into tears, her hands clutching and kneading at the wet pillow under her head.

Rodney's voice, sharp and angry, brought her to her feet. 'Where is she?'

'Sumitra?' she dabbed at her eyes. 'She went back to her flat.'

'She told me she's living alone with her old ayah, and no one else is going to know about the baby. She can't do that. Something might be wrong.'

Margaret said, 'I'm going to look after her.'

'You? . . . And a good doctor.'

Margaret said nothing.

Rodney slammed down into a chair. 'Then I suppose she'll find foster parents for her. Probably Max and Janaki. I could become their night watchman. Or chauffeur. They

287

wouldn't have to pay me anything. I have a small pension.'

'No, you couldn't,' Margaret cried. 'They wouldn't take you. They *couldn't*! You must see that.'

Rodney stared at her, his face dark with congested fury. 'You're right. So I'll never see her, touch her. She'll never know I'm her father.'

Margaret said, 'Sumitra is going to give her to me.'

Rodney's brows came down. 'You? My baby?'

Margaret said, 'She doesn't want to raise it herself – not without you. She realises that she can't even have it brought up in India. The strain would be too much for her. So I am to have her, but I must take her out of India within a month, and never ...'

Rodney stood up. His hands were like powerful claws, slowly opening, outstretched in front of him. He took a pace towards her where she sat on the bed. His voice was almost casual. 'She is my child,' he said. He stood directly over her. 'I could kill you now for trying to get her – but I won't. You are needed, until she is born. But if you try to take her away from me then, I will kill you. Do you understand?'

Margaret put up her hand. He caught it, and she heard her bones cracking in his grip. She said, 'The baby is yours, Rodney. She will always be yours. You will need a house-keeper, a nanny, won't you? Are you going to change her nappies ten times a day, yourself?'

'Yes!'

'Are you going to pot her, and mix her bottle, and sit up all night with her while she's teething?'

'Yes!'

'Then, in what place? In a hovel like this, somewhere in the slums of London? That's all you'll be able to afford, if you can't work ... You're a man, Rodney. A little girl doesn't want a man for her mother. No child does. She needs a father who is a man, and acts like a man, and smells like a man. Let the housekeeper do the things a woman must do.'

The grip of his hand relaxed. He turned away. 'All right,' he said, 'but remember, that's all you will be – a nanny. If I catch you trying to become her mother ... Sumitra means nothing to me, except through the baby. You – even less. Is that clear?'

'Yes.'

288

'Remember it . . . When are you starting to examine her?'

'Tomorrow morning. I shall be late back.'

'Good. Are you well enough trained? What do you know about midwifery?'

'Enough,' she said wearily. 'But tomorrow I shall buy a textbook and study it again. And I shall ask to be transferred to the Obstetrical Ward under Mr Dutt. I'll do everything I can, Rodney, everything that she'll let me do.'

She watched his hard face soften slightly. 'I shall find a name for her. The name of a flower. A Himalayan flower . . . ' His lips tightened again and he said, 'I've got to go to work.'

A moment later she was alone.

Chapter 22

Mr Dutt, M.D. (Lon.), F.R.C.S. (Edin.), pulled out a chair for her and she sat down. Then, rummaging around in his desk, he found a bottle of orange juice, and filled two glasses. 'Why do babies always choose three or four a.m. for entry into the world?' He sighed. 'Especially if it's a difficult entry ... You look tired, Mrs Wood.'

She smiled wanly. 'I am.'

'I shall be very sorry to lose you. Too few of our Indian girls can exert that authority in the wards – like a good sergeant-major, if you will excuse me – that you British do ... You are not, of course, pregnant yourself?'

She fiddled with the juice glass. She was too tired to go on pretending. Mr Dutt was a short plump man, bald, with protruding eyes and fat, strong hands. She had learned a lot from him. This morning's case had been a nightmare. She felt queasy, imagining that she might have to deal with such a case alone.

'No,' she said, 'I'm not pregnant.'

'I presume, then, that you are preparing to act as mid-wife for another lady, who refuses for some reason to have proper medical attention?'

'Yes.'

'And from the intensity with which you have studied obstetrics, and have watched and questioned me, I imagine you are worried about it.'

She hesitated. 'It's not the case, as such. As far as I can tell she's perfectly normal and healthy, except for lack of exercise and a slacker abdominal wall than she ought to have at her age. But it's important. Personally.'

'Ah. Personally. You know it is dangerous for a medical attendant to be too involved personally with a patient?'

'I know, sir. But I have no choice. If I hadn't insisted, she would have had no one but her old ayah. She absolutely refuses anyone else. I was going to tell you, when the time came closer, and ask you to be available in case it developed badly. I wouldn't try to deal with any serious complications I've been studying so that I can recognise them . . . but there's really no reason to imagine that there will be complications. Except perhaps that, at the moment, it's a transverse lie.'

The doctor pulled a pad towards him. A lurid sun hung on the horizon, giving out heat but only a confused light. The electric light still burned, though it was past seven o'clock. A long bar of pale-violet light hung over the sky to seaward, and overhead it was dark and heavily overcast.

'Primigravida? . . . I see. Well, with two abortions she's really not a primigravida . . . Pregnancy clinically confirmed? Blood pressure . . . Date of commencement of last period . . . '

Her weariness faded as she plunged into the familiar technicalities. Height of the fundus of the uterus. Pelvic measurements. Ah, a good gynecoid arch! Mr Dutt beamed. His voice became lyrical and his eyes sparkled over a good gynecoid arch the way other men's did over a pair of long, well-shaped legs . . . General health and mental attitude. H'm, that's bad. Drugs. Get these at the dispensary. Doesn't seem to be anything to worry about, except – except perhaps the dates, coupled with the transverse lie. And didn't you say you thought, at first, she might be further advanced? Well, an obstinate transverse presentation can be dangerous. If it's still obstinate close to term it ought to be correct by version . . .

The doctor stood up, yawning. 'Excuse me . . . And, Mrs Wood – do please have the courage to ignore the patient's protests the moment you have any doubts. Millions of women have been happily delivered by midwives far less competent than you, and thousands have died though treated by doctors far more competent than I . . . but there is a middle ground, not large in percentage but far too large in terms of human suffering, when you think what a baby really is – our projected selves, our dreams, our hopes, our future – where a midwife can do nothing, a doctor, perhaps, can . . . I am at your service whenever an emergency develops – preferably before that. Good luck, in everything, and thank you for all that you have done for me – all of us – here at Wadalia. Are you going to see the patient now? . . . Good. Give me a ring at eight p.m. Or come round, if you want to.'

Half an hour later, the prescriptions made up and stowed

into her capacious handbag, Margaret left the hospital. She ate 'supper' in a nearby café, as was her custom on days when she visited Sumitra. Out in the streets the air felt even more close and oppressive than in the hospital. The violet light had turned to a dull purple and was spreading slowly upward across the sky from the west, though no breeze stirred at street level. The sun had vanished.

She took the bus, as usual, to the corner nearest Sumitra's apartment, and walked along the familiar street, through the door, and up the stairs. The old ayah greeted her with a small softening of her wrinkled face. Margaret thought that in herself the old woman wanted to like her, but Sumitra's attitude made it impossible for her to show it. Perhaps also she resented the Englishwoman with her Western notions interfering in a responsibility that had been hers alone.

She entered the big room, and almost before she was inside the door Sumitra cried, 'You again? I don't want to be examined today.'

Her voice was ill-tempered and the dark rings very noticeable under her eyes. She lay on a couch under the window, her feet up on cushions, her belly rising in a hump in front of her, her hands stretched over it, not calmly or protectively, but with fingers outspread, in anger.

Margaret said, 'I'm afraid I must. It won't last much longer.'

She went to the closet and got out the brown suitcase which she had stocked with all the necessities of private midwifery. She washed her hands and prepared for examination, while Sumitra pulled up her sari and lay back, staring at the ceiling.

Margaret set to work. Half an hour later she had half convinced herself that Sumitra must be wrong with her dates. She had looked for the signs that Dutt had told her of; she had measured and palpated; and she felt sure – almost.

After helping the other woman rearrange her clothes, she sat down opposite her on a hard chair. 'I forgot to ask you your full menstrual history, in the beginning. Are you normally regular or irregular?'

'What on earth has that got to do with it now? Will you never stop asking me questions, pawing and pushing? You're not a doctor, what do you know about it? . . . Oh, all right. I have always been irregular.'

'Have you ever had any flow which you have mistaken for a period, but which later turned out not to be?'

'Yes. When I was seventeen my mother took me to a doctor for it. I used to have two-day haemorrhages in the middle of periods. The doctor said there was no physical cause, it was due to nerves. I was very unhappy at the time.'

'Now – the period from which we are basing our calculations, the one of December 24. Was that on time? How long did it last?'

'Yes. No. How can I remember?'

'I'm sure you can remember if you try. A woman who thinks she is pregnant by her lover is going to remember very well.'

Sumitra glared at her. 'It was ten days late. It lasted two days.'

Margaret leaned back. Suppose it had not been a period at all, but a haemorrhage? Then the calculations should be made not from December 24 but from the last true period before – November 17. In that case Sumitra was at or past term now.

'You're dripping sweat on to my feet,' Sumitra said, 'sit farther away, please.'

'I'm sorry. It's awfully hot.' She mopped her forehead.

'What's the matter?' Sumitra said. 'Is there something wrong?'

Margaret rose and found a smile. 'Nothing at all, that I know of. But you may be closer to term than we thought. If you are, then we ought to get a doctor to alter the lie of the baby. It's lying across instead of head down. It's simple to move before labour begins.'

'No,' Sumitra said. 'Ayah will be quite capable of dealing with it, even if you aren't. She looked at me only yesterday and said it was fine. I don't think you know what you're talking about.'

Margaret controlled herself with a huge effort. She said, 'Wouldn't it be much wiser to get another nurse instead of me? I can find a good one for you without any trouble . . . '

'No.'

Margaret let the sweat run down her cheeks. 'Please, Sumitra, let me get a doctor, now. You need one badly.'

293

'For the last time, no! You shall deliver the baby, and if you do make a mess of it – how wonderful that will be, won't it? Or suppose it's born a cripple. Or an idiot. It's yours already, you see. I don't care. I just have to lie here and grow it and give it to you.'

Margaret repacked the case, and stowed it in the closet. Sumitra lay silent under the window, staring at the ceiling. Margaret turned to go. Ayah opened the door for her and she went out.

Her clothes were soaked through with sweat when she reached the tenement, and the purple-banded sky was dark violet in the lower segment, black as pitch to the west. The landlord was standing on the front step when she entered. He waved a hand at the sky: 'Storm coming.'

She nodded and forced her weary legs up the stairs. She prayed that Rodney was asleep. These days he had to make his own meals. The dirty plates greeted her – let them lie. This was her last day of treble responsibility, thank God. From tomorrow, there would be only Rodney and Sumitra. She pulled off her clothes and fell into bed. Must call Mr Dutt at eight.

A heavy shaking and roaring awakened her, and a ketchup bottle fell off a shelf, smashing on the floor. She tumbled out of bed, her head aching, and slammed the creaky window down against the violence of the wind. The sky was now totally dark except for a thin red line across the centre of the sky. She switched on the light and found her watch. Half past five. The window rattled, the walls shook. She found pan, bucket, and cloth and began to clean up the mess. The door opened and Rodney stalked in.

'You were late getting back this morning,' he said, 'I fell asleep waiting for you.'

She said, 'Mr Dutt kept me, and then I had to spend longer than usual with Sumitra.'

'Why? How is it?'

She wrapped the mess into newspapers, dropped it into the bucket, sat down, and tried to explain her doubts. He listened intently. Ever since the day of Sumitra's visit he had eaten little and, though now suddenly beginning to take care of his person and clothes, he had thinned and his eyes had developed a starved, luminous intensity. His movements

294

had become sharp and jerky, and when he spoke it was in clipped phrases.

She ended: 'There might be no cause for worry. But I'm going to go and see Mr Dutt, because a transverse lie at term can be dangerous. The uterus . . .'

'Call it the baby, for God's sake.'

She put out her hand. 'Rodney, it *isn't* a baby yet. It's a foetus, inside a uterus. Even if you don't think of it like that, and Sumitra doesn't want to – mothers never do – I have to . . . She's in a bad state. She ought to be living with a friend, someone she can talk to.'

Rodney stared at her. The longing came over her that he might look at her like that about her own baby – distraught, intense, involved. It would not do to think about it. He shook off her hand and began to pace the floor.

He said, 'This damned foolishness has gone on long enough. If there's the slightest doubt, she's got to have a doctor.'

Margaret said, 'I told you, I'm going to see Mr Dutt. But what can he do if she refuses to let him examine her, even let him into the room?'

'Why don't you smuggle him in? Hide him in the cupboard where he can see?'

She smiled wanly. 'That's impossible . . . If we could only carry out an X-ray examination, we would know what we needed to know.'

'She's got to go to hospital for that . . . I've got it! Make her ill. Give her something that will make her feel so awful she'll *want* to go to hospital. Once she's there the rest's easy. Put her out, for Christ's sake. Give her a knockout drop and have the ambulance waiting outside.'

'I can't do any of those things,' she said, marvelling at his persistence. 'There's no illness I could induce, no drug I could give her, which might not harm the foetus at this stage.'

'No, not that. All right, I'll go and see her. There's nothing else for it. I'll take her to hospital by force.'

'That would really harm the – the baby.'

'I'll . . . I'll promise to marry her. I can't stand this.'

Margaret turned away and began to dress. The misery didn't seem any greater than usual. Perhaps Sumitra had been working towards this all the time.

Rodney said, 'I hate her, but . . . the baby. I'm going round there now. You'd better not come with me. I'll have her at the hospital by eight.'

The door slammed behind him. She sat, unseeing, at the table until half the window shattered and burst into the room on the wings of a shrieking wind. She went again to her brush and swept up the glass. There was nothing to be done about the window. She pulled her bed farther from it and anchored all light objects under pots and shoes. The wind lifted the bedclothes in long waves and, under its howling, in the blackness outside, she heard isolated shouts of fear and the crash of a falling chimney pot. She tried to cook her evening meal, but the wind blew sparks and burning charcoal sticks round the room, so she doused the fire, found some bread, and ate that with butter and jam. The milk had turned rancid and she could not make tea. Twice the light went out and twice came on again. The third time it did not come on.

After an hour and a half of waiting, ten minutes after the light finally failed, she saw a taxi struggling up the street, almost like a man bent against the wind. It stopped and Rodney jumped out. She caught a glimpse of his set face as he hurried across the sidewalk. The taxi waited.

He burst in. 'She's gone. Come on.'

'Where?'

'Ayah doesn't know. Come on.'

She followed him down the stairs, and into the taxi. The taxi drove off, the driver shouting over his shoulder, 'This is my last trip today, even with double fares. Look at that . . .' A chute of heavy slates whistled diagonally across the street, ripped bodily off one roof and sent like shell fire against the upper front of the house opposite, thence to fall shattered on to the sidewalk. Huge drops of rain began to spatter against the windows.

At the apartment house Rodney said, 'Wait here.'

The driver shook his head. 'I'm not waiting, sahib. I didn't want to wait back there.' Before Rodney could pay him he slammed the car into gear and raced away down the street.

Up in Sumitra's apartment the walls creaked under the wind. Ayah squatted in a corner looking fearfully at the blind windows and the darkness beyond. Here the lights still burned.

296

'*Rani Sahiba wapas nahin agya?*'

The ayah rose, pressing her bony hands together. Her face was clammed with fear. '*Nahin, sahib.*'

Rodney flung himself into a chair. 'She left here about five o'clock. She told ayah she was going for a walk. That's all. The *chowkidar* didn't see her go out. No one did . . . She might be taking shelter from the storm, but I don't think so. The storm had just started by then. She went out into it. Where?'

'Janaki's?'

Rodney grabbed the telephone. 'What's the number?'

'24096.'

He dialled and soon after spoke in Hindi. He put the phone down. 'Janaki's out of Bombay, visiting relatives. But Sumitra is not there, and has not been.' He turned to the ayah and Margaret could understand he was asking her who else had visited the flat.

'No one,' the ayah wailed, 'no one!'

The lights failed. Ayah moaned. A long torrent of lightning poured slowly down the sky and in its glare Margaret saw the sea stretching away in violet and white, running mountain high towards the black outline of harbour and city to the left.

Rodney spoke out of the darkness: 'How long do we wait here? And then, what do we do? . . . Nearly eight o'clock. The telephone's going to go any moment. Use it while we can. Get on to Dutt.'

He lit a match and she dialled quickly, asking, 'What am I to say?'

'Tell him first what you learned this morning . . . ' Margaret held up her hand. 'Mr Dutt? It's Margaret Wood . . . ' Quickly she gave him the details. The surgeon's voice was strained. 'Get her to the hospital, Mrs Wood. She must be put under the care of an obstetrician.'

Rodney, listening with his head close to hers, took the phone from her. 'This is Rodney Savage, doctor,' he said, 'the woman is Sumitra, Rani of Kishanpur.'

She heard Dutt's gasp, the Bengal accent suddenly strong. 'Oah, my Goad!'

Rodney continued harshly: 'The baby is mine. Sumitra's disappeared. Went out at five. Please get all your things, come round here in your car, and we'll go and find her.'

'It is impossible.' Mr Dutt's voice was faint but decisive as she strained to hear. 'I have every sympathy with you, but I cannot spend my time looking for a lady who *may* not be in urgent need of my help if we do find her, while half a dozen women are even now awaiting my attentions. I am going to the hospital now.'

'You've got to come here,' Rodney snarled.

'I cannot,' the doctor said. 'Put Mrs Wood on the line.' His voice was loud and emphatic in her ear: 'Mrs Wood, the storm has produced a rush of cases, prematures, frightened women who weren't going to have a doctor and now want one, miscarriages . . . They're snowed under at every hospital in Bombay. Find the Rani and take her to the nearest hospital. Then ring me. Good luck.' The phone went silent.

Rodney glowered at her, his eyes shining in the lightning with a luminous glow.

She said, 'What about the police?'

'Not a hope. They'll be even busier than the doctors . . . We'll go to Janaki's. Someone there might know where she'd go. Come on.'

'Wait!' She dragged out the midwife's case, and he snatched it from her. They ran down the stairs and into the street. 'No taxis now,' Rodney yelled. His hand pressed hard on her shoulder, forcing her forward into the lashing rain and wind.

'This is a hurricane,' he shouted. They struggled to run against the wind along the esplanade, but could only make the slow and painful progress of mountain climbers against a blizzard. On the left the sea battered against the stone retaining wall. Every few seconds, with a heavy shudder that shook the stone under their feet, a wave smashed over the top and poured in dirty yellow froth across the roadway. A few street lights still shone, though most had their glasses smashed and one lay twisted like spaghetti in the middle of the road. Once a fire engine passed, its bell clanging, but it was going in the opposite direction.

After half an hour they reached Douglas Road. There the tall concrete apartments sheltered the road from the wind, and it was easier to breathe. They leaned against a wall and rested. The water poured from Rodney's hair and clothes as though he had just climbed out of a swimming pool. His eyes burned dully behind the curtain of drops falling from his eyebrows. He said, 'Is this case waterproof?'

'Not very,' she shouted back, 'I never expected I would have to take it out in anything like this.'

'Come on.' He lifted the case, grabbed her hand, and pulled her on down the road, now at a run. Fronds and boughs of coconut palms littered the street, and a small car stood in the middle of the sidewalk.

At Janaki's house they had to pull four times on the old-fashioned bell and shout and hammer for a minute on the locked and bolted front door. Then the door burst open, held feebly by three struggling women and two children against the force of the wind. They shot in like projectiles, followed by a shout of the wind and a gunshot spray of palm fronds, mud, and water. Rodney put down the suitcase and applied his shoulder to the door. Slowly they forced it shut and slammed the bolts into place.

Janaki's mother stood near, wringing her hands and crying out in Hindi, 'Ah, Margaret! What misery! What is the matter?'

Rodney turned to her. 'It is Sumitra, *mā-ji*. the Rani Sahiba. She has gone . . . '

Margaret interposed. 'She doesn't know.'

Rodney said, 'She is going to have a baby.'

'*Aiih!* In this night?'

'We don't know. She has run away from the flat where she was hiding. Do you know where she could have gone?'

The old woman waved her hands. 'I don't know. I have only met her two or three times, in the old days. If Janaki were here . . . She is not far, in Panvel . . . If only we could telephone . . . Bring towels, children, bring hot tea. Bring your aunt's whisky. My poor friends . . . '

'We cannot stay, *ma-ji*,' Rodney said, 'you have no idea where she can have gone?'

A dozen women and children and two or three servants were crowded in the hall round the two soaked English. They all stood in a widening pool of water, the sound of the hurricane increasing outside.

'Wait!' Margaret cried. 'When she first came to our house, and I asked her where she would have the baby she said, "at the flat or" . . . somewhere, a beach hut . . . '

'Juhu?'

299

'No, I would have known that. Oh, I can't remember the name.'

A thin old voice cut in. 'Of whom do you speak?'

The dense crowd parted. Janaki's grandmother stood on the stairs, all in white, her thin white hair drawn tightly back from her forehead, her sari looped lightly over it, for she was in the presence of a man of her own class. She made a short *namasti* to him, then her head went up. Rodney knelt quickly, and touched his hand to her emaciated foot. He rose. 'You are Janaki's grandmother, *bari-mā?*'

'Yes.'

'I am Rodney Savage.'

The hooded old eyes opened with a sudden flash. 'Ah! Of you, she spoke, to me, once. To me, alone.'

'*Bari-mā*, we talk of Sumitra, Rani of Kishanpur. Do you know where she or her family have a beach hut?'

The white head nodded slowly. 'Certainly. At Pabal.'

'Where is that, *bari-mā?*'

'It is near Alkhuti. The road turns off at Khed. It is twenty-five miles from here.'

'I know it,' a tall girl of about sixteen broke in, blushing furiously. 'It is a sort of little peninsula, an island at high tide and in the rains. There are four huts on it. I have been there, but did not know that one of the huts belonged to the Rani Sahiba.'

Rodney said, '*Bari-mā*, is there a car here we can borrow? We must get out there at once.'

The mother cried, 'In this? It is madness, children! Wait till tomorrow. Get . . .'

The old matriarch raised a wrinkled, spotted claw of a hand. 'There is my son-in-law's car. Take that. You, you — see that it is filled with petrol.'

Rodney knelt again, and again touched the old woman's foot. She put her hand lightly on the top of his head, and then he stood up. He picked up the suitcase, and turned to Margaret. 'Come on.'

She said, 'Wait!' She turned to the young girl. 'Do they have electric light out there?'

'Oh, no!'

'Fresh water?'

The girl went pale. 'I think so . . . Not out of a tap.'

Rodney said, 'We'll have a long way to walk. We can't

carry water. We'll just have to hope. There'll be kerosene oil and lamps, or Sumitra wouldn't have gone there. We have a torch . . . Come on.'

They fought their way out the door and along the front of the house to the little garage. Inside, one of the servants poured fuel from a two-gallon can into the tank of the pre-war Austin, then Rodney slipped into the driver's seat, pushed the case over into the back, and started the engine. Margaret got in.

'Hurry, hurry,' she said, 'I have an awful feeling that we're late already.'

'Got to wait till the engine's warm, tonight,' he said. He switched on the headlamps, while the servants stood ready by the double doors. Minutes later he called out, *'Darwaze kolna!'*

The servants struggled with the bolts. She muttered, 'Rodney, I'm frightened.'

He turned his head and for a moment she thought he was going to curse her for a cowardly slut. Instead, his hand went out and rested on her knee. 'No, you're not,' he said gently, 'you've never been afraid when you're with me.'

The doors flung open and they drove out into the storm. Almost before they had left the shelter of the garage something struck the window beside Margaret's head with a heavy crash. She ducked, crying out. Rodney's smile was cheerful in the thin light from the dash. 'Coconut,' he said, 'it hasn't broken the glass, has it?'

Trembling with relief, she looked at the pane, and saw that it was starred from its centre, but not broken. In the road Rodney turned north, the windshield wipers hurrying across the streaming glass and the lights boring a short, enclosed tunnel into the rain. The road lay inches deep in water and debris, and their wheels threw up angry waves on either side. For a time they drove without hindrance through factory and suburb, but the speed never rose above fifteen miles an hour.

'Get that road map out of the pocket,' he told her. 'And the torch out of your case . . . Note the mileage. We started at 3419. How many, on the map, to Khed? – Then look for the turning from 3438 on. That's about the only way we'll recognise it tonight . . . Have we got everything the baby will need after she's born – blankets, clothes, food?'

'Yes . . . *Why* should she run away suddenly? And how could she get there in this?'

'Why? – God knows. Perhaps she'd decided she couldn't let you have the baby, after all. How? – At five the streets were probably full of taxis still. She'd have just about reached Pabal before it got really bad . . . How long will it be before we can take the baby away? One week? Two weeks?'

'It depends – *look out!*' The car was already stopping under the hard pressure of the brakes, throwing her forward on to the dash. A blue flash lit up the wet road, flailing trees and a line of hovels to the right. Another flash followed, and another, each one lighting up the inside of the car with a livid glow. Dimly seen, giant snakes coiled in the road ahead.

'Power cables,' Rodney said, 'two, three . . . Take the wheel. Give me the torch. Follow the light.'

'Rodney, we can't!'

'Yes, we can. Just follow me, put the right wheel where I shine the torch.'

He got out and the door slammed. In the interval when the door was open another flash lit the car and she heard the crackling snap of the short circuit. For a moment blue fire ran along the seething gutter. She slid behind the wheel.

The thin beam of the flashlight shone down. Clear in the headlights she saw a looping coil of high-tension cable lash down and across the road, curled like a whip by the wind. Rodney stepped back without ducking, and shone the flashlight upward. The cable had looped into a tree, its end pouring out smoke. The other cables lay across the road. Rodney turned and signalled her on with the flashlight. She slipped the car into gear and crawled forward. He was standing close beside the cables and she saw that there, where the light shone, they lay flat in the water, hissing and sparkling. To the left they rose in waving coils. He jerked the light and she drove over the cables. The lights flickered and came on again, and her hands tingled on the wheel, then it passed, the door beside her opened, he was pushing her across the seat. The car moved again, faster now.

The car lurched steadily on down the empty road. Three times Rodney and she had to get out and pull tree limbs out of the way. 3431. 3432.

The headlights shone on a heavy truck drawn across the road. A wildly swinging red lantern hung from its side. Rodney got out, the door slamming behind him. She saw him walk past the truck, return, go to a hut beside the road, bang on the door. Eventually the door opened and he disappeared. Five minutes later he returned.

'Bridge gone,' he said; 'it's not much more than a culvert, but it's gone. They say we might be able to cross on the railway bridge.'

He turned the car and they went back the way they had come. After a mile a cart track branched off on the left. He changed down and turned on to the flooded cart track at an even pace. Side-slipping, skidding, but always moving, they came after a mile to the railway. Rodney turned on to the tracks, and began a slow bump bump bump northward along them, the catenary wires of the electrified line arrowing down the upper blackness, the lights glinting along their undersurfaces.

'Here it is,' he said. He took the torch and jumped out. She saw him walk across the bridge, the torch flashing to right and left. When he got back into the driver's seat she said, 'Is it all right? Can we get over?'

He said, 'It's two bridges, one for each track, so we can't go on down the middle, like this. Damn narrow. Guard rails inside the running rails, so there's no room for the car wheels. I'll have to put one wheel on the outside. Get out. Take the torch and the case. Walk over. If I don't make it, get back to the main road and bribe someone to take you on.'

'I'm not going without you!' she cried. 'We can't go on if it's as dangerous as that.'

He pushed her forcibly out into the wind. She started across the bridge. Her head swam, for though it was a short span it had no railings and no side path. An inch below the concrete lip black water ran towards the sea with a sullen roar.

At the far side she turned and waited. By then Rodney had forced the car up on to the rails. The headlights crept towards her, heavily tilted to the right where one pair of wheels rode on the narrow band of ballast outside the rail. If he slipped off that, he must lurch into the flood. The lights came on, bigger and brighter.

They reached her. She pulled the door open and sank into

303

her seat, shuddering and weeping. 'Rodney,' she moaned, 'it's not worth it, nothing's worth it . . . We don't even know whether she's there, whether she needs me, whether I can do anything!'

The car bumped over the ties, and again his hand fell on her knee. He said, 'None of us can do more than his best. That much we must do.'

Soon they reached a grade crossing and, turning sharply on to another waterlogged track, regained the main road.

'What's the mileage now?' he asked.

She peered at the speedometer: '3437 – five to Khed, allowing for that diversion over the bridge.' The car ploughed on.

Houses loomed up in the slashed blackness, all lights extinguished, and the street covered with bricks, slates, tiles, and balks of timber. At a crossroads in the centre of the town the lights shone on a black arrow pointing left, and the message: *Alkuthi* – 5.

'Across the Salsette Marsh,' Rodney said, 'the wind will now blow – for a change.'

The road ran at first among the walls and bending trees of small farms and market gardens. The palms danced like madmen in the headlights. Every few yards one or both of them had to leave the car to drag wreckage out of the way. They were both as wet as swimmers, but they had been since leaving Sumitra's apartment. After two miles the palms and the walls and the spectral huts cowering in their lee vanished. The road became clear.

They were out on to the open marsh. The untrammelled wind struck the car on the left side. Rodney swung the wheel sharply to present the front to the wind, and at the same time stood on the brakes to avoid running off the road. Margaret's knees shook so violently together that the bones hurt. If she tried to speak just now she would scream.

Rodney looked at her in the dim light and said, 'That was a bad one . . . Open the back windows. We've got to reduce wind resistance – it's coming straight from the side, across the marsh. No more trees or other shelter till we reach the coast, probably . . . But take the case out of the back and hold it on your lap. There'll be a lot of water coming in.'

She did as he ordered. As soon as she began to wind down

304

the windows the wind shrieked through like a crazed animal, and she huddled forward beside Rodney, her body spread over the case.

He said, 'Suppose it's a difficult delivery . . . and you have to use forceps or anything like that . . . it won't affect the baby, will it. I mean, her bones or head or anything?'

She said, 'Rodney, you must stop thinking so far ahead, about the baby. We've got to get there. We've got to find out how Sumitra is. She may still have a month to go . . . '

He didn't seem to be listening to her, and she allowed her voice to die away. The little car moved on in a universe of wind and water, the world of human beings drowned or blown away. The lights shone down a straight causeway, shiny-wet with water, the surface mottled by the bursting of the rain drops upon it. To right and left stretched an ocean, also black, also shining, also mottled, but marked too by long wind streaks and, over all, a dense curtain of driving spray. Straining her eyes ahead Margaret could only just tell the difference between the causeway and the flooded marsh, whose waves lapped over the road.

The car crawled on, lurching over to the right under the rhythmic pulse of the wind, crunching back on its springs, grinding on in low gear.

The lights went out. The Austin squealed to a stop. Rodney got out and dragged himself forward along the side of the car. When he returned, he beckoned her to the driver's seat and bawled in her ear: 'Glass blown in, bulbs smashed, all of them. Follow me.'

She looked at him, her eyes almost closed against the rain and wind that poured past his bulk. It was impossible to go on, it was madness. She smiled into his eyes. 'All right.'

The beam of the flashlight crept forward and she engaged gear. Following at five paces behind him, she saw only his legs moving slowly, one after the other, down the left side of the road. He was leaning so far to the left, against the wind, that his upper part, seen dimly in outline, looked like one of those movie trick shots where a comedian leans over, past the borders of reason, on nothing.

After ten minutes the light swung in a pendulum arc and then shone its beam left. The road made a full left turn. She inched round, more than ever conscious that she had no guide but the torchlight ahead. Now she could hardly see that. She could detect no difference between the texture of the road and the flood.

When she finished the turn the torch was almost under the wheels and she jammed on the brakes. Rodney was doing something but she could not make out what – fighting, wrestling . . . one leg rose in the air, kicked forward, then shot back. She heard and felt a crash as the wind threw him back against the hood. The light disappeared and she tugged at the door.

The light came again, low to the ground now, but moving forward. The dim aura above was the shape of a man's back, a man on his hands and knees. Rodney was crawling into the wind.

In that instant she knew they would reach the hut. No one else could have done it. Only this man, her man, Rodney Savage, could drive body and will and machine through such opposition as this. The spine of a book appeared before her straining eyes, the moving flashlight in the middle. She saw the title – *Meru* 1911–1921 – above the author's name – *Peter Savage*. Now her father's face – *the light in the middle of his forehead* – talking always of mountains from his arm-chair. Herself, pigtails, twelve, thirteen years old, rainy day – *the light jerking on behind the swinging wipers* – red binding, heavy book, idly leafing through, rain on the window, liner siren mournful in the Mersey . . . pictures, old-fashioned to her eye; reading a few pages until fear came, with dark visions of terror; the fear was not of the blizzards and precipices, it was fear of the man who wrote, his remorseless advance against overwhelming fate. *The light crawled on.* She had put the book away, never opened it again, never till this moment on the Salsette Marsh recalled it, or associated the name with her own man. He must have been Rodney's father, who died the day before Independence.

She gripped the wheel more firmly. Perhaps she had shown Rodney something of determination, too, and could show him more.

The road made another full turn, to the right, resuming its original westward course. Rodney struggled to his feet and walked on. Half an hour later he signalled her to stop. The wandering flashlight shone on an uprooted palm, others struggling in the grip of the wind, a house. The light vanished. She waited alone in the heaving car, keeping the

306

engine running fast. The light reappeared, flickered, now shone in her eyes, now downward on the water through which he splashed back towards her.

He tumbled in and flopped forward over the wheel as she squeezed away to make room for him. His breath came in long shuddering gasps. She put out her hand and stroked his streaming hair. He did not shrug her off – but perhaps he did not notice. After a time he raised his head. 'Alkhuti,' he said, 'she came through just after six, and went on to Pabal. The taxi came back at once, without her . . . But we can't take the car farther than this. Tarmac ends – sand track beyond, all flooded now.' He edged the Austin into the lee of a hut and switched off the engine. 'Close the windows . . . Ready?'

She braced herself. 'Yes, I'm ready.'

'Here, carry the torch. Walk on my left, hold it in your left hand, hold me with your right. Straight ahead to the beach, a couple of hundred yards, then right, quarter of a mile on beach road, over bridge.'

He forced open the door and got out. She passed him the case and then struggled out herself. Hands locked, they began to walk. Walking was hard, breathing harder. The wind blew so strongly that sometimes it sucked the air out of her lungs and sometimes rammed an emulsion of air and spray down her throat, at a hundred miles an hour. She could only breathe through clenched teeth, but she needed more oxygen than that to move. Rodney, the heavy case dragging and flapping in his right hand, often at arm's length, dragged her forward. The wind came in an alternating pattern of shriek and roar as they passed among and between the hovels of the village. All the time they walked in wind-whipped water, shifting sand under their feet below. All the time, too, a heavy throbbing, deeper than the boom of a liner's siren, deep as the deepest thunder, grew steadily louder and closer, and above it a rising hiss. The water in the wind now tasted salt, there was froth on the road, and the palm trunks were rimmed with white. The last trees fell back and without warning they came upon the sea.

It offered no hold to any sense except hearing. The beam of the flashlight could not reach even to the nearest outflung fingers of the waves. Smell and touch were numb. Only through sound did she know that it had passed the high marks of the highest tides. In sound she 'saw' the short waves

307

crashing down, hurling forward with the long sibilant hiss, being dragged back, hissing louder. In sound she 'saw' the deep swell from a thousand miles out, slowly rising and falling under the surface waves, twelve waves to every surge of the swell. In the upper registers she heard the wind dragging the surface off the water, as one drags a carpet off a floor, and hurling it inland, to coat with salt the palm trees and the huts.

Rodney dragged her round to the right and immediately she found herself floating in huge strides, the wind forcing into her back and up under her buttocks in violent thrusts. In the jumping light she saw that they were being carried like sail planes down a beach road that ran along the top of what was normally a high, flat dune, now a ridge hardly above the level of the water. Rodney, offering more surface to the wind in his body and in the case gripped in his right hand, flew in longer strides beside her, and twice pulled her off her feet so that she dived on her face into the flooded sand. Then the wind held her down, and it took their combined strengths to get her up. On again, the sound of the sea lessening . . .

Rodney leaned back, pulled hard at her arm. 'Bridge,' he screamed against her ear.

She swung the light and it picked out a wooden railing in the sea. Waves raced past – not full ones, or nothing could have survived, but short, steep waves, near the end of their force as they rushed up into the long re-entrant leading to the marshes.

'Walk behind me,' Rodney shouted, 'hand in my belt.'

They went forward into the water. Ten feet out the railing began. By then the water was up to her knees. At the railing he leaned forward, grasped it firmly, and extended one foot to the right.

'No, left,' he shouted. He transferred the case to his left shoulder, gripped the railing with his right hand, and again carefully extended his foot. 'O.K.'

They advanced slowly. The waves surged past at waist level, the crests tossing over the top of the railing. On, one foot at a time, feeling for the surface of the bridge under the water, curiously placing some weight on the leading foot, then more, then all. Shine the light forward, past Rodney's

308

body. Anxiously look at the case, the white tension of his knuckles.

'Hold!'

She braced against a wave that almost knocked her off her feet.

Rodney moved a little faster. He jerked downward and she lost her grip on his belt. The weight of the case dragged him sideways. The railing shuddered. He recovered his balance. 'Surface gone,' he shouted. He edged left, away from the railing, two, three, four sideways paces. Tried again. 'O.K.' On. Railing ended. 'Bridge may have gone, too.' Test . . . 'O.K.' One pace, another, another, the water thrusting like an animal against her, between her legs, wrenching at her skirt. Sudden step down, stumble, scream, regain footing. Shallower, shallower, up on to sand, churned sand strewn with foam and wreckage.

'We've done it! Rodney, we've done it!'

The flashlight showed a hut at the head of the beach. They struggled up the steps, banged on the door, shone the light through the windows. Empty. Fifty yards farther, another hut. Empty. And another. The light picked out a chair, a couch, a pair of feet, Sumitra's face and wide frightened eyes.

Rodney said, 'Door bolted from inside. Through the window. No glass . . . ' He hoisted and pushed her headfirst through the small window, which had never had any glass, only shutters now torn from their hinges and vanished. She hurried to the door and jerked back the bolt.

Sumitra's voice called feebly, 'Who's there?'

'Margaret,' she shouted, 'and Rodney.'

The only response was a long-drawn fluttering moan. Rodney came in. Together they pushed the door shut and refastened the bolt.

Margaret hurried to the couch. 'Is there a lamp here, Sumitra?'

'I don't know,' the voice muttered, 'doesn't matter.'

The flashlight hurried round the room. A cupboard in one corner, an *almirah* in another, two cane chairs, some deck chairs stacked against the front wall, door at the back. Rodney ran to it, opened it . . . the light shone on a small kitchen, shelves stacked with cans – and a hurricane lantern, matchboxes. Rodney brought them out. Margaret found

Sumitra's hand and gripped it. A match scratched, the glow of the hurricane lantern spread through the room. The gurgle and slap of oil as Rodney shook the lamp. 'Almost full,' he said. 'More oil in the kitchen.'

Margaret said, 'Now it's my turn.' She said it aloud but no one heard. The light showed bare walls, the open window through which they had made entry, water lying below it. The wind howled into the room, the rain spattering her where she sat beside Sumitra. 'Block that window,' she said.

Rodney dragged and pushed the *almirah* in front of the window. Margaret noticed another door beside the front door. 'What's through there?'

Rodney opened it, and the howling wind entered. He peered into the outer darkness for a moment and closed the door. 'Bedroom, but most of the roof's gone there.'

He came to the couch. 'Why did you run away? Were you trying to have the baby secretly and get out of your promise to us?'

'Don't worry about it now, Sumitra,' Margaret said, throwing a warning glance at Rodney. 'When did the pains begin?'

'A long time ago. I don't know. What time is it? . . . I thought I'd give you a fright. You were going to get everything. I didn't believe . . . I'm frightened, Margaret.' Beads of sweat broke out on her forehead and a groan was forced between her writhing lips.

Margaret said, 'Hold me . . . Rodney, get sheets out of the bedroom. Knot one into a rope. Tear up others for rags and cloths. I've got to have hot water, too. Quickly.'

When the pain was over, Margaret asked again, 'When did they begin?'

'The waters broke just before I got here, in the taxi. Six o'clock.'

Margaret looked at her watch and started with horror and astonishment. Half-past two. They had taken over five hours getting here. Sumitra had been in labour eight and a half hours.

Rodney gave her the knotted sheet. She tied one end quickly to a leg of the couch and gave the other to Sumitra. 'Here, pull on that.'

Rodney said, 'No fresh water. The tank outside's been overturned. I can boil salt water. Make a desert cooker with

310

sand and kerosene. It'll take about an hour to boil any quantity. A basinful. That's all there is to boil it in.'

'I can't wait that long,' Margaret said, 'I must examine her now. Take off her sari. Put a sheet or blanket under her.'

'No blanket. The sheets are all soaked and filthy, like that one.'

'Leave it then. Go and get the water boiling. I'll need it later.' She took Sumitra's wrist and felt for the pulse.

Pulse 109, temperature about 101. She took the surgical gloves out of the case and began to spread them with Dettol.

The couch on which Sumitra lay was a cane-bottom lounger, its end curved up to support the head. Margaret pulled her chair closer and said, 'Raise your legs. Spread them. Tell me when you feel a pain coming.'

'It hurts all the time now.'

Margaret bent forward . . . Transverse presentation for certain. That showed from the markedly transverse arch of the swollen belly, quite unlike the usual downward pointing egg. Gently she inserted her right hand into the birth passage. Feeling cautiously upward through the thin rubber of the glove she came upon a small protuberance. She slid her finger over it, and bent her head to stifle a gasp. She had felt a hand and part of a forearm. 'Hurry,' Sumitra cried. Margaret slid her hand farther up and tried to feel inside the pelvic cavities to the right and left. She could not, because both appeared to be filled, the foetal head and shoulder being in the cavity to the right. She withdrew her hand just in time before Sumitra's pain began.

Slowly, with the vast force of the mother's reserves of birth power, created for this final act, the hand and wrist of the foetus came into sight. She saw Rodney, passing with a kerosene oil can full of sand, pause and stare. His dark, drawn face turned pale.

Margaret got up. Whatever might or might not have been done earlier, Sumitra had now arrived at a situation where the amniotic fluid had long since drained away, and could not perform its function as a lubricant of the birth passage. The foetus, pushed downward by her contracting muscles, had jammed sideways into the pelvis, one arm out-thrust. Every succeeding pain would impact it still more firmly.

Black smoke and particles of oily soot swirled round the room. Quickly she pulled Sumitra's sari over her upraised

311

knees, sheltering the vulva. 'What are you doing?' she called. Sumitra began to gasp, tugging at the knotted sheet.

Rodney called, 'It'll be better in a minute. I'm going to wedge the front door open an inch or two, and the kitchen door the same, to make a draught.'

She heard him pushing and pulling behind her, the scrape and creak of furniture, the roar of the wind. The smoke lessened. She shook her head, willing herself to think of nothing but her medical task.

She must try to turn the foetus, though it was almost certainly too late to do so. If she failed, an expert obstetrician, with all facilities ready at hand, would be needed immediately. Suppose she sent Rodney back at once . . . he could reach Khed in about three hours. Supposing he found a doctor at once, he could be back in three more . . . six hours. But suppose the bridge went? And how could he drive across the flooded marsh alone, without lights? She would lose them all then – the baby, the mother, and Rodney. That she must not think about. Her responsibility was the mother and child . . . Six hours was too much. She must act sooner than that, and when she did she would need an assistant.

Rodney stood beside her, staring fixedly at the hand and wrist of his child protruding from Sumitra's body, just visible under the arched sari. Sumitra saw his face concentrated only on her loins, and closed her eyes.

Margaret took his arm. 'Come over here.' In a corner of the room close to the door, where she had to raise her voice to be heard above the bellow of the sea and the roar of the wind, she said, 'I am going to try to turn the foetus. You'll give her chloroform. Move that small table to be ready beside you, at her head. Five drops on to the pad, and when I nod, hold it gently on her face. Hold her pulse in the other hand, and count it aloud, so that I can hear. At "ten" raise the pad, and don't put it on again until I say so, and then only for a count of five. Do you understand?'

'Yes . . . My hand's shaking . . . What's the matter?'

'I can't explain now . . . hold the pad loosely. Don't tense. If I say stop, take the pad off at once. It means her pulse rate is getting dangerous. Pull her sari up – right up. More Dettol on the gloves. That's enough. All right, there's the chloroform, and the pads. Get ready.'

She bent over her patient. 'I've got to put you to sleep for a bit now, Sumitra. Count aloud.'

'One – two – three – '

'Head back. Relax. Just breathe easily, between counts, not too deeply.' She saw that Rodney was ready, and nodded. He lowered the pad on to Sumitra's upturned face.

'Seven – eight – nine – ten.' The counting turned to a mumble and died away.

'Pulse,' Margaret snapped.

Rodney jumped, took Sumitra's wrist and began to count. Margaret inserted her right hand into the birth passage, pressed her left hand firmly into the drumlike belly from outside, forcing down until she felt the head and shoulder of the foetus. She began to try to turn it out of its position . . . The hut trembled continuously, the bottles and instruments rattled on the flimsy table. Rodney's voice intoned on, sharp and nervous, counting beats of the pulse. The patient moved. 'Pad,' she said.

She had never done this before. This was a doctor's job, always. Once, at the Royal Mersey, a sardonic young intern had told her to feel the position, so that she would know what they were up against. The forces of the birth pains, which had been spaced apart, had now become a steady bursting pressure, like an over-inflated balloon. The sweat ran down her face, but her body was clammy and cold. Using all her strength, pushing up from inside and forcing up from outside, she could not move the foetus an inch.

She stood up. Rodney kept his eyes down, counting on. Pulse rate rising. She would be conscious in a moment or two. Temperature still raised.

'What's happening?' Rodney said, breaking the rhythm, – 'five, six, seven – for God's sake, what's happening? – eight, nine . . . Is the baby all right?'

She did not answer. Should she bring Sumitra round, knowing that she would have to put her out again soon? How strong was she? Not very. She'd have to come round. Coming now . . .

A long moan. 'She'll be sick,' she said. 'Hold her head. Wash her face, then clean up.'

She turned away. Behind her she heard the sound of retching mixed with groans and, later, Sumitra's faint voice, 'I'm alive . . . Margaret.'

'Yes?'

The hot hand reached up for hers. She smiled, with-drawing her hand. 'I can't touch you, Sumitra . . . gloves.'

'Margaret, there something wrong, isn't there?'

Margaret held the smile on her face. 'Not exactly wrong – just a little difficulty.'

.'Don't lie, Margaret . . . I'm not afraid now . . . I think I have nothing to live for. You can save the baby, at least? Then I will live on, through her. He'll love that much of me, all the rest forgiven . . . '

Rodney's face, tortured into ugliness, stared at her across Sumitra's body. Margaret turned away and gazed at the *almirah* that blocked the window, willing her vision to see through it to the open air beyond. But beyond there was a storm of wind and rain, night, and the sea, no peace, on distant view.

Only a Caesarean could now save the baby. It was a major operation, only to be performed with safety by a trained surgeon in a well-equipped theatre, with all the proper assistants. She looked at the thin catgut and fine needles in the case, suitable for the repair of a minor post-parturition tear, never for a Caesarean. She looked at the muddy slop on the floor, the streaks of sand and mud on Rodney's face, the filth and stain on her own blouse and skirt.

She remembered a film where some man marooned on a cabin miles from anywhere had done some tremendous operation directed by a doctor over the radio. But that was a film, this was real. She knew more than the man in the cabin had known, she had seen many Caesareans performed under her eyes. She knew too much. There was the sheer skill at the cutting and sewing, the time in which she must complete the resewing before haemorrhage killed the patient. If it were a matter of life and death, with no alternative, then she would have to try. But there was an alternative. She could cut the foetus in pieces and deliver them, one at a time, through the birth passage. Barring infection under these appalling conditions, that would save Sumitra.

But supposing she *could* do the operation? Once she cut into the skin would not a miraculous skill come to her from God, from her experience, lending her for those vital minutes the incisive certainty of Mr Dutt, Mr Mackenzie at Royal Mersey?

She looked at her patient. She needed another ten minutes to recover from the anaesthetic before she went under again. No more, as the pains were coming close now.

She said to Rodney, 'I want to look at that hot water . . . We'll be in the kitchen, Sumitra, and I can see you from there.'

In the tiny kitchen she stood pressed close to Rodney in one corner, by the open door from the big room. In the opposite corner the wind whipped flames and oily black smoke round the basin set on the kerosene oil can. She said, 'We don't have much time to spare, but you've got to understand. The baby can't be born normally because it is jammed. A surgeon in an operating theatre could perform a Caesarean, but I can't. So . . .'

'Of course you can, Margaret! I can help. My hand will be steady, for that.'

Again the temptation assailed her. She saw the film, the trapper's hand moving surely over the bare skin . . . Her own hand shook and her voice, when it came, was high-pitched and tremulous. 'I can't! I'd have to cut through the skin, through the fat, through layers of tissue, and finally into the womb. The womb's bursting under pressure, the covering is as thin as paper! As soon as the knife cuts into it, terrible arterial bleeding will begin, gushing out everywhere. In that I have to extract the foetus – the baby – and the placenta, sew everything up from the inside out, layer by layer – with those needles! I've seen a surgeon with an assistant, three trained nurses, and an anaesthetist only just finish in time, and the woman on blood transfusions afterwards, actually during it. We cannot give her a transfusion. *I . . . I . . . I dare not and will not do it!*'

'What do you want to do?'

'*Want* . . . I *must* remove the foetus, in pieces, by the normal passage.'

'But that's murder! . . . Can't you wait? It's past three. Someone will be here in the morning . . .'

'No. Her womb is stretching thinner with every pain. In an hour or two, if I don't take out the foetus, it will burst, and she'll die in a few minutes from loss of blood . . . Help me, Rodney! Give me the courage to do what I must do,

315

the way you did getting us out here from Bombay. How do you think *I* feel?'

Rodney pressed back against the wall away from her. Past his tense, bitter face she saw Sumitra lying still on the couch.

She stretched out her hands to seize his arms, to dig her nails into his flesh. The sheen of the surgical gloves caught her eye and she jerked back her hands, but they hovered in front of her face, between her and Rodney, the fingers crooked and tense. She cried, 'Do you think I don't know what this means? But what kind of future can we have, paid for with her blood, and my respect? She said once, twice, three times, that I was nothing but a woman, in love with you. I believed her. But now, here, I've learned it's not true. I'm also a nurse, Rodney.'

Sumitra began to stir uneasily, her legs moving up and down, down and up. Slowly Rodney's head swung to the right, then to the left. Then he turned completely round, looking away from her. But there was no help, no other solution but the echo of her words, and the wind.

Her voice came out flat and unemotional: 'We must start now.' The water in the basin looked to be hot but not boiling. Since she had no cold to mix with, that would be good. 'Bring the basin through, put it at the foot of the couch. Then get ready to use the chloroform again, same as last time. It will be very bad to watch. I would give anything to save you that, at least – but I can't. I need you.'

She walked into the big room and began to make ready.

From the case she took the razor and, kneeling expertly, shaved off the lower part of Sumitra's pubic hair. This she had done a thousand times, she thought with weary bitterness . . . if this were all! She spoke to Rodney: 'Put the basin down here beside me. Pour in three capfuls of Dettol.' She dipped her finger in it. She'd never heard of sea water being used for sterilisation and cleaning, but no reason why not – except for the sand lying in the bottom. Must wait for that to settle. And it would sting. Since it wasn't boiling, sterilisation of the instruments would have to be done in pure Dettol. Sumitra was deadly pale now, not far from the final collapse of exhaustion.

Margaret carefully washed her gloved hands, then washed the exposed vulva and extruded hand. She stood up.

'Head back, Sumitra, look at the ceiling . . . think o think of sleep. Ready, Rodney. Start counting . . . When wake up this time it'll all be over.'

Sumitra said, 'The baby . . . baby . . . ' Her mumbling died away under the pad as Rodney's hand came slowly, shaking, down.

Margaret took up the bottle of Dettol in one hand and in the other the long surgical scissors. From Rodney she heard, amid the dead monotone of his counting, a falling sigh that sounded like the stifled scream of an anguished child. She poured the antiseptic liberally over the scissors, put down the bottle, and bent over between Sumitra's raised spread legs.

Half an hour later she stood up. At once she clutched the side of the couch to prevent herself from falling. On a torn sheet at her feet lay the separated head and body of Rodney's child, with the placenta and umbilical cord that had so long nourished it. A pool of blood congealed under Sumitra's body and the cane latticework of the couch was sticky with blood. Rodney stood like a dead tree, brittle and white, at the head of the couch.

Margaret dropped the scissors into the basin, dipped her hands, and began to massage the outside of Sumitra's belly. As she worked steadily away, neither seeing nor feeling anything, Sumitra returned to consciousness. 'It's over,' Margaret said dully. 'Look at the ceiling! Rodney, do this . . . dig in with your fingers, not too hard, knead gently . . . '

Rodney stepped forward, two wooden paces, and did as she told him. Margaret knelt to gather up the sheet bearing the remains of the baby.

Rodney said, 'I'll do that.'

She stood up. Rodney was right. She should stay with Sumitra – but to expect him to carry his own dead, mangled child was too much. He went into the kitchen and she heard the door being forced open. The wind seemed to have lessened a little, though it was still strong. He came back, lifted the sheet, and went out. She closed the door after him and returned to her place, massaging to help Sumitra's uterus in its contractions.

Sumitra's voice was faint. 'Was it a girl?'

'Yes.'

'Is he burying her?'

317

'Yes.'

She filled a syringe. 'I'm going to give you an injection in the arm. It's to help contract the womb. There.'

'I . . . I think I'm going to sleep. I'm terribly, terribly . . . tired.'

'Yes. Sleep. I'll be here.'

She sat down on the hard chair and waited, watching the other woman. After a time she picked up a wrist and felt the pulse. Still weak but rebuilding. Ought to give her some hot tea when she awakes. No water. Temperature still high. Ought to get her to a hospital at once, too. Penicillin. Hardly could have avoided infection, in these conditions. Janaki and Mr Dutt would come. When? Noon, perhaps. Rodney was being a long time. Burying his daughter. Burying his future. And hers. Where had he gone? He should have waited for her. She had to stay by the patient, an hour at least, after the delivery of the placenta. That was the rule. More if no one else was present. Past four o'clock, everything absolutely blank, no smell, no hearing, no touch, no taste, no emotion, sight fading.

Five o'clock. Six o'clock. Dawnlight, green and pale, the patient sleeping soundly. She rose stiffly and went to the door, opened it, and looked out. Something moved along the dunes on the mainland, about half a mile away. It was a Weasel, one of the army's small amphibious vehicles. She watched it as it came closer, and at a quarter of a mile recognised the bald dome and round figure of Mr Dutt, standing up in the back with Janaki and a sepoy. Two more soldiers were crammed into the front seat.

She turned, walked through the room without another glance at the patient, and went out the back door. The peninsula was covered with palm trees, sparse beach undergrowth, and patches of long grass. The trees waved and swung in the wind but now merely with energy, instead of frenzy. After ten minutes the palms fell back and she came out on the final point of sand.

The wind blew strong, the sea heaved and plunged to the horizon. Driving sand thrust sharp arrows into her skin. The beach was littered with wreckage, wreckage of huts, of trees, of a world. At the farthest point of the peninsula, where the sea raced past, furious and yellow and deep at

318

the edge of the steep slope, a man stood, his back to the land. She went out to him.

When she reached him he spoke at once, as though he had been expecting her. 'I never knew I was a coward until now.' His voice was loud but full of doubt, like a man who shouts and does not know whether he will be heard. 'I've been here since I buried her. I meant to come, walk into the sea, keep on walking. I wouldn't have lasted a minute. Look at the tide, look at the sea! . . . I couldn't do it. I was lonely.'

She took his hand. 'I'll go with you,' she said. She had taken his life, she would give him hers in return. She felt so weak she could hardly stand. For her, it would last less than a minute because she could not struggle even if she wanted to, and she did not want to. She had killed any hope of his love far more effectively than Sumitra had done. Without him, there was nothing. She knew now inside herself exactly what he had felt during those long months: nothing, absolutely nothing.

She walked into the sea and he followed. The sea tugged greedily at her ankles. Another step and it fondled her knees. The hand was restraining her, pulling her back.

'Wait,' he said. She stopped, head down, unfeeling. 'You didn't give me time to tell you. A few minutes ago before you came, I found that though I didn't have the guts to die I could find the guts to live. What I saw and did tonight turned from an ending into a beginning . . . from a final, terrible experience into a command for the future. Look, my hands are strong, my eyes steady. I can learn.'

'What?' she asked dully.

'To be a surgeon.'

She turned and stared at him. 'You? A surgeon? It takes a long time . . . Yes. You could be a surgeon. You have the nerve . . . Let me go.'

'No. I need a housekeeper. Someone who will earn a living for me, too, while I learn.'

'Is that all you want?'

There was no answer, and after a time she raised her head again and looked at him. He was smiling. At the sight of her the smile, shining white in his dark, filthy, weary face, turned into a low, long laugh.

She said, 'But . . . but you said you'd never laugh again!'

His face returned to its seriousness, but without any trace

of sadness or bitterness. 'My baby's dead, yet I can laugh. It's like a funeral in the army. We march to the grave in slow time, with arms reversed and the pipes playing a lament. We come back in quick time, the bugles blowing and our heads up. You know, all those things that you did for me, all that you have been, and are – I didn't feel them at the time, but I did see them. They have been stored away, like film – waiting to be developed. I've been doing a lot of developing, standing here on the brink . . . Well, will you take me on – for life instead of death?'

The hand pulled her steadily out of the sea and along the sand. The small waves lapped at her feet and the spray tingled in her eyes, but the wind lessened as they turned the corner of the point and reached the lee of the peninsula.

THE END